GW00391609

WILD ELUSIVE BUTTERFLY

An intense and sensuous allegory of the complexities of love and attraction, told with guile and compassion by John Park

Kevin Sampson, novelist

A hugely rewarding novel, many-layered, and sad and funny in all the right (unexpected) places

Gill McMullan, bookseller

A wide-ranging and engaging novel, covering a ship's disaster, a shadowy and elusive agent, a bizarre civil service, a birth and an inheritance where nothing is quite as obvious as it seems. It is profound and witty, slipping adroitly between magic realism and realism itself. Sits neatly between Kafka's Castle, and Joyce's Ulysses

Fabian Acker, journalist

A dystopian fairy tale in which characters use each other recklessly

Audrey Nicholson, teacher

Beautifully crafted, and absorbing, Wild Elusive Butterfly explores deep and disparate territory. Grief, desire, passion, and hope are laced together in a poetic, dreamlike tale of wonder and disconnection. John Park husbands joy, despair, and literary craft into the twenty-first century

David Collins-Rivera, playwright

Alice in Wonderland with filth

Jeremy Drakes, actor

Wild Elusive Butterfly

John Park

This paperback edition first published in Great Britain in 2019

ISBN: 9781521107447

ebook edition first published 2018

British Library Cataloguing in Publication Data is available.

Cover design by Debbie Bright

The play Wild Elusive Butterfly © John Park 2007 is registered at the Library of Congress ref PA0001752754 for

Sarita, Mariele, Lesley, Josephine, Isabel, Mike, Martin, George

Love? Do I love? I walk
Within the brilliance of another's thought,
As in a glory.

Thomas Beddoes:
The Second Brother

I am working on the completion of the dream
book; a small collection of dreams – harmless,
absurd dreams; calculations and speeches in
dreams; affects in dreams

Sigmund Freud
to Wilhelm Fliess
1 August 1899

An investigation of modern love

Lawrence Durrell
of The Alexandria Quartet

Foreword

by Professor Alyson Ruskin

ONE AFTERNOON, STUCK at Crewe railway station, I found the manuscript of this book in a cardboard box.

May I explain? You might agree that I am right to worry, but I promise you will have nothing to worry about yourself.

My name is Alyson Ruskin and I explore ontology and ethics with students contemplating their PhD. Ontology is concerned with the nature of being, and ethics with what you do with it, but we won't be troubled by either. They have recently added emeritus to my name, so I am officially old (60).

Have you been to Crewe? It's a damned nuisance. Not the town of course, nor the people, nor the kind station staff, and not the station itself – it is hardly the station's fault. It's simply that whenever something goes wrong with trains in the North, Crewe is where everything piles up.

I'd been in Manchester lecturing on Jacques Derrida (pipe-smoker, Algerian). At Crewe we all got out. Two hours wait for the London train.

Fortunately there was plenty to do. I was writing a – new, and I believe exciting – paper on the Electra Complex, having squeezed at the last minute into a late afternoon matinée of Electra (the

1

Euripides version) at the Royal Exchange.

Buying a sandwich (not bad) and coffee (really quite good) I set off to find a quiet place to think.

Perhaps I would have better not.

Crewe is vast, with a long bridge over all the tracks. Crossing it, I could see in the distance a quiet platform, deserted and – in its way – attractive.

There was a single bench. Leaving it, a small girl carried a little suitcase, holding hands with an old man.

Long experience of old men has led me to the percentage conclusion that most of them are dirty ones. My paedophilia antennae bristled. Had I a whistle, I might have blown it. I'm joking. I'm afraid I do occasionally. An old man with perhaps his granddaughter, evidently happy together, going home.

That is what I thought.

When I climbed the steps down to the platform, I found it not only deserted, but almost derelict. There was grass between the tracks. No sign of the couple, but the bench was real enough.

I'd been sitting for half an hour, reading, chewing, dozing a little. How peaceful a station can be when you don't have to rush. I put the empty coffee carton on the ground, to take with me when I left. Stooping to do so, I noticed a box under the bench.

I picked it up because it looked as if it had been left.

I am now certain that it was.

It is – I am looking at it – an A4 cardboard box, sold enclosing 500 sheets of paper. Inside were two packets of paper.

The first contained about 100 pages, neatly typed almost to the edges, single-spaced, page-numbered. I guessed 80,000 words, the length of The Secret Garden.

The other had a jumble of sheets, typewritten, handwritten, every side covered, no page numbers, everything out of order.

The first is the novel in your hands.

My train was suddenly announced. Stuffing the box in my bag I ran.

Back in my London hotel, I began to realise that the badly-written manuscript was very original indeed.

To reassure you, I wrote at once to the lost property office at Crewe, without reply. In the present unfortunate times, I imagine they have worse things to attend to. I felt responsible to the writer – unnamed, but I have given him a name on the cover of the book. The 'him' is significant, as you will see.

Unusually, this wasn't printed, it was typed – the first part very neatly. Hammered out in metal keys against a clean ribbon. Perhaps this was the only copy, with a writer somewhere searching frantically for it.

Whoever that might be, I decided to find him, or as I began to be certain, her.

I had a week's leave and had planned to meet old Girtonites (useless English degree, good mates). A couple of them joined me for a spot of literary analysis – a game which gradually became serious.

Very bad, was the verdict. Probably written by two people. Most of it – the better stuff – by a woman. The dirty bits certainly by a man.

A name for the writer? We tossed a coin for male / female. It landed on male. We gave him a name, an Apostle (old Cambridge joke), plus what we were looking out onto – a green open space.

It seemed likely from the second tranche of papers, that the book was planned as the first of a set – a trilogy or quartet – with many of the characters recurring.

There was therefore such a density of characters and plot lines in this first book that we felt a 'story so far' or at times preparatory note at the start of each chapter would help the reader considerably. It would be useful too, to have at the end of the book a list of characters, and notes to explain the many references littered throughout the text The first was achievable, the second less so and therefore omitted.

And that is how you will find this book, which has now enjoyed the success of reprinting.

Three things worried me, the smallest first.

First, the old man and the girl on Crewe station appear in the book, just as I saw them.

It was a shock, but there could be simple explanations. Perhaps the manuscript was left deliberately to be found. Perhaps it was, or parts of it, a story from life.

In any case, the writer should be found.

3

How? Over the months I advertised extensively. There was even a tv interview. Nothing.

I was tempted to forget it, until reading more carefully a page I hadn't paid attention to.

The manuscript included an endless list of acknowledgements. Acknowledgements in novels strike me as pretentious, but in this case could be a first-class route to the writer.

I began to study the list name by name, and recognised several. And then one which, as they say, made my blood run cold.

My own.

How would you feel? I am still not certain how to describe it. Worried, yes. Very. Disturbed, angered, questioning – these, in varying strengths. Frightened? No. I don't frighten, never have, pointless.

I couldn't explain it. An elaborately-constructed trick? Impossible. Who could know I would arrive at that particular place at all? I didn't know myself until I did. The book includes some reference to an existence beyond this one – as a lifelong atheist I am unaffected by supernatural whims. Concluding that some things simply occur, I cast it from my mind.

I contacted a number of the people in the acknowledgements. No-one knew anything about the book, or the possible identity of its author.

The book had found a place in my mind and wouldn't shift. I don't know why, but I felt a sense of obligation to the unknown writer, whoever s/he might be.

As the author, co-author, contributor to some fifty books over the years – my agent and publishers are all grateful for the royalties – I was able to interest a publisher in producing a short run of printed copies. It would have felt wrong to publish a typed manuscript other than in print. All royalties await the author in a dedicated account.

The success of publication, perhaps because of the story behind the book, perhaps of the novel itself – heaven knows, there are enough inept novels in print (I confess to two of them) – justified the modest gamble. And, should I live to decipher them sufficiently, the publication of the remaining two or three.

It was while the book was being printed that the third

disturbing event occurred.

There is – there was, I should say, for Guido's has gone now – a happy little café on Kingsway. Kingsway has been a favourite street for anarchists since the times of the Gordon riots, and is now for students demanding to be heard in demonstrations and sometimes more.

The rest of the time, it's a street of the London School of Economics, Peacock Theatre, bits of Kings College, offices – and cafés, where they all meet.

You could sit outside Guido's to smoke, inside to eat. Students, office workers, taxi drivers, their cabs parked in the rank in the middle of the road opposite. The food was cheap, the coffee – we said – the best in London.

This was a very pleasant autumn evening. I sat outside smoking a cigarette.

A woman leant towards me for light.

She had a lovely face, I can see it clearly now, gentle. Blonde hair, short but not too, pretty blue eyes and a quiet smile. I held the lighter to her cigarette and felt the touch of her hand as she steadied it.

She kept her hand on mine for a moment.

In one of those gestures complex to describe, easy to happen, she lit the cigarette, questioned if she may join me, yes of course, and sat, all without words.

We chatted, I've no idea of what or how long. The time passed most delightfully and – I can't remember why, it was a joke – I wrote my name on the back of her hand and she hers on mine, so we'd know should we meet again.

But I've never seen her since, and I've often gone back in the hope of finding her. Partly to ask the explanation. But more, I know, to be with her.

∘ ∘ ∘

As we spoke, for some reason I turned and looked away from her up the street. When I turned back, she wasn't there. There was no sign of her anywhere, in the café, in the street. It was as if she had disappeared.

I looked at my hand, where she had written her name:

Sarah Carpenter.
I know her quite well now.
As you will find, she is one of the characters in the book.

○ ○ ○ ○ ○

Part One

1

In a time of subterfuge and insecurity, shifting values and social upheaval, Bettina Ballantyne attends the funeral of her husband Captain Ballantyne, accompanied by Daisy, Rachel and Rowena, brought up as their daughters. The navy is strongly represented at the gathering which includes the officer held responsible for a tragedy in which a naval submarine dragged a trawler to the sea bed killing all aboard including Daisy's father.

DAISY AND RACHEL managed not to be late, a triumph and almost a first.

The Church of the Madonna of Sorrows stands halfway up Exhibition Road on the left hand side, after the post office of the Science Museum and before Imperial College, which wraps around its back. Stylistically it has no relationship to its neighbours, except perhaps to the exuberant faïence of the Royal College of Organists and the twirls of the Victoria and Albert Museum.

Up in the skyline there are – yes! – onion domes, and not with the vulgarity of Westminster Cathedral. On the other hand, there is none of the solemnity of the Brompton Oratory round the corner, nor of the newness of the Mormon church across the road. In an unlikely way, it settles comfortably in the street; grand, cheeky – and polite.

The church was enormous, and Daisy wondered how she'd never particularly noticed it, because when you did, and stared at it, it was really quite outrageous. As if a Muslim architect setting out to design a mosque thought twice – perhaps invoking Hagia Sophia – and accidentally built a catholic church.

Rowena Ballantyne sat on one side of their mother in the front row; Daisy and Rachel sat together on the other.

At the cue, Rowena and Daisy walked the few paces up the aisle and up to the lectern. Rowena spoke first. Daisy counted the crowd – a thousand and a half. There was a television crew in the gallery. She didn't dare look at Rachel in case she laughed. Rowena hated Daisy so it was an effort to stand next to her. Rowena hated Rachel. 'Rachel Fonseca is a communist' was one of her smaller insults and it was true. Rachel ran Bound To Be Red down the road from Seven Dials, with easy-to-read novels for a pound in the boxes at the front, and hardcore socialism in the basement. 'Rowena Ballantyne is a bitch' would be Rachel's reply, and that was true too, and it would be with a laugh. There were some things that Rachel took easily, which included anything about Daisy. Daisy, more thoughtful, would agree – sometimes. But she realised now that Rowena was about to cry. Not a blatant, look-at-me cry, but the welling-up cry of someone who couldn't cry. Without thinking what she was doing, Daisy slipped her arm around her sister, and cuddled her. It surprised her to have done it, and more that she wasn't pushed away.

∘ ∘ ∘

'Well. Did you see that?'

There were a couple of men in the gallery. The tv crew didn't pay any attention to them and they didn't seem to be connected with them.

'I certainly did. Extraordinary', the other man replied.

'Something of a breakthrough.'

'Quite.'

∘ ∘ ∘

'We would like to thank you, on behalf of our mother and the family.'

It was Daisy's turn, and she didn't take her arm away from her sister for a few moments. She read the opening of St John's gospel and the passage from St Paul about the dead being in another room – didn't everyone? There was a faint smell of incense which she found inspiring, as if her heart might rise with it.

'We loved our father.'

Many of the audience – it didn't seem right to call them a congregation, being in the way of a special event – were in uniform. All kinds of uniform: naval – surface, submarine, marine, airborne; merchant marine – cargo, passenger; and from all around the world.

'The Captain – we didn't actually call him that at home, you'll be glad to know' – laughter – 'was Dad to us. I was lucky to have two of those, and if my first Dad had known my second Dad, I know he would have loved him as much as I do.'

It came effortlessly. Looking back, in a way it had been acting. But there had been love, real love, there was no doubt in her mind about that. Learning to act at the age of six was, she thought, a good thing. How funny never to have put it into clear words until all these years later, making a speech in front of a thousand people. She had taken her arm from her sister, but was aware of her closeness. Which one of us, she wondered, which of the two of us is it who can't feel? I'd always thought it was her. And then: do they clap at the end?

She waited for Rowena to say something when they went back to sit with the family, but she didn't, simply sat down on her mother's left side as before. Daisy passed her mother to sit next to Rachel. 'Well done, he would be' her mother whispered, 'he will be very pleased.' She turned and spoke to her other daughter, probably the same. Daisy thought: can't you talk to her first, for once? Must it always be me? To be fair? No, it's fair to put your real daughter first. Can't you see she needs your love? That that only makes it worse between us?

Rachel nudged her, and they were small again, pushing each other, whispering, laughing, being reproached, nudging each other. Rachel would kiss her easily. One day when she was seven, eight, Rachel picked her up – picked her up entirely – and stood her on a bench so they were the same height, eye to eye. She put her arms round Daisy, held her tight, kissed her. 'I love you little Puddleduck' she said. 'I love you. Don't you forget it.'

Rachel whispered: 'It's a great church, I want it for my funeral. Good organ.' Rachel's whisper was anybody else's stage whisper. 'Not too keen on the little-boy choir.' The choirboys were queuing up for communion in their black robes and white surplices, some tiny boys, some older. 'Sodomy with the choirmaster? Inevitable.'

'Rude girl! Anyhow, it's buggery. With lubricant.'

'For the beginning of my funeral I want Chopin's Prelude Number 20 in C Minor. Sombre. Easy to play. Coffin, maybe on wheels? Bizet's Agnus Dei with ladies singing in the choir?'

At least she was really whispering now. Daisy thought of Dad Ballantyne smiling with the resigned look of an man in a house of three, four, women.

People began to queue for communion and Daisy was away in her thoughts with no-one to call her back. She was wearing Chanel on the jetty under the wing of a Catalina flying boat. The master of ceremonies in the church, a thin man with a sculpted nose and hair slicked down over a partly bald head was out of his cassock, into the neat and becoming uniform of a steward and manservant; her batman. 'Is this Rawalpindi?' Her accent was impeccably edged.

'It's Heathrow, madam.'

'It looks like Rawalpindi. It's everything I imagined. Great-wing-spanned birds in black, sweeping low to scavenge. The beaks of a pair of vultures. And look – aren't those vultures? The Maharani's palace.'

'We're late, madam.'

'I like to be late. I'm late in several different time zones. Eastern Pacific Time. Central European. Quebec. Lima. Alaska Standard. Hawaii-Aleutian Daylight. And almost certainly Greenwich Mean.'

The server on the altar, reasonably good-looking, improved by make-up, became the pilot, irresistibly handsome. 'Permission to land is such an arbitrary idea' he observed, putting on his gloves and locking the aeroplane's door.

The customs officer, brusque, faceless: 'Undress on the floor and point your iris to the beam of my torch.'

Really! But Daisy was magnanimous. 'Th
congratulated. Book me a passage to Tang
might stop over at Mumbai.'

Rachel whispered 'This is a fucking madhou
out?'

'When they get you to pray.'

'Anyhow. Mozart's Lacrimosa from the Requiem in D Minor.
"Lacrimosa dies illa, qua resurget ex favilla." I love favilla, what a
fabulous word, it means ashes – did you know?'

'I can't know everything. That's your job.'

'"On that day of tears and mourning, when from the ashes shall
arise, all humanity to be judged. Spare us by your mercy, God,
gentle Lord Jesus, give them rest."'

'I thought you didn't pray.'

'I can't think of anything better than rest at the end of it all. To
be able to sleep. Oh, and Chopin's Funeral March. Too
grandiose?'

The four of them stood together at the grave, a mother with
her three daughters: unconcerned in her love and that of her late
husband with the sisters' technical relationship as natural, cousin
and adopted. There was a moment when Daisy and Rowena
brushed against each other, but Daisy felt the stiffness of
Rowena's body. There wouldn't be a repetition, the small
conciliation had been – what? – an accident? – a deliberate
encouragement to be rejected? She searched for a sign of triumph
on Rowena's face, but all she could see was nothing. Rowena sad,
glad, angry, happy looked much the same, except that Rowena
didn't make a habit of being happy. Cold, yes, but sometimes
Daisy wondered if it wasn't a screen, something that Daisy herself
had created by her unwanted arrival? Her intrusion?

Next to the church was a courtyard set in a quadrangle formed
by a high brick wall separating it from Exhibition Road, the
church, a grand hall, and the house in which lived, Daisy assumed,
the priests who served the church and perhaps a squadron of
nuns. A flight? Did they live together and possibly have sex? The
courtyard contained a dreary formal planting of trees and shrubs,
but the house was built around and above an archway through

she could see a pretty garden with flowers – racy,
vagant flowers – astragals and wild fruit trees.

o o o

'Madame, may I? You will not remember, I am Emilio.'

'Emilio. Emilio Podro, of course I remember, from the
Embassy.'

'Mrs Ballantyne, you have a remarkable memory. But with such
a beautiful woman it is not at all, if I may say so, surprising.'

'Dear boy – no, no, you're a boy to me, after all – Ballantyne
always said you were a spy. You can be frank. This is after all a
party, wouldn't you say? Look! Everyone well dressed. Eating.
Drinking. It must be a party. So you can tell me in complete
confidence if you are a spy and I certainly won't tell anyone. In
any case I am far too old to be believed.'

'Madame. If I said I am not a spy, that is probably what a spy
would say – wouldn't you say? So I will tell you that I am a spy
and then you won't know whether to believe me. But it wouldn't
be true because everyone at an embassy is a spy because that is
what an embassy is for. I prefer to say I am mysterious.
Unfortunately my job and my pay are prosaic.'

'Do you know anyone? I'm not sure that I do.'

'No. But as I am with the most beautiful woman in the room
why should I care?'

o o o

A couple of bees flew across the courtyard, chatting – more in the
way of passing time – on their way to Hyde Park.

'A social event?'

'They are well-organised.'

'So they say. Pollen collection is satisfactory. It is most likely
that there shall be sufficient honey for the non-productive
months.'

It was a difficult matter to raise, but Marika could no longer
keep her thoughts to herself. 'Anabella, have you ever considered
living alone?'

There was a long silence. They had passed Imperial College by
the time Anabella replied. 'We can't talk about this.'

'We must.'

14

'We are a community. There is no future for the individual.'

'I love you, Anabella.'

They had come to the Royal College of Music before Anabella felt able to reply. She turned, and appraised Marika. Her beauty in flight, in person. 'I love you too. But there is only Mother.'

It was true that each morning at the meeting when tasks were assigned they stood in their hundreds and recited 'Hail! Holy Queen! Mother of mercy. Hail! Our life. Our sweetness!' And our hope; hope that we shall survive another winter. And the plague.

'I am sorry.' It was inadequate, but what else was there to say? She was filled with sorrow.

∘ ∘ ∘

Rachel was thinking that the hall was more village than grand. The roof was pitched and there were skylights high up near the ridge. The space under one of them was divided off, with buckets underneath it, half full of water. There were tall windows, and the sun made it bright. A little too bright, to be honest, and quite hot.

Daisy said 'Who's the man talking to mum?'

'Lanky man. Milkman eyes. Who is everyone?'

Rowena came past. 'Who is the man with mum?'

'We don't know.'

'It's too hot, I'm going to see if Paul is all right.'

As she left, Rachel whispered to Daisy 'I'm sure she fucks that dog.' Daisy giggled and pushed her away. 'You are so unclean.'

'Who's that woman? Did you see that?'

∘ ∘ ∘

Paul sat outside. Rowena had provided him with a hat and tied it carefully so that he didn't need to adjust it with his front paws. There was shade nearby and a clean bowl of water. She was considerate, and he appreciated her thoughtfulness. In turn, he tried to look after her. It was comfortable in the sun. It was good to go to church. They hadn't been to this one before and she had left him at the back with an old man who wore a similar collar to his own. He had wondered if it would be polite to take him for a walk, but the old man did not appear to have a lead.

As they sat together, Paul was considering the question of Pan. Pan had been sent to prepare the way for the arrival of God. Yet

15

there were people who worshipped Pan as a god. Pan was not a god. And Pan was dead. There was one God, and only one. He wondered if the old man knew.

Out in the sun, Rowena sat down next to him. She took off his hat, felt the temperature of his head and stroked it. Sometimes, if she was not in a hurry or he was full of mud, they would shower together. On days that were rushed, she'd stand him in the garden and hose him down, or lift him – keep a straight back, woman, don't hurt yourself for me – and set him on his feet in the bath. Either way she's first feel the heat of the water with the back of her elbow. She was careful with soap near his eyes; always considerate. Sometimes he would sleep on top of the duvet alongside her. This was often hazardous: she was a restive sleeper with sharp claws. On the whole he found it more comfortable to sleep in a basket. In the middle of the night she'd get up and he'd wake to find her squatting next to him, simply looking. Living is dreaming? Too philosophical. Paul slept. In the morning he could find her lying asleep on the floor near to him, a big clumsy thing, mouth open and – he was sure – uncomfortable, her hand resting on his fur, and he'd know what it meant to love and be loved. Now they were together, and warm.

∘ ∘ ∘

A couple of tourists wearing shorts and carrying backpacks strolled into the courtyard. The woman had a camera. They walked hand in hand through the open door of the hall.

The man spoke slowly to the first person he saw, an old, angry-looking woman. 'I wonder. Could you tell me the way to get into the church?' He looked more carefully at her as she did not reply immediately, wondering if he had pronounced the words correctly. He guessed her age at her late 70s. She carried a large handbag. Her eyes were pale blue – intelligent or psychopathic, perhaps an average of the two. The tops of her cheeks were rosy, dissipating lower down into splintered veins and a liverish colour. She had a faint odour. It wasn't as strong as the smell of someone who had slept in her clothes, more as if neither she nor her clothes were frequently washed.

'Are you German?' she said.

It was the woman who replied. 'Yes. We are German.' She

16

moved her arm round the back of her companion and held him protectively.

'No photographs.'

'Thank you. That is useful to know.'

The old woman turned into the room and started to push her way through the crowd. The couple looked at each other, whispered, and laughed. They left the hall and walked across the road.

○ ○ ○

'You are a flatterer, Emilio. But an old lady has no objection to flattery.' Mrs Ballantyne was not preening; she was too practical to preen. But the difference between Mrs Ballantyne preening and not preening was, on this occasion, slight.

They had been joined by the weapons officer of a destroyer, brisk and precise. 'Is it not true, Mrs Ballantyne, that you were a student of the Royal Academy of Dramatic Art, The Rada?'

'Certainly not. I was a dancer at the Folies Bergère.'

'Ah you see Madame.' Emilio Podro glided smoothly into the conversation. 'Only a dancer could display such elegance of deportment.' He winked at her and leant closer, whispered 'A moment when you have time, to speak about your other daughter', kissed her hand, nodded to the officer, and stood back to make way for other guests, including the admiral commander of Ark Royal.

'Your husband was a remarkably fine.' But in what way remained unsaid as the old woman with the large bag pushed the admiral aside and stopped square in front of Mrs Ballantyne.

'You don't know who I am. Do you?' Her voice was loud, definite, but not a shout, not mad, not quite threatening. Enough though, in her voice and in her aggressive holding of herself. to frighten an elderly and recent widow.

Mrs Ballantyne didn't move, didn't step back, her body didn't stiffen, she didn't draw herself up. Nothing changed in her face. Her grey eyes looked straight at the old woman. It wasn't a facing-down stare, more an appraisal. She spoke in a calm voice.

'I am very glad that you have come.'

'You don't know who I am.'

'This is a good day to be at peace. A time for resolution.'

17

'You have no idea who I am.'

'It depends what name you would like to be introduced in. Instructor? Captain Verry? Or just Verry. You were court-martialled, stripped of your rank, sentenced to eight years in prison and got out in four. I'd say on the whole that you were lucky. A cheap price for five families. Oh, and you killed the father of my daughter.'

The old woman didn't reply, shriek, scream, abuse. She took two steps back to be able, it turned out, to extend her arms. She withdrew from her bag what the gunnery officer immediately identified as a 25mm-gauge flare pistol. Holding it with both hands, she brought it up to level at Mrs Ballantyne's chest and pulled the trigger.

At the same time as the assassin had stepped back, so, in paso doble, had Mrs Ballantyne. As the assassin's hands and weapon moved up, so did Mrs Ballantyne's right leg. In synchronised connection, foot – impelled by Mrs Ballantyne's full weight – connected with hands and pistol-butt. It drove them upwards so that the shot fired at an angle of 60 degrees. This proved exactly correct for the flare to smash through the leaking skylight – dropping glass harmlessly into the fenced-off area below like a tail of crystal stars – and soar upwards into the sky, describing a perfect arc symmetrically about the elaborate facade of the Church of the Madonna of Sorrows. Across the road, Gretl Lorelei, the female of the German tourists, caught the precise moment with her favourite Leica lens which she had just attached to the Pentax body of her camera, and her photograph became the headline story for the national news.

'Oh God!' said Marika. 'What the hell is that?'

'There is no God' said Anabella. 'You must correct your language or you'll get both of us into trouble: you for saying, and me for listening. There is only Mother. Oh.' She paused.

'What?' said Marika, who disagreed. Anabella's hesitation made her think that it was not the time to discuss theology.

'A green flare. You know the meaning of a green flare.'

'No I don't. And I don't care.'

'Precisely it means "I relinquish command". The Queen must be dying. The Queen will be dead."

18

'We're free!'

'Free? We still have to fly. Is that freedom?'

'Free to be together. Free never to go home. Anabella We love each other. The hive is dead.'

As a Labrador, Paul wasn't bothered by guns. Vacuum cleaners irritated him; bangs and flashes he could take or leave. But he was worried about Rowena. She was sensitive. She would be afraid. Among all the sudden raised barking he tried hard to distinguish hers but couldn't. His fur prickled and he realised his hands and feet were tensed to spring into action. Intellectually, he realised there was nothing practical he could do. If he ran in to find her, they would miss each other, she would come out, find him gone and panic more. On the other hand there was a chance he would find and rescue her. It was a difficult choice. She couldn't look after herself. He decided to stay where he was – uneasy in mind.

Mrs Ballantyne had completed her manoeuvre by locking the old woman in a head-hold till she was taken away. There was a general conversation involving the admiral and gunnery officer about the trajectory of the flare which both agreed was technically a parabola, and the significance of a green flare. The choice of weapon over bullet they dismissed – Very flare for Verry by name – as not worth consideration.

'Classically "Cleared for take-off"', the admiral remarked. 'For aircraft' she added, in case the difference in prestige between an aircraft-carrier and a destroyer had not been clearly established.

'We use it to mean "Safe now, you can stop searching"' said the gunnery officer, adding with a trace of superiority – though with suitable deference to rank – 'It is particularly useful in our humanitarian work.'

'Susanna, did you notice when she raised her leg?' the admiral's husband whispered.

'Knickerless and well-trimmed' replied the admiral. 'Just what you'd expect of a navy wife.' She fondled his bottom.

'I think we've missed the point' said Mrs Ballantyne 'by being too technical. Green for victory, that's how it's used every day. She wanted a victory.'

'Mum, mum are you all right?' Daisy had finally pushed through the crowd, and held her mother in her arms.

'What really annoyed me was the idea of losing my daughters. You will be my daughter still, won't you darling?'

'For always.'

'Forgive your old mother.' She felt Daisy stiffen in her arms, and stroked her hair as she had done when she was a little girl. 'No, forgive her. One day. Try to do it before it's too late. You've seen what can happen. You can, you know. I know you quite well.'

'You know me better than anyone.' It was a conversation that had come up from time to time, and one which Daisy had always resented. But now, when she had nearly lost the mother she loved, she muttered, not sure if she meant it but resolving to say the words: 'I'll try.'

'By the way, where is my other daughter?'

'Gone to the dog.'

They both laughed. Her mother laughed loudly. Daisy was glad to see her laugh – and there must have been fear, unshown – and feel the tension ripple out of her body. 'She knows her priorities.'

A man with white skin and hair, with socks and shirt to match, but a black tie and suit stood by the door and caught Daisy's eye. She winked across the crowd at Rachel who had turned slowly from talking to a priest. There was a hotch-potch mixed buffet, and Daisy chewed a quarter-sandwich, all she could manage to keep down. Rachel didn't seem hungry. Daisy looked at her watch. 'We can slip away' she said. 'Skunk's here.'

Paul felt an overwhelming relief to see Rowena. He stood up to meet her. She lifted his face to hers and held him tight. As always, she didn't smell great, and her breath was rank, but she meant well and for a minute they remained silent in each other's arms; happy, alive, together.

○ ○ ○ ○ ○

2

The late Captain Ballantyne chairs an official inquiry into the fatal encounter between naval submarine Defender and civilian trawler Turmoil – a naval exercise which goes wrong. His professional detachment is tempered with distress for the families wrenched apart, particularly for 6-year-old Daisy who has lost her father.

THIS IS HOW Daisy's first father came to die.

One crisp night with a red sky, Aloysha drove off down the cinder track and wiped the mist from the screen with the back of his hand. It was nine o'clock, and she'd gone to sleep easily at eight. He grinned, it was a story that worked well for sleep, one of her favourites. The magical look on her face, a little perturbed, concentrating, her mouth slightly ajar – he could remember that. It was a good memory, he would remember it tonight, into the morning and cold.

Verry (who would be referred to as 'Instructor' in the official report by Captain Ballantyne, Chief Inspector of Marine Accidents) climbed down into Defender. That slight sensation of enclosure. Not exactly claustrophobia, which would be an irony after so many years, but the combination of being wrapped – and held. Defender pulled away from her berth and dropped to the bottom of the ocean.

Aloysha (he would be referred to as 'Reculver') took the wheel and Turmoil inched out into the sea, a lazy-bottomed trawler with a roll like a bitch in heat.

Daisy (even Daisy would be renamed by Ballantyne – 'Miss Reculver') pretended to herself to be asleep, but her head was full of the Box of Delights. And she was awake, she was sure of that. She sat comfortably in the railway carriage, The First Nowell playing in her dreams, watching the wolves running by the side of the train on the wall of the nursery. No, Daisy's bedroom – she was far too old to have a nursery. There was school tomorrow. Daisy decided that, on the whole, she liked school. There were exceptions, but most days were quite nice, and – generally – the other children too. She was certainly awake because she could see her night-light on the wall, a red carrier bag lit so you could see the shadows of the toys inside. Though she had a boat, which was a different shape, and her daddy – dad, now that she was grown up, but sometimes daddy – had a boat. He was out on it now, but he'd be back in the morning to take her to school.

If Turmoil and Defender were side by side – there would be no good reason for that – Turmoil would be seen to be a quarter of Defender's length. If Defender stood upright next to Nelson's column – and it would have a right to, being a submarine of the Trafalgar class – it would be one-and-a-half times Nelson's height. If they had gods, Defender's would be Demersus, who scraped an existence on the water bed. And Turmoil's Pelagos, guardian of the surface – and latter-day patron of the dolphin-friendly trawl.

It was one o'clock in the morning. There were three of them out over the trench. A mile more or less north-north-west Briardeus made a comfortable 10 knots with her trawl fully deployed. To her south and perhaps a mile from Turmoil, Ramona III was beginning the turn, the point at which she would be most vulnerable. The trench formed a natural feeding ground, providing a regular tonnage of fish for a small number of trawlers, so that at any time there would be three, four, five at sea. More would be unsafe, with the danger of snagging each other's trawls, particularly at the turn. Each would sweep slowly along the length of the trench, turn along the short side, and up along the other side, always keeping a safe distance of three-quarters of a mile to a mile. At the turn, the skipper would always be in the wheelhouse, the starboard window open in any weather to check the operation of the winch, the searchlight switched on. From time to time the skippers would chat to each other on the local frequency, but mostly they'd keep radio silence, tuning in to the shipping forecast on the hour.

Ten miles away Defender laid a trail of mines. Rebuke, a Leander-class fast naval frigate equipped with Ikara anti-submarine missiles and a Westland Lynx anti-submarine helicopter, found Defender on sonar and prepared to attack.

Verry (Instructor) stood back, watching the student Mary P – who would be called Student One, abbreviated to S1 as the report progressed – accelerate Defender to her full 32 knots. A natural. It was joy to watch her weave Defender starboard to port and back, pause, and turn her neatly round on her tail. By minute 10, the chase was reversed to check mate, and five tubes loaded with Spearfish torpedoes aligned on Rebuke. S1 gave the command to arm, and prepared to kill.

Daisy slept.

A Beaumaris shark approached the trench, thought better of it and turned away. Mackerel and lancets, pilchards, herring continued to swim contentedly, even in a self-satisfied way – the pelagic zone, after all, belonged to them, and it was good to have a name for where they lived. The trench had a name too – Fitzroy – from the man who discovered how weather could be forecast, though there was no weather tonight. Ended his life with a stropped razor across his throat in depression. No depression tonight. The furies sat in the cumulus, peering down, toying with the idea of a water spout, tiring with the effort of thought, joshing each other, flying away. Defender slipped into the trench.

There were five students aboard Defender. For this exercise, command of Defender was passed from her captain (Captain) to the course commander (Instructor). Instructor passed full command of the vessel to the student under test who, under Instructor's supervision, had the title Duty Captain for the duration of the test. This was the final stage of the student's training before being certified fit to command, and there was no doubt in Instructor's mind that Student One was outstanding.

Instructor withdrew to discuss Student One's performance with the captain in private. One other person was there, described in the report as Guest. The identity of Guest was not disclosed – not in the report, to the inquiry, nor to the judge in the criminal trial – because, the report acknowledged, the presence of Guest had no effect on the event. Guest had no authority. While the two officers conferred in the presence of Guest, Student One and Student Two chatted as Student Two prepared to be called to command. The one had ceased to be Duty Captain, the other in waiting. In this short period, the report was to conclude, and with Defender proceeding at a crawl speed of six knots, no-one was in command.

'Oh and by the way are you down the pub later?' It was a running joke over the radio between Reculver and the skipper of Briardeus. They neither of them drank. 'It's your round.' Turmoil approached the end of the trench and Reculver signed off to navigate her into the turn. With the trawl fully extended she presented a length of half a kilometre, the trawl some 30 metres wide and 25 metres deep. Altogether Turmoil and nets accounted for a volume of around a quarter million cubic metres – below the surface an unmissable target.

'Yes,' replied Marcus D (Student Two). Mary P had asked if he was nervous. 'Don't be' she said. 'You'll be fine. Once you get command it all slips into place.' It was a question of marking time, but not a long time. There was, after all, no hurry. Instructor and Captain were taking time to dissect her performance. A lacuna. Being outside time, a lacuna could last for unlimited time, but the time for this was seconds.

There were two perceptions. Within Defender it was the sudden smashing and dragging sound against the hull as her fin snagged and dragged a warp attaching Turmoil to her trawl.

In the wheelhouse of Turmoil, Reculver had a second of thought that Briardeus had collided. Too far away. A shark? His attention was so completely on the turn, on the avoidance of the twin warps crossing, on the trawl lifting from the bottom of the trench and remaining unentangled, on the note of the winch engine, on the rudder staying hard to starboard, the engine staying full ahead, Furuno radar and sonar fully functional, all hands safely below in the crew cabin, that till the end of the second he didn't think that he was dying.

It was only as Turmoil was wrenched under the sea and clattered against the hull of Defender that he forced himself to admit death. Nothing to be done but to take the breath of water. Daisy safely tucked in bed, nothing to harm her.

For a moment the vessels were aligned. A knowledgeable fish – a cod who'd travelled, perhaps – would be able to witness that, yes, Turmoil would fit four times into Defender and that Defender was, at the bottom of her keel, 60 metres below the surface. That the four hands of Turmoil were dead, having failed to open the escape hatch above them to the deck. That the Beaufort 6-soul inflatable life-raft had tried unsuccessfully and for the same reason to race to the surface, even to float there empty. That Turmoil lay on her starboard on the floor of the trench at 150 metres. That Reculver lay beside her on his back, eyes open and available for consumption by passing dragonet, bib, bull-rout, and whatever else Demersus might entertain.

Immediately following the noises against her hull, Defender stopped engines to listen, her position was recorded, and Instructor took command. She concluded that Defender had caught a trawl, most likely with her forward fin. In the silence a brief noise was detected, possibly the concluding spin of a propeller. Instructor took Defender into a turn and took her away from the area to make sure she was clear of other vessels before surfacing. 30 minutes later, she took Defender to periscope depth, sighted Briardeus and Ramona III fishing normally and handed command over to Captain to bring Defender to the surface.

An hour after the collision, Defender surfaced. Rebuke, alerted, searched the area and reported that nothing appeared out of the ordinary. Captain observed Briardeus and Ramona III continuing to trawl. An attempt was made to contact both vessels on VHF without success. Captain and Instructor noted some damage to Defender's fin consistent with cutting a trawl. In the absence of wreckage, survival aids or disturbance, Captain logged the incident as an encounter with marine debris. He reported the incident to Southampton by radio, took Defender down to 25 fathoms and handed command to Instructor who resumed the exercise.

It wasn't until four days later that Aloysha's body washed up on Reculver Bay, later to become his pseudonym. By that time Turmoil, on its separate journey, had rolled and kicked its way along and out of Fitzroy Trench. It had tumbled to rest where it would be found – wrapped in its trawl with its bodies and life raft – and brought, in an expensive operation, back to the surface.

Ballantyne's reaction on arriving from Southampton was dispassion. As chief inspector of marine accidents, it could not be otherwise. But he was also human – another requirement of the job. As he examined evidence, attended the identification of what remained of the bodies, listened to careful statements and excuses, he felt a revulsion at the pointless loss of souls, at the destruction of families. At the inquiry in Chancery Lane, he looked up from time to time at the public gallery. A merchant marine officer sat there, a handsome man perhaps in his twenties. Next to him sat a child, as tightly next to him as she could, upright and looking ahead. Ballantyne knew who she was. If he didn't, he thought perhaps that he would have guessed. What would happen to her, he wondered? What would happen to the little girl?

○ ○ ○ ○ ○

3

Daisy Ballantyne's first father died when his fishing trawler was dragged to the sea bed by a naval submarine on exercises. By adoption at the age of 6 she joined the family of Captain and Mrs Bettina Ballantyne as one of three nominal sisters. The others are their natural daughter Rowena and her cousin Rachel. As adults they have recently attended Captain Ballantyne's funeral.

TOM DEVINE SAT astride his kitchen stool at his porridge, not a square meal or easily made, because he wasn't a skilled cook. He used a spoon which was clean, but mottled from long use. The set face he had developed, accompanied by the frown that he gradually put on, served mainly to reflect his precision. He had completed his sleep log, his clothes were laid out, toothpaste on his electric toothbrush, and all was ready for the day. He would be nervous to see Daisy, but not yet. He contemplated a peach (unbruised), but decided against eating it. There could be too much. He ran a bath, took it, shaved, took a bus, a tube, sat at his desk, commenced his meditation.

Reilly turned the car off Shaftesbury Avenue, pulled up beyond Seven Dials. Rachel said she didn't know when she'd see Daisy next – so busy – almost forgot to kiss her – she was already in her mind opening boxes of books, pricing, sorting, shelving –

remembered to, got out of the car. 'Don't slam the door.' She didn't hear, slammed the door. Daisy winced. Rachel banged on the window; mouthed a kiss, turned away, the car drove off. Daisy liked the smell of it, stretched her toes in her shoes. She wasn't nervous about meeting Tom; she would be, but she wasn't.

'What are you doing today?' Rachel had asked.

'Seeing a ship. A massive, massive ship. And my little Turmoil. She's a tramp, and I love her. And my captain. I love my captain too.'

'I wondered why he wasn't there.'

I enjoy my expensive car, and I am not nervous about seeing Tom Devine. These are two realities, and they will do for the moment.

An hour later they arrived at the office in the port. It was sad to have left Tilbury, sad to have packed up what had been her father's office from the old days; but Daisy knew her father. Be big, be audacious. When she asked what audacious meant, he said 'Bold. But audacious is a grander word.' Be grand too. She had practised audacious, and would sometimes whisper it in his ear when he read to her at night, and they would both laugh. She could hear his laugh now. It was a good laugh.

Tom Devine walked to Fenchurch Street and took the train out to the port. Looking at his hands in his lap, he wondered if she'd changed. It was two years since he had last first seen Daisy Ballantyne sitting across the court waiting to give her evidence. The hearing was in Chancery Lane in the old commercial court building, an arbitration between the owner of the Countess Constanza and the owner of her cargo – she as an expert for one, he for the other. His lawyer Jill Jouvry had sat next to him for encouragement. He had never appeared as an expert witness before and he was nervous. It had seemed disproportionate, too, that there should be an argument, and for so many days, over the loss of cargo when there had been such loss of life. She'd been a tramp ship – his speciality – a storm, an accidental breach between the holds, explosion, some survivors, the dead not drowned but incinerated. He knew he should shudder to think of them now, as he did then, but couldn't. It was possible to feel the pity intellectually, possible certainly to put himself in the place of the dying, at least in imagination. But really to feel? No. His father had seen to that. Not, he quickly corrected his thoughts, in life. A good and kind man? Gentle too. But in death.

Tom Devine knew exactly who Daisy Ballantyne was and had not been honest. There was arguably no reason to be honest and he told himself it was for the best reasons not to be. He could argue to himself that it was not dishonest not to tell everything – and there he was, wrapping himself into a double negative again; he spent a lot of time arguing inside his head. What he couldn't argue with was that his affair with Jill Jouvry had been excellent, and in its now sporadic way, continued to be. Jack, her husband had become a friend – that was the best way to put it. A dealer in anything, Jack Jouvry. And that when Tom Devine had seen Daisy, he knew that he was utterly, completely, ridiculously in love with her; which wasn't practical as he had no time left to spend on loving. The hours of the day once necessities were subtracted – demurrage, charter parties, their enforcement, the ceaseless detail of loading, unloading, the possibility of sleep snatched across time-zones – didn't allow love. No time! No time!

Daisy took a port car the short distance to the quay and boarded the pilot vessel. It was a sleek boat with a dusky orange superstructure on a black bottom and it moved fast through the lanes, out into the sea, turned and ran alongside the enormous hull of China Lines' Strident Bucephalus, 400 metres long, 16,000 containers, carefully matching its speed. She followed the pilot up the ladder and took the lift up to the bridge. The captain – an old friend who had invited her aboard to show her around – got up from his reclining seat, shook hands with the pilot, kissed Daisy.

'I take it you've come to buy my ship?'

'If you're part of the deal. I'm not going to drive it myself.' She sat down at the back of the bridge out of the way as the captain and pilot took Bucephalus to its anchorage. The first officer took over to supervise the unloading of cargo, releasing the captain to carry out his inspection of the perimeter, a loop of a mile. Inviting Daisy to accompany him, his obvious delight in showing her his ship and pride in every new thing it could do made her smile.

'Boys don't grow up.'

'Nor do girls.'

'I think my father would have completely loved this.'

'I'd never have been able to get my hands on the wheel.'

'She doesn't have a wheel. By the way.'

'Useful to know.' He nudged her. 'Aha. Isn't that one of yours?'

They'd reached the stern and watched the pilot vessel take its way out to Turmoil. The sea was roughening, small waves, and it bounced from trough to crest, making a fast pace.

'Pöl Stuyvesant at the wheel. And Turmoil does have a wheel.'

'A very small wheel.'

'A wheel. And you're seriously taking her round the Cape? Does he know the way?'

'I think Captain Stuyvesant is reasonably competent.'

'Listen. I taught Pöl Stuyvesant. Okay okay, he taught me. If he has a compass he'll be all right.'

'He's just done Cuba-Leningrad. In the old days it was anywhere: Bilbao-Freemantle, Riga-West Africa, West-Africa-Shanghai. I think he'll manage.'

She was silent, watching the pilot go aboard. He knew she was worried, kept the silence with her for a while, judged the moment to speak.

'It's the last time, isn't it?'

'Yes. She's done us very well, but it's time now.'

'Will you carry on?'

'I'm not sure I want to. I couldn't find a replacement for Pöl. He is, he's been – everything.'

Pöl Stuyvesant in leathers, crash helmet, Rudge 500 motorbike. 'Daisy, whatever happens, I'll be here.' He'd never said the words 'Your father is dead.' That had been a police officer, and she'd said it in a different way. He had always, from the absolute first time she had been carried by him, had an aroma of being clean. 'Pöl Stuyvesant was the first person to come and visit you. You'd only just been born. He said you looked quite nice. Quite nice for a chimpanzee.' A trace of bay rum on his cheeks from shaving. Smart uniform. Three rings with diamond on his sleeve. Four now. The last voyage. And then?

Turmoil stood alongside, a third of the length of Bucephalus.

'17 knots' said Daisy. 'Want a race?'

○ ○ ○

On the drive from the port to her mother's house in Upminster, Daisy and Stuyvesant discussed the turnaround and departure for the final voyage. Unloading would complete in a couple of days. By the weekend they'd be off Kent, coming round into the Channel. She was worried about her mother and knew she didn't need to be. Half pay, now that Dad was dead, perhaps a little more. No mortgage; there were savings. She could help her mother. And Reilly? Her father had managed to manipulate a small salary for Reilly from the Maritime Board on the pretext of his sometime need for a driver on official duties; had made up the rest himself. I can justify a driver. Could she? And some money to her mother? Her mother who would refuse? How to give her money without her knowing? She'll be tired now.

Mrs Ballantyne was far from tired. She looked as if she could dance all night and Daisy knew it was Stuyvesant. Charming, handsome, 65, suave, flattering. Mum was behaving like a girl. Flirting. Embarrassing!

Paul was pleased to see Pöl. It always amused him that they shared the same name. He stood up to greet him, because Pöl was a man you wanted to greet formally, on all fours. Pöl was obviously pleased to see Paul. Pöl looked happy – very happy – you could tell. That was certainly a smile, no doubt about it, no matter what other people might say.

Rowena had named Paul after Pöl. Daisy wondered why she'd never thought of that before. Her mimsy sister, a crush on a man twice – three times – her age.

Later, her mother took her out into the garden. 'A quiet word my dear.' Daisy thought whether now would be the right time to raise the question of money. Her parents had never talked about money. They'd argued about it together with the door closed. Rowena and Daisy had sat together on the stairs, afraid at the raised voices. They hadn't always been distant. There were times of armistice and, thinking more carefully, Daisy realised that the truces were perhaps much longer than the periods of warfare. Were they that different from natural sisters? Natural brothers and sisters? In a way their family was odd, but weren't all families odd? How could anyone know what was normal? Perhaps they were good sisters after all. She resolved to try and be better to her sister, to make her more like a sister in her mind. To forgive. To forgive? Wasn't it she who should be forgiven? The interloper? 'Rowena is a bitch.' Was it me? Am I the bitch?

'The man from the embassy.'

'Oh yes, the man with the dozy eyes.'

'The man from the embassy, anyhow. He says your cousin. He thinks she is your sister. I kept trying to tell him she is your cousin. I have quite enough daughters. Far too many indeed, when you count them up.'

'There are only two of us.'

'But I have the worst possible daughters. Perhaps I should have had sons after all. It's probably too late now. On the other hand science is remarkable. One never knows. I believe my breasts are adequate.'

'The man from the embassy.'

'The man from the embassy says your cousin Rachel is making bombs in the basement of her shop and the police are going to arrest her under the Defence of the Realm Act 1914.'

'I don't imagine that is still in force.'

'Exactly what I said. "Emilio" I said. "Don't be ridiculous." Well. He corrected me. "And in any case" I said. "That was all about not flying kites to warn the Zeppelins." He said they've brought it back in. At least she's not being accused about that.'

'What?'

'Kites.'

'How does he know this?'

'Do you mean that it's true?'

'I mean, how does he know about this if it's true?'

'I certainly hope not. Oh they all talk to each other. Special Branch, whatever they're called. Diplomatic Protection dah de dah. Gossips. Nothing to do all day but gossip. He frankly admitted to me that he's a spy. Ballantyne always said he was a spy. "Emilio Podro" – I remember it clearly, it was the Ambassador's leaving party in Grosvenor Square. First class chandelier. They say it's by Nicolas Poussin.'

'He was a painter, mother.'

'When you say "Mother" I know that you are reproving me.'

'A painter.'

'He could well have dabbled. So many of them did. Botticelli. Da Vinci.'

'No chandeliers. They were all painters. Ok the occasional vase. Who cares?'

'"Is a spy." Your father was always right about those things. I wish you will tell her to stop.'

'I think it's highly unlikely that Rachel is making bombs.'

'I would like you to speak with her.'

'I will speak with her. I wanted to mention the question of money.'

'How much do you need?'

'I mean, for you.'

'Oh I'm quite all right thank you. Thank you dear. You are a good girl. Quite often you are a good girl. Your sister is a good girl. You are not good girls always at the same time. If I was doing this again I would ask for daughters who were more – enmeshed.'

Pöl Stuyvesant was staying with her mother and Daisy had given Reilly the car to take home. Rowena was somewhere. Daisy decided not to disturb her. They had both loved their father, but he had, first of all and absolutely, been Rowena's alone. Daisy was uncertain what to do, remembering the giving of Rowena's body in the church and her later return to normality at the reception. Would it be the normality of the future? No, Daisy thought. We have nothing to hold us together now. Mum, yes. But Dad's gone. It's not the same and we won't really be related any more. There isn't any reason for us to see each other much again. Sometimes, for Mum. That's decent. And after Mum goes? Daisy felt a touch of righteousness, as if that was not simply the way it could be, but the way it should. Her sister had constructed her own fortress. Sister? Let's be honest, she is not actually my sister.

Daisy had closed the front door. She walked down the drive and shivered slightly. It was hardly cold, and she would soon become warm. She heard the door open and expected her mother to call out that she'd forgotten something or to push a bank note into her hand – 'You'll need to get something to eat'. But it was Rowena.

Daisy stopped, uncertain what to say. A confrontation? 'You won't need to come back now. You won't need to come back again'?

Rowena was clutching something in her hand. 'This is yours.' She said it awkwardly, didn't know what to say. Daisy thought how difficult the words sounded. She knew what she was holding. All the years stopped.

Rowena was looking at her own hands. She said – suddenly, in a rush, as if she had rehearsed the words and would not be tongue-tied nor read them from paper on the night – 'I am sorry.'

Rowena leaned forward and kissed Daisy on the side of her face. As her face approached, Daisy had imagined it would be an inept, stubborn kiss, but it was surprisingly gentle, and for a terrible moment of contained and shrieking laughter Daisy thought – like she kisses her dog. But she didn't laugh. She didn't know what to do, nor what to say.

Rowena backed away from her, touched both her arms with her own, gave her approximation to a smile, turned and walked back into the house, quietly closing the door.

Daisy thought: I'm not at all afraid of meeting Tom Devine in the morning. Why should I be? He's just himself. And that's all I am. She had successfully distracted herself for the few seconds it took to clear herself out of sight from the house. She looked down at the pencil-case in her hand and burst into tears.

○ ○ ○ ○ ○

4

As the owner of an ageing cargo ship, Daisy Ballantyne prepares for its final journey carrying a cargo for Tom Devine. Tom is a methodical, practical man, pragmatic in business as in love. An earlier encounter with Daisy, however, has put him off balance.

ON THE WALL there were clocks for Eastern Pacific Time, Central European, Quebec, Lima, Alaska Standard, Greenwich Mean, a few others, and his favourite – Hawaii-Aleutian Daylight.

Tom had never been to Hawaii and wondered if they had garlands. Probably not. Never been to the Aleutian Islands. Probably never would. Never would see Unalaska, never board the Alaska Marine Highway ferry, never see the Pacific Ring of Fire, never go to the Russian Commander Islands, never meet an Aleut. But it was good to see their time behind, to know that in Fairbanks and Bethel, Anchorage and Valdez, on the Yukon river and across the Bering Sea they could still be enjoying a peaceful Sunday night while London sat briskly at its 6am desk on a Monday morning.

Daisy felt sick, had been sick, showered and felt better, rinsed out her mouth, gargled, flossed her teeth, brushed her teeth, packed her briefcase, was driven.

The office was off City Road, in the dirty bit of Worship Street.

It was a four-storey building which started smart at the ground floor: a shopfront with little square window-panes let out to a greasy spoon. A glass door which could do with a clean led up to a couple of office floors. Above them was the top floor – from the street it looked rank and possibly unsafe – with a dormer window set in a high-pitched London roof.

Out the back was the depot, and trucks shambled along Curtain Road, past the bomb-sites and derelict buildings, taking cargo to the port.

Tom was quite certain he wasn't nervous. He had mediated and changed his breathing from chest to diaphragm, taking deep long breaths and holding them to the count of seven, expelling them to eleven. His brain was fully oxygenated, tie straight, shirt clean, shirt ironed, suit excellent, shoes not at all scuffed. Shirt and tie had taken thinking about, but in the end he'd gone for plain white respectively, and deep red. Black tie, for her period of mourning? No, because it must not be assumed that he knew – though it would be ridiculous not to have known – and could look obsequious. Cuff links? Only one pair would do – the simple gold discs. Not for this occasion the Las Vegas matched breasts.

When Daisy walked into the room, she knew at once that she had lost. There was no point in telling herself that it was irrational – she knew that. He wasn't extremely handsome. He was fairly handsome, in a way. His hair needed to be crushed down slightly, it had habits of its own on top but was well-behaved at the sides. Good eyebrows and eyes, and considerate surroundings to them. Funnyish ears. Clean shirt but one of the sides of the collar bending up – should she tell him? Girly mouth. It was insupportable to be in love with him. Anyhow – she glanced at the clocks spread around the room – there was no time. She shook his hand.

'I'm happy with your terms. No arguments about that and thank you, very clear. I understand also that you will be travelling with us? That's a pleasure. Will it be the first time for you?'

How to tell him?

'My father always insisted one of us was there at the far end. I've usually flown over, but – it's special, this one. That's very dangerous water. Can't wait.'

'On the plus side, it's safe from attack. That's pretty certain. As for the weather? Plenty of lifeboats.'

They laughed.

'There's no weapons?'

'Not on the way out. Bucephalus has a couple of guns and a navy crew to go with them, some light arms and a small detachment of marines but in the end you can't defend a merchant ship, they're too unmanoeuvrable. And it invites trouble if they know you're armed. On the way back, sure, that's different, we'll have a navy escort and five holds full of munitions. But that's cargo, locked down. Captain Stuyvesant doesn't like weapons on board, not even side-arms. We don't have them on any of the fleet.'

'How many have you got now?'

She was thinking of terms and lies. She was thinking of his clothes. I like your clothes; they are – right. You are more than your clothes. I am more than my clothes. I want to dance. I want to rock and roll with you. And lies? Why do we tell lies?

She'd said five, that was true.

He'd gained confidence. 'May I ask you a personal question?'

'Try me.'

'Your father?' And he carried on for a while. She thought again: why do we tell lies? Living, working in the vestry of lies, the borough. For good, to avoid hurting people. Always for good.

Oh! It's simple, but Ballantyne is my family name, out of respect for my father who is, was, my stepfather. He was looking at her, and she realised she hadn't spoken the words, did so.

'I read in the paper. But I should have guessed, your black dress.'

Daisy thought, why should he be circuitous? She knew exactly who his father was, had been. 'He wasn't my actual father.'

There was no reason to say this, he hadn't asked. But she knew he wanted her to say it.

'My actual father was drowned. He was skippering a trawler that was snagged by a navy submarine going back to Faslane.' I must slow down my voice. 'Just north of the Isle of Man. They were all killed.' Only a small lie, a change of location. It was time for some truth, that was fair, but not all truth, that would hurt.

He wondered why she was lying. He knew who her father was. She couldn't know who his father was. There was a game, but it wasn't teasing.

He brought out the right phrases, looked sorry. She looked graceful. A Victorian parlour game, played correctly.

'It's appallingly tactless to ask, and excuse me, but what happened to the bodies?'

'They – left them there.'

She never saw the body of her father. Pöl had taken her to Reculver but that was later. Aged nine she had asked to go, and her new father agreed. It was after that that she asked to be given the name of her new family. One day, she thought, she would be called Reculver. It was a good name, a good place, the place where her father had come home.

She thought how awful it must be for Tom. I will protect you. Can we change the subject? I don't want to tell any more lies.

'I was six. I got a new father, and a mother, and a sister. I've just lost the new father. They don't last.' She laughed. 'I wear them out. Ships are more reliable.'

What I have learnt is: love is an unreliable quantity. You love people: they leave you. It wasn't worth setting out to learn. When I think, there is an accusatory person inside ticking me off. Bitch stole my pencil case. And you from her? Her father? Her security? She was a little girl too. Not much of a trade.

His eyes – annoyingly gorgeous.

She pulled a biro from her briefcase and was about to scribble her signature on the contracts when he spoke.

'An item.'

He was, though, absurdly pedantic. She gave him her quiet look, but he only smiled back and continued.

'I have a preference. A couple actually. Sorry, it may seem stupid.' Come to the point.

'Let's get on.' It was safe to be brisk.

'I prefer to sign in ink. I'd be grateful if we could sign using a fountain pen. This.'

It was white, the surface marbled with a gold filling-lever on the side, a gold nib.

'It was my father's.'

38

He opened a drawer of the desk, took out a bottle of blue Quink, filled the pen, offered it to her. Her fingers were practical as well as fairly slim. Not exactly piano-playing hands, and not girly hands, not robust fingers and certainly not pork sausages – he laughed, and she looked at him as if he was laughing at her, which he was, and he quickly said he was laughing at being so pedantic, which he wasn't sure if she quite believed. I want to hold your hands. To kiss your hands. He settled that they were dry hands, not in the sense of skin flaking, but in the sense of not being limp and wet; elegant fingers; so, all in all good hands; but hands which could tie a rope to sheet a load; tie a cow hitch, a cat's paw. A blood knot.

She made a gesture, you first. He signed the first copy, the second copy, watching the ink, wet. I have to have it wet in my hand. I need to see it flow. When the ink squelches on the parchment – can't you hear the sound? – it's as if the spirit of the deal is bleeding. I prefer red ink for the apparent authenticity, the likeness to haemoglobin. My blood, your blood, intermingling.

She took the pen, looked at the clear italic of his signature. The precise hand of a precise man; scrawled her own.

'OK.'

She handed him the contracts. I could be heartbreakingly dirty for you.

There were schedules to be cross-checked. She finished hers in a quarter of an hour and got up, stretching as he continued. The meeting room was on the second floor and looked out over the street. She was surprised it was clean; from the outside it looked old and dirty, but the windows were sparkling clear, and the paint inside bright white; the sashes worked, one a little open. She supposed it had once been a house, with the warehouse added later. The back window of the room was still there but now looked into the warehouse, and she looked down, watching the loading and unloading. A woman crossed the floor, shifting a palette on a trolley, stopped, unhooked it, skipped up into a forklift and stacked it into a shelf just below the window. She wore a t-shirt and shorts turned up below her knees, safety boots and helmet. Her breasts were plump, well-disciplined. Their eyes met for a moment, she withdrew the forks, spun the truck round.

He finished. She said 'Will you arrange sealing?'

'That's the other thing. I like to use this sealing wax. Do you have a lighter?'

'I prefer matches.' She pulled out a box, passed them to him, looked in her case for the company seal. 'Be careful, they're white phosphorous. If you strike them too hard, little globules of flaming phosphor spray over your hand.'

There was a stick of red wax in the drawer, held to the seal with a rubber band. He melted the wax and impressed the seal next to his signature on each of the copies.

'What's the shape on the seal?'

He handed it to her.

'Oh, it's a flower? Is it a significant?'

'No. Can I see yours?'

She sealed the contracts and passed it to him, watched as he examined it carefully, putting on his glasses. Do you need to examine my nipples? I could open my shirt?

'It's a flower. Is it significant?'

'No.'

∘ ∘ ∘

Across the road, towards the bend into Curtain Street, a pink-purple lupin had grown up in waste land. She inclined upwards, listening carefully as God spoke to her. She nodded and told the dandelions who were nearby 'He says he'll make it rain quite soon.'

'I should think so.'

The dandelions were wilting, so couldn't really be blamed – the lupin thought – for being tetchy.

'Was that all?'

'He said, hang on, it's going to be lively.'

'Lively, eh? I don't mind that at all, speaking personally. There's precious little that's lively round here. I'm not dying of thirst. That would be a ridiculous exaggeration. But I'm bloody thirsty. That's certainly true.'

The dandelion leant over and told the dock leaves, who in turn told the nettles. Generally, there was a feeling of expectation. There was no need to look up at the clouds. Rain was promised:

rain would come.

What came was more than rain. It was as if everything that could possibly have been accumulated in the heaviest clouds which the densest air could by supreme effort have supported suddenly released itself – crash. It flattened the lupin, the dandelions, nettles, daisies, primroses, dog-roses, none of whom minded as they were supple and would stand again, or their successors, and the water would drain into the earth, which would dry itself, refreshed.

∘ ∘ ∘

In the office on the second floor they heard a loud impact, followed by cracking, a thump to the ceiling, the sound of materials – slates, little timbers? – falling and hitting the floor, which held, with a little plaster falling into the room. Daisy ran to the door, turned, Tom didn't follow.

'For God's sake, man.'

He sat down. There was no time to deal with him. The ceiling looked as if it would hold, that he would be safe. She assessed the stairs to the top floor – unsafe, probably competent. Carefully, she mounted them.

The roof was higher than she had expected. It would have been a clear three metres to the beam at the ridge. It was broken now; the dormer to the front had collapsed on the floor, and lay surrounded by slates, gypsum, bits of wood. Part of a chimney had fallen into the room. The rain flooded through onto the floor, turning the rubble to slurry, and suddenly stopped.

There was a soft noise on the stair and Daisy turned as the woman she'd seen earlier stood by her side. Her face showed a light sweat from the climb and she took off her helmet, shook out her hair, all in silence. Daisy was aware of the scent of her body, reassuring and pleasant, the fresh aroma of a body used to cleaning itself with sweat from manual labour. She had a name tag on her belt which Daisy couldn't read without staring. White socks peeped from the tips of her Tuf boots. I do like your hair, Daisy thought. Smoky smelling and tousled. Black and tangible.

'I've seen you before.'

'I'm the cargo supervisor for Strident Bucephalus, Ms Ballantyne. Berthonella.'

41

Daisy smiled. The formality was correct and polite. The captain of Bucephalus was rigorous about the non-use of first names between ranks. But that was on board ship, and in any case, the woman didn't work for her. Most likely, she'd never see her again. And Daisy wasn't an officer. She said 'Daisy.'

The woman relaxed, smiled back. 'I'm Isabella. Isabella Berthonella.'

'This is a mess.'

'We'll get it cleared up, Ms Ballantyne. Daisy. I can handle it.'

Daisy didn't know what to say. She felt, but didn't want to put a name on what she felt. And all the time under it she was thinking of Tom. Cowardice?

'Thanks.'

Berthonella carefully led the way down the stairs. She turned to see that Daisy was all right and carried on down.

Tom sat at the desk, contracts in front of him, schedules – all as she'd left him and them. He wasn't reading; his head was turned to the window, but he wasn't looking at it, or beyond.

There was no roundabout way to tackle it.

'It's all right' she said. 'It's all right Tom. It's all right to be afraid.'

He waited. She knew that he wasn't toying with her, making a statement by a grand silence; that she was pulling him back from his thoughts.

'I don't go up there, you see.'

No excuses made. He didn't bother to say he wasn't afraid. He spoke as if it was quiet common sense and that she would understand.

'It's where my father hanged himself.'

○ ○ ○ ○ ○

5

Daisy Ballantyne's first father died as a result of a tragedy in which his fishing trawler was dragged to the sea bed by a naval submarine on exercises. Tom Devine's father, who had been a guest aboard the submarine, later hanged himself in the office where Daisy and Tom have just completed a business agreement engaging her merchant shipping company to transport his cargo. During the signing of the contracts a storm has damaged the office roof. The subsequent trauma has inadvertently thrown up the hitherto unacknowledged connection linking Daisy's father and Tom's. Isabella Berthonella has been working for Tom to broaden her experience of the merchant shipping business.

THEY SLIPPED OUT the back of the depot into New North Place, took a left at Toto's past the Old King's Head on the corner of Holywell Road and Scrutton Street and on by the Fox into Epworth Street and the City Road.

Carrick's were doing stew today. They decided on that.

For a moment he'd felt relief, that it could all come out. But what reason could she have to care about his feelings? It was her childhood which had been taken away, not his. And that wasn't true. His father's depression had choked their lives – mother, father, son – like a poisonous cloud. Finally, for him, to extinction. It wasn't that his ghost lingered; it didn't. Tom remembered – slightly, a few flashes – his father's normality. And it wasn't that there were not periods of happiness: again, flashes.

Carrick's didn't call it stew. It was Veau Marengo, pretty and delicious.

'I make it so often. No, sometimes. Veal, tomatoes, mushroom, onions, garlic, orange, thyme, basil. They should all be Provençal. Olive oil, but that's from Italy really. That's where I had it first. Have you been there – Provence? It's quite nice. You have not to think about the small cow. Veal is cruelty to a lot of people. Do you feel that way?'

She didn't need to fill in the spaces but he didn't mind. He could listen to her talk for as long as she talked. He thought her voice was musical in the same way as a piano: most of it took place around the centre, with journeys up above middle C, occasional visits down towards bottom E for effect, then up to top A for hilarity, leaving the ends unexplored.

'Just a coffee thank you.'

She seemed calmer now. He wondered why he had blurted it out. Knowing her – did he? – it couldn't have been to break the dam. She was too held-in for a little trick. She had tried to speak. He could see she'd been on the edge of saying 'I'm so sorry. I'd no idea' – but hadn't, because it would have been another small lie. Not the sorry, but the no idea. Instead, a couple of words – he couldn't remember what – palliatives, neutral, correct. Then they were out of the office door and mainly in silence till they had sat down in the restaurant.

Carrick's was a gloomy old place with stained grey tiling to the front, the name in raised and serifed Roman lettering above the ground-floor plate-glass windows, and again in red neon above the upper floor – daringly without the apostrophe. Coffee downstairs, meals above, a sign in the window saying Traditional Restaurant and a menu from the beginning of time.

Every day Tom worked for his father they'd come here, sat at the same table facing the stone fortress of the Honourable Artillery Company and the tombs of the Nonconformist burial ground. After his father died, the day after he'd come into the office and found a note telling him not to go upstairs and why – which naturally made him go there immediately – he changed to another table. The view was similar, though with less artillery and more tombs.

Same view today. Same waitress, same uniform – black skirt, black cardigan, white apron, white cap – same pleasant manner of enquiry. Same menu though some days it was Boeuf Bourguignon: same recipe: beef for veal. Fridays Bouillabaisse, ditto, fish. Coq au Vin. He shuddered.

Jack. Tomorrow night he would have to face it. He sighed.

'Are you all right?'

'Yes of course. I'm so sorry, is it all right?'

Her pretty face. It would be out of the question for her to love him, even to think twice about him. I'm ashamed of this place, ashamed to have brought her here. She must think me incredibly drab. I am ordinary, I am dull. All of the men in her life must be exciting. I'm not exciting. Predictable, not handsome, not attractive, overweight? Underweight? I can never get anything right except lists, bills, calculations.

Daisy was angry that she hadn't faced it. The moment had gone so fast and so immediately that for a moment she laughed – inside – at the idea of it running away as fast as it could, on two little legs, hiding somewhere, never coming back. It had been pointless and ridiculous to lie about a detail. My intentions were good.

Now.

'It wasn't the Isle of Man. It was the Fitzroy Trench off the South East Coast, the submarine was Defender, your father was Guest. I didn't want you to know that I knew.'

'You knew when we first met?'

'Yes.'

'Why not just have said?'

'I knew when I was 18. My father told me. I didn't know about you. Just about your father, and my father said that he was innocent. It wasn't till a while after we'd met that I realised you must be his son.'

'He was telling a joke. It seems trivial, doesn't it? He was telling them a joke. They weren't paying attention and killed your father.'

'My father – my second father – was clear that it was the

responsibility of the instructor and after her the captain. No-one else. Your father was just that, a guest.'

'My father hanged himself because for twenty-five years he blamed himself for killing your father and the crew.'

'When we first met, did you know who I was?'

'Yes.'

'It would have been easy to have had this conversation then.'

'It's not easy now.'

She thought, you're right. I told you to relieve myself. I've made more problems. I've set up a wall between us. I will learn to shut my mouth. I can't take it down now, it's setting. It's set.

'On second thoughts, it is.'

He was suddenly light, put his hands in his pockets, pushed his chair back. She thought he was going to leave.

'What?'

'When he killed himself I realised two things. How horrible his life was. That he'd waited till I'd grown up, seen I could manage. That's all.

'He loved me.

'We blame people who commit suicide, but he couldn't go on. For twenty-five years he couldn't go on, but he did. He waited till he'd given me everything he could, then he left. OK it looks selfish to kill yourself in the office, but wherever you do it, someone has to find you. My mother? Some poor stranger? He knew I was strong enough, loved him. I would understand. He was right. I understood. Perhaps I was strong enough.

'I took him in my arms. Laid him down to peace. Like a sacrament. It was somewhere that he felt safe. It was not as if he haunted the building. More as if he blessed it.'

Daisy examined his hands, which were stronger than him. He was weedy – it couldn't be avoided – but in quite a manly way. Perhaps not weedy; simply not very assertive. I only like people who are assertive.

But for a moment he had become resolute and she thought that was attractive. The trouble was, all of him was attractive, and the logical mismatch of qualities she required against what was presented didn't bother her. I am what I am rather than what I should like to be, and that's how he is. There's nothing to be done about it except stay as far away from him as possible.

'What's the time? I can't stay any longer. I'll get the bill on the way out. I insist.'

She didn't go. Half an hour later they were still there. Carrick's final courses trampled rather than trod familiar paths but Black Forest Gateau for two was messy and good for the destruction of dignity – Maraschino cherry-marks on faces and hands. A plate of cheese. Coffee. An hour.

He asked when they were meeting next, reluctant to break the mood.

'I'll see you at Jill's tomorrow night.'

'Oh.'

He couldn't make the connection; suddenly it came.

'Of course. The Constanza.'

'Yes. We got to know each other. And Jack.' She thought it was getting too close. Too closed in. I'll phone him and get it over with. Completely?

He thought it was getting too close. Phone Jack? Get it out into the open. Is that fair? Only to relieve myself? Pissing over her, him? Defecating? Defecating It's important to get the small things right, but shitting over both of them isn't small.

'Share the joke?'

'Coq au vin.'

'Do they still make that anywhere?'

'They make it here, for sure. And tomorrow night. It's the only thing Jack can make. He is the master of Le Coq.'

'Something to look forward to.'

The only thing.

They shook hands at Old Street tube. Tom took the long way back to the office. He'd spend an hour going through orders with the warehouse manager. He'd work out what to do about tomorrow. The nagging temptation to phone; the easy way out.

Then I will sleep with my ancestors, dreaming of trading coal on tramp-ship routes. No airless holds crammed with slaves, sold by their comrades, battened down, crewed by Lascars, sailing for California. Far too exciting. My family's dull cargoes are and always have been logged by quartermaster Masefield. Bauxite and copper sulphate, chocolate, silk, soft fruit, beer, potatoes, milk of royal mares. The bulk hold is full of sulphur rocks, for crushing to flowers and the stink of hell; occasional points of blue ignition releasing yellow fog. My family: Huguenots from Revolution to Spitalfields. A thousand years of history, built on dullness and clever marriages.

Their house had been in West Sussex; it still was. His mother lived there, both of them getting old but the house having the edge. Tom supposed he'd keep it when she died. I don't have the imagination to do anything else.

At the office they'd repaired the roof. Rubble had been bagged and removed, bags neat by the loading bay. The floor looked swept and washed. All shipshape and Robertson Dawley! I can hear you saying that, father, never dad. It was new.

Tom took a chair upstairs and sat alone in the room. My father's – what? – launching pad? My family. Piracy, shipwreck, insurance, negligence, arbitration; loss of vessel, cargo, precious life.

War. The Somme. Dynamite. Gas and bullet ships solid across the Channel.

They say you could hear the guns of the Somme in Sussex.

Comfortable socialists Beatrice and Sidney Webb rented our house. The sound of a generation wiping itself out distressed Beatrice. Oh, they'd demur they were comfortable. They were visited – so the family legend has it – for a week or two by George Shaw. Bernard, if you don't mind. It was where he wrote Heartbreak House. You used to point out where when people came round. An allegory of the collision of the great European powers. Later recorded as Hotel by the King.

Apparently – were you joking? – Beatrice would squeeze her pudgy hands together and her eyes would fair pop from their sockets with self-delight: 'We knew Virginia Woolf and all – lots of important people.' And little Sidney would pipe up – they often finished each other's conversations – 'Lawrence of Arabia – on and off his bike. DH Lawrence.' 'And his fat German whore' Beatrice would add. 'And of course Lady Ottoline Morrell. She had absolutely none at all!'

What a riot!

'Mr Devine.'

He looked up.

'Isabella.'

She stopped, as if she didn't know what to say, or what was the correct action. He stood and felt awkward, but for her, because he realised his face was covered in tears.

'I have a terrible allergy to pollen.'

It was a damned good improvisation. He was sure she wasn't even slightly deceived, but it gave them both a gambit.

'There must be a.'

She didn't mean to interrupt in a rude way, he knew. To help him out.

'I must go now back to my ship.'

He tried to place her accent, although he knew. At the moment he couldn't remember items. The contents of a charter party would be impossible to recall, for example. But that wasn't called upon. This was a simple transaction. He had only to focus.

'I didn't want to leave without thanking you. Thank you for the opportunity.'

'It's been great for you to be here. I do hope you'll pop over and join us for as long as you want next time.'

He wanted to concentrate, but another thought intruded. I have to face up to Jack.

'I would like that. I have learnt a great deal.'

They weren't sure what to say next. She had a white bag in her hand with lettering on it, perhaps the name of a shop.

'I don't know what is correct here. At home to say thank you we like to give a present. Oh!' She looked worried, but gave him the bag. 'Can you eat nuts?'

There was a joke here, but he kept his face serious.

'Yes, I can eat nuts.' He opened the bag. 'And I love cantucci. But most of all I love cantucci al miele.'

'You know what it is?'

'I know what it is.'

'If it was Christmas, I would have given you panettone.'

'Do you make it yourself?'

He smiled now because she looked shy; not an emotion he'd have expected.

'Yes.'

49

'Is it forbidden to make or eat panettone outside of Christmas?'

'It is a mortal sin.'

She laughed now, a big open laugh.

He wasn't sure how to conclude. It seemed correct to shake hands, just as he had with Daisy. He couldn't kiss someone on both cheeks, a kiss which by repetition he felt meant and was meant to mean nothing, and in any case it would be completely out of context. They looked at each other. They looked at the packet of biscuits in his hand. She stepped forward and kissed him robustly on his cheek. One cheek. She stepped back and walked with surprising grace down the stairs.

○ ○ ○ ○ ○

6

Daisy and Rachel are sisters of sorts. Rachel runs a bookshop and is being watched, suspected of making bombs. Jack, Jill, Daisy and Tom are entangled in a sexual labyrinth which is beginning to unravel.

'HE'D BEEN IN the shop before and thought I hadn't remembered. You know me, photographic memory.' Rachel laughed. 'Unlikely. Anyway he was standing there and I was up the ladder, right up at the top. He looked up at me. I said "Are you looking up my dress?"'

'You are so embarrassing.'

'He looked – awkward. He said he wanted a copy of a book by Graham Greene, a second copy.'

'What's the book?'

'By heart: The Human Factor. 339 pages. 1978. Hardback. He had one and wanted another – must be identical. I ask you. I said – just a soupçon coyly – "Do you like what you can see?" He said "I am not looking up your dress." He went red.'

'Poor chap.'

'My arse. He was a sexual deviant. Absolutely no question. Not really. Rather cute. I liked him for going red.'

'Not another.'

'I'm very discriminating. Anyhow I came down the ladder,

opened a drawer and put a book in his hand. I said "Like this?" His face! He said "That's incredible. It's just like mine." I said "It isn't. It is yours. You left it in the shop last time you came." I did laugh. He didn't. He went red again. He's called Adam.'

'Poor Adam.'

'Anyhow it was his fault. I ran after him the first time, to give it back. He'd disappeared. He's quite sweet actually.'

'And?'

Rachel drew her finger along her lips. 'Perfect seal. Off to see the fat one?'

'She's pregnant.'

'She's fat when she's not pregnant. All right. Comfortable. Large and pleasant. And the man has teeth like a wolf.'

'One slightly prominent canine tooth.'

'Vulpine. I'll give you a present of a dictionary. Marxist or plain?'

'Jill is lovely.'

'A bloater. And the man wears peculiar trousers. Also he must have a massively large dick, it's more of an – elongation. Boxers. Briefs wouldn't contain it. Quite a hunky cock, all in all. And it probably has been.'

'I'm sure that Jack is very maritally faithful. He adores her. You can see it. And she loves him. That's wonderful.' Daisy stopped. Rachel was sniggering. Daisy thought it better to laugh. She said 'We shouldn't laugh.'

○ ○ ○

Jill Jouvry sat flopped in an armchair like a fat Martian experiencing Earth's gravity. She wondered what trousers her husband would be wearing. The loose cavalry ones? He came into the room. Yes. Not the snug tailored fit of the cavalry officer, more the rough durable khaki twills for mucking out. Boxers, penis loose. Deliberate?

'Some people are repelled by pregnancy' she sighed. 'But the rest of us – we're enthusiasts. All the normal people.'

'I'm certainly an enthusiast, darling.'

'Jacky.' Why not? A little twist of the knife might liven the incredibly dull evening ahead.

'Jack.'

'Darling.'

'It's certainly drawn us closer together.' Why not, he thought? A little twist of the knife might liven the incredibly dull evening ahead.

'It's not an it. It's a little she or he.'

'I'm not Jacky, I'm Jack.' Oh the joy.

'Touchy, darling. What are you creating for us tonight?' Fucking chicken in red wine.

'I thought chicken in red wine.'

'Wonderful.'

'Mushrooms, chicken of course, a flamed bottle of Medoc, bouquet garni. Shallots.'

'Darling, remind me. How long does it take?'

'Exactly one hour, 20 minutes.'

'Don't you think – darling – if we're all going to eat tonight, you'd better go and strangle the cock?

There was a thud on the door because neither of them had repaired the bell.

'That'll be Tom.'

Jill yawned. 'Don't spend hours in the kitchen talking about football.' Jack hated football. He went out to open the door.

The Jouvrys had bought in Brockley when it wasn't fashionable, and remained there as this continued. Jack had picked up a big shambling house in a deal, front door, room to the right (styled a fraction pretentiously by Jill as the library), dining room ahead followed by a conservatory (new), a short garden and a summer house. Kitchen to the right of the dining room, no serving hatch (Jill considered this, ruled it bourgeois) – complete privacy for cooks, conspirators, lovers, friends. And high worktops because the Jouvrys were tall.

Jack was a neat cook. The tools and dead chicken were laid out as after a murder, before cutting and parcelling up the corpse.

Tom took a couple of deep breaths. He'd rehearsed thoroughly what he was going to say. He had been careful not to build it up into a mountain. Or rather, he had visualised it as a mountain, but approached by a series of little hills, so that one might ascend gradually in fragrant air to the challenge of the final ascent. He wimped out.

'What are you doing?'

Jack glanced at him and continued chopping. The chopping board was white, the knife substantial.

'Dicing shallots.'

'Ashamed of being gay?'

'I'm not gay. Pass the cottage cheese.'

'You've still got a cock in your hand.'

'It's a chicken, Tom.'

'But note, the male chicken. There's a cock in au vin.'

This had taken entirely the wrong direction. If only he'd spoken, said the hard, necessary words. Fought, if necessary. But he hadn't. Postponement of the moment of action is what I do. I am a coward.

'Get it out, Tom. I make money. I sell ordinary things. I don't pretend. I don't go to celebrity parties. But I provide. I'm married. I bought this house The woman I love is having a baby. What is wrong with that?

'You're fractionally up your own arse.'

'Or, before you answer. What exactly have you achieved? You're clever. But at the centre of your life, you won't commit. Why is that? Because you're a child. You're stuck somewhere between nought and fifteen. Still putting off the day when you'll face up to your adult responsibilities.

'Let me take these points one at a time.'

'No, Tom, because I'm not interested. And let me save you the time.'

'OK. Peace. Peace. Peace. Give me a job to do. I can clean mushrooms. I can dice onions.'

'Shallots.'

'Shallots. Fuck, man, I taught you this recipe.'

'Peel the potatoes.'

'I prefer them scrubbed, myself.'

'Peel the fucking potatoes.'

'OK.' One day I will have the courage to say what has to be said. I know that is not true.

'And wash your hands first.'

There was a thud at the front door and Daisy came in.

Tom had remembered to bring an expensive bottle of wine, because Jill would price it. Jill took a prominent position on not drinking alcohol in pregnancy. 'Baby's needs come first.' She received the visitors in turn in the library till Jack struck the gong.

'Rather lovely in its own way; an auction in Lots Road'.

Tom looked at a reproduction of Jan van Eyck's Wife of Arnolfini and tried to imagine Jill a few sizes smaller fitting into the frame. Daisy didn't quite miss catching Tom's eye and knew he was trying to keep a straight face.

The books on the aged-oak shelves which went from the expensive Isfahan Rugs to the reproduction Adam ceiling might have been bought by the metre but cleverly the spines didn't match and they might have been read. Tom thought it was spiteful of him to sneer at their taste and felt guilty, but it passed quickly and he sneered again and enjoyed it.

He caught Daisy's glance. She looked gorgeous, and he felt inferior.

At the end there was warm sloppy Camembert. Tom remembered the biscuits the woman had given him which were still in his bag. Jill approved.

'Cantucci. How wonderful that we have a little Vin Santo. Jack?'

Jack obediently got up and returned with a small bottle of sweet dessert wine. Daisy took one of the biscuits, put it in her mouth. It was honey-sweet and solid, delicious in expectation.

Jill shook her head. 'I won't have any wine myself. Baby's needs.'

Daisy looked surreptitiously at Tom, couldn't contain her laugh this time, and accidentally swallowed.

She started choking, thinking it would stop, but it didn't.

She tried to breathe and couldn't.

Logically she knew not to panic, but logic went, and she knew she was going to die. She was going to die as her father had died, unable to breathe.

She tried again and her lungs tried to force her, but the breath was blocked, and she began to faint.

Tom was on his feet and round to her. He was ready to hit her on the back, but Jack, quicker, pushed him aside, lifted her gently from behind and kicked her chair out of the way.

Putting his arms under hers, he leant her gently forward and tilted her head down. He made a fist with one hand and covered it with the other in the centre of her ribcage up above her stomach.

Tom knew this was the wrong position, but Jack had exuded an authority which was impossible to resist. He watched Jack's hands thrust firmly against Daisy's breastbone, inwards, downwards.

Suddenly the biscuit came out of her mouth, and she sucked in great draughts of air. There was water round her eyes and her face was red, but she wasn't crying. She leant back on Jack and for a moment her held her, his hands over and slightly above her breasts. And Tom suddenly realised why he hadn't put his hands lower, hadn't applied pressure onto her stomach. It was how to handle a pregnant woman.

Which was natural. Jill was pregnant. Jack Jouvry had adapted himself, as he always did, to the exact circumstances he encountered, like a leopard in the snow. Or perhaps that was a different kind of leopard, Tom wasn't sure. It didn't matter: if Jack was a leopard and the deal needed it, he'd change spots for white, and include his old skin as a down payment.

After dinner Jill received in the summer house.

'If you don't mind, darlings, I will excuse myself from the removal of the debris and retire to the belvedere.'

It was a lot more than a shed, more of a Greek temple. Sometimes she called it the Acropolis.

Jack said he'd bring coffee and started to clear up. It was the moment for Tom to find him alone and speak, and Tom was afraid. He had seen Daisy in Jack's arms, strong arms, resting for a moment against him; failed when quick, immediate and correct action had been needed; been tossed aside by the better, more competent male. He felt stupid, useless, unmanned. He followed Jill into the garden.

o o o

Daisy helped Jack clear the table and went with him into the kitchen. She closed the door.

'Nobody noticed. Some people say they can tell within a couple of days. A little plumpening around the face.'

56

Jack cleaned food from the plates into a gleaming tall stainless steel bin, and ran water into the distressed Belfast sink.

'What's the news?'

'You're going to be a daddy two times over.'

'How do you feel?'

'Frightened.'

'Why be afraid? It's been done a few million times before. There's plenty of books.'

'I'm frightened of the explanations. And what people are going to say.'

'Yes.'

'Does that disgust you?'

'Nothing about you would ever disgust me.' He laid a plate on the draining board, turned to her. 'I'm looking at the woman I've longed to meet since the day that I was born.' The words slipped out easily.

Daisy wondered how often he'd said them before. But it was a brief wondering. She was thinking of something more fundamental. Do I love him, and if so, how much?

'You're an un-healable romantic.'

'If I have you, I have everything.'

'And how do you know that you have me? How do you know that you'll keep me?'

'When would you like me to make the announcement? Or you?'

'I love you.' Do I?

'Actually, I knew that already.'

'You're very presumptuous. For a tradesman. Will she divorce you?'

'What do you think?'

'Easy. She's hot, passionate, rational, and devoted to the people she loves. Loyal, and completely unpredictable. Also a little mad. It's really a matter of tossing a coin.'

'Thank you.'

∘ ∘ ∘

The grand façade of the summer-house consisted of a pair of naked caryatids sculpted in stone in tribute to an idealised and slender version of Jill. They carried – in Corinthian order down to the last grape – a stone entablature supporting a stone pediment.

57

All in all it was quite like the Parthenon, but with a slim terrace of York stone beneath and French windows behind.

Jill reclined on a chaise longue covered by a Mandarin throw. This was possibly with Lillie Langtry in mind, but it looked more to Tom like a fat version of the Death of Marat.

Lowering her head and looking up at him – more or less seductively – Jill sighed.

'I'm desperate. Desperate. Desperate. Desperate for the taste of your lips. I'm desperate for your charm and your wit.'

'I'm glad to hear it. It was redundant in the kitchen.'

She lifted herself onto an elbow, her face registering slight alarm against a broader background of excitement.

'You didn't tell him, did you?'

'Heavens, no. I'm not suicidal. Though as you know, I'm always up for a new experience.'

'Kiss me.' She offered her lips, parted.

Tom felt what he always felt when she said that – though he'd always tell himself not again – a powerful shudder of desire.

'Like this?'

'More.'

'Like this?'

'Better.'

'Like this?'

'Almost perfect.' She wiped her mouth with her hand, and asked brightly, 'When are you going to tell him?'

'Jill, it's not a question of "When am I going to tell him?"'

Tom knew Jill well enough to recognise familiar patterns to her strategies. This particular sequence was usually wet or wettish passion – for which there were sub-routines – followed by the point. What that might be, was generally clarified by commands, often issued in the disguise of questions.

'Or actually, not when, but how, are you going to tell him?'

And there she had him. The confrontation he had run away from – which now approached like an express. Chess was one of the many skills Tom knew that he lacked, and trying to think of what to say, what she would say, and how he would score the winning goal – football was another missing talent – preoccupied him.

Jill was getting restless, which was dangerous. I'm going to say something like: for many years now, while masquerading as your friend, I've been having an energetic affair with your wife. Jill would reply: energetic affair? Is that all it is to you?

And the answer?

I hope it was more. I hope I really loved you once. I know that I don't love you now. Not because you are not good, kind and gentle. I know you to be all of those things, sweet and generous too. But because I'm in love with Daisy, and it will never go anywhere because I'm not good enough for her. And if I'm not good enough for her, I can't love you, because that would be to reduce you, and you are not to be reduced. You belong at the top of somebody's tree. Jack's, perhaps. But not mine.

'I'll think of the right words at the right time.'

'When? If I was still your lawyer.'

All those frenzied nights spent ripping the pink ribbon from her immaculate briefs.

'I would insist that you proceed without delay.'

'You have to appreciate, Jill.'

'I'm not a client, Tom.' She spat it out.

'OK. Jacky.'

'Jack.'

'Jack is a trader. He'll hate the situation. But he'll accept it. Provided he gets something in return.'

'A timeshare of my cunt? Or why not divide me another way? He could have the exclusive benefit of my mouth.'

Some merit in that.

'Buying something in exchange for my baby?'

'Hang on. Two minutes ago it was our baby.'

'I have given up my career to be a mother.'

'For a few months.'

'No Tom, not only for a few months. I intend to be a full-time mother.'

'What about your career?'

'Do you mean, what about the money?'

'Of course, what about the money? Money comes into everything.'

'And yet Jack can accept that. Without a second thought. So far as Jack is concerned, if I choose to continue soaring to the pinnacle of the legal profession, that is my concern. If I choose to become a full-time mother, he will support me. He will support us. He will support our family.'

'It's not his family.'

'In exactly what sense isn't it – his and my family?'

'Do you mean to say that there's any doubt? I thought you told me, that apart from some – temporary activity – around the time of conception.'

'Do you seriously expect me to live with a beautiful and good-looking man, and not make love?'

Suddenly, Tom saw clear sky.

A little later he went to the library to pick up his bag and found Daisy there doing the same.

'Hang on. I'll just say goodbye.'

She ran out into the garden to the summer house and knelt down beside Jill.

'You look beautiful.' Jill spoke softly. 'Your face is – radiant.'

'Ha. Running.'

'You look adorable. I want to feel. Yes. Yes. Rub me? Of all the people who have touched me physically, throughout my life from the first moment that I can remember, there is no-one who has your touch. Nor of the people who have kissed me, your kiss. No-one makes me feel more complete.'

'You are gorgeous.'

'You don't need to look so surprised. I'm still beautiful even though I'm pregnant. I hadn't realised how much pregnancy transforms. The skin glows. The body exudes power.' Jill paused, added almost in a whisper, 'Sometimes I get depressed.'

'Silly.' It was time to go and Daisy stood up, her voice as practical as a head girl. Never get depressed, her second father had said. Or if you do, try for it not to linger. 'Any pregnant mum's going to face problems. Among the people she knows and loves. Readjustment.'

'We don't know the future. There's no point worrying about it.'

'Jack always says that.'

'Yes. He does, doesn't he?' Jill snapped. She looked directly at

Daisy. She must know. Perhaps she'd known all the time.

Tom was waiting for her outside the front door.

'I thought I'd get out of there. It looked like those two had things they needed to talk about.'

She was glad he was there, felt safe, needed safety.

'I got that too.' She made her voice sound bright.

'When do we meet next?'

'On the ship? Talk tomorrow?'

'Do you want to share my taxi?'

'I have a car.' She pulled keys out of her pocket. 'Nice, isn't it?'

'Fantastic.'

'I got it from Jack. Part of a deal. You want a ride?'

○ ○ ○ ○ ○

7

Daisy and Tom are linked by a tragedy which ultimately has caused the deaths of their respective fathers. They have just completed a business agreement engaging her merchant ship Turmoil to transport his cargo. At the end of a tense and destructive dinner party with friends each harbours an unspoken, impractical attraction to the other.

ONCE IN THE day and once at night, once a week, the bombers flew in a cross, visibly unarmed. Daisy drove fast and reached the ferry across the Thames before the last sailing. There was a message on the phone which at first she didn't disclose, too much was going through her mind. Tom sank back in the passenger seat, and she wondered if he was scared of her driving, drunk, or didn't know what to say.

Always two planes. One flew at 400 metres, comfortably above the tallest remaining building in the City, low enough to intimidate. The other a thousand metres above it. They'd sweep from east to west: Cranford and Hanwell, Brentford and Ealing to Poplar and Plumstead, Rainham and Grays, Canvey Island. Then south to north, from the Epsom Downs and Carshalton Beeches over St John's church in Caterham, past Norbury High Street and Streatham Market, the Tower of London to the Angel, Parliament

Hill and Hadley Wood, Barnet Museum and Enfield. Then in tandem up the spine of England, splitting left and right to Carlisle and Newcastle, out to sea and round the north of Scotland, passing each other and returning south, one to the west side, the other to the east. Neighbourhood sirens would activate before their arrival, and stop as they passed over, linking the suburbs and centres, and each village, town, island and city through the country in a winding up and winding down whine. If anyone was expected to rush to the air raid shelters, nobody did. It was, after all, nothing more than a grown-up fire-alarm drill, and who had ever cared about those? If it served any purpose, perhaps it was to keep everyone on edge, but that, Daisy thought, would be cynical. The road signs said: dip your lights.

'Unfortunately I nearly killed you tonight.'

Well, he'd tried a joke. Better than silence. One of the ferry crew in a yellow jacket signalled her to a space at the front end. They got out and stood at the rail looking back at the cars and trucks driving onto the ship from the drawbridge. She thought how neatly the crew positioned each of the vehicles big and small, sparing on limited space, almost touching, completely apart.

She thought of saying: that would make it two nil to your family. Father, son: father, daughter. But there was no need to be cruel, even to be funny, and she didn't want to hurt him. She didn't want to love him either. The question was whether that was inevitable like a collision or could be escaped. Such a small amount of time in which to compress the amount she had to live. Long or short made no difference – it was what would fit into whatever there was. Waste it to fit in another pointless love affair? Everything came to an end.

'You're taking responsibility for the biscuit.'

'It was my biscuit.'

'It became mine when I accepted it. A basic contract. Buyer beware.'

They watched the ferry detach itself, sweep round and clear in an elegant dance with its twin going in the opposite direction.

'I felt useless.'

'Why?'

'I was going to slap you on the back. All wrong. He pushed me out of the way, and it's a good thing. He knew what to do. I didn't.'

'You are stupid.'

'Yes.'

'No. It was my fault. It got sorted out. If you want to worry, worry about something real.'

Back in the car, she started the engine. There was something sweet about his words. Or the tone of his voice? Or being able to know that he was inadequate and to say it?

'Like what?'

'Like Turmoil is re-routed right up round the top and down to Liverpool because the Channel is, apparently, suddenly not safe.'

'So we take a few more days. We part-load in Liverpool, far better. I'll truck up half the scrap and they can crush it there.'

She decided. It wasn't sudden. Realistically, she'd known from the moment she'd seen him again; and before, in the expectation. If I am to commit, there isn't an alternative.

'It'll be you.'

'You're not coming?'

'It means new paperwork. I'll fly down and join her somewhere along the route.'

He knew that it meant that she wouldn't come, and he'd expected it. All a waste of time.

She dropped him off outside his flat. He didn't know how to say goodbye, knowing it would be goodbye. He didn't risk to kiss her, in the end shook her hand, worrying that his might be damp.

It was midnight when Daisy arrived at the port. Pöl Stuyvesant was waiting for her in the office. They went straight to the charts.

'It's too far south to be safe.'

Daisy grinned, loved him, knew his over-caution.

'Is it do-able?'

'Yes.'

'Then we'll do it.'

They stood by the dock watching the stevedores load the cargo: crushed scrap from broken cars and girders, the metal debris of bomb sites. She stood on tiptoe and kissed him goodnight, feeling always safe to be with him. At least there is one certainty in my life: always there, always has been, always will be.

64

It was two o'clock, and she was too tired to go back to Hillfield Road. Instead, she drove to her mother's house, let herself in with her key, showered and went to bed in the room which had been hers since as a child she came into what she always thought of as the second part of her life.

And what, she thought as she fell asleep – and when – will be the third?

○ ○ ○ ○ ○

8

Bettina Ballantyne has three daughters, not all related: Rachel, Daisy, Rowena. Rachel runs a bookshop and is being watched, suspected of making bombs. Daisy runs a shipping company; her vessel Turmoil is contracted to transport a cargo of scrap metal for Tom Devine for whom she has an inconvenient longing. Jill, friend and lover to both Daisy and Tom, and married to Jack, is pregnant.

'YOU WILL TELL me, won't you, when you need help?'

There was no point in trying to eat. Daisy pushed the plate of bacon, sausage, egg, tomato, mushroom to one side and tried to avoid her mother's eyes. Your pellucid eyes, yes, pellucid was the word, but what did it mean?

'Old girl?'

Old girl! The old girl is you. What will I do when you die? Who will there be, not what, to call home?

'I don't know what I'll do when you die.'

'I am not intending to die at the moment, as you can well imagine. Do I look like someone who is about to die? I can assure you that nothing is less likely. All told. It would also be useful if you would spend a little more attention on your religion. But that's as much as I'll say or you'll be bored and tell me to shut up.

However I will not be silenced.'

When you need help. It was not if, but when. There was no point in speaking the words – no doubt that she knew, but the fact of the words not being spoken gave leeway between the two of them. Three including Paul, who strolled over, gave a reassuring push against Daisy's leg and stretched out under the window in the sun. She wondered if dogs thought, and decided not, obviously. Religion? All the holy pictures in the world won't save me now.

'Where's Rachel?' I must see her. If I can talk to Rachel, pour out my heart, it will all be all right. Rachel.

'Your sister stroke cousin has a man. Adam, I believe. I know nothing about him and she is in Oxford, I'm quite sure. A lecture of some kind. When Rachel becomes evasive I don't pry. That would be counterproductive, clearly, Rachel being as she is. There will almost certainly be trouble.'

'Has that dreadful man being saying things?'

'Emilio is a good man and was very fond of your father. Now that I am a poor widow, the attentions of any young gentleman are welcome and as a matter of fact rather than speculation I have invited him to afternoon tea. There will be, I fancy, Battenberg cake and possibly scones. It depends on cook and the maid.'

'We don't have either.'

'We can always pretend. I have always pretended. One must have a fancy otherwise life becomes so incurably dull.'

'When did Rowena go to work?'

Paul looked up at Rowena's name, put his head back onto his paws and closed his eyes. She had been a late child – a miracle, her mother would say – fifty years old when Rowena was born. Sometimes she would add: in the footsteps of Mrs Abraham.

'A miracle. And then the gift of my second daughter.' The eyes again, loving. 'And a half if one counts a cousin and from time to time, I do. A variable girl, but on the whole satisfactory. I have no complaints, only gratitude. I have been blessed.'

∘ ∘ ∘

At exactly 15:30 with Daisy long gone, there was a polite strike of the door knocker – quiet, almost apologetic.

Emilio Podro could have been born in one of a variety of years, lost in the middle ages of 35 to 50, a short man, possibly jolly in appearance, but not quite, with prominent whites to his eyes so that they seemed – only slightly – to bulge, and the irises to float in them like poached eggs. He carried a box.

'Three years in the oak and fifty in the bottle, my heavens Emilio this is a vintage well beyond extravagance.' Mrs Ballantyne held the bottle to the light, taking care not to disturb the sediment.

'Nothing as vulgar as price will disturb us in its consumption, dona Bettina. Do you have with you the necessary?'

'I do.'

The dining room looked out on a pretty garden with a picket fence and beyond it a slope down to a field where an old jenny donkey grazed and – from time to time – brayed, but more one sensed for the hell of it rather than because she wanted to say something important. The table was laid with a lace cloth, bone china plates with a blue trim lined with a fine gold line, cups and a teapot and milk-jug which matched, silver apostle spoons, small bone-handled Sheffield knives, a pair of linen napkins in silver rings, a cake-stand with cucumber sandwiches, currant scones, plain scones, a silver dish of unwhipped double cream, an unmatching dish of raspberry jam. Two port glasses.

'The secret – I believe – is lightly buttering the outside of the bread. A glaze, almost invisible. A more thorough buttering on the inside, but still not to excess.'

Mrs Ballantyne went to the kitchen and returned with a Battenberg cake on a plate, and a knife which curved up at the end.

'In the old days it came in a tin.'

'But dona Bettina is too young and beautiful to remember the old days.'

'I am far too old not to remember them.'

'I meant the very old days. Captain Scott.'

'Buried the horses to eat but they were rotten when he came back. Thawed.'

'If only they'd had tinned Battenberg from the Expatriate Trading Company. All would have survived. It was good enough for Sir Edmund Hillary and Sherpa Tenzing on the top of Mount

Ararat. The only requirement would be this.' He flourished a Swiss Army penknife. 'With the electrical circular-saw attachment to open it which unfortunately this one lacks.'

Mrs Ballantyne took a packet of cigarettes from the sideboard, lit one and tossed the pack to Podro. He lit hers with a petrol Zippo and then his own. The ashtray was a boy holding a plate behind his back. There was a complicated partly-concealed system of tube-work beneath it and between his legs, the effect of which was that the heat of a cigarette being stubbed into his back made him appear to urinate. All in plastic, he wore a blue sailor suit, had blond hair and on his chest the words Souvenir of Ceylon.

'I can see why Ballantyne liked you.' She stood at the French windows looking at the jenny, who ignored her. 'Ballantyne loved a good story. Emilio, you are a bullshitter. This is a compliment. He used to say "Never spoil a good story for the sake of the truth". Off duty. On duty, his life was the truth.'

Podro inhaled, held the smoke in his lungs and released it slowly in a cloud of Latakia. 'Dear dona Bettina, the essence of diplomacy is the spontaneous ability to bullshit.'

'I have some competence myself. Now, tell me exactly what my niece has been up to.'

'Shall we sit down?'

'I think this is something I should take standing up.'

'There is a man.'

'Adam something. What is he? Special Branch?'

'Mr Brook is evidently a civil servant and nothing – apparently – as glamorous as that. Some quite straightforward department of the Home Office I imagine, no more. It's mainly rhetoric at the moment, is it not? But it might be useful if you were to have a word.'

'She won't listen.'

'I would suggest that she does.'

A few days later Daisy woke to the voice of another mother: 'It's no good the kittens mewling. The cat is dead.'

A dream? A memory? She packed an overnight bag and took a train.

∘ ∘ ∘

69

Tom sat on a train to Liverpool to join Turmoil listening to a woman saying she was a chemist. 'I often don't tell people because they then tell you what's wrong with them and I have to explain that while I am of course sympathetic, I don't work in a shop, I work in a lab and write papers.' He wondered if the journey would be her life history.

And what am I? Bank clerk, English tutor. Bad poet. Shipbroker – I'll never escape the family.

'If I told them I did politics or English or economics they'd feel happy to pitch in with an opinion. That's on the basis that if you accidentally read Maynard Keynes on holiday, or a novel by EM Forster, you're an expert on economics and literature; and politics you just make up as you go along.'

That's me. One day, they'll find me out. He leaned round the seat to see the voice. A pretty woman, putting bright lipstick on her mouth while talking, holding a small mirror just so.

'Science apparently is complicated. Nobody reads science on holiday. People don't care about science so long as it behaves itself. I don't care. The moment I tell anyone what I do, they change the subject and I don't have to talk about work.' She snapped the compact shut. 'Nobody gives a flying fuck about valency.'

He remembered the story on the news about a man who had burnt to death in a car. If it was only charred bones could they still find DNA? For a moment he was tempted to ask the chemist.

Since he'd known about Daisy's father drowning, he'd carried a picture of it in his head. Never wholly away. He was there – vividly – catching the moment at which the expectation of drowning switched to the certainty. And then the fact.

Drown or burn? Which would be quicker?

Crossing the bridge at Crewe, Tom saw a girl standing at the far end of a platform. It was empty apart from her, and he noticed that the rails beside it was stained brown with rust, as if trains no longer used them. She wore a mackintosh, a child with a leather suitcase, curiously out of time. She stood by herself, but it was more than that – she was alone, there was no question.

Absurdly he thought of sandwiches. Had she been left with sandwiches? A refugee?

○ ○ ○

At Liverpool Lime Street he changed stations and trains, and the two-car diesel rattled along an old single track to the docks. He wondered why the patterns on the seats needed to be dull. The sun flickered over the water, bouncing moiré lines from the oil, making rainbows.

There was a time when the Thames bristled with armadas. Spaniards reached the Houses of Parliament! The Mary Rose sank in front of Henry the Eighth. They renamed her Turmoil. No, that was wrong. Pull yourself together. Seven wives was bound to be too many. The break with Rome, age of Rationalism, foundation of the Protestant church, the Troubles, Civil War, execution of the Regicide judges, posthumous execution of Cromwell, Restoration, loss of faith, rise of Islam. It's all so modern. Look at the route of our vessel. Bound to end in tears.

The Port of Liverpool had machinery to mince up steel and iron scrap into smallish pieces. In the end he'd trucked some up from London, and found the rest locally with ease. There was no shortage of debris now in the major cities, particularly those which could load and unload ships.

The docks here had specialist cranes fitted with orange-skin grabs for loading metal – rather than magnets, which could upset Turmoil's electrical and navigational gear. Turmoil's cranes were the same, but the docks' were larger and quicker, reducing the cost of anchorage and delay to the voyage.

Turmoil had two suites for the owners, one nearby for the master, and another for the chief engineer. Elsewhere there were single-berth cabins for the crew, mess rooms, a sick bay. Accommodation was to the aft of the ship: below the bridge and above the engine room.

A steward took Tom to one of the owners' suites. He wasn't expecting luxury, and wasn't disappointed: plain walls, a desk, a bed, and a couple of rectangular windows. Bleak and functional as an office.

The steward was an older man with an un-weatherbeaten face.

On shore, Tom would have taken him for a bank manager in a medium-sized town, reassuring and not particularly active. But he climbed the companionways easily enough and looked good for another few years.

'Hopefully you won't need these.' The steward pulled out straps above and below a bench seat between the windows. 'Part of the refit in London, on account of the exciting route.'

The steward smiled, sat on the bench and strapped himself in. Two of the straps came up between his legs, two more over his shoulders, meeting in a round metal centre-piece with a D-shaped ring to one side like a parachute release.

He pointed to the loudspeaker in the ceiling. 'As soon as the alarm sounds, it's into the life-jacket, onto the seat, strap yourself in, and wait for instructions. At the all-clear you release yourself by a sharp tug on the D-ring like so.' He released the straps and re-fastened them. 'And if that doesn't work there's a back-up which is to hit the centre of the ring with your fist, and again, you will be released.' He got up. 'If you're called to the lifeboat get out of the door as fast as you can.'

'Do you know when the owner will be joining the ship?'

'I wouldn't know that, Sir. Ms Ballantyne communicates directly with the Master. Be sure to pick up the telephone if you need anything. Will that be all?'

Tom felt as if he'd been in the same room all his life. The same four plastic-covered walls; the same faint smell of fuel – heavy oil or diesel regardless. Same flat air-conditioned air pumping from the ceiling, same wooden bed bolted to the wall and floor.

The same life.

And would be forever. All his small departures, attempts to become himself, had brought him back to the identical position of limited failure. He couldn't even succeed at that.

He unpacked – neatly – allocating each category of clothing to a suitable hanger, shelf or drawer, took a shower and lay down on the bed. She might come in the end. How much he loved her.

He remembered the first time he had seen her, sitting outside the courtroom. And later, properly, as she stood outside in Chancery Lane smoking a Black Russian cigarette. Their eyes met, just like in the films.

She was laughing. Was she? He was laughing. Why? Not an explosion, revelation, flash – none of the words for sudden, inescapable immediate love. Smash! Like a car crash, not a bad crash, best-ever car crash, and both of us damaged forever: good damage.

In the instant, he knew that she loved him, and the word was recognition. Not as their names, as the children of their families, the history of all that. But as the two human beings who had been made to fit together.

Then – immediately – realisation of the complications. That love would involve adaptation, new lives. It would take time and be – frankly – inconvenient.

So, as practical people, they didn't give words to thoughts. They exchanged pleasant remarks – briefly – and continued with how the day had been planned, and after it, their lives. Time and experience had so deftly covered the memory, that Tom wondered if it had ever truly been the moment that now came into his mind; whether there had been that second of mutuality; or whether he was only conjuring up some excitement into his life where there wasn't any; daydreaming as must even a mediocre poet.

Would she come? There was nothing to do except wait.

o o o

Daisy walked from the tube to the building in West London. There was a need to think in fresh air. The room was on the first floor, drab as a hotel: wash-room, cupboards, desk – for writing a will, suicide note? – a vase of artificial flowers. And a bowl of plastic fruit to complete the mise-en-scène? The window looked out to the front and she could see the protesters – the police had been asked to move them across the street – silent in prayer. She took a shower and lay down on the bed. There was nothing to do except wait.

o o o

On the first floor of the house in Brockley, Jill lay on her bed, naked except for a towel over her bottom. Magda, au-pair-in-waiting, tall, elegant and pretty with long, thick black hair tied back in a ribbon, massaged the bulk of her as a vet might seek to

73

reinvigorate a stranded whale.

'So what is Poland like?' Jill grunted.

'I don't know.'

'It's your country isn't it?'

'Is Stoke on Trent a wonderful place?'

'How on earth should I know. I've never been there. I never will be there I shouldn't think. It's up North. There. Yes there, that's wonderful.'

Jill writhed, a smile spreading across her face.

'So tell me about Poland.'

'I have never been there.'

'Of course you have. Why not?'

'I'm Russian.'

'Ah yes. I thought your passport looked funny. How on earth do you understand the writing?'

'I come from Novosibirsk. The architecture of the famous Novosibirsk Glavniy Train Station on the Trans-Siberian railway is inspired by a steam engine. Novosibirsk is the capital of the Federal District of Siberia as well as of the Oblast of.'

'Yes, yes. I'm sure that's very interesting. Time for the other side and gently. I'm going to turn over.' But she knew she was hateful. If there was some way I could become better, kinder, I would. I don't know the way.

She was afraid, too.

Jill turned over, careful of her content. Terrified rather than afraid, but bottling it in. If she could isolate her fear, give it its precise and legalistic name, it would be the fear of fucking up. I must not fuck this up, whoever is to come out must come perfectly, whatever he or she is like, however perfect or imperfect this little one is, but the birth, my contribution to it, must be perfect. I must do better than my best.

She lay on her back, ignored Magda, felt her soothing hands on her body, closed her eyes. There was nothing to do except wait.

∘ ∘ ∘

In Oxford, Adam Brook sat in the van, looked at the screen. Another car had followed the bus from London to check that Rachel didn't get out on the way. The van was parked off Beaumont Street with a couple of officers inside and he watched

Rachel on the screen walk up from Gloucester Green bus station into the building. Passing the time he re-read the printout of the news about the man who'd burnt to death in a car. They switched on the sound and sat back to listen to her. On past form, she'd talk for an hour, and they were ready to wait.

○ ○ ○

Tom woke, not sure why, looked at the time. He'd only slept for a few minutes. No reason to fall asleep; none to fall awake. But the sleeping time was better: there could be dreams. Mentally he slapped himself round the face. Be a man. His father had never done nor said that; a gentle man. Perhaps he'd needed someone hard, would now be less of a drip.

Mind you, he thought, being a drip isn't bad – and immediately counter-argued that yes it damned-well is. It's time to stand up and be counted. I will face the future and its great adventures, and I will face it now.

He knew why he'd woken up. There was a pulse to the ship, the beat of the engine. Turmoil was under way.

○ ○ ○ ○ ○

9

Under the pretence of blossoming friendship, Adam Brook, Home Office employee, is watching Rachel Fonseca who is suspected of making bombs. Tom Devine is accompanying his shipment of scrap metal aboard an old cargo ship, Turmoil, on the vessel's last assignment. He has tender hopes that Turmoil's owner, Daisy Ballantyne, will join them. Jack and Jill Jouvry are looking forward to becoming parents, supported in their comfortable if unconventional domesticity by their Russian au pair, Magda.

RACHEL STEADIED HERSELF to the table. She was fine, there had been a headache or two – no more than that. Some blurring to the eyesight – only when she was tired. She wasn't really dizzy – probably a touch of nerves.

Rachel was confident of what she would say. Not too many people in the room – 30, 40 or 50. Ready.

The camera wasn't ideally placed. There hadn't been enough time, and it was a balance between seeing and it being seen in the relatively bare room. But the sound was perfect, and the vision adequate for evidence, should it come to that.

○ ○ ○

Sitting in the van, Adam thought she probably wouldn't care anyhow. She'd suspect that she was watched, however cursorily; would be insulted if she wasn't. It amused him that CS Lewis had lectured over many years in the same room, perhaps dreaming up Narnia.

He watched Rachel cough, the cough of a speaker about to start, and the room become silent.

Adam thought it was ironic that Narnia made Lewis famous. After that, did anyone read his books on the problem of pain and a merciful God, the nature of the devil, the finding of belief? And that he'd chosen to lecture in the resolutely humanist rooms of Concordance House, in the footsteps of Shaw and Jeremy Bentham.

That morning, Adam had stood at Lewis's grave in the churchyard of Holy Trinity Headington Quarry, requesting a burial.

'No room for more on the south side of the church, I regret. No corporeal burial. But a burial of the full body may be possible on the north.'

And perhaps, the vicar added, a cremated burial next to the hedge on the south side, in sight of Lewis's grave. With the news article in his pocket, Adam thought that would do – cremation already done.

The vicar pointed out the adjacent grave of Merry Kimber, exponent of the concertina. The annoying tune of Poppa Piccolino passed through Adam's mind. "As welcome as an accordion at a funeral" – wasn't that the expression? He wondered what Rachel would look like at the end of a rope, hoped it wouldn't happen.

o o o

Rachel began to speak.

o o o

In Brockley, Jack Jouvry lay under a Lagonda car up on axle stands. Carefully and using the slightest twist on a toque-wrench he loosened the eight bolts securing the sump, which he had drained of oil. He finished by hand, gently removing them and reaching out to put them into a tin he'd left by the side of the car.

As the last came away he eased the cover off, being careful not to tear the sealing gasket, and laid it by his face on the ground. A few warm drips of oil splashed his cheek.

He reached for the camera he'd left on the ground just clear of the car, took it to him and photographed the underside now exposed. He reached out for the tin to put in the final bolt and realised it wasn't there. He felt blindly around for it and the bolt was taken from his hand. A hand held his hand and a mouth kissed it.

o o o

The camera in Concordance House showed Rachel clearly and – as important, Adam now realised – the table in front of her. On it there were pieces of car mechanism including a starter motor and key switch, with various lengths, colours and thicknesses of wire. The lights were crude bright fluorescent strips, unflattering to the faces, but bringing out every detail of the machinery.

She picked up the motor and continued: 'There's a couple of ways. The ignition lock closes a low-amperage circuit. This is a typical starter motor. This part – the chuck – is thrown by centripetal force into the gear system which starts the engine.'

A 12-volt battery stood on the desk. With a heavy crocodile clip she connected the wire from one terminal of the starter motor to the battery, and laid its body across the other. There was a jolt, bang, a flash of sparks, as the motor fired and the chuck whizzed to the end of its spine.

'That needs a heavy traction current, hence this relay. A simple modification diverts the traction current to this bit of kit. It's a heating coil round a pump attached to a reservoir – here – typically a couple of litres, easily concealed.'

Adam thought of the man getting into the car, turning the starter switch; the doors locking, petroleum gel squirting from the centre of the steering wheel over his body, the realisation of death. Ignition.

'This is a specialist application. Questions?'

There were a lot. Rachel answered them directly and without notes.

She wrapped up the meeting with a quote from Proudhon.

'"If I can call slavery murder, why can't I call property theft?"'
'And that's in 1840. I commend him. Thank you.'

∘ ∘ ∘

'I have brought you a cup of tea' Magda said, but that was with her mouth. Her body spoke differently, and Jack was grateful. From where he lay alongside her and under the chassis of the car he could turn his head and see her feet balancing her body as she squatted on the ground to place the cup and saucer. He pulled himself clear.

'Russian, I suppose.'

She wore a long dress, and remained low, next to him. He liked her cunt, and wondered if he was in love with it – her? – or in love with her, or just enjoying the ride. He hoped it was more. He liked her pants, thought the colour suited her, and stroked them down the front and between her legs. He had seen it described as a fig – believed that was the Italian word, fica – gentler than cunt, which seemed too concrete, too brusque for something so graceful. The cloth of her underwear made a pouch of it, and he decided that pouch was the best way to think of her in that place.

'I like this place' he said.

'No. It is English. I am in England and if I make tea or drink tea, it is in the English way. With milk. I have put the milk in later, that is I think correct to preserve the temperature. Two sugar lumps, a cup and saucer. Some people say a mug is not right. There is a Nice biscuit, in fact two, in the saucer.' She shivered politely. 'I am glad you like this place.'

She ran her fingers over his trousers, but he moved her hand away and continued to stroke her. She squeezed his hand with her thighs. Last night had been for him. Today, he wanted to give to her. She gave him the camera. 'Photograph me' she said. 'I only know me from above.'

∘ ∘ ∘

Deep in Turmoil, the chief engineer was cleaning oil from his hands as Tom came into the engine room. He finished by washing them in a sink with soap, rinsed and dried them on a clean white towel, held out his right and said 'Welcome, Mr Devine. Prepare for the grand tour.'

Tom was surprised by the public-school voice, and felt guilty for his snobbery in assuming that all chief engineers were Scots, Irish, German, West Country – any of a number of parody accents, and not the additional one he heard now. As if engineers were inherently caricaturable by voice, kept below decks as below stairs while the upper-class officers enjoyed the upper air. That this man must in some way be lowering himself to have dirty hands, which in fact were clean.

What a mess I am. I can no longer see that people are what they are. As if I ever could.

'It's very good of you to find the time, Chief. Thank you.'

'The name's Beacruft. Doggy, naturally, but only to the master and we get on surprisingly well. We're supposed to hate each other: chiefs and masters etcetera. Unfortunately we don't. It breaks the mould and surely that can't be right?'

'The master sends his kind regards.'

Tom laughed. Beacruft had a twinkle in his eyes that was infectious; a tall, rangy man with faded brown hair; the classic weather-beaten face of a mariner, and a trace of freckles.

'Good of him in his dignity. Duty keeps me below, or I'd visit him from time to time and see if there's still a sun in the sky. This is the sewage plant, feel free to shit, it will be looked after robustly. Here is the engine, Wärtsilä, four-stroke, big chap, low vibration, economical. And that's about it.'

'As a matter of interest, what happens if it breaks down.'

'We're fucked.'

'Wouldn't that be serious, given the course?'

'There isn't much we can't repair underway. We know most of what we're doing here and there's a few of us.' He indicated the engine room crew. 'One or other of us generally knows what to do. Here you see the fresh-water system, highly efficient? Fire pumps, ditto we hope. Air conditioners less so. To be honest, more in the way of mechanical air handling rather than true air conditioning.'

'Two propellers?'

'Single screw. No tricky manoeuvres from the bridge, we're not a navy ship. Turmoil likes to go in a straight line with occasional turns to left and right. That's the nature of the merchant marine.'

○ ○ ○

Adam Brook crossed the stub end of the Strand from Aldwych station, threaded his way past Australia House, risked the road crossing and walked to the lacklustre office block on the east side of Kingsway backing on to the London School of Economics where he and Sarah Carpenter shared an office, along with a couple of hundred other assorted civil servants.

He had more or less affectionate respect for Sarah Carpenter; and she less or more affectionate respect for him. So on balance there would be parity, if it were ever possible to achieve balance between two sets of emotions and intellects which sometimes flowed in the same direction, often not.

Sarah Carpenter would say she was the boss of Adam Brook; he would agree: there was paperwork which confirmed it, and a salary structure which hinted at it but was compromised by a differing entitlement to on-the-job expenses. Item, hire of truck with complement of officers, analysts of film footage; item, travel expenses to Oxford; item, lunch away from office.

It was undeniable that Sarah Carpenter's salary was higher, but they ignored that for going out together at work or if necessary outside of it, taking turns to pay, never splitting bills – which they felt by unspoken agreement was divisive – and not following a strict rota of payment – that would be anal.

Sarah Carpenter would put her hand on what in someone else would be a heart and say she neither cared nor wanted to care what Adam Brook did and Adam Brook would say the same. They were completely independent and she told him what to do and he did what she said. Except it was more complicated than that, so, generally, they avoided discussion and got on with what the day might turn up.

'You see, Sarah, I simply don't believe she's done this. It's all made up. She's an amateur.'

'You're in love with her.'

'I don't think I am. The trick with the starter motor. There hasn't been a starter motor like that in 50 years. They don't work like that any more. Sparks, flashes. It isn't real. It's theatre. She's an ingénue.'

'OK from the film it doesn't look as if it can be done. Not

realistically. You're talking about a container for – what? – two litres of gel – this big – taking out and rewiring the ignition; and a pump; and a hole to squirt it through that someone sitting in front of it isn't going to notice before they're covered in sticky stuff and burn to death?'

'Exactly.'

'There's a way to find out.'

A couple of nights later Sarah Carpenter couldn't sleep because she was afraid. Before going home she'd asked Brook what he was doing; he'd said he was playing squash; she'd asked who with; he'd said 'Podro'; she'd said 'Report what you say'; he'd said 'Of course', grinned, slung his kit over his shoulder and left the office; she'd gone home, gone to bed, couldn't sleep.

Sarah Carpenter's bed was wide and long, with a firm mattress and a soft flouncy duvet. Her pillows were duck-down and she kept them separate, one to bend in two and put under her head, the other to cuddle. She'd pulled up her knees. This was no way to behave. She told herself to sleep. She couldn't face now what was to come, only when it came. And fear was natural, it would be silly not to be afraid, it would show she wasn't normal.

She didn't feel sick, just scared. She would handle it when it arrived. She deliberately stretched out her legs, worked through her body tensing and then relaxing every toe, finger joint and muscle including the fugitive ones trying to stay hidden in her shins, wrists and scalp. Finally she began to breathe deeply, letting her stomach rise and fall, feeling her body relax and encouraging her mind to follow.

It was a bright morning and she felt indifferent to being alive. As she strolled early along Exhibition Road, she thought that the people who felt glad to be born because the sun was shining were bonkers. People about to be burnt to death weren't gladdened by something large and incandescent, no matter how far away it might be. She noticed a big church she'd seen idly in passing a hundred times, thought it fine, wondered if you were allowed to walk in. What would be there? Religion had never interested her; it didn't seem practical. Although I am practical, she thought, I am not a dreamer. She turned left into the gates of the Imperial Institute, showed her pass, and walked into the laboratory.

Through the observation window she could see that the car they'd found was the same model. It didn't sparkle as new, but it was clean and wasn't marked. It looked as if it had been used perhaps three or four years. In other words, like every car on the road except for an external release lever fitted to the driver's door by the laboratory technician.

She wondered if it would make a difference to her life to have a car. She could get a permit. She decided not, and knew she was distracting herself so she wouldn't face up to what was next.

Sarah Carpenter was five foot seven and stocky. They had a suit ready to her measurements and helped her into it. The breathing cylinder fitted comfortably into her back, the belt a snug fit round her waist. A mask with microphone included went round her mouth and nose. The suit was made from aluminised glass fibre cloth with a vapour and heat resistant lining stitched with Kelvar thread; there was a hood, visor and helmet. She had short hair and could see clearly. She put on the gloves, wool-lined, insulated; the boots with Nitrile soles. They tested the microphone; she thanked them, opened the door to the fire room, closed it behind her, waved back to them through the fire-proof window, thought she knew what it was like to be a chicken in an oven, and walked to the car. She was good for 800 degrees.

She unlocked the driver's door and opened the bonnet. The screenwash pouch had been removed and the gel pack and heater stowed in its place against the bulkhead with electrical connections activated from the ignition switch. She slammed the bonnet shut and inspected the interior. The seat had been pulled back to accommodate the extra bulk of the fire suit and oxygen pack and the air bags had been removed. Visually there was no difference except for a small neat hole in the centre of the steering column which with luck and hurry would remain unnoticed. She got in, pulled the seatbelt over her shoulder, shut the door, put the key in the ignition and turned it to the first position. Doors and windows locked with a click.

She turned the switch off and tested the doors and windows. They remained locked. She turned the key all the way. The engine didn't fire and there was no sound of the starter motor, which, correctly, had been disconnected.

At this point, she thought, the driver would be irritated and if under pursuit, begin to panic.

There was a short delay as the gel heated and became liquefied, then a gush of fluid from the centre of the steering wheel. She wiped it from the visor, and watched it spread over her.

He would smell it now and be afraid. He would be brushing it from his body and trying to get out. He would be thinking, there isn't a spark. There was a flash beneath the steering wheel and a rush of flame as the gel ignited all over her body.

She thought what he would do, and released the safety belt. Perhaps he wouldn't have put it on? Only if everything had seemed normal. She tried the doors in case they released automatically with fire. They remained locked. The fire began to melt the plastic fascia. She wondered at the beauty of herself in flames.

She began to count.

In three minutes he would be dead, and for that time he would be conscious She began to count to a hundred and eighty. At sixty the windscreen shattered, the fragments showering into the car as the fire consumed the oxygen inside.

She continued counting.

If he'd passed out momentarily, the rush of air would revive him and increase the temperature of the flames across his flesh. She reached a hundred and eighty, and smashed the weakened glass of the driver's window with her elbow. She pulled the release and the door fell from the side of the car. She stepped over, and walked away.

Adam Brook said 'You switched off the microphone.'

She said 'Yes. In case I screamed.'

○ ○ ○

Daisy lay on the bed in the nondescript room, the curtains drawn, feeling over. An early memory, a staying memory, was – is, because it arrives in the present and becomes the present – the smell of petrol. She is looking down as her father looks up at her from a brown wooden boat with an outboard motor, smiling, to hand her down into it. Daisy can hardly wait in her excitement.

His short-sleeve loose shirt. He's glowing with some sweat, smells of exertion, not body odour, a manly body smell. He is oily maybe, she's in rough clothes – they both. He pulls the cord of the motor. They're going on an adventure.

○ ○ ○

They stripped the suit off Sarah Carpenter, took her into the shower room, and left her with Adam Brook. There were benches and he sat on one. She undressed and stepped into the open row of showers. They were built for decontamination: dropped a heavy load of water onto her and fired jets from the sides.

She said 'I'm sweating like a pig', and he said they don't sweat much. She said 'I'm sweating like one who does'; he said they were clean usually, by preference. She said if they were that smart they'd avoid being bacon, that talking of bacon did they do breakfast here? He said he thought so, watching her strip and thinking she looked OK dressed and naked.

Sarah stood head up into the downpour like a child in the rain, innocent and having fun, feeling the water properly as no-one had felt it before.

Adam thought her body looked firm, strong, not overtly muscular, but – competent. The competence of a runner's body: a sailor's perhaps.

There was only carbolic soap and she washed her hair with it, scratching her scalp, rinsing, washing again, washing her face. He thought her body was a bit like a man's, but not in an unfemale way. Resolutely a woman's body. Not large breasts but right; her bristle of pubic hair like a toothbrush; her firm bottom and legs; her armpits shaved – which was in one way a surprise, and in another in keeping.

Sarah said, I have clean clothes and I have no towel. Adam said, here, and gave her a big soft clean white towel from his bag. She said, I hope this isn't sweaty from squash last night. He said, I'm offended, it is clean for squash tonight, but I may not want to use it after you have. She took the towel and laughed. She said, it'll be all the cleaner, and dried herself, transforming back into the day, and for the moment of transition becoming curiously vulnerable.

In the canteen, Sarah Carpenter drank a half litre of cold water and they ate colossal fry-ups, with a mountain of chips which they shared. She finished with a huge thick strawberry milk-shake, sucking it through a straw.

'You can do it much simpler' he said. 'It's an electric petrol pump in that model. Disconnect it this side of the carburettor, run a tube up the edge of the windscreen concealed in the trim, fix a perfume atomiser on the end. The second you turn the starter, it sprays all over you. No gel, no complicated electricals, no pouch, no concealment, and the liquid's already sitting there for you in the petrol tank, as much as you like. She has no idea. She's irrelevant.'

'Feelings getting in the way?'

'In your imagination. Not in the facts.'

'I don't pay attention to facts.' She was, as always, calm. As always, this annoyed him. As always, she knew this. 'It depends too much on who is defining them. I go on what happens.'

He looked away.

'Why were you so mad as to do that?'

Sarah found it difficult to read Adam's face, and for a reason she couldn't explain, she felt moved. She knew not to show this, and replied in her normal matter-of-fact way.

'What happened is a man burnt to death, and Rachel Fonseca is telling people how to do this. She may tell it differently because she doesn't know and is grandstanding, or because she wants to mislead. I incline to the latter. Time and careful observation will tell, and the meantime we can look on her as a useful fool. Through whom, perhaps, we shall learn a great deal.'

'And why were you so mad as to do that?'

She sucked the last of the milk-shake noisily and said excuse me. She put it down, straightened the cutlery on her plates and stacked them, pushed them slightly away, put her hands one on the other onto the edge of the table, and looked into his eyes.

'Because when I come to question her it will not be enough to know what she intended to do. I had to know, and now have some knowledge of, exactly what the man was made to suffer in order to die. Then I am in a position to try to begin to understand why a mother would allow that to happen to her son.'

○ ○ ○ ○ ○

10

Bettina Ballantyne's daughter, Rachel, is suspected of seditious activity and is being watched by an undercover agent of the state. Meanwhile, Rachel's sister, Daisy, is planning to join her merchant ship, Turmoil, as it carries a cargo of scrap metal on its final voyage. The owner of the cargo, Tom Devine, is already aboard the vessel anticipating Daisy joining them. Daisy and Tom share a tragic episode of family history which took the lives of their respective fathers. They also share an undeclared attraction which each feels is about to climax.

MOST DAYS, GRETL wears a blue dress. Whatever she wears she looks pretty, and most of all in her blue dress. Today she is sitting at her desk chewing her lip and swearing quietly in German. Gretl is 26 and I can't tell her I love her because I am much older than she is. If I was 18, Gretl would be disparaging because I'd be a child. If I was 26, Gretl wouldn't count me because I'd be immature. If I was 30, I don't know. It's unfair – what is the right age for me to be able to say to Gretl – I love you? I should cry, but I smile, or rather, I chew my lip because also, I'm Gretl's boss, though we don't work like that, and we are, all of us collectively, facing a big problem.

So I quietly know I'm in love with Gretl and it's truly the love that must not speak its name. When she is happy, she talks to me. When she is sad, she talks to me. Sometimes, when we are working together, she'll say 'Can I talk to you about something?' and I can see she wants to cry, so I smile and say in that older role I know she wants me to switch into, 'Just cry, get it out'. And add 'Everything will be all right.' My instinct as she weeps is to cuddle her, as with a child, and I control it, I must not. The love I feel for her is gentle, sexual, protective, motherly – all kinds of love tugging in separate directions, well beyond expression by the triangle of forces. As I listen, and make soothing understanding animal noises that can't be written down, I say that everything will be OK, in the end, and soon. I keep saying it, in different forms, and it's a lie. I don't say that life is horrible, depressing; I don't say all the rottenness and despair that lies ahead in the most ordinary lives; nor that my sorrow is for those who truly have suffering, beyond the normal tragedy of regular lives. What would be the point? And I don't say, I'm waiting to die with relief because, believe me, there is nothing to look forward to. And of course, I don't kiss Gretl.

Gretl says 'Helen, can we talk in private?'

'Is it going to take long?'

'A bit.'

'It's urgent, yeah?'

'Yes.'

o o o

Helen Landesman led the way into one of the glass meeting rooms off the open-plan office of Lapraman Landesman Architects and closed the door behind them.

'I'm really sorry to disturb you. I know how busy you are.'

'I mean to say, Gretl, I think I know.'

'It's Diana.'

'Right.'

'It's astonishingly awkward.'

'Gretl.'

'OK we're all friends. But at the end of it I'm an employee.'

'I mean to say, we are friends. You are a good friend. You're worried, yeah?'

'Helen. Diana is sick in the head.'

88

'This is a long way beyond employer-employee.'

'I know.'

'OK in confidence.'

'Helen, she needs to go to hospital.'

'She does.'

'I can do some of her work. It's all going onto you. I want to help.'

'You can't. Gretl I mean to say you're fantastically bright. I'll embarrass you and be honest.'

'You're always honest to me.'

'Diana is better than me. Cleverer. These are facts that can't be changed. More talented. And she's my partner. Without her, I don't see that I can carry on.' Unsaid: aren't I allowed to be loved?

'How's the Jouvry job coming along?' she added brightly. 'When's the baby?'

○ ○ ○

The jenny thought that the secret of fulfilment was a well-drained and well-watered field. She looked around hers and saw that all was good. When the rain came, the grass became green. As it drained peacefully away, the grass became good to eat. A comfortable shed provided shelter. There was no rope to tie her. A mild gradient at one corner of her field provided scope for mild exercise. Mrs Ballantyne sat next to her smoking a Cohiba cigar. Both were content.

'We have to face it, Dulcie' said Mrs Ballantyne. 'We are both old, we'll be dead in due course. The question is, will we go to heaven, or alternatively, the other place?'

The jenny, who accepted the name Dulcie with a polite lack of enthusiasm pointed out, as she always did when this topic arose – regularly over the thirty years she could remember – that donkeys only had to show the mark of the cross on their backs to be admitted without fuss, on account of carrying him at least twice and probably other times that hadn't been written down.

'I'm glad about that, Dulcie. You're a good old thing' replied Mrs Ballantyne, as she always did. 'I suppose if I tag along with you they'll let me in.'

Dulcie agreed they probably would.

The days passed in a leisurely way. She supposed Bettina was right and that it wouldn't be long. What was best for the girls? If she went first, they'd have no-one to comfort them when Bettina died. It was, she concluded, her duty to remain. She smiled thinking of when they were little – always in her memory – but it had to be faced that time moved on.

Home was her shed, and she was grateful. The captain had made it, explaining to her as he did so that the most important thing was the damp-proof membrane under the concrete. It would keep her dry when she lay down to sleep. At first she didn't make sense of the sounds he made, and couldn't make her meaning clear to him. But as he worked and showed her what he was doing, they began to understand each other and she realised that spending time in her company meant something to him.

It was in this way that she'd first heard about Daisy, a child suddenly without a father. Bettina told her that Daisy must come and live with them, and what did Dulcie think? And so Daisy came, and Dulcie was patient with both of the girls as they clambered on top of her and kicked their little heels into her sides.

'Would you like a hat?' asked Mrs Ballantyne.

'No I would not, Bettina' said Dulcie. 'I'm not a fucking variety act.'

'No need to be tetchy.' Mrs Ballantyne picked a bunch of thistles. Dulcie accepted them and the small dispute was over. Sometimes the offence was the other way round and Dulcie nuzzled. In this way, amicably, they had fallen in and out over a lifetime.

'I'll be honest with you, though' said Mrs Ballantyne. 'It's Rachel.'

Dulcie smiled at her name. One shouldn't have favourites, but Rachel – good, kind, gentle, loving Rachel – was. There had never been a time when Mrs Ballantyne hadn't fretted about Rachel and whatever mess she was in at the moment. The answer was to nod diplomatically.

Rachel and clean straw. The shed would be cleared, the old straw burnt, the floor swept, and Rachel would come in with armfuls of new straw. 'There you are Dulcie. Nice and comfortable.' She'd kiss Dulcie on her forehead and ruffle her coat.

'I'm worried about Rachel' said Mrs Ballantyne. 'I think she's got herself in a lot of trouble.'

○ ○ ○

Turmoil was out in the safety of the Atlantic, marked as neutral and land far beyond the horizon. They'd come through Biscay with the sea unusually calm and were now at 40 degrees latitude – south of Oporto and north of Lisbon. Tomorrow they would reach Gibraltar.

Tom was now used to the rhythm of the ship. The names of her parts – human and inert – and the language of command and response were becoming familiar. The mate was Mr Mate to the fourth mate, the master Sir to all. Pöl and Dog – sometimes Andrew – between the chief engineer and master. Greasers for all below decks. Beacruft was Chief for first to fourth engineers. The first engineer, curiously, addressed as Second. The first officer, Number One to the master. All in the engine room – too confined for formality – addressed by their first names from Beacruft. The bosun was in charge of the deck hands, able-bodied seamen. Donkeyman, someone in the engine room. The steward – he must be in his sixties and, Tom now knew, with the ship from her birth – nicknamed Roger the Cabin Boy. Cook, cook. The master, informally, Old Man.

Tom sat in the Old Man's cabin, waiting for him to come from the bridge. Stuyvesant had told him to make himself at home. The first thing that struck Tom was how much smaller it was than his own cabin and – if possible – how much plainer. A simple desk and bed, a shelf containing seven books, a cupboard, perhaps with drawers inside – there were no others. Off the room a lavatory, basin and shower.

It was rude to look at people's books – like looking at their diaries – particularly when there were so few, but there was nothing else to look at except for the room's three luxuries: two comfortable leather armchairs and a matching sofa.

Walden by Henry Thoreau, 1854, the textbook of freedom which had inspired Walt Whitman with his poems of the open road, and Frank Wright into the floating slabs of Fallingwater and, Tom thought, left Thoreau trapped in history in the hut by

91

the pond.

A new translation of The Four Gospels by Émile Victor Rieu, 1952.

Zen and the Art of Motorcycle Maintenance: An Inquiry into Values by Robert Pirsig, 1974.

The Republic by Plato, 380 BC.

Letters to His Son on the Art of Becoming a Man of the World and a Gentleman by Philip Stanhope, 4th Earl of Chesterfield, 1774.

My Idea of Fun by Will Self, 1993.

The Beach Beneath The Street, The everyday life and glorious times of the Situationist International by McKenzie Wark, 2011.

Modern books, none.

Pöl Stuyvesant came in.

'Oh, the books. You're looking at them and looking at me. No no, dear chap I don't mean you'd be so rude.'

Stuyvesant waved him to an armchair, dropped onto the sofa.

'Don't worry, they're not the windows of my soul. I have a young woman in my life who since she was, I think when she was this tall', he put his hand just above the ground, 'has set out to improve me. I'm afraid she's failed. Every time she comes on the ship I find a new set of books on the shelf. At first there was no shelf. Then came one day the shelf, later the books. Sometimes there are three, seven, sometimes five. Daisy has evidently a preference for odd numbers. I've never asked her why, come to think of it.'

The Dutch accent was still there – faintly – and Tom struggled to put a word on how it made the English phrasings sound. Not ironic, quaint, not archaic. Unaware, perhaps of the slight strangeness of the sound of the accent and the words. The voice carried authority – a seasoned and relaxed authority, with the kindliness of experience examined and learnt from.

'And I'm afraid I have never read any of them.'

He looked tired and Tom wondered if he had slept.

'Is this really to be Turmoil's last voyage?'

'I don't know how much you know about Turmoil, how she started?'

'I don't know much about anything.' Tom laughed. 'I never

seem to learn. I'm sorry, that's introspection.'

'Do any of us?'

'You have. I think so.'

'I wonder.'

'Tell me about Turmoil.'

Stuyvesant slouched back in the sofa, hands in pockets, stretched out his legs. 'Aloysha Krestyanov saw the future and built her. That's it in a couple of words. The long version is Canning said – I read one of Miss Daisy Krestyanova Ballantyne's other books – 'I called the New World into existence to redress the balance of the Old.' Aloysha did the opposite.'

'Is she anything like him?'

'She's got the brain. Aloysha Krestyanov was my best friend. He was older than me, gave me all my opportunities. We met forty years ago when everything was all right. Long before all this. Different world.

'Something I'd say about Aloysha. He wasn't a saint.' Stuyvesant chuckled. 'Certainly not. But he a was a good man in all the ways you might think of that. Someone you could rely on. Rock steady. You could look up to him, and you wouldn't be disappointed. I suppose when you lose a friend – your top mate – you're going to idealise them, but the trick Aloysha had was that he was a real leader. Often enough you didn't realise you were being led. Or maybe you did and wanted to go along with it.

'He bought his first ship a year later, made her work for her living, soon enough he had another. Everything was containers, there wasn't a cargo carrier that wasn't containers, at least not of any significance.

'One day he thought, what about if you arrive in a port and there's nothing left: no cranes, no infrastructure, no container trucks, no railway lines, all suddenly gone in mid-voyage, never knowing what you'd find when you arrived? So he looked at what they did the last time, pulled out the old designs, picked the best, and here she is.

'She can take any cargo, carries her own derricks, heavy lifts. She can turn up anywhere and unload herself, take her cargo anyway it comes, slip out of the harbour, and she's away. Engine that's mean on fuel, efficient, low maintenance. And when she needs a quick turn of speed, she's got it. She'll do another 5 years, maybe a bit more, but she's coming to the end. Daisy'll sell her after this run and buy something bigger. You can't be sentimental about ships.

'And this will be my last command. You can't be sentimental about people.'

'Did you know my father?'

'Not to speak to. Was he alright?'

'More or less.'

'Mine was coldish, it was the fashion then. Still, you have what you're stuck with. Aloysha wasn't like that. He was a hundred percent.'

'Is she coming?'

'Soon enough.'

'By plane? Where to, Gibraltar?'

'Not just a plane, dear chap.' Stuyvesant relaxed, kicked his legs up onto the sofa, lay back and sketched an aeroplane in the sky. 'This is Aloysha's pride and joy. Personally I think he must have seen Steelyard Blues at an impressionable age although that was a Catalina and this is an Electra. Anyway he got the idea of restoring it. Chamberlain went to Berlin in one, Amelia Earhart disappeared another. It doesn't sound good does it?'

He roared with laughter.

'Aloysha reckoned they'd used up all the bad luck. It was pretty, so he decided he'd have one. Except he then died which left Daisy and me to put it back together for him. Which we have, over 30 years. Strengthened for aerobatics. Me, Daisy, and a lot of Skunk.'

'He must hate you calling him that.'

'Loves it. Reilly was Skunk back from the old days because he was black and white and he stank. Black suit, clean white shirt – he was particular about that. Unwashed feet, unwashed socks, stale cigarette breath, Vat 69 mouthwash.'

'He smells all right now.'

'Daisy introduced him to laundry. He gave in but it was grudging: "Aye, very well. But it goes against nature." And that accent! Tipperary meets Brigadoon.'

Stuyvesant yawned. Tom wondered if he needed to sleep, but

he stretched and carried on talking.

'Skunk's an albino. He's been lucky with his eyesight. They fixed it when he was a boy. He's a fighter, that lad. Covers up in the sun but it didn't stop him becoming a marine.

'He's got a couple of plusses. Being an ex-marine he can drive most things on wheels and in this case fly a plane. And he's devoted to Daisy. So when I'm away, she's safe.'

∘ ∘ ∘

It was 4 o'clock in the morning when Daisy saw the moon. She had driven from Mill Lane and was passing the Hoover Factory at Perivale when the clouds pulled back and showed it. High, speckled with tiny clouds – big, beaming, and not at all sinister. A cheese, bright as a clean white Cheshire cheese – not pussy – smiling. I'm a friendly moon, she seemed to say – definitely she. Nothing unpleasant here, I can assure you. Bon Voyage!

Reilly had arrived at Northolt at 2 am and filed the flight plan which Daisy had prepared as navigator. It would take them towards Bristol, along the north coast of Cornwall, out into the Atlantic, and south, well clear of the mainland, six hours in all.

They walked round the Electra inspecting the fuselage, checking the elevators up and down with their hands, the ailerons at the wing tips, the twin rudders at the rear, the landing wheels. They sat together at the twin controls, working through the list of pre-flight checks, testing the instruments, checking the fuel in the regular tanks and the additional tanks fitted for increased range and finally starting the two propellers. As the plane rose they turned west, flying into the moon.

By the time they reached the Atlantic the sun was low enough to light and give shadows to the waves, modelling them into three dimensions; and high enough to bring them into colours – blues, greens, aquamarines, subtle half-tone greys – completing their make-up with sparkling highlights, ready for the curtain call. Monarchs of the sea, Daisy thought? Drama queens, every one.

The airspeed indicator showed 190 knots, the altimeter 1,800 metres, the aircraft's cruising speed and height. There were no clouds. Reilly glanced over at Daisy and said 'Bored?'

'Only slightly' she said, 'so far.'

'Right. You first?'

She shook her head. 'You have control.'

'I have control' he repeated, and took the Electra up high. Plunging down at speed he banked it over to the left and Daisy, looking past his face down the port wing, stared at the water. The plane continued its rotation till it was upside down, then on to its starboard wing, and finally back to its upright position, in a perfectly-executed barrel-roll.

Levelling out, he said 'Ready to loop? You have control.'

'I have control' she said, and climbed to 3,000 meters. She allowed it to cruise for a few minutes to regain its balance, then drew the control column towards her, lifting the nose of the plane. It continued to rise till it passed the angle of stall and then dropped suddenly as the smooth flow of air under the wings spun into whorls.

She eased off the power till the port and starboard engines barely rotated and the Electra hurtled down towards the ocean through the roar of the air.

Daisy had eaten porridge for breakfast with treacle, and fruit, three boiled eggs, five thick slices of toast and butter, peanut butter, apricot jam, unpasteurised Jersey milk coffee – two thousand calories plus plus plus – and thought that she was glad it was fully digested.

She could taste nothing as she moved her tongue around her mouth, no sweet and sour, and best of all no sick. I will never be sick again. That is a statement of fact, or at least, a resolution.

As the sea hurtled towards her, she thought that she could see clearly down to the bottom of it. If she did nothing, they would hit the surface like concrete. The plane would smash and they would be crushed to death without waiting to drown. She wondered how long it would take to die: instant or minutes? No coming back: nothing after, after all.

Daisy breathed in deeply, loved the smell of fuel, bracing as oxygen. The control column was a half-wheel covered in white leather. She had bought the leather and Skunk had stitched it. His needlework was meticulously neat. Never a loose thread. And pretty colours, from the bright silks and cottons in his sewing kit. Did he want to die? His hands rested on his knees, relaxed. He sat back in his seat admiring the view; no sign of a sudden readiness to grasp the controls. She knew that he would accept whatever she decided to do. She gazed dreamily at the sea.

She calculated from the feel of the fall that the Electra was at terminal velocity and recited to herself that the gravitational pull now equalled the resistance of the air. There was a Reynold's Number to be estimated, a quick summary of Poiseuille's Law within the conditions of Newton's, a glance at the air-speed indicator and artificial horizon, and the overwhelming sudden realisation that at last – I am glad to be alive.

At 500 metres Daisy opened the throttles wide and pulled the column towards her, this time with all her strength, sucking in her stomach to prevent the blood rushing to her head and losing consciousness.

The fuselage shuddered under the stress but the nose lifted and the aircraft rose vertically till it pointed straight up to the sky. She slackened the power and it continued to turn backwards, making her feel as if she was floating – light, sensuous as orgasm. Then upside down and facing back. For a moment she could see clearly into space, out beyond the spissatus, beyond the mare's tales of the troposphere, gazing into heaven.

Then once more down towards the sea, and finally as she opened up the engines, back the right way up, flying ahead.

○ ○ ○

The sun came up into the top of the sky and passed overhead, making a flash off the silver wings. As they drew level with Morocco, Daisy banked the plane to the left and turned below Tangier, up into the Mediterranean and back in a gentle curve towards the airport at Gibraltar.

She turned to Reilly. 'Colman' she said.

He knew it was serious by the use of his name, reflected, and decided on silence.

'You don't smell any more.'

'Aye' he said. 'Things have taken a turn for the worse.'

Daisy grinned and patted her hand over his. She was ready for Tom now. He would be waiting for her. She felt resolute, no fear, no hesitation, no ambiguity. Time for action. Nothing to go wrong any more.

○ ○ ○

Gretl Lorelei was nervous because she was slightly afraid of Dianita Lapraman. Dianita was all contrary to start with – it was a baby version of Diana, and there was no baby present in Dianita. She was strong, from her strong cheekbones and short black hair to her strong arms and legs – built like a warrior from a race of warriors born to the saddle and hardened from the savage winters of Mongolia. Slender, too, with dark passionate eyes and a ravishing mouth as if she'd stepped out of a risqué version of Kubla Khan.

Diana Lapraman lived on the top of a high-rise in Kensington. Gretl had never been to her flat before, which made her twice as nervous. She pushed the button for the 31st floor. The press conference for Square Mile City was scheduled for 10 am the next day and she was delegated to rehearse Lapraman in her speech, take her photograph, smell her breath and check the dilation of her pupils.

She rang the doorbell. It didn't work. Gretl paused, knocked on the door. There was no reply. She banged hard on the door. There was a crash from inside. A deep voice boomed 'Come in.'

○ ○ ○ ○ ○

11

Merchant ship Turmoil docked in Gibraltar awaits the arrival of her owner, Daisy Ballantyne. On board, Tom nervously awaits his reunion with Daisy for whom he has a simmering, and as yet undeclared, passion. Meanwhile, at the controls of a small plane Daisy performs some perilous but calculated aerobatic manoeuvres and realises that she prefers to live knowing that Tom will be waiting for her. In London, in a society that is on edge and unpredictable, Rachel Fonseca enters a relationship with Adam Brook, unaware that he is an agent of the state investigating her for sedition. Lapraman Landesman Architects face crisis: as they embark on the replacement of the City of London, Diana Lapraman, the creative partner, becomes mentally unstable.

IN THE GRASS by the ruin of a house at the perimeter fence at La Linea airstrip a cat too starved to deliver milk to her infants lay on her side to die. Daisy looked up from her to the electric fences and through them in the distance to the imploring faces on the mainland side of the border. Minutes ago she had been determined that nothing would spoil this moment, and part of her explained calmly that other people's problems must remain their own. It wasn't rational, and it wasn't fair, to assume that the difficulties of the world were necessarily the difficulties of the individual.

On the other hand, it didn't feel like Casablanca. Not the real Casablanca, which lay half an hour across the water, but the one where Daisy was Ilsa Lund with unforgettable music – though arriving by plane instead of leaving. Ingrid Bergman was undeniably beautiful, so that was OK. Humphrey Bogart – say what you like she thought – ugly and not very tall. Tom was taller and not quite ugly; otherwise the characterisation was pretty much exact.

But unlike Casablanca, no Rick. Daisy walked through Customs trailing a suitcase expecting Tom to be waiting. He wasn't. On the circuit before landing she'd seen Turmoil at anchor in the harbour. She tossed in her mind to walk or get a taxi; lost, and set off on foot.

∘ ∘ ∘

Gretl Lorelei pushed open the front door of Diana Lapraman's flat and passed through an open-plan kitchen with a pile of used plates and a rancid waste bin. The door to a bedroom was open: rank rumpled sheet and duvet sprawled half on the bed and half on the floor, windows curtained and closed. She passed a door which was shut, and entered the living room.

Diana Lapraman stood in a dirty kimono over jeans. Behind her was a glass door open to a narrow precipitous balcony, with an alarmingly low balustrade.

'I wonder if you would like some coffee?'

Lapraman's voice was now much quieter, almost delicate; sensuous.

They shook hands. Without asking, Gretl opened the closed door: a bathroom. She inspected the shower and turned it on, checked the temperature. She found a bath towel in an airing cupboard and put it in Lapraman's hand, guided her to the shower and closed the door.

In the kitchen she put water in a pan, warmed it, added a small amount of sugar and stirred it till it dissolved. She found a bottle of olive oil and took the pan and oil into the living room.

In the bedroom she found clean underclothes and put them

over a chair, and a white shirt which she ironed. She rooted through the cupboard and came out pleased with a dirndl in greys and black, the skirt cut long.

There was no coffee, so she poured Indian ink from Lapraman's design desk into an expresso cup which she placed on a clean saucer. She cleared the balcony of a convincing stone Buddha which turned out to be polystyrene, swept it, put a chair at the far end, and unpacked her make-up kit.

Lapraman came out of the bathroom and sat on the edge of her bed while Gretl dried her hair. Gretl wetted it with the sugar solution, poured a teaspoon of olive oil into her palm, massaged it into the hair until the texture had the slightest cling to stay in place, and an even sheen. She opened the door of the bathroom to wash her hands, paused, looked in the bin, retreated without comment, and went instead to the kitchen. She watched Lapraman dress, intervened to tie the sash of the dirndl, took her into the living room, worked for a quarter of an hour on her make-up, and finished the styling of her hair with a comb.

Gretl took Lapraman onto the balcony and positioned her at the end. Lapraman stood with the chair behind her as if she'd got up to contemplate the view. Coffee cup in her right hand, saucer in the other, she looked out over London with the sightless stare of the visionary.

Gretl slipped an ultraviolet filter over her Leica to kill the morning haze and, lowering herself below Lapraman's eyeline, photographed her against the sheer drop to the panorama below. Pulling out a notebook from her hip pocket, she scribbled 'The peasant girl from the Karakoram Highway with London at her feet'. She put a wavy line under girl: not right, but woman wouldn't do, nor peasant by itself. The headline would come.

She took a couple more shots with Lapraman sitting down and moved in for close-ups. Satisfied, she took her by the hand, guided her off the balcony and sat her down in the living room.

There was a thump on the door and a woman came in towing a case, said 'I'm Dr Tillett', unpacked some apparatus and inserted a needle to take blood out of Lapraman's arm.

Lapraman vomited over her dress.

Gretl packed her make-up bag. 'Someone will have to wash her hair as well' she said. 'If you want samples of bodily waste for analysis, there are plenty in the bathroom. Along with the end of a bottle and a couple of needles in the bin.' She was about to put her camera away, but on second thoughts fired off a dozen shots of Lapraman and stopped to look at them.

'That was cruel' said the doctor.

'It's an alternative press release. Why not tell the truth?'

Gretl wrote in her notebook: 'My story, the star that crashed to earth.'

'I'll examine her now.'

'There's nothing wrong with her medically, I'm sure. You're the doctor.'

'She could do with a little love.'

'She needs a hard slap on the face and being told to pull herself together.'

Lapraman sat up and wiped her mouth. 'I could have you fired.'

'Fire away. I don't cry.'

'I'm the. Ideas.'

'And no guts. Look at yourself in the mirror. Preferably the one you haven't smeared with shit.'

Lapraman closed her eyes. Dr Tillett put on gloves and scraped a sample of stomach fluid into a lab jar. 'Is she left- or right-handed?' Gretl shrugged. The doctor broke open a sterilised pack and used it to clean and puncture Lapraman's left thumb. She squeezed out a bubble of blood, extracted it with a pipette, transferred it to a small machine, waited, and noted the reading.

'She has a press conference tomorrow.'

'There's not the slightest chance.'

'You can give her a shot.'

'I'm not that kind of doctor.'

Gretl said 'Make sure she doesn't drink the coffee' and left, closing the front door.

∘ ∘ ∘

It wasn't anything new for Tom to feel ashamed. Shame was always in the background, there to run to when the world wasn't spinning correctly on its axis – and that had been for most of his life. Running away.

He sat on the 9-inch gun at the top of the Rock and sweated in the sun. It had taken three hours to come by the Mediterranean Steps to the summit. The road was easier, but he had a head for heights, and brushing past the pretty white narcissus and esparto grass made the climb worthwhile.

From a distance out at sea, Cadiz had looked flat, and here in Gibraltar the Barbary apes – he corrected himself, macaques – had syphilis. There was nothing to be done about either. Geology accounted for Cadiz, and the macaques were responsible for their own behaviour. I should be responsible for mine.

Gazing into the sky, he saw the Electra from a long way off, and heard the gentle drone of its twin engines. A Lockheed Model 14 Super Electra – and the basis of the Lockheed Hudson light bomber – he corrected himself. For once, he wasn't bothered that he was a nerd. His other defects were more pressing.

The Electra made an elegant sweep of the final circuit and came to land in perfect balance. He watched it taxi from the runway and the propellers wind down. Daisy climbed to the tarmac, took off her helmet, and shook out her hair. She looked around. For him? He hoped it wasn't for someone else. He knew that he should be there, and felt ashamed. Afraid.

∘ ∘ ∘

'You want it straight, Helen?'

Gretl sat across the desk from Landesman.

'She's incapable.'

'I see.'

'And there is a single alternative, who is you.'

'Yes, I see that.'

'You have a speech?'

'No.'

'I've drafted this.' Gretl took papers from her briefcase. Landesman put on her glasses. She read them carefully, tapped them neatly together and placed them on the desk.

'I mean to say it's certainly comprehensive.'

'O'Brien can do his piece on the landscape of dreams.'

'I mean to say it's not how an architect speaks.'

'How might that be?'

'Ladies and Gentlemen, it isn't often that an architect has the privilege of addressing the Royal Society.'

'They know they're men and women, they know where they are, and they're not interested in you. Cut to the action.'

'Good morning.'

'They know it's morning. They're waiting for you to finish so they can get drunk.'

'This is one of the greatest projects.'

'Absolute ban on 'projects'. Cliché alert. Absolute ban on 'less is more' – in case you were tempted.'

'I wasn't.'

'Try and be interesting.'

Helen Landesman took off her glasses, put them in their case. She twisted her hands together.

Gretl crossed her legs and looked out of the window. The silence wasn't oppressive, and she didn't care one way or the other. She thought about when she might be paid. She'd been in the job for a fortnight and knew she had made an impact, knew they'd never had someone quite like her before. She guessed how far she could go, wondered how long it would be before her newness wore off, what she'd do next.

Helen Landesman had been generous to her in giving her money up-front to pay her rent. She thought about Ingo and was pleased that he loved her. She didn't take it for granted that he loved her nor that she loved him. With his job and hers, there was plenty: with one job there was enough. Or they could move on somewhere else.

Or stay here? The Jouvrys were promising. They had money. They seemed to like her. Helen wanted her and the thought neither revolted nor filled Gretl with enthusiasm. Helen was a cripple. She'd ask her about it before long. She'd need to dress right for tomorrow, be told how to walk up to the rostrum with just enough emphasis on her disability, and not too much. Her hair would need work, but the material was good; and make-up. A press release to tell a story about Lapraman – just enough to leave a faint implication – a tease. A photograph?

o o o

It was warm enough for Rachel Fonseca to wear her favourite light summer dress, and she strolled along the Embankment on the north side of the Thames. Then it was cold and rained. She corrected herself. I am always ready to exaggerate – it is chilly. There is a sprinkling of water.

Rachel had a song more or less in her heart, but the words weren't clear. 'The sound is elegant, delightful and charming. The music of our lives.' She began to run gently to its rhythm, really no more than a walk. I am trotting. Je fais le trottoir? Perhaps, and – who cares? 'And from a feeling of prettiness swing such flowers as blossom forever.'

It definitely rained, she ran. It rained hard, she ran hard, her dress raking up round her thighs. If people stared, what did it matter?

The night before, there had been a bar by the canal which sold thirty different kinds of jenever. There was a kitchen at the back that that made poet's stew from potatoes, carrots, an onion and cheap cuts of lamb.

Upstairs was a room where you could dance. Adam Brook poured a glass of water; Rachel took an orange juice and followed him. A fair-haired woman sang the blues; there was a band. People who'd danced sat round the dance-floor flopped out in chairs, hands over the sides, legs open – like actors who'd finished and taken off their strings.

Rachel and Adam danced. It was the first time they kissed.

∘ ∘ ∘

Captain Stuyvesant and Chief Engineer Beacruft wore overalls spattered in oil. It was peculiarly silent in Turmoil's engine room apart from the small noise of a generator providing enough electricity for the ship's basic systems. The main engine was off, the propeller shaft still. The circulating water pump had been removed, and parts of it lay on the workbench.

'It'll take a couple of days' said Beacruft.

'We don't have them.'

'A bearing is a bearing is a bearing, Pöl. In dock, I can fix it. At sea, I can't.'

'Andrew, we don't have the time.'

Beacruft reflected that if the master was calling him by his real name, he was worried. Probably he was tired. The two men seldom argued. Stuyvesant understood machinery almost as well as the chief engineer. He could strip an engine and make a decent job of it. There was no point making concessions for the sake of peace. Better to be safe and stick out for the time needed to get it right.

'What do you want? You say "Full ahead" in the Southern Ocean. This', he indicated the bronze components of the bearing in front of them, 'seizes up. No cooling water to the engine. The engine seizes. Full stop. You want to be on the bridge in a ten-metre wave with no power?'

'Two days?'

'Perhaps a day and a half.'

'Do what you can.'

Stuyvesant cleaned his hands at the sink, hung up his overalls, left without saying thanks.

The First Engineer kept quiet, reckoning it was better not to let the Old Man blow more steam than necessary, and put on the kettle.

It was an engineer's kettle: sparkling bright steel, with a smudge of oil to match the surroundings. In strict protocol, making tea was a job for the lowest greaser, but Dog Beacruft's engine room took its tea seriously. The first engineer was the recognised expert, and by unspoken election official tea-maker for officers and crew alike. A colour chart on the wall showed everyone's shade of milk and tea, with notes on timings and sugar allocations.

And no humdrum conventions of type. There were Ceylon and India teas, highland and lowland, green and other tips; caffeinated, decaffeinated; ginger and ginseng; loganberry; blackcurrant burst; cranberry, elderflower; mixed berry; mango; raspberry and strawberry bliss. A jar of instant coffee for occasional use. Some regional variations when in Rome: chai, yerba mate. Traditional biscuits: digestives, Nice, custard creams, Garibaldi, bourbon. And chocolate digestives – milk and plain – kept in the fuel-analysis fridge.

Beacruft drank tea and thought that it was a shame that relations with Stuyvesant were – for the moment – chilly.

Not because of friendship – that was old and strong; as waterproof as oilskin. But because it cut the engine room off from the upper world of the deck, where officers wore white and

106

you could see the sky.

And more importantly, from the gossip.

Not general gossip, but the question of romance. Everybody knew that Daisy was in love with Tom, and Tom with Daisy. Except them.

As soon as Daisy arrived, she'd come round everyone to say hello, just the same as she'd done since she was a child. Turmoil was her family – her real family, never mind a family on land. It was her father's ship – which he was never to see – now nearing its end but still home. Everyone wanted her to be happy.

Tom was a drip but he was our drip, was the feeling. He knew his cargoes, and that earned solid respect: loading and unloading, trimming, roping, sheeting, cargo stability, testing, inspection, inventories, minimisation or elimination of demurrage. And he was polite. Didn't talk down or up; direct, not arrogant, looked you in the eye. Handshake occasionally limp, but no-one was perfect. Moody since boarding, sometimes enquiring with an indifference which fooled no-one whether Daisy would join the ship and if so when. Increasingly eager at the prospect, scared since the reality. It was love, no question.

Beacruft washed his mug out in the sink, dried it on the tea-towel and put it back in the cupboard, neatly arranging it with the others. There was no shame in ritual. When it came to the need, ritual could save a life.

○ ○ ○ ○ ○

12

Rowena Ballantyne, unlovely and so far unloved, is the Cinderella sister to Daisy, owner of the elderly cargo ship, Turmoil, which has just left Gibraltar following repairs carrying a cargo of scrap metal for Tom Devine. For some time Tom and Daisy have been circling each other in a tense emotional stand-off, each expecting this voyage to bring matters to a head. A third sister, Rachel, has embarked on a relationship with Adam, unaware that he is an agent of the state investigating her for sedition. Lapraman Landesman Architects face crisis: as they embark on the replacement of the City of London, Diana Lapraman, the creative partner, becomes mentally unstable.

'I THINK IT'S distinctly possible', Mrs Ballantyne's voice came in waves over the ether, surging to full volume and receding almost to a whisper 'that Emilio Podro is taking an interest in your sister.'

Daisy put up her feet on her cabin desk and looked at Tangier as it passed the window.

'Hardly. He's a lot older.'

'I think not, you know. Careworn. They work them most frightfully hard in the Corps Diplomatique. It's highly likely with a good scouring that he'd turn out to be very much the same age.'

'He's ugly.'

'We must face reality. Emilio Podro may be our only hope of unloading her.'

'True, but he's still ugly.'

'Nothing that can't be improved by perseverance.'

○ ○ ○

Off Oxford Street near Bond Street in a small street of restaurants, fruit stalls, coffee shops, and street hawkers with hot pans of roast chestnuts and candied peanuts, Rowena Ballantyne sat opposite Emilio Podro in a pâtisserie, both eating big mille-feuilles oozing custard and sipping hot chocolate covered in whipped cream.

Rowena said 'I like this. Thank you.'

She felt awkward. She knew it was because she wasn't used to being in the company of someone else. She felt as if she had no small talk, that people were looking at her. Her words ground to a halt and she wasn't sure if there were any more.

'I like this too.'

Emilio smiled at her but didn't hold the look. He knew from the years of embassy parties, that sometimes it was good to fill silences with words. And sometimes – rather than reassuring somebody shy – it could overwhelm. Occasionally, it was good simply to look at the other person, to allow them to feel appreciated, even evaluated – anything better than ignored. Other times, to look was to frighten. Delicate judgments. Inconsequential chatter could work; interrogation; gossip about public figures as if from the inside; a story; or silence. He decided on silence. But an encouraging silence.

'I.'

Rowena was setting out to say that she didn't go out much, and realised that made her sound unwanted. I am unwanted. I don't know why I'm here; I don't know what he wants.

He smiled again. It was a reassuring smile. She felt welcome.

'I'm sorry I'm not very interesting. You must meet a lot of interesting people.'

Humiliating to talk like a child. What right did he have to make her feel like this? How stupid to be tongue-tied. He's smiling as if I am an idiot. He is humouring me.

'I'm in the company of one at the moment.'

'Hah.'

It was meant to be a light acknowledgement, but came out as a report. I don't have my sister's grace. I don't have the easy fluency of my cousin, the confidence of my mother. I have never got anything right and I never will.

'Don't be shy.'

'I'm not. There's nothing to be shy about. That's stupid.'

'I was a very shy boy.'

'I can't imagine that.'

'Ah. You're smiling.'

'I'm allowed to smile.' It came to Rowena that she was flirting, and it felt all right. The prison bars had opened, and wide enough to walk through with a touch of confidence.

'I think so. It's quite a reasonable smile. In my opinion.'

'You were never shy.'

'I was small, fat and shy.'

'Why did you ask me out?' She thought, fuck I've blown it. Why can't I be like everyone else and know what to say?

'I thought someone with such an admirable dog must be a superior kind of person.'

'Paul is my best friend. He's very intelligent. He understands everything.'

'And you?'

'He understands me better than anyone.'

'Perhaps he's the person you allow to understand you.'

'I'm not sociable.'

'I hadn't noticed.'

'Look, what do you want? Why am I here?'

Podro looked down at his finger-nails. He thought that they needed cutting, and that his suit smelt slightly of dry-cleaning fluid. He'd picked it up that morning from the cleaners on the way to work, and changed at the office. It wouldn't last much longer, and he couldn't afford another one at the moment – not till the treasury at home went back to paying their salaries in full and on time. No point in grumbling. He was all right for money. German Embassy party tonight, food probably digestible, wine usually chilled. With luck an early night.

'I want information. There is some information that we need and which you possess or are able to acquire for us. It was decided that I should approach you informally to see if it may be possible to make a trade.'

'You're taking the piss.'

He grinned. 'I'm taking the piss.'

She laughed. It surprised her that it was an easy laugh. There wasn't anything that was going to improve the way he looked. Some people had the right kind of face. He didn't. Fat eyes. But he had a way of not taking it all particularly seriously. He was slightly fun. Perhaps I can be slightly fun too.

○ ○ ○

The auditorium for the press conference held 1,000 people. Not large, but this was a particular audience. Eminences, grey and otherwise, of the Royal Society of Arts, the Royal Society, the Royal Academy – a royal flush. The Financial Times, The Times, The Fortean Times. Square Mile City would stretch a mile into the sky, replacing as much of the City of London as remained.

Gretl sat in the dressing room with Helen Landesman hearing her speech for the tenth time.

O'Brien walked onto the stage. There had been no announcement, no tricks with the lights, and he drew no deliberate attention to himself. As ever, he was relaxed, a slight smile on his face. A calm, almost welcoming figure, strong.

Conversation faltered as the different parts of the audience realised his presence, drained away to silence. O'Brien seemed not to notice the quiet. He looked around the audience in a leisurely way, so that each person felt that she or he had acknowledged him, and in turn been acknowledged.

He spoke.

'In all of our dreams, there is a horizon. I mean dreams that happen when we are awake, not stupid sleeping dreams. Let it be our creative delight to allow the formation of unchained dreams. Horizon. The limit – but is it? – of our vision, and, mentally, our aspiration. Perhaps before, we have been blind. Oh – seeing of course – but blind. Our eyes have stopped at the horizon. Now we shall rise beyond it. Our eyes are suddenly open.'

111

As Turmoil headed south through the Atlantic, Tom Devine and a member of the deck crew, both wearing white overalls and breathing kit, unlocked the hatch to the number one hold located at the front end of the ship and climbed down the metal staircase to the bottom.

This hold carried small scrap – such as the more expensive metals from broken-up electrical machinery – boxed in cubes on pallets and stacked with spacers so that one didn't touch the other. Temperature at the middle and top of the hold was monitored from the bridge, and the air analysed – both to ensure the absence of electrochemical reactions and poisonous or inflammable gas. Periodically the crew examined the cargo directly.

The master noted Tom's enthusiasm for joining inspections – which took him for long stretches of time to isolated parts of the vessel and therefore avoided any chance of him running into Daisy – with a smile, but he kept his thoughts to himself. He noted too that when Daisy wasn't at her desk, she'd taken to helping out aft in the engine room – hair tied back, boots, smeared overalls. Well clear of the holds, and Tom.

○ ○ ○

The number one dressing room to the auditorium contained a shower and lavatory – both of which had been used – and Gretl Lorelei had dressed Helen Landesman from bare body to full package.

One wall was a full-height mirror and there was a tilting cheval for the back view. Landesman stood looking at herself as Gretl completed her transformation.

Gretl had coloured the hair black to remove touches of grey. She had been sparing with make-up at the upper face to give maximum impact to Helen's sharp green eyes. Shoes were simple: plain, black. A Shaker dress (black silk) from neck to ankles. It was close enough to sketch in the curves of her bottom; loose enough lower down to conceal her deformity. Higher, it gathered to emphasise the fullness of her breasts.

Helen smoothed her hands down her body, turned sideways to the mirror.

'I mean to say, not bad'

112

From where Gretl stood in the wings listening to O'Brien she could see part of the audience. All eyes were upon him; bodies still. They'd given everyone a glass of wine and a carrier bag with nuts, chocolates and blurb. Nothing had been touched. They were entranced.

There was silence when he finished. He'd withdrawn his presence and left them to themselves. They were alone. Then the applause. They rose to their feet – but no whoops and whistles, no cheers. The clapping of two thousand hands, a nod from O'Brien, his exit, the audience seated, a feeling of sorrow. Gretl walked on stage to a dead room.

She knew how she looked. Dressing Landesman, Gretl had made sure that Landesman would shine – to whatever extent she could – and that her own appearance would be of lower status. It would accord to her position – introducer, facilitator, announcer, master of ceremonies – the glue of it all. The tone of her voice would be quiet: authority without bombast. They would like what they saw: someone who knew her place. Someone you could trust.

On the screen above Gretl's head was the photograph of Diana Lapraman looking out from her balcony.

'Ladies and Gentlemen. I am about to introduce Helen Landesman. She will tell us what Square Mile City will mean. Not just to us. But to everyone in our country. And indeed throughout the world.

'Before doing that. Circumstances have arisen which mean. Well. May I talk with you in confidence?'

Gretl stopped. The house lights were up, and she could see every face all the way to the back of the auditorium. She had them.

She turned away and looked up at the projected image of Diana Lapraman. She joined her hands behind her back, her arms loose, her head tilted up: respectful, innocent admiration.

'Isn't she beautiful?'

She faced them. They looked uncertain, waiting for what she would say.

'When Helen Landesman and Diana Lapraman – we call her

Dianita – met at college, they resolved to set up an architectural practice based on idealism.

'They believed that architecture is not about buildings. It is about people.

'Helen Landesman would tell you – as she tells everyone with great humility – that genius in their partnership is Dianita. That Dianita's graceful designs astonish and delight. That you experience wonder when you walk around her cities and buildings. From the micro to the macro. That the same magical dust is sprinkled on everything she touches.

'Helen Landesman would tell you that – apart from fist-fighting and smashing furniture over each other's heads when they have the – actually small – creative disagreements which flavour all artistic relationships – they never have a cross word. That they love being with each other, marvelling at the creation of beauty.

'And all of this is true.'

∘ ∘ ∘

Some of the trees in Hyde Park had changed for winter, dropped their leaves and stood without the slightest embarrassment As one tree put it, 'I have no clothes on. I'm naked. You could say I'm nude because I'm a work of art. It's a free country and frankly I'm free as the air. I have no shame and no reason for shame. What's wrong with being stark completely unclothed whenever you want to be?' Another tree said 'But we only do it in winter.' The first tree said 'That's true.' For a while neither spoke.

It was brisk with dry intentions, an English day and therefore hard to predict if the overcast sky and occasional breaks of warmth meant a sudden drench or the bursting open of the clouds for the sun to fill the world with light and implied optimism.

Regardless, Hyde Park was filled with people. Some were in groups queuing for the pedalos on the Serpentine, some strolled among the Italian fountains at the Long Water dam. Families gathered around tables at the café on the waterfront. There was a cluster around Peter Pan; the bemused and agitated at Speakers' Corner.

There were twos too, because the weather didn't kill romance or pairing generally: rather, a slight encouragement. Hostile twos in the finals or semi-finals; business twos elsewhere. Spies hoping to be untapped as they exchanged codes and carrier bags. Twos of birds (and bees), roach and rats.

One two was Rowena Ballantyne and Emilio Podro. At a fast glance they could be separate people walking together.

The man had a worn-out tweed suit – unfashionable, though clean, and some less-than-invisible mending – and worn-down polished brown shoes. The woman wore jeans and a clumsy black jacket with a red woollen cap, red woollen gloves and a matching long scarf down her back.

But there were indications that the state of apparent discreteness was unstable. Ballantyne had glanced at Podro, Podro had glanced at Ballantyne – both when the other wasn't looking, the glance held for more than a second – and the glances had been repeated. At first they strode, later slowed, now strolled.

Sometimes, accidentally, they brushed together.

∘ ∘ ∘

The photograph above Gretl's head began to fade.

Her voice became practical.

'Helen Landesman would tell you those things because she is modest. She is loyal. She is, like the best of best friends, protective. How much we all long, Ladies and Gentlemen, for a good friend.'

Cautious smiles of agreement. The screen went black.

'Yesterday I visited Dianita Lapraman at her flat. I took the photograph that you have just seen with the intention of issuing it to you today to accompany her speech. Thinking about it later, I realised it would be a lie. What I found was this.'

A new photograph. Diana Lapraman lay slumped in her chair, hair ragged, bile and half-digested food over her clothes and lips, a needle in her arm and the blurred profile of the doctor squatting beside her.

They were too sophisticated to gasp. Here and there, hands went to mouths. On most of their faces, a visible conflict between respectful attention and the delighted enjoyment of another's humiliation.

'Dr O'Brien has expressed to us, Ladies and Gentlemen – and

I think we can agree that he has done so most eloquently – that what is here today is something greater than has ever been achieved in the history of the world.'

The slide flicked off.

'And we need to begin that journey in truth and under leadership we can trust. The first of two realities is that Dianita Lapraman has – most sadly, and human weakness is something we all share and can therefore sympathise with – become sick.

'Her sickness is specifically a dependence on alcohol and injected drugs – established and increasing over, I am afraid, a long period of time.

'Again we clearly must feel empathy for a fellow human being.'

Some of the audience were eating chocolates. She had their eyes.

'But that needs to be – I am sure we will all agree – detached. Please rest assured that Dianita has already begun to receive the best treatment. And that will continue until she is able once again to lead an independent life.

'The second reality is that the talent and creativity, the drive and execution – the inspiration – of Square Mile City, has for these past several years come from the last-named – and not the first – in the partnership of Lapraman Landesman.

'Ladies and Gentlemen please put your hands together for Helen Landesman.'

∘ ∘ ∘

Adam Brook stopped the car outside Rachel Fonseca's house.

'Coming?'

He shrugged.

'I'm allowed visitors.'

He smiled.

'There's a signing-in book, of course.'

She found her key and opened the front door.

He started to say, 'I believe'. She held up a finger and he stopped.

'I didn't realise you had beliefs. How exciting.'

He followed her inside.

∘ ∘ ∘

116

At home in Upminster, lights off, curtains drawn, dog fed, Rowena Ballantyne stretched out in bed.

She thought of sun, wind, rain, and Emilio Podro.
It had been a lovely day.

○ ○ ○ ○ ○

13

Daisy Ballantyne is the owner of elderly cargo ship Turmoil, heading east after stopping at Gibraltar for repairs, carrying a cargo of scrap metal for Tom Devine. For some time Tom and Daisy have circled each other in a tense emotional stand-off, each expecting this voyage to bring matters to a head. In London, Lapraman Landesman Architects face crisis: as they embark on the replacement of the City of London, Diana Lapraman, the creative partner, has become mentally unstable. Supported and encouraged by her assistant Gretl, Helen Landesman prepares to deliver to prospective backers the crucial introduction to the project. Jack and Jill Jouvry look forward to becoming parents, supported in their comfortable if unconventional domesticity by Russian au pair Magda.

THERE WERE NO equator virgins aboard Turmoil. All aboard had crossed it before, most of them many times, so officially there was no-one to initiate. But in the last couple of days openly – and previously in secrecy – the ceremony had been prepared. On the day, in the heat of the afternoon, two substantial thrones appeared on deck, constructed by the engine room from papiermâché and enriched with gold paint.

So it was when Turmoil was level with the Gulf of Guinea that Daisy met Tom.

Officers and crew – cross-dressed in pinks, blues, crêpes, netting and rubber – soaked each other in cheap scent from Gibraltar. A command. A roll of drums.

Captain Stuyvesant, dressed as King Neptune, cardboard trident in his right hand, ascended a throne. More drums. Chief Beacruft appeared as Queen Amphitrite. He wore a long evening gown, tiara and Wellington boots.

At a whistle from the bosun, flour from the cook's stores was poured into buckets of water, and everyone issued with a bucket. A second whistle, and the contents of the buckets were thrown. Soon, officers and crew were covered in sticky white liquid. At the third whistle, a ration of rum was issued and a toast given to the king and queen.

King Neptune rose to speak. He praised the beauty of his bride. Beacruft looked bashful – to applause. Neptune commanded a queue to be formed in two lines, for the king and queen to present certificates of commemoration.

Whether by careful plan or accident – no admissions were made afterwards – Daisy and Tom came to the front of opposite queues at the same time.

Daisy wore a Harlequin costume with an old-fashioned sailor's hat. As she knelt to receive her certificate, she looked at Tom. He had chosen a flimsy dress of torn cloth and coloured paper over bare legs. Over it, he wore a shawl made from streamers, topped with red and green feathers. She burst out laughing. Seeing Daisy bedraggled, wet and covered in flour, he joined in.

Daisy had been determined to remain aloof. Fleetingly, she felt that she should be annoyed; and realised that she wasn't, and didn't care. No point in holding back. It achieved nothing.

Tom felt something like relief.

∘ ∘ ∘

The first cape petrels arrived next day. An entry was made in the log. Tom watched them trot along the waves to take off, and return to peck at the water for krill. They dived under and leapt

119

out, white bellies rearing up. Their cross little black heads spat at each other as they fought over food, their elegant underwings suddenly exposed – white, black-edged.

'It'll be cold soon.'

He hadn't seen her approach. She stood beside him, but not close.

'There'll be albatrosses in a couple of days.'

He thought how stupid he sounded. But he'd avoided the Ancient Mariner.

Daisy managed a cool expression and looked over the sea. Can you kiss? Mornings I wake up equating. I could dream about love. But when I jerk awake at four, I'm calculating demurrage. I do commerce, I do nothing for the common weal. I should at least be sidling towards goodness.

She said 'Imagine swimming across the Atlantic.'

Tom wasn't sure if he should move closer, thought it best to stay where he was. I fell in love with you. The actual fall happens around four in the morning 'when old men die, and armies attack'. You wake up and drop, suddenly. It can't be love – I fantasise about you. I wank to you. When you're in love, the loved one is beyond the physical.

'Beyond physical endurance.'

'Yes.'

She wondered if he wanted her to be there. I used to fall in love often. In a bad week, at least twice. Usually on Sundays after a hangover when the world seemed innocent. And Mondays if I needed to. Sometimes twice a day. Practice, practice, practice – never perfection. Every time it was real. Every time it would last for ever. I'm always late. On time for opportunity. Too late for affection.

I never have time. I will never be found.

'Are you interested in pulp wood?'

She turned to him, caught his expression and laughed.

'No.'

'Baled pulp?'

'Guilty or not guilty?'

He looked puzzled.

'Out on bail.'

'Oh, I see.' He laughed.

'Anyhow, when we get to Shanghai, I have to inspect a warehouse full of it. Pulp wood and baled pulp. Somehow I don't think you'd like to join me?'

'That's exactly right.' She smiled. 'But I'll expect a full report.'

He watched as she walked back along the deck. There was an elegant and natural sway to her body with the rise and fall of the ship.

With a little extra swing to her hips.

○ ○ ○

On the floor of the Jouvry library, Magda said 'Come again Jacky. I want to drink your jism.'

Jack raised his face from her clitoris, licked his tongue along her stomach, said 'I love you. If I have you, I have everything.'

'Dirty boy.'

'Go on then. Give me your political analysis of the consequences of the 30 Years War.'

Magda stretched out and closed her eyes. He rested his head against her belly, kissed her. She stroked his hair and for a while they lay together in silence.

After a while she left the room and returned with a handful of pages from her dissertation.

Jack lay on his back, a cushion under his head. Putting the papers on his chest she sat astride his legs and began to read quietly aloud. His penis was hard, and she took it in her hand.

'The peace to the 30 Years War took five years to negotiate because ambassadors had to return to their countries to consult on every point. Travel took months, especially to Spain and back. The treaty gave fixed borders to what would later become Germany and Poland. But it blocked a way to the sea. Other countries were placed across the mouths of Germany's great rivers – the Rhine, Ems, Weser and Elbe. This land-locked Germany.'

He brought up his knee and she began to rub against it.

'Shall I go on?'

'You must. In detail. Just a touch faster.'

'And stifled its access to world trade. The formation of modern Germany under Bismarck in 1890, defeat in the First World War and national humiliation created pressure for the invasion of Poland in World War 2. However the exact moment of the signing of peace in the 30 Years War halted troops at the mid point of the King Charles Bridge in Prague prior to their assault on its citadel. In the shadow of which Franz Kafka would later be born. Indeed his major work The Castle describes the citadel exactly.'

Magda felt the rise of his orgasm, and her own. She pressed herself against his knee and lowered her voice to a whisper. 'The Castle extends to 850 pages. Tomorrow I will describe it in some detail.'

She bent down to kiss him.

'Soak my face in your love-water.'

∘ ∘ ∘

Pöl Stuyvesant's great-grandfather looked relaxed in a naval captain's uniform. The photo had been taken on the bridge of his warship. He stood next to a push-button steering mechanism – at the time, revolutionary.

Stuyvesant wondered what the captain would make of Turmoil's steering wheel. A step back? And that on the bridge, he'd find the same paper charts and the same sextant for navigation. Back of the bridge, the same radio operator tapping Morse code. Even grandfather would be amazed.

Stuyvesant's father, who had seen the change of the times, would not.

Pöl Stuyvesant had trained on GPS and Glonass, just like all of his contemporaries. They'd read about navigation by the stars, quaint as a fairy-tale. Gradually, it had seemed pragmatic to learn how to do it. Suddenly, it had become essential.

∘ ∘ ∘

The rounding of the Cape was uneventful. Huge seas and savage winds threw the ship about, but that was the nature of the Cape, and Turmoil was built for weather.

Stuyvesant navigated on dead-reckoning. The sky had started overcast and continued for the passage, leaving him unable to fix their position from the stars, sun and moon.

It was true that ships in their thousands had done it before. It was also true that ships in their thousands had sunk here. Stuyvesant shook his head, more at himself than at the times. Daisy called him a pessimist with added gloom. Clear of the Cape, the weather would open and the sextant would do its job. And if it didn't, everything would be all right. Of course it would.

∘ ∘ ∘

Gretl had written Landesman's speech with precision, and Landesman was doing it well. Competent. Thorough. If O'Brien was the candy-floss, Landesman was the meat and two veg. They would believe in her.

Gretl sat in a row near the front with Francesca Casine, head of client entertainment. Jill Jouvry sat on the other side of Casine. Beyond her, and dwarfed by her fortress-like presence, were several smaller clients. Gretl's work was done, and she was exhausted. She snuggled against Casine and closed her eyes.

Jill Jouvry whispered to Casine. Within minutes, Gretl was driving Jouvry's Lagonda sports car fast through the traffic to Queen Charlotte's Hospital. Impressed by her calm, she glanced over at the expression of pain on her face. There was a bumping in the engine, quiet at first then louder. Gretl recognised a big-end bearing about to go, and hoped they'd get there first.

On the incline where Marylebone became the Oxford Road, a car jerked out in front of them. With no time to brake, Gretl swung right and put her foot to the floor.

There was loud bang as the bearing shattered and the engine seized. She floored the clutch and coasted into the side, missing cars and bumping up onto the pavement.

'Jack will be furious.'

It was such a ridiculous thing for Jouvry to say in the circumstances that Gretl nearly laughed. One look showed Jouvry about to cry. Gretl zipped her lips, phoned for an ambulance. In her thoughts she was stripping down the engine, straightforward; and delivering the baby, less so.

'I knew I would fuck up.'

'Everything will be fine' Gretl comforted. She wasn't sure it was true.

○ ○ ○

Turmoil was at the centre of the Southern Ocean, approaching the longitude of Madurai. She had passed well below the Madagascar hurricane belt, and measurements in the clear sky had confirmed her position.

Strident Bucephalus also headed east on a course well above Turmoil, up in the Indian Ocean with better seas and wind. This was made possible by the support of a Russian-built destroyer and her own complement of armed marines. Hostile shipping was even further to the north, but the captain of Bucephalus briefed Stuyvesant by radio and advised him to continue along the far southern latitudes.

Daisy and Tom stood at the rail of the outside bridge, the length of the deck ahead of them, as Turmoil ploughed the Roaring Forties.

They'd expected sharp, cold air. Instead – freak weather – it was hot and running-wet humid. The engine room was boiling, and there was little relief in the cabins.

All the crew were on deck preparing for the storms of the Forties. Holds hatches were double-checked tight and waterproof. At the fo'c'sle, a sailor re-sealed the spurling pipes of the anchor chains with a pudding-plug of rags and sandy cement to prevent the bows from sinking. Mobile cranes and pivoting derricks were locked against movement. Hoists were lashed to eye-bolts. Each of the lifeboats was checked secure and complete.

A pair of albatrosses raced from stern to bows, outpacing the ship.

Daisy wore an old t-shirt over loose blue jeans and sea-boots, a faded blue cotton cap. She stretched, closed her eyes, yawned.

'I'm going to my cabin. I need critical sleep catch-up before the Southern Ocean. And these supposed hurricanes, sorry, cyclonic storms. Come on, I've done the Forties before. They're not that bad. Believe it when I see it.

'What does the master say?'

'"You'll see it, Daisy. Hopefully on tv, otherwise we've made a serious miscalculation." The master can be very straight at times. Particularly about cyclonic storms.'

She giggled. 'In the film, the captain would be Jack Hawkins.

He's dying of cancer, they've drilled a hole in his throat. He uses it to smoke Capstan Full Strength. He talks by burping Morse code. Ask him how the sea is, and he's guaranteed to say "Cruel". He prefers cruising in convoy, scanning the waves with high-powered binoculars, looking for the wake of a periscope. He wears a duffel coat with the hood down, a white polo-neck coarse-wool oiled sweater, and Wellington boots. At nights he strides the poop looking for whales, the steel of the deck echoing to the tap of his wooden leg.'

I'm not quite ready, still sore, still shocked. Not sure what I've done. Not sure of anything.

Tom was listening, laughing.

'The stars are different in the Southern Hemisphere.'

It was the best he could manage. You couldn't see them: the sky was once again overcast and it wasn't even night.

'Not really, it's just that we've moved.'

Do you wear a dress? Perfume? If we're old and cruising will you wear a shawl? I'd hate to be on a cruise. I hate wearing a tie. When I fall in love I'll tell everyone. I couldn't have a secret love. The idea of sharing life with a person who isn't me. Shocking, and I should be shocked. I am not natural. And I am afraid. I can't think of the words. My voice would falter. It would all be a disaster, and embarrassing. Why would you want me anyhow?

I love your innocence. You man, you're completely unspoiled and un-calculating. I think you don't know how beautiful you are, in your face. And in your mind. I'd love you just the same whatever you were. But most of all I'm glad that you're you. I will never want to change you, or perfect you.

She said 'Anyhow, I'm going down.'

He didn't know whether to nod, smile, say something. It would be ridiculous to shake her hand. I'll go down in the Southern Ocean. I'll go down anywhere you like. I'll drink your piss. No, that's going too far. And I don't want to be the water in the bottom of your lavatory. There have to be limits to love – at least, initially. I don't like strong body smells either. Napoleon and 'Don't wash, Josephine' isn't for me. Nor the exile in Elba – where was Josephine and her odour then? Don't mind smoking. I'm not putting limits on what I won't change. But it's reasonable to indicate a perimeter.

Daisy couldn't remember if he'd answered. It didn't seem to matter that she'd spoken. She made no effort to leave, kept looking ahead, lost in time.

She thought it was funny how incidents came back, unrelated.

Late one night on the tube I saw a woman, quite old, certainly 28, plain – let's be fair, ugly – slight acne on her face, clean teeth, something respectable like an accountant. She had plump legs in black patterned tights, a smartish black coat. Her face was lying back on a younger boy's shoulder. Her fingers were red, no rings on them, never will be, her left hand rested on his inner thigh. They were both drunk, not out of it, but him enough for beer-glasses and her enough to mask gratitude, and I thought – she's needed this a long time. Tonight she'll be in heaven.

'Anyway, it doesn't matter about the storms.' She laughed. 'Our guardian angels will look after us. That's what mum would say.'

'Don't forget tonight.'

She was to host dinner with the chief engineer and master in the owners' private dining room – the only time it was used. Normally the officers and owners ate together in the officers' mess. Once in a voyage it was traditional for the owners to entertain the principal officers in private.

'I won't.'

She smiled and turned away, climbed down the companionway to her cabin.

Under his breath, Tom muttered: 'Guardian angels. And flying pigs.'

∘ ∘ ∘

As it happened, the two relevant guardian angels were a couple of hundred metres off to starboard.

John Lewis sat on a wave, repairing the wing of an albatross – a feather or two had come loose from a badly-judged landing. His companion Peter Jones sat beside him, chatting with the bird, whose name was Abena.

Peter Jones had once lived in Oxford Street and John Lewis in Sloane Square. By coincidence, there had been department stores of the same names in the opposite locations, which had once given rise to jokes.

Happy days, they would say reminiscently. And doesn't it seem long ago?

'Well! Did you hear that?' said Peter Jones.

'I'm not even listening, dear. Now Abena. That's the best I can do with glue. You'll have to be careful with your slope-soaring till your new feathers grow. And remember to compensate with your stall angle when you come in to land.'

Abena thought, I think I know how to fly. She said a polite thank you, flapped her wings experimentally, and took off. It was not one of her best – the port wing wobbled – but as she rose with a thermal she found the correct trim. She turned carefully and flew back over them, dipping each arm in turn.

∘ ∘ ∘

In his mind, Tom was back in the old house. When I was small I always wanted to live in a lighthouse. That is different from – for example – a water tower. One is round, and the other rectangular.

'Furnishing a rectangular room is easier' remarked John Lewis, who had strolled onto the outside bridge with Peter Jones.' But both are towers, both have a hell of a lot of stairs. And both have only one room on each floor – so a man – or woman – can live in self-indulgent isolation several times in the same place.'

'And a lighthouse looks like a cock' added Peter Jones.

'Please ignore him.'

A new seabird appeared, one that Tom hadn't seen before. It was black, sensual, a great-wing-spanned bird, sweeping low to scavenge. It drifted across the ship like an omen, turned, and flapped lazily to the fo'c'sle where it paused, sat, and looked back at him.

Daisy put the cabin air-conditioning on high. I feel sick. It's not sea-sick, I've been on ships forever. When I was little, I thought the world was made up of bays. I'd sailed every one of them, from Shanghai to Baikal, Boston to Trincomalee. Now the world's made up of my mistakes, things I haven't done. From laguna to lacuna. And the ship is called Turmoil.

She felt too lazy to put on the kettle and make tea. Always remember to drink at ambient temperature. Drink warm in the heat.

I grew up rubbing against every nationality. Most of all, I liked rubbing against Poles. My first mate was First Mate. Age 14, I sucked on a Fisherman's Friend. My first tastes were salt and fish. I am guilty. I am empty of my loss. I am calculative of my gain.

o o o

Tom lay on his bed. How many people have masturbated in this bunk? Sailors wank all the time. Coming into port after a long voyage, the decks covered in seamen. What do they think about? Are they all gay?

'Sailors vary' commented Peter Jones. 'It's not all rum, bum and concertina. No time to beat about the bush. Make a move.'

She couldn't ever love me. She's too perfect.

'Samuel Pepys said', remarked John Lewis, '"Even my Daisy shits." His mistress. The "shits" is right. I'm guessing about the Daisy. Time to leave the lighthouse, Tom.'

There are no faults to her. She's supremely self-confident. She's in a different class from me. She'd be disgusted. I can't think of any words. If I said anything – I'm certainly not going to do anything – she'd be horrified. Wouldn't she?

o o o

Daisy lay down.

Smear me with engine oil. Roast me. Baste me. Debase me.

o o o

'A cunt's a cunt' said Peter Jones.

John Lewis sighed. 'Such a romantic. Sees life through rose-coloured testicles.'

Tom sighed. This is the woman I love. She probably doesn't have one.

o o o

Daisy sighed. Don't move fast. Slow your engines, half ahead. Be ready to go full astern in case of disaster. Seduce calmly, take time, and I'll be your animal forever. A stoat for protection, a horse for you to jump, a cat to stay awake, kitty to lick you asleep. A monkey to find bananas when your erection fades. Dance. I'll be your May Queen.'

She ran the shower. My careworn body is vulnerable and soiled.

128

She undressed, paused at the full-length mirror. I long for the rustling of ecstasy. I'm inclined to texture, velvet.

Peter Jones whispered 'Darling, it's obvious to us that you're in love. It's written in the evening sky – bright red from the horizon to the zenith and all the way down the other side. Mottled with blue. Quite like the head of a knob.'

John Lewis pushed him gently aside. 'You're a butterfly dear. Not part of a display. Not gassed, not pinned. One that flies. Life's only a few days. Find him.'

'Consider the fishes of the sea. Salmon marry for life, and travel together all the way from the Tweed to the Atlantic. Eels go in pairs, sticklebacks and Tigris Fish. Blow-fish blow kisses. Cod say there's a place for us. And pollocks.'

Daisy turned in front of the mirror, gave a pert and approving look back at herself.

'I'll wear perfume tonight. I'll wear a dress.'

∘ ∘ ∘

Tom's trousers were soaking from the deck.

Peter Jones said 'Make an effort, dear. This isn't Das Boot.'

Matelots and flares? Why flares? Wet flares must have been hell. Hornpipes, pigtails, keel-hauling, rigging, losing your hands in the capstan, jolly Jack Tars, Billy Budd, buggery, Peter Pears, Aldborough, Jeremy Thorpe. 'My gun jammed.' Andrew 'Gino' Newton, Rinka, 'Bunnies can and will go to France.' Norman Scott.

'Focus, dear. Focus' said Peter Jones. 'Seduction has to be planned. Go for the back of the neck. Like a cat with a rabbit.'

'We're aiming for breakfast in bed' added John Lewis. 'For a lifetime.'

I hate marmalade.

'A cup of Morning Kick, or Lapsang Souchong if you must' said John Lewis. 'With lemon. Is refreshing. And as much fruit as you can manage. For you know what.'

I hate tea.

Peter Jones grunted. 'No-one has ever done suicide after a hearty meal, a good night's sleep, or a satisfactory evacuation of the bowels.'

129

The sea was rising, Turmoil riding it comfortably. Daisy dried herself from the shower in a big warm towel, felt luxurious. She stretched out on her bed. There was no hurry. The pillow was soft.

I could hang myself on that hook. Slicing the wrist should be done along the vein, not across. Tom, give me some of your blood – supposing I don't have enough to lose? I can slip over the side and dive deep. I'll breathe in fast – get it over, drench my lungs. I'll sink forever, I'll never be bored, I'll fall to the bottom of the sea. It's the end of being afraid.

She went to sleep. We can ride off into the sunset together. But once out of frame, we'd be on horses in the middle of the prairie. In the dark, and no lamp.

∘ ∘ ∘

John Lewis leaned over Tom and whispered 'Reveille!'

Tom woke with his clothes sticking to him, hair tousled and his body wet, his mouth unpleasantly dry.

'Hands off cocks and into socks!' said Peter Jones.

'Shit. Shave. Shower.

'And don't bend over for the soap.'

Tom hadn't switched on the air-conditioning, but it was cooler now with the setting of the sun. He opened the window, stripped, and inhaled the evening air, feeling uneasy at what the evening might deliver. But the shower was full and powerful, and as he soaped his body, he began to feel strong and alive.

∘ ∘ ∘

Daisy dressed. Peter Jones sized her up.

'Perfume, dear. Back of the ears. And a tiny touch of eye-liner. White shirt.'

∘ ∘ ∘

I feel pretty. There's a whole country in my cunt.

∘ ∘ ∘

Tom shaved, debated after-shave.

'Trust your instincts' murmured John Lewis.

'Clean your shoes. Do up your zip. Quick check in the mirror. Ready to go.'

130

o o o

Tom and Daisy were the first to arrive. He thought it was a funny old room. Wallpaper? Something with texture, off-cream. Mahogany table. Fake Louis Quinze chairs, white and ornate, details picked out in gold leaf. A tablecloth (discreetly clipped to the table), polished silver cutlery, crystal glasses.

'Tom! Tom. You look amazing.'

'Daisy!'

I have never before had my breath taken away.

He gave her a coy wink. 'Oh, this old thing.'

She laughed. 'You look good.'

'You. Um you look good.'

'Southern nights.'

The door opened and Pöl Stuyvesant came in, took off his cap.

'Daisy. I'm really sorry. I can't join you. Chief can't leave the engine room. Sends his apologies.'

She put her arms round him. 'You OK? You look awfully tired.'

'Fine, fine. You know all this stuff. It's normal, bloody bloody normal – can you hear your dad saying that? Normal Southern Ocean chaos. The weather's everywhere. We know the size, we know the speed. We don't know the direction, because it keeps flicking around.

'We're trying to keep well away. And we probably will. Double watches all night. Any problems I'll call you. Make sure you strap in the bunk tonight. Tie everything down. Sorry Tom, you too. Talking to the boss.'

'Master's quite reliable, Tom. We'll probably be OK. Came to see me when I was one day old. My God-father. Lots of pictures and films of me tormenting our glorious leader on lots of ships.'

'Brings a tear to the eye. Must go. Bon appetit.'

She closed the door behind him, sat down at the table and looked quickly at Tom. My stupid brain is jelly, I never meant to be in love. I can't look at your pretty eyes in case the jelly spreads to my knees, and I fall into you, ie your arms, and embarrass you and confuse me. It isn't chemistry, it's possession.

'Avocado pear.'

'Yes.'

The table was set for four. Tom cleared away two sets of

131

cutlery, glasses and plates, and restored each to its cupboard. He lifted the lids of a steel bain-marie the size of a kitchen range bolted to the floor and inspected the contents. Sense of order satisfied, he sat down opposite Daisy.

'It's quite an achievement to have avocado pear on a ship', he ventured.

'Yes. Keeping fresh fruit and vegetables fresh is an engineering challenge.'

'Vinaigrette?'

John Lewis and Peter Jones strolled outside the ship. It was only fair to give the potential lovers a clear start, but the wait was maddening. John Lewis was the first to break.

'Should we go and peep?'

'There's nothing more we can do, dear. We're not Christof, and he's not Truman. He's got to take his life in his own hands. He has to become a man.'

'Some people never grow.'

'He's not Peter Pan. He has to learn for himself. He can't hide in that silly tower. Even Rapunzel let her hair down.'

'You're right. It's so annoying. You want to bang their heads. Young people! Never in a hurry. You have to be. It slips through your fingers. And your last words are, "Is that all?" You're as wonderful as the day we first met. Why can't everyone have what we have? I'd like them to.'

'Because there aren't many people as lovely as you in the world. Come on, romantic. Little peep.'

They peered through the window, feeling like voyeurs.

'Such a sweet girl – just right for him. Lovely hair. Pretty earrings. Washed her hair.'

'It needed it, John. Didn't you notice? Lank. Split ends. Wash it in beer, dear. Rinse with lemon. And our boy could do with a blow-dry; hair's clean, though. Thank heavens he's ironed those trousers.'

o o o

Mulligatawny soup.

Daisy said 'We're both orphans.'

'There's no-one around at the end. In practical terms there's no-one around at the start. Although you're inside your mother, and your father's put you there, neither of them can live your birth for you. Or your life. So even if parents are alive, at best they're accessories. We're always alone. Do you miss your father?'

'Every day. Most seconds.'

'Do you ever feel his presence?'

'I can't make that kind of jump. This table's here. You're here – and that's good, Tom. It's good you're here. All the rest is conjecture. There are no spirits. No concrete fantasies. Our imagination is chemical reactions.'

'The cheek of it', muttered Peter Jones.

Daisy thought for a while. 'I can only deal with pragmatics. The rest is madness. I'd love to be another person. Someone who can dream.'

Peter Jones nudged John Lewis. 'This could be positive.'

'Dreams aren't all they're cracked up to be.'

'Oh for heaven's sake man!' John Lewis kicked Tom.

'Ow!'

'What's the matter?' asked Daisy, startled. 'Are you OK?'

'Did you kick me under the table?'

'Of course not. Would you like me to?'

'OK.'

'Ow!'

'You can kick me back. Ow! Not that hard. Look what you've done to my leg.' She stretched it out, looked up at Tom.

'This is it.' Peter Jones could barely conceal his excitement. 'We're going in.'

Tom knelt beside her.

'Shit, I have. Your poor leg. Thigh. Shin.'

He stroked it experimentally.

'I'm not a sheep. Lower. Higher. That feels lovely. That feels a lot better.'

'Pretty socks.'

'Fortnum & Mason.'

'I thought they only did food.'

'And high-class ladies.'

'I thought high-class was hookers?'

'You may be in luck.'

'Depends on the rate.'

'My rates are high for stroking.'

The loudspeaker in the ceiling screeched, followed by the first officer's voice.

'All crew to stations. Survival aids. Stand by.'

Tom looked up at Daisy. 'All hands on deck.'

'All hands are fine where they are. My life-jacket's in my cabin. I'll get yours.'

'I'll go.'

'I'll come.'

As they ran down the corridor Turmoil gave a violent lurch. Daisy stumbled, fell against him, said 'Shit.'

'Hold tight.'

'Don't worry. I'm not letting go.'

He got her to his cabin, pulled the life-jacket onto her.

'That's yours.

'I'll get yours. Stay here. Strap in.'

The voice of the first officer came over the Tannoy.

'All passengers strap in. Confirm.'

Daisy pushed the intercom. 'I'm in Tom's cabin strapped in.'

'Where's Tom?' It was the master.

'Getting my life-jacket.'

'When he gets back, secure the cabin door. It's moving up to 10.'

'How long?'

'All night? Don't sleep. Out.'

○ ○ ○ ○ ○

14

Daisy Ballantyne is the owner of elderly cargo ship Turmoil, heading east after repairs at Gibraltar, carrying a cargo of scrap metal for Tom Devine. Tom and Daisy have been circling each other in an emotional stand-off which is beginning to relax. A violent storm comes upon the ship in the Southern Ocean. In London Jack and Jill Jouvry look forward to being parents, supported in their comfortable if unconventional domesticity by Russian au pair, Magda.

JILL JOUVRY – TIRED, mighty, serene – sat propped up in bed at Queen Charlotte's Hospital, West London.

Miss Jouvry, 3.3 kilogrammes – healthy, average but not large weight – sucked at her breast.

Jack Jouvry loved two women: his wife, and the Magdalene.

Jill said 'Darling, are you fucking Magda?'

'Isn't that what she's for?'

The both laughed. He felt a shit, but equally, he didn't. Jack was expedient, and it was an expedient reply. He loved Magda, and it would be an insult to her if she were not worth a decent lie. But he felt slimy, and realised that it must be a deeper and less practical love than he'd thought.

He looked at Miss Jouvry and realised that he loved three

women. She was beautiful. What an unworthy and meaningless word with which to describe someone of such glorious and triumphal delight, little heart-melter, little gift to the future, angel and princess – again, useless words. Herself.

No name. They had agreed that she could have – must have – the freedom of being unnamed for as long as possible. To be, and to establish herself on her own terms. She was evidently strong, and already with a twinkling of humour: gaiety. A girl who would thrive in her long life, and bring in turn to others that joy which she brings to us now.

Who would flourish.

'Where is Daisy?'

'Tom and Daisy are – they should be – right down in the Southern Ocean. The clipper route, I believe it's called.'

'It's an old ship. Isn't that dangerous?'

'It's over-insured.'

They both laughed.

Jill Jouvry looked at her husband in simple love, as he looked at her. The baby lay in her arms, hands and feet like her mother's, eyes and colouring too. Her father's nose and mouth. Jill smiled and closed her eyes.

∘ ∘ ∘

Three or four hours to the east of Turmoil a giant wave built, dwarfing its companions. Two furies watched it form, the naked imps of the sky: mothered by the earth, it was said; fathered by the air.

First one and then the other dropped from sky to wave in the way that a tick drops – suddenly, vertically. Swooping along the top of the wave, they examined its indigos, browns and greens, its crown too sharp to foam, its roll and force. They flew west with the sea, faster by far – its hours their minutes – unbattered by the wind.

Arriving at Turmoil, they held hands, skipped around her and pried into her windows.

∘ ∘ ∘

A degree of normality – the normality of an emergency – had returned to life aboard.

136

It was a great storm, but Turmoil was a great ship. She was built for the ocean, her crew strong men and women, each in every way a master of the sea.

Master, wheel crew and navigation officer were at the bridge, the radio officer behind them. First and second officers were ordered to rest. Non-essential crew were stood down, ready for instant recall.

Nothing stopped the galley making food. It was the policy of Mrs Patropi, the cook, to deliver meals at exact times, regardless of the angle of the floor. She fed all, fed fully, and fed equally.

From the outside, the furies watched the frothing of yeast, the commencement of a sourdough poolish with seven days to go, the spiking of racks of lamb with honey and garlic, the rise of a dozen perfect soufflés, the butchery of a dead pig, the baking of Florentines.

Through another window, they witnessed First Officer Renn making critical notes to Lady Chatterley's Lover. Her degree was in English literature and it was her firm belief that Herbert Lawrence's insistence on private publication in France had robbed it of the rigorous edit which – her proposed doctoral thesis would argue – it needed.

Elsewhere, they watched intrigued as sailors female and sailors male – in private and in company – performed sex solo and combined. Rising and falling. Spurting. Yearning.

○ ○ ○

There was something languorous too in the mounting of Turmoil on the ocean, riding the waves in her thousands of tons.

For moments, the whole of her deck submerged. Then she would rise and shake it off, like a whale preening itself. On the great swells, she climbed the sea to the top and freewheeled down the slope, meeting the next sea as it came – the opposite of Coleridge's idle ship on a painted ocean. And no-one had shot an albatross.

Daisy looked anxiously at the door, hearing the sounds of the outside as if for the first time. Throughout the ship, the noise of the sea was a constant presence, separate from the throb of the engine. In calm water, it could be as gentle as a whisper. Sailors might talk of it as a sigh.

Now it was a roar. It pounded and pulled against the bottom and sides of the ship. It scraped the metal as if with giant fingernails, banged and resonated the holds. It battered from above, ebbed as it drained from the decks, and came back renewed as Turmoil crashed into the oncoming sea.

Tom came in with her life-jacket over his shoulder.

'Thank God.'

She didn't know if it was her thoughts aloud or a prayer.

'Get over here man. Strap in. Captain's orders are don't sleep.'

He put it on and looked unalarmed by it all, casual even.

'Can you keep up all night?'

He grinned. 'Depends on the company.'

'I've slept through worse than this.'

He strapped into the seat beside her, took her hand.

'It's OK to be afraid.'

'I have never learnt that.'

'No gentleness?'

'Gentleness, yes. No place for weakness.'

He squeezed her hand, touched the side of her cheek. 'It's not weak. It's being alive.'

∘ ∘ ∘

The furies were at the window.

'We're the bastard children you'll never have.'

'Now that you've spat in the face of God.'

Seeing them, Daisy froze.

'Surely God is merciful?'

Puzzled, Tom replied 'I've no idea.'

'Can't you hear them?'

'Voices in the wind?'

'Can't you see their cruel faces?'

'Here's work, sister' said Fury Two. 'To saw and hack and snap. The Devil's here, and us. Lord God and hosts. Turmoil.'

∘ ∘ ∘

'Dante', Daisy muttered.

Tom was about to say Beatrice, but thought better of it. She was clearly in shock, terrified of the storm. Following delusions wouldn't snap her out of them. It was better to focus on the real, practical calamity.

'What if you lose your ship?'

'I'm buying another.'

'Who owns half of this one?' He knew that much.

'Jack.'

'OK.'

'Why OK?'

'Didn't know. Curious.'

'Don't be. It's business. This is personal.'

'You could lose your ship.'

'My ship, your cargo.'

'Everything is a commodity.'

'Every person?'

Tom stroked her hand. 'There aren't any rules written about you.'

'You can let someone in. Is love just for girls?'

'You're the girl.'

Daisy laughed. 'How do you know?'

'You've got all the things girls have.'

She widened her eyes. 'How do you know?'

'And you smell like a girl.'

'How do we smell?'

'You've done this before. Different from a boy.'

'You've done this with a man?'

'I surrender. You fuck Jack?'

o o o

Peter Jones threw up his hands in despair.

'Oh for heaven's sake, man. Haven't you any self-control?'

'Unbelievable' said John Lewis.

o o o

Daisy thought for a while. Finally she whispered, 'You don't have any right to ask that.'

'Quite right' said John Lewis. She filled him with admiration. 'You tell him, dear.'

'You didn't have any right to ask that up till about half an hour ago.'

'No no no no no' said Peter Jones.

'You're going to have the right to ask it.'

'No he isn't.'

'So I'll answer it.'

'Grief' said John Lewis.

Daisy sat upright, looked Tom straight in the face.

'Yes.'

'Oh.'

Tom looked at the wall. Did he move away, flinch? It was so slight that Daisy wasn't sure. She wondered how she could tell such a tiny difference in the space between them against the violent movement of the ship. But she couldn't stem the flow of words. It must be all, or the whole thing must be lost.

'There was a past. I've let it slip away. Those are emotions. Do you want facts? I aborted his baby. Is this more than you wanted to hear?'

∘ ∘ ∘

'What a magnificent woman.'

John Lewis clapped his hands.

'Think of the courage it took to come out with that. Risk everything.'

'It's about the most stupid thing I've ever seen anyone do', Peter Jones replied. 'He's never going to touch her now. She should have lied.'

'You wouldn't do that.'

'How do you know? Maybe I lie all the time. Maybe I'm out on the Heath every night when you're asleep.'

'Maybe I've seen you there. Are you the one in the balaclava?'

Peter Jones kissed him. 'I love you.'

'I love you. I love your integrity.'

'In the end, it has to be the truth.'

'Why accept anything less?' John Lewis looked Tom up and down. 'But he doesn't have the moral courage. Look at his face. He's going to drop her like a hot chestnut.'

'Coal.'

'Brick.'

'He's revolted. He knows he can never trust her. He's going to wimp.'

'What about him fucking the woman? He's going to lie his way out of that. Look at him. Creep.'

'He doesn't deserve her. Look at her fine features.' Peter Jones smiled at Daisy. 'Noble face, strong firm mouth.'

'Her vagina's completely different.'

There was a pause.

'I hadn't made the comparison' said Peter Jones. But you're right, it is. Her vagina's quite slack and rubbery. It's like a big crimped flange with a loose seal, like double-glazing that's been badly-fitted, or worn with the passing of time. Or a slack mussel in a freezer bag of moules. It's a perfectly good colour – I've only ever seen them in pink – and it's a pretty pink. Not much hair, but some people like that.'

John Lewis held out his hands.

'If you drop the second finger of the hand that you use down to the ball of its palm, and measure the distance from where it reaches to its tip, that's supposed to be the length of your cock. When I first met you, I was surprised by how big your cock was, because your hands are quite small.'

The remark, well-intentioned, stung Peter Jones.

'No they're not.'

John Lewis stroked them, restoring calm.

'I love your hands. They're eloquent.'

'These are 11-note hands. I can span C to octave D with either of them. As well you know. Very effective for arpeggios. I was delighted by the size of your cock. Its thickness. It reminded me of a cannon at Aix-la-Chapelle.'

'Maybe that was the good news they brought from Ghent to Aix – "The cocks are thicker here".'

Peter Jones gave a happy sigh.

'First time I rubbed your cannon, it fired a good metre.'

'Long time ago.'

'Happy memories. Happy present. Happy ahead.'

'He's preparing to make a statement.'

∘ ∘ ∘

Hesitantly, Daisy took Tom's hand.

'Don't hate me.'

'I'm astonished.'

'You look as if you want to tell me something.'

141

Tom squeezed her hand, let it go, folded his arms, unfolded them, looked ahead.

'I've never met anyone who tells the truth.

'My father was a liar. My mother was a liar.

'Not big important lies, little lies about prestige. Small, social lies. Everyone I've ever met tells lies, trivial things, business lies. Am I pretty? Of course. Shall I part my hair behind? Absolutely, it suits you. Was that good for you? The best I've ever had.

'I've never heard the truth. And I just have.'

'I owe it.' It was almost a whisper, and Daisy felt as if she might cry. Not at all from sadness, but somehow – illogically – from hope. That, and release.

He looked away. 'I have to tell you something. I'd like to think I would have, some time, but I don't know if – when it came to it – I would.'

'That's a long conditional.'

It had come to the point of disclosure, at which everything he had longed to gain might be thrown away.

'I've had a relationship with Jill for years. She's pregnant of course. The baby may be mine. I also had a long relationship with Jack. It was passionate.'

'Well' said John Lewis.

'I had no idea.'

'You had an abortion? Are you all right?'

'What's all right, Tom?'

'It's complicated.'

'I'm glad we've told each other. What will you do if you're a father? Do you want to be with Jill?'

'Do you?'

So he knew.

Daisy reflected on that, and took it into her heart.

'I've acquired other priorities. A formal way of putting it, but I can't think of another way. Love is a formal business. There are conclusions and beginnings. Lines need to be chalked on the ground.'

'I don't want to be with Jill. I want to be with you.'

∘ ∘ ∘

'Applause!' shouted Peter Jones.

142

John Lewis pursed his lips.

'She's not going to buy this. Look at her mouth. She's not happy.'

'Happy! She thought he was straight, turns out he's a bender, so's she, and he's co-shagged both the people she was shagging and simultaneously deceiving. This is Olympic-class competitive gay adultery.'

John Lewis looked from Daisy to Tom, and back again. Things didn't look promising.

'All the cards are on the table. He's no surprises to play with. It's screaming for diplomacy. Our boy's not strong on diplomacy.'

○ ○ ○

Daisy cleared her throat.

'I don't think that's going to be possible now.'

○ ○ ○

Chief Engineer Beacruft ran a well-ordered engine room. Machinery was serviced and efficient.

Here, at the bottom of the ship and permanently in the deeper currents under the outside water, the noise of the ocean was as loud as the drawn-out explosion of a volcano, powerful and low as an earthquake. Whether they spoke, or whether – as now – it was necessary to shout, the voices of officers and crew remained calm.

Turmoil's engine ran smoothly. It was the manufacturer's claim that a cup of coffee – or tea – placed on any of its horizontal surfaces would remain unspilled. At present the engine room itself tilted between 30 degrees down from level and 30 degrees up – an arc of 60 degrees over one to two minutes, matching the rise and fall of the sea. This was recorded in the log, taking its place among the record of commands from the bridge and the engine-room's actions in response.

Beacruft had a tendency to poetry, seeing in his machinery the rhythm and flow of verse; and in the life of the sea a wealth of classical references. He believed in fallibility – that whatever was mighty must have a flaw, a path of hubris. Hercules and his Augean Stables, Queen Cleopatra and her asp; Saul and David;

143

Samson and Delilah. There was Achilles too, and his heel; then Paris in turn, and the consequences of his Judgment.

But most of all he believed in bathos: that it was always the ridiculous which brought about the end. And so with Turmoil, he kept an ear to the bearings of the circulating water pump.

Every piece of machinery had instruments to measure function, flow, malfunction, foible. There were indicator lamps, hooters, switches, valves, optics, dials. There was also a broom handle. He took this now, put one end at the casing of the bearing and pressed the other against the tragus of his right ear. He could hear the rotation of the pump and the flow of water. There was a slight irregularity too, a periodic squeal which disturbed him. He picked up the phone to the bridge.

∘ ∘ ∘

Peter Jones slipped his arm round John Lewis. Together they regarded Tom – silent, brooding over what Daisy had said. 'You have to like people' said Peter Jones. 'He's a single-occupancy man at heart. You can only comfortably fit one person into a lighthouse.'

'The keeper.'

∘ ∘ ∘

Daisy and Tom looked in different directions.

The storm, via Turmoil, continued to throw them against each other, and apart.

∘ ∘ ∘

Shyly, Fury One approached Peter Jones.

'Excuse me, have you got a cigarette?'

Catching sight of herself in a mirror she realised what he must see – what he must think. She tugged at her wild hair, trying to unlock the strands, embarrassed by her uncut fingernails – not talons, please don't let him think that. Him in his lovely smart clothes, beautifully cut. She wondered if it was all right to be naked.

'Roll-up OK?'

Peter Jones took a pouch of Golden Virginia and a pack of green Rizlas from the pocket of his Harris Tweed sports jacket.

And he was nice! He didn't look her up or down, didn't

evaluate her, didn't scorn. Just did what she asked, normal as can be. Sweet face.

'Cool, thanks. I'm Fury One, my friend Fury Two.'

'Peter Jones, my friend John Lewis.'

'May I?'

He snapped a silver Zippo and she took a light from him.

'Thanks. You're the pair of queers from the water tower?' She checked her language, hoped it was OK. His expression didn't flicker, and she began to relax. 'Seen you around. Always wanted to meet you. Is it a single staircase all the way to the top?'

'It was a hell of a job getting it in' said John Lewis. 'Each of the flights was handmade off-site. Solid oak from Italy. Weighed a ton. We had to hire an enormous crane. Blocked off the street. Winched it in from the top. Anyhow, it looks wonderful.'

'That sounds really lovely. Timber floors?'

Peter Jones smiled.

'John's very stripped-wood, and uncomfortable chairs by anyone German. I'm more fabrics and throws – traditional poove. But I think there's a breath of humanity in that. You been following this?' He tilted his finger towards Tom and Daisy.

Fury Two spoke for the first time, her voice softer than Fury One's.

'Like, half-heartedly. They're so into themselves.'

'Plus we only really work if you believe in something' said Fury One. 'God. Satan. Even the Enlightenment. But if you're nothing or humanist – forget it. They don't notice.'

'There's only one thing worse than being talked about and that's not being talked about' said Fury Two.

She added, unsurely: 'Oscar Wilde?'

'The one and only.' Peter Jones roared with laughter.

'Hey that's great, I really really like him. I like you! Oh. Sorry.'

She looked down, ashamed.

'Steady' said Fury One.

'Sorry.'

'She oversteps the mark.'

'I'm always embarrassing her.'

Peter Jones grinned at Fury Two. 'Don't be silly. It's not embarrassing.'

'Are you two – together?' asked John Lewis.

'Well' said Fury One.

'She's really really shy about being out' said Fury Two, laughing. 'We've been together ages now. Yeah, we're together. How long you two?'

'Years and years. And all of them happy.'

'Oh, that's so lovely.'

'You'll have to come over for dinner. Are you vegetarian?'

'I'm not, she is' said Fury One.

'Typical, isn't it. I love meat. Peter faints at the sight of it.'

'I still have to cook his bloody steak when it's my turn.'

'We try and take domestic chores in turn. I cook for a week, he cooks for a week. I must say he's very good about handling meat.'

'Oo-er. Pardon my friend. Terrible in company.'

'We'd really really love to, that's so sweet' said Fury Two. 'I'm so into Modern Movement, Bauhaus, Mies Van Der Rohe. I'm like you John Lewis. Frank Lloyd Wright was way way way too fussy for me. Sorry. I'm talking too much.'

'Oh you must, dear' said Peter Jones. 'You must express yourself. But I have to say – to a lot of us – Frank Lloyd Wright was a god. I love comfort. I love excess. You can never have too much excess.'

'Did Oscar say that?'

'My dear. Oscar would have killed to have said that. I must modestly admit – it's a Peter Jones original.'

'Modest! Ha!' said John Lewis.

∘ ∘ ∘

Stuyvesant picked up the bridge phone.

'Yes?'

'The top bearing's about to go.'

Turmoil rose in the water. There was a sudden break of clear sky to the horizon ten kilometres away. Heavy seas, but with a sound ship, nothing impossible.

In half his mind, Stuyvesant listened to Beacruft. An unconscious process calculated the possible endurance of the engine against the period of the waves, their height and direction, the speed of the wind. If it came to it, he wondered if she'd snap in two like the Derbyshire. And it was reasonable. A ship

146

voluntarily in the world's most dangerous ocean.

'Give me a time.'

'One, maybe two hours of full power, if we're lucky. If we're unlucky, minutes.'

Stuyvesant pictured it. A cylinder a man's height and a bit less wide. Inside, an electric motor with a broken bearing, the water pump below it undriven. Next to it, the great engine of Turmoil – big as a shop on two floors. No water to cool the pistons. They overheat, expand, seize against the cylinder walls. The engine is destroyed. With no power, Turmoil drifts, is thrown by the sea. Drowns.

○ ○ ○

Fury One looked diffidently at John Lewis.

'I like reading books. Do you like reading books?'

'Nothing too difficult.'

'I'm reading All The Pretty Horses by Cormac McCarthy.' She searched his eyes for approval. 'There's no punctuation.'

'Gosh.'

'It's hard to read. I'm not making much progress.'

'I have a copy of Black Beauty. Would you like it?'

'Oh.'

'That's about horses. Horse.'

'I.'

'Yes. It's probably too – narrative. Usually I love not knowing where I am. I want to question the reality of what's going on. I don't want anything concrete. Oh dear, that does sound pretentious. But it's a good read. I promise.'

'I like to know exactly where I am.'

'This is what she is' said Fury Two. 'You are, love. I have to tell her all the time: "I love you." "Do you love me?" "Yes of course I love you." "Do you really really love me?" "Yes, I really, really love you." I like that, though. I do love you.' She kissed her.

Peter Jones beamed.

'Ah. That's so sweet. But you're right to demand it, Fury One, it's crucial. You have to keep saying "I love you."'

'They're not simply words' added John Lewis. 'It's the affirmation of word.'

A smile spread hesitantly across Fury One's face.

147

'That's how the Bible starts. I keep quoting from the opposition, but to give it its due, it's not bad. "In the beginning was The Word." Admittedly that directly means God, and the next sentence "And The Word was God" actually says that. But it emphasises the sacred aspect of speech, which is something we can all agree on. We have to say what is on our mind. It's no good thinking it. Mind-reading can be ambiguous and just plain wrong. Speech is exactly what you say, John. It's affirmation.'

o o o

The giant wave rolled towards Turmoil, thirty minutes from the point of encounter. Just beyond the visible horizon, and already taller than the ship, it continued to grow.

o o o

The silence between Daisy and Tom enclosed them. It created its own kind of intimacy: a cocoon within the greater noise of the tempest.

It was Tom who broke it.

'I can't blame you. Oh, hell, I'm simply sorry. I knew I couldn't get it right.'

o o o

'So internal' muttered Fury One. 'Seeing her in his own terms. What about her needs? For crying out loud, she's just had an abortion for him. Can't he see she's done it for him? To give them a future together?'

John Lewis nodded vigorously.

'He has an inability to do anything in practical terms. He's misunderstood, and there's a danger he will never be understood. He can't make decisions.'

o o o

Tom rose to his feet. 'Right. I've made a decision.'

Daisy looked up. 'What are you doing?'

'Wait.'

'What do you mean, "Wait"?'

He phoned.

'Jilly? It's me. Yes. Bit of a storm. Listen, I'm with Daisy. Can you guess why I'm? And you can talk? Right. OK. Right. Oh look

148

I'm absolutely thrilled. Oh that is such good news. Oh that's lovely. Oh, I'm so happy for you both. That's wonderful. Yes, it's for the best. So looking forward to seeing you both. Sorry, really bad reception. Just wanted to. Yeah. Got to go. Much love.'

He sat beside her. 'It's Jack's.'

Daisy hesitated.

'Is it a boy or a girl?'

He said nothing.

'You didn't ask?'

He wondered if she'd seen her aborted baby, knew whether boy or girl, thought of a name. He said quietly 'It's a girl.'

'Oh, she's had a girl.'

Daisy was on the edge of tears. 'That's – lovely for her.'

'We've both been honest.'

'There isn't any more truth to tell. I feel as if my stomach's been ripped open.'

Tom felt unsure to take her hand. Cautiously, he laid his on hers, let it rest for a moment, took it back. 'It has, in a way.'

Daisy didn't move. 'I admire what you've done, but I wish I didn't know any of it. You must wish the same about me. And it opens up a lifetime of questions of fact – who fucked who just after who fucked who? And where are the loyalties?'

'No.'

He jumped to his feet.

'It does if we let it. This is the chalk line. We have to be grown up and cross it, and say, what's behind is the past.'

'Will you hold my hand?' She stood next to him, slipped hers into his. 'Shall we cross that line together now?

'Ready?'

Two adults, skipping forward hand-in-hand like children in a playground? And he didn't care.

'Line crossed.'

'And what if we're dead?' Daisy spoke very softly. 'What if we go down? What if we sink? What if we drown?'

He held her face in his hands. 'If we were lovers, our love would last forever. Because forever would be short. And we'd never be unkind. Across the Styx. Another ship, another captain. Me still the passenger. You still in charge: codename Beatrice,

149

codename Dante. You get the better part. Except we're dead. This is morbid.'

'I know how to change the subject.' She touched his face. 'We're almost strangers.'

'I hardly know you.'

She held him.

'Then know me.'

There was a rap on the door and one of the crew rushed in, her face and life-jacket smeared with oil.

'Madam. Proceed to the bridge.'

'Right away.'

'Sir. Stand by for a call to Lifeboat One.'

Stuyvesant's voice over the Tannoy: 'Daisy. Bridge please.'

'Yes sir.'

'Kiss me', Tom whispered.

'Later.' She released him gently and ran for the door. 'We have a lifetime.'

As he watched the rogue wave approach from a distance, Stuyvesant faced a judgment which at one level was simple. The two principle lifeboats – one port, one starboard – could each carry everyone on board, and there was a third smaller boat aft of the bridge. In a rough sea, it would take half an hour to abandon ship and get the boats clear from being smashed against her sides. A giant wave was survivable with luck and an engine. Lives were safer on the ship.

It became more complex with detail.

Stuyvesant guessed 25 metres for the height of the wave – a titan. Most likely, there'd be another a couple of hundred metres behind, and maybe a third. He ordered the wireless operator to alert shipping. If the engine held, he could steer Turmoil into the wave and minimise the risk of capsize, hoping to ride it and survive with broken windows. If she crested successfully, running down the far side might sink her at the trough.

If the engine failed, she'd sink at the first wave.

In the present sea, it would be impossible to launch the boats.

The only decision was to stay with the ship.

○ ○ ○

As Daisy arrived, breathless, Stuyvesant gave the command to evacuate the engine room. One look at the wave was enough, and the same calculations flashed through her mind. Minutes later, Beacruft stood alongside Stuyvesant, driving the engine from the duplicate controls on the bridge.

'Full ahead.'

'Full ahead.'

Pöl Stuyvesant clenched and unclenched his hands, tensed and released his body from head to feet. He'd learnt to face every crisis of his career relaxed. In this way, he'd survived and he intended their survival today. It was Aloysha Krestyanov who'd taught him that deep breaths oxygenated the brain and allowed it to think at maximum efficiency. Stuyvesant had no idea if this was true, but like most of Aloysha's theories, it worked. He breathed deep and slow, and said a silent prayer of thanks to whoever might listen, that First Officer Renn, keeping Turmoil's snout directly into the wave, was the best helms-woman in the fleet.

Daisy didn't ask why he'd called her to the bridge. She understood. The arrangement between them had always been that no reality was withheld. They would see it through together. She didn't feel afraid. When things went wrong in her much smaller world, her father would put her on his knee and confide into her ear, 'Strong girls sometimes cry', with a kiss that that made things better. She wondered if he was here.

Turmoil's lights flickered. Beacruft said 'The bearing's gone. Start counting minutes.' The lights went out and came on again full. 'Emergency generator on.'

'Maintain full ahead.'

'Full ahead.'

Three waves to go. Two. And then five storeys of water stood in front of them. Turmoil rose into the sea, higher and higher, creaking, straining as if she was climbing a roller coaster a notch at a time. Her bows drove into the water but the upsurge of the sea rejected her, carried her to the summit.

For a moment Turmoil stood at the top of the ocean.

The second wave was reassuringly modest in comparison. Turmoil swept down the tail of the first and met it fully in power and head on.

Ploughing into the crest of the second wave, a mast wrenched free and collapsed into the bridge, killing the master and chief engineer. Slithering down the far side, Turmoil broadsided. She tumbled upside down, righting herself beneath the water. For a while she surfaced. She sank gracefully, her lights bright, down to the bottom of the sea.

○ ○ ○ ○ ○

Part Two

1

Daisy's merchant ship Turmoil is lost in a storm at sea. Aboard Turmoil and moments before the disaster, Daisy and Tom finally revealed their love for each other. In London, Daisy's adoptive cousin Rachel Fonseca is investigated for radical activities. The mental illness of Dianita (Diana) Lapraman separates her from her business partner Helen Landesman. Their architectural practice is designing Square Mile City, the enclosed area which is to replace the bombed-out City of London. Daisy's adoptive sister Rowena – by nature withdrawn, and inseparable from her dog Paul – blossoms under the attentions of Emilio Podro, a South American diplomat who is informed about the investigation into Rachel. He is an old acquaintance of Rowena's mother Mrs Ballantyne.

SHE WAS BEING kissed. The kiss lasted for ages, and emptied everything out of her. The lips on her lips enclosed her, smudged her face as if it was a cartoon face sketched with pastel crayons, wetted, and only the brightest colours. The irises of her lover were grey, a brown grey, a light sienna, her lips full, her taste sweet pomegranate, her hair lustrous, tousled, black. Her name?

'Here she is.'

155

Something shouted, another voice. Freezing cold, her sleeve torn open, her arm bared. Drowning.

'Here she is.'

It was warm now, very comfortable. There was the question of opening her eyes, but there were two opinions about that. Being dead was a new experience and opening her eyes would mean acknowledging it; plus she wasn't sure she'd like what she saw. On the other hand she may not be dead, but if not, where was she? Better, on the whole, to keep her eyes shut. She tightened them.

'Come on, sleepy head.'

The fingers of two hands cupping her face, stroking her forehead; the most gentle fingers imaginable. How she longed to be kissed again. Warm breath over her face; clean, practical breath. A kiss on each of her eyelids.

'Now you're playing.'

She smiled, couldn't help it, opened her eyes.

'Here she is.'

Daisy looked up into the most beautiful face she had ever seen.

The sheets were damp with her sweat. Her face was sweating, her hair lank, wet with sweat. There was a strap around her hips, not tight, not unpleasant; and a strap around her arm. Into the inside of her elbow – my port elbow, she corrected herself – there was a cannula, held in place with white surgical tape. Its valve was open, and a drip – she looked up – was attached, which in turn – she strained to look back – was fixed to the top of her bed, a bed with a tubular frame.

'We are rehydrating you.'

'Surely I don't need more water.'

'Surely you do.'

She noticed there was a strap around her other arm, a cannula leading into the back of her right hand, a drip to another bottle. Morphine?

She was suddenly concerned.

'Tom?'

The woman was silent. Daisy said nothing, looked at her face (her lovely face). She noticed for the first time that she had been crying, that there were tears ready in her eyes. She looked at

Daisy, said quietly. 'Everyone is dead.'

Daisy knew she should be sad, but sadness wouldn't come. It was there as a thought, but wouldn't translate into something that could be felt. Curiously, she did feel for the woman in front of her, for the evident distress she was trying to conceal (for whose benefit? Her own? For Daisy's?).

'Oh.'

The woman said nothing, leant forward and kissed her.

'I feel lovely' Daisy whispered.

'Sleep now.'

Daisy thought that was right. She was drowsy and closed her eyes.

'You're Isabella' she said. 'You're Isabella Berthonella. Just what are you doing here?'

○ ○ ○

On his second visit to Rachel Fonseca's house , Adam Brook was shown around the bedroom of her son – Gary Malanuik, absent.

It was on the ground floor and faced the front door – allowing the occupant to come and go unnoticed, and – it occurred to Adam Brook – keep a check on anyone else. The bedroom door was elaborately decorated with pretty and intricate filigree panels in a rococo frame.

Rachel opened it and switched on the lights.

The first thing Adam noticed was the stained-glass windows, mainly because they were the most restrained items in the room.

A heavy, gold-threaded embroidered counterpane – carpet? – covered the bed. Some of the oil paintings on the walls – he counted twenty – had picture-lights above.

Ornaments – most of them porcelain, some in silver, gold – littered every item of furniture: Limoges, Portmerion.

A Thomas Crapper lavatory commode. A Victorian wash basin with wash jug. A horse-hair shaving brush, after-shave, eau de cologne, cut-throat razor, leather razor strop strap, all from Taylor's, Jermyn Street. A cigar humidor: polished walnut with expensive marquetry in light and dark woods, modern.

A 'Perfect Date' inflatable.

Fortnum & Mason house-champagne bottles lay in a rack. Champagne glasses. A leather travel-alarm-clock – wound and

157

working with a red second-hand sweeping round – stood on a French-polished writing-desk. Bookshelves were stuffed with books, mainly contemporary, but a few old by the look of their leather covers, and possibly rare. A pair of big, rough, used monitor speakers stood in adjacent corners.

'It's very clean.'

'I have a cleaner. As a socialist it embarrasses me a little, I won't hide that. If Marx was alive he might conceivably have a cleaner, but I admit it's not reasonable to use hypothetical reality as justification. It's not having a servant. I'm not exploiting the working class. On a separate note, the cleaner is Mainland European and so arguably outside the class system. It's a question of a fair wage for a fair day's work. I don't come in here. I don't not come in here, but I'm trying not to be a creepy mother who obsesses over her son's things. I don't stroke his underwear. What did you expect – model trains?'

'Why not?

'He might have had them in the past. Sure. His father was the type who could easily have had a live steam O-gauge Gaston du Bousquet articulated locomotive and a scale model of the Peking-Hankow Railway concealed in the wainscotting of his sitting room.'

'I didn't have model trains.'

'I didn't either. No Trix. We're probably only half-formed.'

She picked up a copy of The Human Factor.

'You wanted this.'

She opened it, flicked through the pages.

'Pencil marks everywhere. Why has he done that?' She handed it to him.

Adam laid the book down, shrugged. He wandered around the room, looked up a large painting on the wall. It was an oil painting of a naked woman – graphic, almost pornographic, her legs splayed wide, eyes gazing provocatively at the viewer. At the artist. It was signed GM.

'This is you?'

'Why not?'

∘ ∘ ∘

Tom wasn't clear how he came to be on the beach. It was certainly a beach. He wasn't wet. He was wearing a tee shirt, shorts and plimsolls. Plimsolls! He'd never worn plimsolls in his life. But here they were, laced up and comfortable. All of him felt comfortable. And it was warm.

'It's hot' he said to the man next to him. 'It's warm. I like to be warm.'

'People often find it hot or warm, on their arrival' the man replied.

He was a handsome man, with smartly-cut grey hair and gray-blue eyes, late forties or perhaps early fifties. Tom noticed his eyes. He looked at Tom with full attention, but in a way that contained neither obsequiousness nor threat – a polite welcome.

'There's no oil.'

'Not in the sea. There's no oil here, Tom.'

Tom wondered how he knew his name. He felt as if he was in a mystery – a perfect setting of his imagination. But the man was real enough, and the ground solid under his feet.

'Are you a doctor?'

'No. No no no no no no no. I have a doctorate. Of course. Everyone has a doctorate. Friday.'

'Friday! Then I shall be Caruso.'

The man gave a big, wide laugh as if he'd never heard the joke before.

'Wrong! Wrong altogether and such a common mistake.'

He lowered his voice. 'Thursday lives next door. Shhh. All the days of the week live here. And the months of the year.' He put a finger to his lips. 'We must be secure.'

'From what?'

'Who knows?'

'What are your hobbies?'

'Quaint. Activities to pass time. But no-one has time. Did you have time, Tom? Do you?'

'I don't think I had time.'

'I had Morgans. TVRs. AC Cobras. My lover and I were wont to get pissed. We fucked best pissed. Sorry', Friday paused, suddenly embarrassed. 'OK to say "fuck"?'

'Of course. Please. Fuck.'

'It's easy to cause gratuitous offence by a careless word or gesture.'

'Good manners are surprisingly rare. But never wasted.'

Friday produced a bottle of Johnnie Walker Black Label whisky and a pair of tumblers. He filled each a third full, placed one in Tom's hand, raised his in good health and sipped contentedly.

'My chickadee and I loved to drink and drive' he reminisced. 'You should have seen his face. We were shit-faced. You know they say people go white with fear? He was darkening his trousers! Excrement was flooding out of his botty! Absolutely no doubt about it. He was caking himself.'

It was Tom's turn to feel embarrassed. He hesitated to correct his new friend, but it must be done.

'Cacking.'

'Of course. A cake is a sweetmeat?'

'In the Middle East, certainly. In Northern Europe more likely made with wheat-flour and allowed to be leavened with – for example – bicarbonate of soda – commonly known as baking-powder. The Turkish versus Greek Delight is a separate topic, as are their coffees.'

'Remarkable. My, we shall have a capital time.'

'I'm sorry Dr Friday. I interrupted.'

'Oh, but I'm so glad you did. Cacking himself. Rigid with fright as the chassis of our Jaguar. Still made with a chassis! A triumph of engineering. Made by the Germans! What a turn-up for the books! First they bomb the Coventry production-line in '43. By the turn of the century, they're making the cars themselves!'

'Uncanny.'

'Ironic. And so much better.'

They were alone, but Friday leant forward, whispered:

'Are you a Roy Orbison fan?'

'I do think – creepy? The dark glasses. Was he blind?'

Once again, Friday gave a grand laugh.

'Ha! A popular myth. No, of course not in the least. I felt his duet with kd lang – Crying – defined loneliness. Are you lonely?'

'I think I'm easier alone. In life, I mean, rather than at this second.' Tom realised he was happy. 'It's very good to have your company.'

'The matching of their voices. Sublime. She's a lezzer', Friday said with affection. 'Of course, being blind, maybe he didn't

160

know. But as he wasn't blind, he probably did.'

He paused, lost in memory, came back with a jolt.

'Blotto! We were six sheets to the wind. Smash! We wiped him from the road. Man, it was splendid!'

'It sounds a terrible accident.'

'Fabulous! No-one expected anyone to walk out alive.'

Tom knew that he shouldn't approve. On the other hand, Friday was such a charming man that it seemed cruel to spoil what for him was evidently a happy recollection. A change of subject would be tactful.

'Friday. Have you noticed? It's usually only men who have names in the week. Woden's day. Thor's day. And only women who have months? Avril, May, June, Juliet.'

'Augustus.'

'A chubby lad. Fat, rosy cheeks.'

A children's book? He couldn't remember. Now that Tom came to think about it, he couldn't remember anything of himself at all. Best to keep talking.

'And all the women are from sunny months. Hope. Expectation. Fecundity. Nothing from autumn.'

'Octavia. October. The Octavia Hill Housing Trust – a lamp shining in the darkness of social deprivation. At once-fashionable Notting Hill. Where all the murders were. Christie. Absolute Beginners.'

Tom closed his eyes, saw the Embankment lamps, the dancer, the man in the trench coat alone with a Strand.

'I love David Bowie. Not met him. Some things don't occur.'

'I love Neil Hannon. I have one of his records on the gramophone. Would you like to dance?'

'Are you a homosexual?'

'What!' Friday sounded astonished. 'In the South Seas?'

Tom offered his arms.

'Dance?'

'Very well. But we shall wear these.'

He donned a pair of Sennheiser studio headphones and gave a second set to Tom.

'Thursday is writing a book. His autobiography – The Man Who Was Thursday. But he's not conceited, at least, not very. He

161

did promise all of us will be mentioned. Who knows? Perhaps he'll forget.

'Come.'

He put an arm round Tom, joined their free hands, closed his eyes.

'In Pursuit Of Happiness.'

○ ○ ○

Diana Lapraman was young and pretty when she first met her.

Dianita.

Dianita was soft to the touch and had a delicate aroma. Dianita had excellent taste in deodorants, perfume and make-up generally. A gentle voice, sweet eyes and smile.

If it could truly be said of anyone that she could light a room with her presence, Dianita was the light.

Lovely times: much better than good. Far better than average.

Helen Landesman smiled.

'We've not had a cross word. That's a lie. We've shouted and screamed. And we've always made up.'

They had never been embarrassed by each other's nakedness, and she wasn't embarrassed now. Shyly, Helen stroked Diana. Dianita.

She kissed her.

'I love you.'

○ ○ ○

'Would you say that we are customarily stepping out together of a Sunday?'

Rowena Ballantyne put her arm through Emilio Podro's.

It was so stunningly cold that Rowena had put on two sweaters, mountain boots, two pairs of mittens and her thickest coat with a big fur-lined hood tied at the bottom in a discreet bow. All that appeared of her face was something small but – she hoped – significant.

Rowena had tried unsuccessfully to put a coat on Paul. She had given up entirely on the little covers for his paws. Emilio wore a coat with the collar turned up, no gloves, dilapidated shoes.

They strode past the Duke of Wellington's house and down into Belgravia, Paul ambling behind and sometimes alongside.

162

'Probably, if this was Quality Street.

'It might be "walking out"', he added as an afterthought. 'No, you're right, "stepping out".'

'If it was Quality Street you'd have a much smarter coat.'

'And a cane.'

'To beat me with?'

'I hope not.'

Rowena giggled, put on a Cockney accent. 'Excuse me sir. Where do you live?'

Emilio drew himself up. 'I don't live, madam. I reside. Here, in Belgrave Square.'

'Seedy.'

'Declining. Aren't we all?'

'There's a Waitrose.'

'A substantial place of provision. Big as Uranus.'

'Uranus?'

He looked down her back. 'And that's – pretty large.'

'Can I be your wife?'

'I've no need.'

Rowena looked crestfallen.

'I could be your mistress. I could be your maid.'

'No time. No time.'

'I could be your pander.'

'I loathe furry animals. Particularly with smudged and appealing eyes.'

He stopped, looked at her

'Actually, you have appealing eyes.'

'They look quite ordinary to me. But then, they're my eyes. You have nice eyes.'

He cupped her face in his hands and, very gently, kissed her eyes closed.

'I wonder' he said. 'Can I be your husband?'

∘ ∘ ∘ ∘ ∘

163

2

Daisy is the only survivor of the wreck of her merchant ship Turmoil in the Southern Ocean: she and Tom had just declared their love for each other. Tom is among the dead; he is welcomed to an afterlife by Dr Friday, a fan of Roy Orbison. Gretl works for Lapraman Landesman Architects who are designing the replacement for the bombed-out City of London. Jill and her husband Jack have both been lovers of both Tom and Daisy. Daisy aborted the pregnancy she had with Jack to be free to love Tom. Jill has given birth.

THE HELICOPTER FROM Strident Bucephalus landed at Harbin Taiping.

They carried her the short distance to the Electra, which took off almost immediately for the overland flight to Irkutsk. Reilly and the engineers had fitted the fuselage with long-range tanks and a couple of bunks for the spare crew, covering the journey in rotation. There was a bed for Daisy. She slept till they circled Lake Baikal and landed to refuel. She ate a little.

Another landing at Abakan: the smell of gasoline. Novosibirsk Elitsovka: she wondered if Magda had come home. The long flight to Surgut: she felt cold. Murmansk: she managed breakfast. Out to sea: safely clear of Finland, Sweden, Norway. Newcastle:

final refuelling. A smooth landing at Northolt: a stretcher, an ambulance. Sleep.

o o o

'The range of his ways of talking about love!'

It had been an excellent dance.

As they disengaged, Friday returned to the subject of Roy Orbison.

'The Big O!

'What a corker!

'His adoration of The Other in Blue Bayou – forbidden trans-racial love. His drowning pearl-driver in Leah. His indictment of the American gambling industry in Penny Arcade which – in his odd intonation – he pronounces "pinny".

'What a crackpot!

'What an artiste!

'Does the very pronunciation contain a hidden meaning? His mother's apron-strings, perhaps?'

Friday paused mid-tirade as a skinny youth sidled up to him. He wore a tattoo of golden claws. Friday pumped his hand enthusiastically.

'And now Tom! May I introduce you to – Sugar Popsicle?'

'Hey ho, that's me. Sugar Popsicle. I make all your dreams come true.'

Tom looked away and put his hands in his pockets. Absently he remarked, 'I find that unlikely dear, particularly as you're a man. On this desert island.'

Sugar Popsicle shrugged.

'There's no desert.'

It was a difficult situation. Tom noted that the new arrival had been careful not to deny that they were on an island – this could now be assumed as a working hypothesis. Forever? If so, it was rash to pick quarrels with fellow maroonees. He would appear polite.

'What about features of local interest? Architectural high spots?'

The shadow of his initial indifference evidently remained. Again, Sugar Popsicle shrugged. It was a slighter shrug than the first, and that – Tom recalled – had been a small one, as if even a

165

shrug was an effort.

'None of those.'

'Do you have a lighthouse?'

'No.'

'Water tower?'

'We're surrounded by water. Islands are.'

Again, the confirmation of island status.

'I don't like it.'

'There's a lot I don't like. But I make a fist of it.'

'I'm sure.'

'I wave my wand and magic is certain to follow. I could wank you off for a – five shells. I could suck you for 10.'

Tom realised that he was being challenged. He must make a stand – though not in those particular words.

'No thank you. I'm fully respectful of your life choice to be gay. But I think it's filthy and perverted. Buggery! Ugh!'

Sugar Popsicle looked at him patiently, as a teacher might size up a promising child who had not fully taken the point but who might do so, with encouragement and careful explanation.

'We use shark-fat for lubrication. You won't feel a thing. And when you come, I'll smear you in marmalade.'

'Marmalade?'

Tom's imagination filled with an image of Nell Gwyn's exuberant breasts, bullet nipples and basketful of oranges.

'It's a South Seas tradition.'

'Started by Robert Louis Stevenson', added Friday.

'RL Stevenson? The blameless Scottish farceur who died of consumption?'

'In this very house.'

'You'll be staying in the Robert Louis Stevenson Suite' said Friday. 'Do you know what his last words were? No-one has the slightest idea what he meant. "I wish I'd invented The Rocket."'

Sugar Popsicle turned away. Tom looked down at his taut buttocks and recoiled in dismay.

'There are flecks of shit on your knickers.'

'Tokens of exhausted love.'

Sugar Popsicle seemed ready to forgive Tom his initial indifference. His tone had become philosophical and

166

introspective to the point of weariness, leaving no trace of belligerence.

'Lots of people only come here for the racing. Round the island. 300 kph. No, I'm confused. That's the Isle of Man. I do them all. Out of season, I'm in season.'

He stopped, despondent.

There was a plop from the sea and a cheerful head emerged in a spout of water. Sugar Popsicle beamed.

'Hello, Porpoise.'

'Hello you fat tosser.'

'That's very rude' said Tom.

'Oh! No, not at all' replied the porpoise. 'Here in the South Seas it's considered polite to add mild insults – it's all the wrong way round, like Erehwon. You fat cunt.'

'That's not mild. That's brazen.'

'I was joking.'

'It's a very offensive joke.'

'My, we are touchy. I'm touchy-feely. I was the Alnmouth Dolphin. Strike a chord? Ta-ramm. No? Sic transit gloria. Even though I'm a porpoise. Women played with my penis. Men too. One was arrested. In court, do you know what he said? "Your honour, the penis of a porpoise is a means of communication." Would you like to play with my penis?'

'Certainly not.'

'Would you like to ride on my back, you Guardian-reader?'

Tom bristled.

'No thank you. And I read The Independent.'

'I was being playfully insulting.'

'There's nothing playful about being mistaken for a Guardian reader. They supported the government of the time over the invasion of Iraq. That's a war crime.'

'Heavens, you are un homme sérieux. Why the long face? That's the punch-line of a joke.'

'I know. But I can't remember the joke. I can't remember everything. Some things I remember completely.'

The porpoise looked dreamily out to sea. 'In Baikal, everything makes sense. They make shotguns, and the lake is crystal clear. Hop on my back and I'll take you there.'

'No.'

'You're right.'

The porpoise sighed, as if at the pointlessness of existence. Tom noticed for the first time that there was the trace of an Australian accent. Or New Zealand? One had a whine and he couldn't remember which, or if it was important.

'A lot of the time I swim underwater and you'd drown. It's natural to me, you shrivel-faced prune. I'm a fish. We are incompatible. However much we may seem to have the potential of friendship, our spec-ial difference makes true understanding impossible.'

'Gosh' said Tom, impressed. 'It's like listening to Jean Paul Sartre. Do you smoke a pipe?'

'I'm not an end-of-pier show. In fact, I am. I hang around near the shore hoping to entertain, hoping that my coy antics will attract attention and – who knows – friendship? It's – risible.'

There was a poignancy in the porpoise's words which hurt Tom. It was his own dullness which had depressed the poor animal – mammal? – and he felt sad to see what he took to be tears, although they could be water.

'Don't blame yourself.' He inserted as much comfort as he could into his words, though it was often hard to tell when enough was enough, or if one had floundered – a tactless word to a porpoise, and Tom was glad it was unsaid – into over-familiarity.

'In the end, none of us is loveable. Except to ourselves. And that's – a groovy kind of love.'

'Shane Fentone and The Fentones!' shouted the porpoise. 'Are you a fan? I had all his records once. The 60s! What an era. We shall never see their like.

'Marianne Faithful. She could have played with my penis as a means of communication.

'Yves St Laurent – all the French clothes-makers. Why do they eat snails? Who knows? It's a mystery! The Marie Celeste – that's another.

'Was Marat wanking in his bath? That's a mystery! Or Jim Morrison? And Mama Cass – choked on her vomit stuffing a sandwich into her mouth, or a heart attack? That's a mystery.

'That's far too many mysteries! Talk to me and you only end up confused. Everyone says that. I'm mad, me!

'See you later, alligator. I hope not, actually. Alligators leave indelible marks – usually on corpses.

'Phew! I need a swim. Not surprising – I'm a fish! Cianara, you loafer!'

'Oh. Cheerio.'

The porpoise lingered.

'A lot of underwater life, a lot of fish, are religious. Definitely. Ever since Jonah lived in the Whale. Mind you. Tom Jones – the singer – he lived in Wales. Jones? Wales? Exactly. That's how that one started – if you ask me.'

The trio watched as the porpoise leapt into the air and dived, surfaced, waved, and disappeared.

Sugar Popsicle gazed far away and murmured, 'Pieces of shit – little flecks of poo – are gifts of anal love.'

He looked at Tom out of the corner of his eye.

'Shall I show you my bum-tricks? I purse my lips round cigarettes and spit them out – lit. The old Thai hooker stunt. Anyone can do that.

'But I can hold, stuff, tamp and light a pipe with my rectal doors and gases. My dear Watson – it's alimentary.'

Tom knew that he should be grateful to have two companions; and tolerable ones at that. But it had to be faced that an island with no escape was a cage. 'The Prisoner had a number.'

'Six.'

'Not that it helped him. He couldn't escape. I'm trapped.'

'There's a steam packet every week' said Sugar Popsicle. 'It's there now. Look! If you run, you'll catch it.'

'Where?'

Eagerly, Tom looked around. His heart raced.

Nothing.

'Poof! It's gone.'

'Oh.'

'I'm such a tease!' said Sugar Popsicle. 'Voilà!'

Suddenly, the boat was alongside.

'Do go.'

Tom ran aboard.

'I'll come again' he called back.

With a blast on the whistle, the packet departed, gaining speed as the island raced away.

Sugar Popsicle's voice came to him over the waves.

'There are fat women in Baikal.'

∘ ∘ ∘

'Apparently you have pleurisy.'

Mrs Ballantyne's inflection suggested that Daisy was getting off lightly.

'Would you have preferred pneumonia?'

Laughing cost a surge of pain from her lungs and a violent shuddering though her body.

'I've brought you these, dear.'

Her mother tipped up a carrier bag and a couple of white woolly socks fell onto the bed. She regarded them for a moment with quiet approval, lifted a corner of the sheet and glanced at Daisy's legs. She leaned forward to inspect them in detail, each in turn.

'Yes, the skin has taken a battering. It was always so smooth when you were little. Your sister was the same. My own skin has never given me particular trouble. But also I have never been – immersed. Not, at least, for a period of time.'

'I can't look at them.'

'The exposure to – and ingestion of – large amounts of salt water is seldom beneficial. There are boils. They will go away. On the whole I would prefer you with boils rather than, say, dead. I imagine your sister feels the same.'

'I wouldn't bank on it.'

Mrs Ballantyne smiled. She lifted Daisy's arm – cautiously, not to disturb the drip – and placed one of the socks under her hand. She did the same with the other.

I have two hands, two socks, two feet. There are other important things, but I will remember these first.

'Alpaca. Very soft, you can see that. Comfortable animals, sociable by nature. I've often thought of having one or two in the garden.'

'Dulcie wouldn't like it.'

Her mother thought about this for a moment.

170

'Ah. Now Dulcie. Although she's never been able to stand the name. Personally, I sometimes wonder if Rowena would have been better as Dulcie. The names, that is, not the creatures. Mind you. On the other hand, it's uncertain whether Dulcie would have tolerated Rowena. Poor girl, she could be most difficult at times. But on the whole, marvellous.'

'You're speaking of her in the past.'

'My darling. There's a time for all of us. Not you, not at all. Heavens.' She looked for a safe part of Daisy to touch, and not being certain, stroked one of the socks. 'Touch wood. Myself, perhaps at some point. Now, certainly not. The fact is. Dulcie decided it was the right time. Quietly, in her own way. So she's gone up North.' She raised a finger upwards.

Daisy burst out laughing. An avalanche of pain. A great shock of pleasure. A cascade of tears. There'd been no time to cry, and finally every sorrow and lost opportunity, every incident of her own stupidity, could be released.

Part of her – still at work – measured the evacuation of sea water against the income of clinical saline, and the consequent volume of tears at her disposal. Everyone is dead, she thought. Even the beasts. And it's hilarious.

'Paul?'

'Paul is alive and independent. Rowena has plans for a bow tie for the wedding. It will not be tolerated. That is an entirely safe prediction. There is also the question of the chief bridesmaid.'

Her mother took her hand gently in hers and kissed it.

'The general opinion seems to be that she will survive.'

Mrs Ballantyne sat for a while in silence. She closed her eyes. It was a look Daisy knew well. It meant she was preparing to say something that her relevant daughter would hate.

'Now dear, prepare yourself for a surprise. I know it won't be pleasant. But it is something I feel must be done.'

It came out of the sun, so far from reality that it had never – never? – entered Daisy's mind.

'I want you to go and see your mother.'

Daisy, wordless, simply looked at her.

'I have found out where your mother is. She is in a home. It is a place for alcoholics and so on, people who haven't quite been able to deal with life, and we must have a good deal of sympathy for that, though not in a condescending way.'

'No.'

'Try not to be difficult, dear. It is extremely important I believe, now that everything.'

'Not. On. Your. Fucking. Life.'

'The proprietor is a Mrs Riskill. I haven't spoken to her myself. Now that everything has gone so horribly.'

'I am not going.'

'Please let me finish. Look. Awful things have come to you. Things I couldn't begin to imagine, and you know how dearly I love you. I am sorry for your life. There have been many burdens. And now this terrible, terrible reality. We must complete the circle. It is I believe essential that you confront – only once, I promise you – the way in which, through whom, you started your life. And for this wretched woman, it would be an act of charity.'

o o o

Another day Jack visited her.

She listened carefully to what he had to say.

o o o

A few days after leaving hospital, Daisy took the earliest train from London – the sooner to get it over with, and return the same day.

Mrs Riskill was a thin woman with a pinched face and mean expression. Daisy thought that life had either passed her by or was in sight of doing so. Her skin had the raw rosy look of a weather-beaten vegetarian, and a sign outside noted membership of the National Allotment Society.

Rows of broad beans and broccoli stood in raised beds. There were plum trees and apple trees, marrows, carrots, potatoes and a septic tank.

Mrs Riskill said that the last witches to be hanged had been trapped in the villages of the long hill which ended abruptly in an escarpment ('The Devil's Leap') and formed the backdrop to the care home.

The home was a Jacobean farmhouse with a patched slate roof

172

and dry-stone walls. A well provided spring water. Residents who were fit enough did some work in the fields. The rest stayed inside. In total there were twenty or thirty, depending on death and replacement.

There was no question of an identification. How could she pick out someone she'd last seen when she was two? Mrs Riskill looked ready to talk. Daisy politely raised her hand.

'I'm not here because I want to be. My mother – Mrs Ballantyne – has asked me to come. I like to do what she says. I don't want to know who the woman is.'

This seemed not to surprise Mrs Riskill, who merely nodded.

'No-one is aware of who you are. You will simply be a visitor.'

'She is not, you see, in any sense my mother. I'm lucky enough to have a real mother. This is just something I came out of.'

Again, Mrs Riskill nodded.

As Daisy followed her around the home, she felt nothing: neither pity nor interest, and certainly no excitement.

Left on her own, Daisy looked for women in their fifties and sixties, but it was difficult to distinguish age. The faces she saw belonged to people who had been destroyed rather than the mildly dipsomaniac. A woman she talked with seemed lucid, but confined to her own world. So am I, Daisy thought, but it's a different one. Another was incoherent. It was time to leave.

Mrs Riskill sat on a plain wooden chair at a pine table in the office. A file lay open. As Daisy knocked at the open door, she wondered if she was reading it or gazing in front of her.

'Thank you. I'll go now.'

Mrs Riskill looked up.

'Did you have any luck?'

Daisy shook her head.

'But I would like to make a donation.'

She took some bank notes from her bag and passed them over, was thanked and given a receipt.

As she left, Mrs Riskill was still sitting at the desk, looking at the money.

o o o

Lake Baikal was precisely as Tom had imagined it, but not as he

173

had read it to be. Reduced to a swamp, the news had said, with 160 tons of liquid waste discharging every year into Chivyrkui Bay.

But standing beside it, he saw it to be pure and magnificent, the bluest of cerulean blue. Deserted too, except for the silver flash of a toy plane in the sky which stirred a memory he couldn't place.

Then it was gone, and a venerable looking man appeared by his side – silent and possibly a prophet. Tom felt it correct to greet him.

'I admire the deep lake and its shimmering colours, and the statue of the Madonna beneath the surface, arms outstretched.'

The old man shook his hand warmly.

'Fasil Iskander. Once a novelist. Well. A storyteller.'

Tom could hardly contain his glee. The author of Forbidden Fruit, Rabbits and Boa Constrictors, and The Old House Under the Cypress Tree – to say nothing of The Thirteenth Labour of Hercules and Sandro von Tschegem which Tom had read in German!

'A great novelist, sir. It is a privilege.'

'Let's just talk.'

Iskander took his hand in his own and led him to the edge of the lake.

'Once I travelled all the way to Moscow and bought my wife some boots with all my wages. They were far too small, but she laughed and kept them forever. I love my wife.'

'Relationships are certainly good for some people.'

'You are some people, Tom?'

It no longer surprised Tom that everyone knew his name.

'I was one of some people. I was nearly one of two. Though two, they say, become one. I am afraid of unity.'

Iskander peered at him.

'You're afraid of fear, perhaps?'

There was a woman. Tom didn't know if she had come from the land or the water, and it wasn't important.

'The lady. Who is she?'

'Tom, you're a small man. She's a large woman.'

'There are fat women in Baikal.'

But she wasn't fat.

'Large in brain, character – clout – is that a word still? Madame La Commissar.'

There was something that must be said, but Tom hesitated. Equally, here were some things which must never be said. It was a mantra that he had been brought up on. He could picture his mother wagging her finger at him to underline the words – although his memory may have been making that up. Or were there? In her blue apron with sketches of summer flowers. He took the plunge.

'My fantasy is. Will I embarrass you?'

Iskander slapped him on the shoulder in a comradely way, taking the words out of his mouth with the ease of a mind-reader. 'Two brawny lasses – Aeroflot hostesses – accustomed to running a burning samovar along the aisle of a propeller-aircraft – and missing communism – locked in a breast-to-breast kiss, sitting on your face?'

'The brazen nonchalance of blubber' said Tom. 'White mounds of suet and wet buttocks.'

Iskander bowed as the woman approached.

'Madame La Commissar.'

∘ ∘ ∘

At half-past-five in the morning, Gretl looked at the day through her bedroom curtains and determined to embrace it.

It could be a day that would have to be ridden until it was thoroughly broken in. They expected her to be German, but it was difficult to be German in that way first thing at dawn.

Gretl tried touching her toes and gave up, got into the shower and scrubbed her hair with her hands, enjoying the soap and heat.

Ingo lay asleep and she thought that she had stopped loving him. His electric shaver sat neatly on the glass shelf. She realised that a man didn't use an electric shaver. A man shaved wet.

Gretl thought of the new sadness in Helen's face. She would help, starting this morning, if only by consolation.

In the mirror, her freckles were still there. How her mother and father loved her freckles! Unsere kleine Gretl. She missed them. Our home in Mendelssohnstraße. She wanted to be dashing with her friends for the tram across the Main to great plates of Ribchen at Wagner's. She wanted to love, to be loved.

At eight in the morning Daisy couldn't sleep any longer and got up. She rinsed her face, pulled her hair back in a tight knot, and got on a train to Brockley. She had spent a week in bed, unbothered to read or wash, eating little. Depression finally got her out of the house.

The tracks between Hoxton and Shoreditch ran out of electricity and the train stopped. There was no-one to speculate about: the carriage was empty. Outside, a sea of wet roofs. She passed the time counting houses, and the houses that were missing.

∘ ∘ ∘

The other day, as Daisy returned from Mrs Riskill on the train, there had been three people whose relationship had puzzled her.

Two women sat on one side of a window table. The one by the window was in her forties; the other called her Francesca and was evidently Gretl. Gretl had a lively face, freckled, straw-coloured hair, sharp eyes. She looked in her mid-twenties. They both wore black. Gretl ignored the man who sat opposite Francesca.

A family returning from a funeral? The daughter quarrelling with her father, and siding with her mother? Gretl didn't look like them, although of course she could be adopted. Either way, the ages didn't feel right; and there was no sense of shun. Gretl got up, stretched, and set off down the corridor.

Crossing points into Crewe, the train slowed to a crawl. The man looked intently out of the window. Daisy saw a girl at the end of a platform. She was perhaps six years old and wore a mackintosh. She stood by herself, a child with a leather suitcase. The man got up and, leaning forward, kissed the woman.

'Goodbye' he said. 'Goodbye dear Casine.'

She held on to him. The train jerked to a stop.

'Dear Mr Beldane.'

As he stepped onto the platform, Gretl returned with a bag from the restaurant and set out two cartons of coffee. She offered a paper plate and a pastry.

'I wasn't sure if you'd want one of these, but I got two anyhow. Apfelstrudel. At home, we eat them all the time. Even though, strictly speaking, they are Austrian.'

She smiled.

'They speak our language. We eat their cake.'

○ ○ ○

Daisy looked across the platforms for the little girl, but she was no longer there.

○ ○ ○

The Brockley train lurched forward.

Daisy didn't want to visit Jill – not yet. She wanted to be a good friend, so that when they met, she could give her best. But in the circumstances, it could no longer be delayed.

'Are you managing to get any sleep?'

Trite and safe, it covered her shock. Daisy had expected a natural loss of weight from birth, but the fat woman was now emaciated. Bones showed on her face. Jill was propped up in bed on pillows, seemingly oblivious that her dressing gown was open, and that her breasts hung empty, a heavy roll of skin loose beneath them.

She stared at Daisy, aware of who she was.

'Haven't we been clever? You needn't have come.'

Daisy smiled, said nothing.

Jill's voice was on the edge of hysteria.

'My ickcle bickle baby.

'Who'd have thought it was so easy?

'All it took was Jack and me! And we did it. So many times. Calendars. Thermometers. So clever!

'And she's so lovely.

'I love my husband. I do love my husband. He's extra-specially loveable. And I'm loveable. I'm extra-specially loveable.

'And jolly clever.'

Daisy judged that it was safe to speak.

'You're both jolly clever.'

Jill's face clouded.

'Are you criticising?'

'I'm being supportive.'

'Because if you're criticising me', she was raging now, 'it's very easy for someone who can get pregnant and just – throw their fucking child away – murder their fucking baby – to criticise.'

'You're absolutely right. I.'

'What right do you – of all people – have to look down on me? A mother. I am a real mother.'

'Yes. You look. Actually fabulous.'

Jill stared at her, lowered her voice.

'I look like a rag doll. I look like a crying, wetting, bleeding doll. I look like a used rag that's been thrown on the floor to wipe vomit. I look like the scum I am.'

'It is normal to be depressed after birth.'

'This isn't a normal birth. It isn't natural! It isn't right. Is it? Nothing will ever be right.'

Daisy cleared her throat. 'Shall we fetch baby?' She said it as naturally as she could, keeping her voice as calm as she could without sounding forced. But she guessed that there was nothing she could do to stop Jill's rising temper.

'I don't want baby. I never want to see baby again.'

'Post-natal depression is – chemical. It's not you darling.'

'Don't "darling" me, you cunt. I. Am. Not. Post. Natally. Depressed.'

Magda came in, pulled Jill's dressing gown together and adjusted her pillows. 'You all right?'

'Get out. You fucking Polish whore.'

Magda grinned. She put her arms round Daisy, their bodies warm together, and kissed her.

'The Madonna offers comfort in the vale of tears', she whispered.

Daisy rested her head on Magda's shoulder. 'I look shit in a veil', she murmured. 'Bless you.'

'Come on darling.' Magda helped Jill out of bed. 'Let's get you sitting down.'

'I'm not an invalid.'

Jill's tone had softened, and it felt right to leave. Saying goodbye could provoke another change of mood, so while she was distracted, Daisy slipped out of the room. She waited by the front door and Magda joined her.

'You're very sweet.' They held each other. 'I don't know what to say.'

'It's love you need. And time. And anger. When the anger

begins to come, the heart is mending.'

'I've nothing to be angry about. Sadness.'

Jill's voice shouted from upstairs.

'You didn't have to come. I didn't ask you to come. Now get out. Don't ever come here again.'

○ ○ ○

Tom bowed.

'Madame La Commissar.'

She regarded him for a while. Iskander had gone.

'Chief executive. The rest are lies. I have a hankering for the good days. But I don't want them back. Nostalgia only works in the present.'

'But commissar – chief executive – of what?' asked Tom.

'I am the managing director of the Baikal Shotgun Factory.'

'A challenge?'

She considered this for a moment or two, turning the idea over in her mind and coming to a conclusion.

'I have everything to prove.'

'I admired Marx.' Tom knew that he sounded like the class creep, but he longed to impress her. His reading of the Communist Manifesto was a long time in the past, and he hadn't got very far with Capital. If there were searching questions – actually, if there were questions – he was doomed.

'Teenagers admire' said the commissar. 'And stupid, head-in-the-clouds teenagers. There is no-one admirable. Basic communist theory: all are equal before the state. There can be no cult of the individual.'

This was getting a lot deeper than Tom had intended. Cool air came to them across the water, ruffling the woman's hair and, for a moment, making her seem girlish.

Encouraged, Tom said 'I would be grateful if you could accompany me on a boat-trip. I believe the sights of Lake Baikal are remarkable.'

The commissar gazed at him, and for a moment he thought she might accept. Instead, she replied in a voice barely above silence, 'Have you any idea how many discrete stages are involved in the manufacture of a single-barrelled Baikal shotgun? A hundred and eighty-five.'

179

'Incredible.'

She raised an eyebrow, half a smile on her lips.

'Are you taking a rise out of me?'

There was a music to her voice, which played with, rather than against, her authority, as if the two weaved together in harmony.

'Where did you learn English?'

'My father was a wood-carver, hewing trees and shaping them to concentric Russian dolls. Hard, but manlier than piano-tuning.

'And when I remember my father, I try to see the silly dolls cupping inside each other as symbols, slap myself, and say – they are just silly dolls. There is a man who will save everything. Magruder of the Yard.'

'Has he never lost a case?'

'Small items, portmanteaus. Irritating wheel-along overnight bags. But never a trunk. Your call.'

'There are no fat women of Baikal.'

It slipped out, and he glanced to make sure he had not caused displeasure. She was scrutinising him, as might an interrogator.

Tom shuddered.

'Corpses in the water bloat through decomposition. The floating body rots, internal gases inflate it. I dream that from a boat I can see her torch, lamp-lighting twenty windows of Turmoil's bridge like Flora McDonald searching for Bonnie Prince Charlie. He was once the coming man. Died incognito on a South Sea island wheezing "Auld Reekie". And no-one understood that it meant something written on his heart.'

The commissar's voice had a certain sensuality, perhaps responding to something in his own.

'There are 185 separate processes. The parts of a modern gun can all be named. Our gun-stocks are carved from the same wood as that traditionally used in the creation of Russian dolls. Polished in the same way. Varnished with a shellac veneer. Baked. Only the product differs.'

She added, quietly, 'Your Daisy is alive. You are dead.'

'In my imagination, we row away and I can see the beam of her torch. To me she's Florence the nightingale searching for the lost spirits of the Crimea, coughing in the sulphur of Berkeley Square. It's a pea-souper. When the fog clears, there is no ship. The lights under the surface stay on, for a surprisingly long time.'

'Tom. Tom. You are dead. Your Daisy is alive.'

'I'd rather leave now. Or communicate.'

'The line is dead. All the numbers are zeroes.'

'I failed to engage.'

'There are 185 separate steps in the process.'

It was too early, if it might ever happen, to think of a change. But something stirred inside Tom.

'No. I will speak. In my self-indulgence I, all of my own choice, turned to myself, my inversion.'

The commissar nodded, as if she understood. Equally, she could be humouring him, but emboldened, he continued.

'Breaking open each outer casing of my self, I found other fascinating facades inside. I didn't notice that each was littler, more trivial, and led inward.

'I should have stood and pulled my shoulders back, so that no-one could be ashamed of me. I should have risked and stood for her, for life. I should have fought. Risking all to love – with honour, but that's not the point.

'I could have chosen love.'

Finally!

And to accompany it, the last magnificent movement of Hans Bach's Piano Concerto No. 1 in D minor, Opus 15, pianist Arthur Rubinstein, conductor Bernard Haitink.

An orchestra in the lake? To look would be a blasphemy. Better to accept, and listen. Benjamin Britten conducted a choir of boys to a translation by Imogen Holst (Her father did The Planets! At the school where he taught, the girls called him Gussie!) and Peter Pears of Amadeus Mozart's The Passion of Saint John.

The commissar's voice, the spoken solo.

'There are 185 discrete processes in the manufacture of a Baikal 12-bore single-barrel shotgun.

'The works collective would recite a listing of the stages in iambic pentameters, and productivity surged.

'As a Westerner, most likely you will laugh at our socialist-inspired manufacturing methods. But we – I – warm to poetry, art, visual, aural, oral culture – and film. Andrei Tarkovsky's Solaris. Yet Tarkovsky's greatest film was never famous in the

181

West. Zerkalo. Mirror.

'A child is born – symbolising the birth of Communism.

'The grass stirs to the orchestral preamble of Johann Sebastian Bach's Passion of St John.

'The baby emerges – our beloved Russia, born to save the world.

'The choir erupts with its triumphant greeting. "Herr! Unser Herrscher!" As Christ would be greeted. "Sire, Sire, Sire. Lord and Master. Unto thee be praise and glory. For ever and ever."

'Sacrilege? I once believed in Russia.'

Tom sniggered. The spell was broken.

'You're laughing.'

He felt a heel, but couldn't resist turning the knife. 'It's such a failed ideology.'

'People fell in love', said the commissar. 'We ate. Even I was distracted by the false allure of diadems – pretty things. And the prettiest thing is love.'

'I found it easy to resist.'

'That it should take a manufacturer of shotguns – a prosaic occupation, surely? – to point out your shocking lack of humanity – is queer.'

'I skated the edge.'

The orchestra had gone quiet at Tom's faux pas, apart from the replacement of strings and the discordant noises of re-tuning. Maestro Haitink was suffering the agonies familiar to anyone who has tried to accompany, spontaneously, an unknown silent film, at the head of a 50-strong orchestra.

But now, that sixth sense which can sometimes come to the aid of the artist in despair, did.

With a nod to Arthur on the grand, and a joyful smile of inspiration and relief, Haitink raised his baton.

Decisively, he brought it down to the opening chords of Lara's Theme from Doctor Zhivago – "Somewhere my love".

The commissar closed her eyes, lost in the music.

'I've skated.

'Arms round beaux on either side,

'In a ra-ra skirt, pink boots, and a fur hat made from a bear we'd shot ourselves and eaten – using a Baikal 12-bore double-barrel over-and-under shotgun, easily superior to a Purdey.

'I divided my heart between each man.

'Boy, because a man – and woman – in love becomes innocent.

'Sometimes my heart would belong to boy A: sometimes to boy Zee. There could be a litany of remembered, or fantasised, loves between.

'It was as if a slider were drawn across my stomach, allocating the pump inside to one, and – a second later – the other; or part and part.

'And all the while – we skated.

'Not expertly skated. We were mediocre skaters, expert shotgun-makers, whole-hearted lovers.

'But skated while loving, loving while skating.

'Through the centre where the ice is thin, risky, to the edge.

'Kissing, too.'

Tom had become progressively more miserable.

'I was a bank clerk. I embraced the Established Church. I've wibbled. And wibbled restlessly.'

The commissar grimaced. 'We in the former USSR have allowed you to sneer at us, in what you consider our inferiority. But now, Tom, pull your shoulders back. You are dead. Your Daisy lives.'

'What can I do?'

'Become a man. Allow your emotions to release.'

'If it was easy, every bank clerk in the world would be doing it.'

'Every bank clerk in the world is doing it – except one. Bank Automated Clearing System – the words carry a pulse. You have none. You are dead.'

'If I knew where to feel, I'd feel a pulse. Surely?'

'You can't feel your own pulse' she snapped. 'That would be a mad world.

'Here in the former Union of Soviet Socialist Republics we deal harshly with cowardice.'

'I am a moral and emotional coward.'

He felt like a whipped dog ready for beating.

But the commissar's voice was kind.

'The admission marks a beginning. And I have an admission –

we are treating you too unpleasantly. It is only with warmth that you will expand.

'Come. Embrace me.'

She enveloped Tom in her arms.

'I've failed.'

'There there.' She patted his head.

'My mother was a fairly large woman.'

'You are feeling a connection to your mother because mothers and communist regimes have in common the spectre of ruthless, unreasoning, uncompromising authority. A mother is a programming, destructive, emasculating, de-feminising monster, motivated in selfishness, self-adoration and self-centring manipulation.'

The bosom of the commissar was an enchanting place to be, and Tom would have stayed there. But someone had arrived and he was let go.

'Madame La Commissar.'

'Mr Magruder.'

A charming man. Everyone was delightful here. A gentle man, with authority, knowledge and wisdom. Elderly?

'Tom.'

Mr Magruder greeted him as one might an old friend. There was a projection of esteem in his manner – not overdone – as if it had been too long since they last met, and how splendid it was to meet again. Tom was sure that they had not. There was nothing familiar about Magruder's face or voice, and yet Tom felt open, that he could confide and reveal to Magruder secrets hidden deep within. A caution, too, that times ahead – though interesting – may prove demanding.

With the same delightful manner, Mr Magruder turned to the commissar.

'Our – obsession – with numbers, facts. Are we making a little progress?'

'There's an ingrained tendency' she said, diffidently. 'When it's your lifetime, Mr Magruder. Very easy for you to.'

'My dear Madame, there is no suggestion – I promise you – I am most sincerely in agreement – in understanding – of course –

and there is no urgency – in your own way.'

'Stalin was the father of the nation. To lose his wisdom. To see it as indoctrination. My whole life, I have served the state, lived the state. The state lives in me. It is to pluck out my heart.'

Mr Magruder put his arm round her. 'We shall transcend.'

'Together.'

She had tears on her cheeks. Mr Magruder took a clean white handkerchief from his pocket and wiped them away.

'Together' he replied. 'In your good time.'

'Tom.'

Whoever Magruder was, secrets could no longer be kept. Tom found himself speaking.

'I don't know how. Everybody knows.'

'That you love her.'

'That I love her?'

'Well, don't you?'

'I've avoided that – word – my whole life.'

Mr Magruder's voice and manner changed.

'See the little cutie hat-check-chick?'

He was a tout, beckoning from an alley, luring Tom to special delights.

'You can't. I beg your pardon. About a – grown woman – as. A cutie.'

'Want some porking action? Come over her face? Eh? Eh?'

'I really find this – tone – this attitude – appalling. It really is – distasteful.'

Tom tried to walk away.

Magruder sidled beside him.

'Want a taste of something tasteful?'

○ ○ ○ ○ ○

3

Daisy's lover Tom and the crew drown in the sinking of her merchant ship Turmoil. Her ex-lover Jill gives birth. Daisy aborts the pregnancy she had with Jill's husband Jack to be free to love Tom. Gretl works for Lapraman Landesman – from which Diana Lapraman has departed – an architectural practice designing the replacement for the bombed-out City of London. Rachel Fonseca owns a radical bookshop in central London. Mrs Ballantyne is Daisy's adoptive mother and Rachel's aunt.

THE DEPARTMENT OF Transport Marine Accident Investigation Branch Inquiry into the loss of Turmoil took place in Commercial Court No 1, Chancery Lane.

In the same court as a child, Daisy had listened as adults debated the death of her father. Today she was the adult. Under examination and cross-examination, she told the story of Turmoil's last voyage from its beginning to what she knew of its end.

Sometimes she looked at Rachel in the public gallery.

At the conclusion of the evidence, in accordance with the regulations of the Defence of the Realm Act (Re-enacted), counsel for the government submitted questions to the court which boiled down to:

Concerning Turmoil in London before departure (with similar questions for Liverpool and Gibraltar): Hull and equipment good and seaworthy? Any defects, if so, repaired and inspected? Holds correctly prepared before cargo loaded? Description and amount of cargo? Weights correctly balanced across the holds? Properly secured against shifting? Amount and type of fuels?

Concerning the voyage: What was the vessel's route? If hazardous, what was the reason for taking it? Did the route contribute to the loss of Turmoil? Was she equipped with the boats and lifesaving equipment required by the Act? What was the cause of the loss? How many lives lost and when?

The court reserved judgment to a later date.

○ ○ ○

Mrs Ballantyne made her own way to the station. She refused Reilly's insistent offer to drive her to London, pointing out that the railway line had been repaired and she was perfectly capable of sitting on a train.

Everything was much slower, of course, and it was two hours before she arrived at Fenchurch Street.

It was dispiriting to look around. One of her favourite churches, St Olave's in Hart Street, had gone. Hart Street too, though it had always been small. It was a matter of picking one's way among rubble without the guidance of familiar landmarks.

Tower Bridge was there.

The Tower of London remained, in part. At least The Tower was being preserved and taken down stone by stone – each numbered for its eventual reconstruction.

So they said. Mrs Ballantyne increasingly doubted what anyone said. Perhaps it was old age. She shook her head. She walked to the underground station at Tower Hill.

At Leicester Square, she took the Cranbourn Street exit and sized up the stairs. A young man – handsome – hesitated – 'May I?' – offered his arm – was accepted. At the top, she smiled.

'Thank you. Getting old.'

'At twenty-one? Hardly.' Definitely a flirtatious smile. A rascal.

She squeezed his hand and strode off briskly.

An excellent start to the day.

○ ○ ○

On the pavement in front of Bound To Be Red, there were open boxes of books for sale – good, solid and well-made timber boxes with sensible lids for the rain. Rachel was bending over them, rearranging and replenishing stock from a trolley.

Mrs Ballantyne noticed that she was – for Rachel – very smartly dressed.

'Rachel.'

A turn, surprise, a broad smile, a warm embrace. 'Mum.' A holding at arm's length, a regarding. 'Is everything all right?'

They went to a shop and ate cake, drank coffee.

'I want to know everything' said Mrs Ballantyne.

'Daisy's afraid she'll be ruined. Financially, but mainly it's her reputation.'

'Bastards.'

'Not really. Nobody was brutal. Even the cross-examination was – courteous, I suppose. It may be naive, but I think they simply want to find out what happened. I don't get the impression anyone wants to crucify her. They can see what she's been through.'

'She'll lose everything.'

'If the insurance doesn't pay, sure, she'll lose a lot of money. But she has four other ships. She's not going to be penniless.'

'If she gets the blame for thirty people dying, it will kill her.'

'She doesn't come into it. She's not the master.'

'She's the one left alive.'

There was something else.

Mrs Ballantyne plunged in.

'I am worried about my other daughter, too.'

'Rowena? She's as happy as a pig in clover. Looks like one, come to think of it.'

'Rowena is a fine girl.'

'It does begin with f. She's a fat girl.'

Mrs Ballantyne patted her hand.

'This one.'

Rachel signalled the waiter, ordered coffee. Like an experienced chess player, Mrs Ballantyne was aware of Rachel's favourite moves. She recognised this one as delay covering the construction of a sturdy defence.

'Adam Brook.'

○ ○ ○

Gretl Lorelei waited to see O'Brien.

Lapraman Landesman Architects had only two private offices, which interconnected. She wondered if Helen would knock them together now. Perhaps she'd do away with them and join the other designers in the big and informal open office in which they all worked.

The headquarters building of the Square Mile City Development Corporation was altogether different – full of impressive people, and in such delightful clothes. Gretl could sit for hours in reception looking at the way that each woman, each man, wore and had chosen their suits, skirts, styles and fabrics.

There was no visible hierarchy of rank in the way they dressed. These gorgeous people seemed to exist without care; their smooth faces free of stress, their pretty bodies relaxed.

Power? Not from the building, she was certain. True, it was a fine building – solid with the barest minimum of glass, and topped with a massive burster slab of prime-quality concrete. But it was the human beings who gave it authority and – or was her imagination taking flight? – life.

'You've come to see O'Brien?'

She snapped to reality. It was just a building. They were simply people.

Arriving at his office she stood, politely, at the threshold.

'Dr O'Brien?'

'Gretl. Come.'

He leapt to his feet and shook her hand sincerely, led her back out of the door and set off vigorously down the corridor.

'You'll like this. It's fun.'

He was lovely. Everyone was lovely. It was a lovely day.

The arboretum took up two floors and one side of the building.

'Dr O'Brien.'

'Jo-Jo. For God's sake, Jo-Jo.'

He had the widest possible smile, fine and even white teeth, a healthy face without make-up, natural skin, prematurely grey hair closely cropped, kind eyes. He stopped and took her by the shoulders.

'All this O'Brien. It's a joke, Gretl. It's a joke, a happy coincidence. It makes people laugh, and laughter is fun. This is all fun. Look. Broccoli. Very successful broccoli.'

It was a good, green, broccoli with thick flower-heads and pliable stalks.

'Bloody good brassica oleracea – good as Chinese, and the Chinese know their broccoli – 9 million tonnes of the stuff. Absolutely. That's what they do. 43 percent of the world's production. OK Gretl, we're not doing 9 million tonnes, but we're growing it. One million people. Something like that, figures pending. We're housing, entertaining, stimulating, giving hope and the potential of endeavour to one million happy souls. And we're feeding them.'

'On broccoli?'

He laughed, she laughed.

It was hot as a greenhouse, the air thick with humidity. Gretl sweated, and the sweat stayed on her skin. She was surprised that it wasn't unpleasant, noticed that he was walking more slowly, taking the pace of the heat. The arboretum was divided along its length by high glass walls, each enclosing a different section of climate. Passing from the tropical rainforest into the next area, the humidity decreased; there was a light breeze. Another compartment was bone dry; hot as the desert. Finally, a mild climate with a brisk wind which lifted the sweat from her body and left her comfortable and relaxed. In each of the areas there was vegetation: jungle, esparto, fruits, sand, vegetables, yucca trees, cactus, yews and planes, tomatoes, barley, wheat, oranges. She tasted one.

'Bitter!'

'Seville! Must be bitter. We must have marmalade. Can't have a world without marmalade! Try this one.' Sweet.

They went back to his office – a cramped and insignificant room off a corridor: not a corner office, not a power office; a harmless place. It said, without him saying, I am the same as everyone else. It was just big enough to contain a cheap table for a desk, another with four chairs around it, a couple of armchairs either lovingly-worn or new from a secondhand shop, a shelf with a kettle and a clean sink.

'Instant?'

He made them coffee in mugs with teddy-bears on the side, indicated an armchair, and sat in the other.

'Now.'

He looked at her politely.

'I'm worried about Helen.'

O'Brien was at ease. She thought that perhaps he always was, and that was the trick. Let other people make the way.

But he didn't peer at her. She had no feeling of interrogation or scrutiny. He didn't leave her with a silence to complete, simply waited a pleasant length of time to see if she would continue, and when she didn't, spoke, his voice courteous and encouraging.

'That is very kind.' He paused. 'In what particular way are you worried, Gretl, would you say?'

'I think she's cracking up.'

'Ah.'

He had no nervous habits. He didn't look at his fingernails, flex his hands, fidget, put his hands in his pockets, cross his legs. Equally he wasn't annoyingly calm – like, for example, she thought, patience on a monument staring at grief, or anywhere else. Nothing like a guru: she couldn't imagine him in the lotus position and nearly laughed, but caught it in time, though she knew he wouldn't mind a good laugh, a big belly-laugh even. It was rumoured that he meditated, but if it was true – she hoped it wasn't – Buddha was absent today.

Nevertheless, he was able to be silent and relaxed without it being noticeable.

'I once saw the dead body of a friend.'

There was the right amount of emotion in his voice – sufficient to show he was human, not too much – a delicate balance, she thought, like judging salt into an omelette.

'It must have been bloody awful for her.' Bloody. Swearing, or apt? She kept quiet, wanted him to continue.

'My – friend. He had committed suicide too. He hadn't, thank God, no, he hadn't fallen, thrown himself, that is, off – what was it – twenty-five, thirty? – storeys.'

191

'Twenty-five.'

'Twenty-five, thank you. Oh God. She must have looked terrible. Poor girl. Poor child.'

'She was over forty.'

She bit her tongue. It was a stupid thing to say. He looked on the point of making a sharp reply, and part of her was glad to see the possibility of spontaneous, uncontrolled emotion in his face. Instead, he nodded.

'I imagine it is very difficult for Helen. I will have a word.'

'I'd rather you didn't tell her I've spoken to you.'

'Of course.'

'I wouldn't want her to think I talked about her behind her back.'

'I'm sure you never would.'

Was there a double edge to his voice?

'Tell me one thing. At the departure. How was she then?'

'We drove up to Leeming. Very impressive, by the way. Who arranged that?'

O'Brien bowed his head.

'Helen driving, Casine, me. The body was already there.'

Again, O'Brien nodded.

'There was a little – service? An air force vicar. They put her on the plane. It took off. Loud.' She put her hands to her ears. 'A very expensive coffin, amazing flowers. Not open – obviously – no glass top, nothing vulgar, no flashy brass. Simple and elegant.' She glanced at O'Brien. 'How many hours to Mongolia?'

'Ten to Chinggis Khaan International and then a local flight to Ulaangom. She was taken to her village by road, and buried. Everything was done correctly.'

'I think Helen wanted to cry. You can't easily tell with Helen. She doesn't clam up, she becomes more polite than ever, till you want to slap her around the face and say "Get it out. Get it out!" But you don't. You say the same polite things back and let her drive back to London by herself, which is what she obviously wanted to do. Does that answer your question? Casine and I went back by train, which took hours. All the trains were diverted via Crewe.'

'Thank you' he said. 'Now. What can I do for you?'

Gretl took out her notebook and a sharp pencil. Flicking the cover back she sat up straight and looked directly at O'Brien.

'I would like to start all over from the beginning and generate a fresh approach. In your own natural words – homespun, if you like – I want you to tell me the story.'

O'Brien looked away, collecting his thoughts. He was silent for enough minutes for Gretl to wonder if he would speak at all, or was preoccupied by what she had said. Suddenly, he got up, put his hands in his pockets and, resting against the wall, spoke rapidly.

'Square Mile City is a pyramid a mile high, a mile long and a mile broad occupying the present footprint of the City of London, located at 51.5 degrees north and as near as makes no difference on the Greenwich Meridian, centre of the world. Am I going too fast?'

He glanced at her pad. 'Gretl, is that shorthand?'

'It serves the purpose.'

'That which the enemy's destruction has left us and which is worthy has been, is in the process of being, or shall be, dismantled and in whole or representative part be preserved within the galleries of Square Mile City.' He paused. 'It's only St Paul's, really, and The Tower of course, Trinity House. Pity about the Guildhall, but it was mainly tat. And the odd church.

'We shall house permanently – the aforementioned – one million people. At any moment it will contain some two million at work, in transit, on holiday, shopping, or simply marvelling. Sufficient food and more will be grown within the pyramid using agricultural methods designed by our engineers. We employ at present thirty firms of architects – Lapraman Landesman is one – fifty of engineers and in total half-a-million design, administration and construction staff. From the present standing start and level – level-ish – ground – we shall complete within five years, and welcome our first residents within the year.'

'Is there a policy of selective breeding and ethnic segregation?'

'I've heard these ridiculous rumours and I can assure you, Gretl, quite emphatically, that this is nothing of that kind. Most certainly not. No eugenics, no profiling, no division along ethnic, racial, religious, social or any other categorisation. This is a building. It is not a society.'

Gretl almost jumped from her seat. She felt like a girl – it shocked her – why so silly? – wanted to bounce up and down. 'I like that' she squealed – squealed! 'I can use that.'

He laughed.

'Hey' she said. 'Why go up? Why not underground?'

'We are human beings. We are life, and life is light is life.'

'Great! Keep them coming.'

'It's not Brave New World, Gretl. There's no Soma. Just good, natural food. It's not Soylent Green. There is no, repeat no, euthanasia, no monkeying around with the dead. Our dead will be cremated, or if they want to be buried, there will still be burial grounds, just as there will still be aerodromes. We are not aiming to do everything. Just as much as we can. It is not 1984. It is not Utopia.

'In Britain, there will never be a utopia. We have too much of a sense of humour.'

'Fantastic. That's the strap line.' She closed her notebook, got up. 'So, no elimination of the retards.'

He jumped to his feet and again took her by the shoulders.

'Never' he said. 'Look at me Gretl. Never, please, that word. Never in anything you write for me to say. Never. Even in private.'

He giggled.

'It's one of Jo-Jo's Nine No-No words.'

He counted on his fingers.

'Cunt. Nigger. Bum-boy. Fuck.' He wobbled his hand. 'That's a So-So No-No Jo-Jo word, depends on context, the rest don't. 'Chav. Mong. Honky.'

She found gentleness in his eyes and her own. She felt faint.

'That's only eight.'

'Tonto.'

They were quiet. She thought you could almost have heard a heart being broken, but it wasn't that kind of silence: more that a heart might be formed.

He broke only the silence.

'You could never be certain what the Lone Ranger meant.'

Gretl was shocked, suffused, thrilled. She had heard of love, thought she had experienced it, knew that anything in the past had been nothing. Never before, this thrill. And better, this magnificent – wonder.

'I want to be your woman.'

'I want to be your man.'

Nothing more to say. She felt, he felt – she would like to take off her, his clothes, in this room – shrine – and love. But for the first time in her, his life, she felt, he felt – no. They would marry, and all their love would be contained within that: the privacy, and fortress.

'I'll resign,' he said. 'We can't both be on the team. And you are more important. They can always find a new leader.'

He tidied papers, switched off machinery, pulled out the plug of the kettle, turned off the light, closed the door and they left.

At reception, he handed over his pass.

'I won't need this again.'

Gretl took off her own, placed it on the desk.

'Neither will I.'

They walked from the building hand in hand. Sometimes they stopped, and looked at each other.

○ ○ ○

Daisy didn't want to visit Jill again, but Jack had begged her.

He'd cried over the phone, and said that she was the only person who could get through to her. Daisy doubted it. She wanted desperately to care, and couldn't. She climbed the hill from Brockley station and rang the bell.

'I was just passing. How are you?'

There didn't seem to be anyone else in the house, which surprised her. They sat in the dining room where – it seemed ages ago – she'd sat with Tom. Different days. How much she felt the loss of his love.

'Have I been unpleasant to you?' asked Jill.

'Nothing important.'

'What's it like Tom being dead?'

'I'm not really in the mood.'

Jill left the room. It worried Daisy that no-one seemed to be around. She couldn't physically restrain her if she harmed herself, let alone Daisy.

Jill was coming towards her, her voice wheedling.

195

'I've brought baby to see you.'

'How lovely.'

'What's it like everyone you love being dead?'

'I can't react to this.'

'What's the matter?'

'I'm trying to.'

Jill walked round her and looked closely, as if examining an animal's coat. She sniffed.

'You smell.'

'I will have a bath. I'll have a shower.'

'You should wash your clothes.'

'I will be very happy to make you. What would you like? Would you like a cup of tea? What will baby have? Are we breast-feeding?'

'Oh yes.' Jill spat out the words. 'We're breast feeding. My breasts are sore with feeding. My breasts are so extremely sore that I don't think I can feed any more with them.'

Her voice rose, to the brink of a scream.

'Heavens! They're absolutely empty. Never mind. Let's have another go. Come on baby.'

'Would you like me to hold baby?'

'Have you ever held a baby?'

'I think I know what to do.' Daisy tried to sound cajoling. 'Why don't you show me properly?

'Thank you. Ooh. We're such a lovely little girl.'

Jill sat square to the table, placed her hands in her lap, looked vacantly around the room. She fixed Daisy with a stare.

'I'd like a coffee. I drink a lot of coffee. I drink it regularly throughout the day. I find it passes the time. Do you drink coffee at all ever?'

'Let me make you some coffee. I can make it in a cafetière. Actually Tom.' Her voice choked. I must control myself. 'I think he liked to make coffee in a cafetière.'

'Do you wish you were dead?'

'I can't remember. Do you take brown or white sugar?'

'You used to fuck me. I used to fuck you.'

'I love you very much.'

'If you love someone, you can't love them very much. It's either love or it isn't. You can't have more than a full jug.'

'Yes.'

'Do you love me or not?'

'Oh certainly. And I love you too. Aren't you a little angel? Aren't you adorable? And such a lovely mummy.'

Daisy was shovelling out any words that would come. Was madness infectious? She had to get out of the house. At the same time, she was afraid to leave Jill alone. There was mania in her eyes; she heard it in her voice. But terror, too.

'I'm very clever. Me and Jack have been very clever. Icky bicky boo. Do you wish you were dead? What's it like being the only one left alive? Did you kill them too?'

Daisy could feel self-control slipping off the leash. I'm going to break this fucking thing's neck.

'Do you know what I want to do?' Jill muttered – whether to Daisy or to herself, Daisy couldn't tell – and ran her finger along the inside of her arm. 'I want to take a blade and cut it. I want to cut. You see like this. I want to saw. And hack. And cut and cut and cut. I want to see if my blood is scarlet. Or red. Or vermillion. It's important to know exactly the right words if you're a solicitor. I am a solicitor. I search relentlessly for the mot juste. I'm in pursuit of the right word.'

'I'd hate it if you killed yourself.'

'I don't care what you think. I don't care what you care. Do you love my baby?'

'I think your baby's gorgeous. Do you want her back?'

'Fed up with her? You didn't even give yours a couple of weeks. After you'd fucked my husband.'

'Yes. I think I'll give baby back to you now.'

'Give me my baby back. Husband-fucker. I'm glad they're all dead. You fucking whore.'

'I'll give you your baby back.' Daisy rose, screamed, threw it with all of her strength. 'If you can scrape it off the fucking wall.'

○ ○ ○ ○ ○

197

4

Tom is drowned at sea when the ship belonging to his lover Daisy is wrecked. He learns about life in the afterlife.

'YOU WANT HOT fucking action?'

Magruder had him cornered.

Tom was appalled.

The Commissar had vanished. The lake had receded. Tom tried to categorise the expression on Magruder's face and finally marked it down as a gurn – something of which he little experience.

'I'm OK with a brisk walk, probably.'

'I got black girls, I got Asian girls. White girls? Under-age? Something special? Greek?'

'Look, I really must object, I.'

'Girl on girl? Dirty pleasures? Liquid refreshment? Glass table? Chocolate sandwich?'

How low would the man sink? Tom felt he should draw himself up to his full height. He tried, but found that his height wasn't much.

'I'm grateful to you, Mr Magruder. But I don't want to have commercial or perverted sex. It's an act of love – not a pleasure that can be divorced from affection.'

'Quite the little fucking prude.'

'I. Look, I really object to foul language. Call me prissy, a prude, someone out of step with the times. But I respect the tongue. This is English, man! It's the palette of Shakespeare.'

'You're saying there's no shagging in Shakespeare?'

'I'm saying, I'm not interested in isolated experiences of sexual intercourse. I'm sorry, I can't be one of the lads. In any case, I'm suspicious of men who are always telling you how much sex they have.'

Magruder slumped. All the pomp and wind went out of him and he looked as ragged as an old and fishless otter. Thinking this, Tom gave a quick look around to make sure that the porpoise wasn't present or near, in case of offence by association.

In a curious accent, Magruder continued: 'Are you getting at me? Is it because I'm Welsh?'

'Definitely not. Everybody loves an Eisteddfod.'

'We're a musical people. Would you like me to sing something from the Valleys?'

'No I bloody wouldn't. I'd like you to fuck off. I'd like you to ram a leek up your arsehole, you sheep-pumping, onanistic Dai Dickhead.'

'Tom, I'm surprised.'

Tom wasn't. He had felt the pressure building, and the relief of release. But looking at the forlorn figure of Magruder, he was ashamed. 'Every now and again my brain blocks with rubbish and I reach up to pull the lever at the side of my head – to flush it – like a lavatory.'

'At our two-up-two-down in Llanelli we called it the netty. It was out the back-yard. Inside, we kept coal in the bath, and a sheep for milk, and wool for the winter.'

'I can't be moved by what you say, Magruder. You simply don't have the ring of truth.'

Magruder looked sorrowful, then straightened up and became the considerate, well-spoken gentleman he had originally appeared. His voice was weary, but Tom sensed a new level of intimacy between them – the beginning, perhaps, of trust.

'I try to be all things to all people, Tom. It's a hell of a strain. I have to remember what I've been to one person, then another,

199

sometimes several in a day. There are psychotics, people with profound but not irredeemable grudges. All languages, all backgrounds.

'One thing in common: luggage. Small items, portmanteaus, irritating wheel-along overnight bags, great storage trunks. Something that can't be let go of.

'And my objective, Mr Devine – my purpose – in whatever language will most readily accomplish that purpose – is to let them let them go.'

'I'm suitcase-less.' Tom was uneasy. 'I'm travelling light.'

'Anything we haven't tackled?'

'No.'

'Are we certain?'

'No.'

'Isn't it worth the leap?'

Perhaps it was. Tom remembered how often he had been told to conceal his feelings. And for what?

'I would like not to be afraid of commitment, of throwing myself into the unknowable. But I am afraid. Always was. Afraid I'd mess up. Be – unreliable. Lose interest. Not be able to respond to complexity.

'Running a woman isn't like running a car. I shouldn't think so. I've never had either for long. A flirtation with something sporty hired on holiday. A brief affair with a soft-top. Servicing – sounds fun, but proves expensive – always more than you thought. That's what people say.

'I've never dipped my toe – my cock – in long enough to be absolutely sure. And never wanted to find out. I'm happy to read about commitment in books, rather than having to experience it.'

Magruder gazed over the lake. Almost under his breath – perhaps remembering other times – he whispered, 'She's a splendid piece of equipment, a woman. Magnificent in her bloods and sweats.'

'So much fluid, so many smells. Too many for me. And all those emotions. I'd be sure to make a mistake. That's what I thought. So many openings. All that liquid.'

'Why be afraid, Tom? Surely, men have gone before you? The

wave of a woman's hand can be breath-stopping. The wave of her hair in the breeze. A permanent wave, a permanent way for the heart.'

Suddenly Magruder's voice became brisk.

'The precise sequence of events?'

'You've changed tack. To catch me off balance? I've answered these questions in my sleep, night after night. You didn't give me any warning.'

'I apologise, no trickery intended. No time, so no need for speed.'

'I lose her, the sensation of falling, and being wet. Seeing Turmoil sink. No time to launch the boats. All the radars rotating, the screw spinning, lights staying on. Equipment crashing from the deck. Floating. Voices shouting – only for a while. So much liquid.

'You lose her?

'Daisy is on the bridge. The master is dead. We roll under water, and – a miracle? – turn upright and afloat. Perhaps we can survive. Impossible? At sea, there is always a chance.

'Four holds remain watertight. The hatch to the forward hold breaks free. The hold floods, and drags us down. Turmoil is dead. Daisy, thank God, survives.'

'Why do you care?'

'Because I loved her.'

'You loved her?'

'Of course.'

'God damn it man. Why didn't you say so?'

○ ○ ○ ○ ○

5

Daisy's lover Tom and the crew drown when her merchant ship Turmoil is wrecked. They had both been in relationships with married couple Jill and Jack. Jill and Jack's baby daughter dies shortly after her birth. Rachel, Daisy's adoptive cousin is investigated for subversive activities.

'YOU SHOULDN'T HAVE done that. Broken her baby.'

Jack.

He must have been in the house all the time.

With Magda. In her room, in his room, wherever they went together.

Daisy felt distaste, but was sure there was no jealousy. Tom had cleaned her of everything that had happened before she fell in love with him.

When was that? At the moment she met him, or gradually?

Cleaning – that was correct. Love for him had erased her past loves – if they were love. Purified the past.

Bleached it.

She laughed, her thoughts dancing. As for Jack and his lover – or, in parity – Magda and hers – she felt understanding. Oddly too, admiration.

Jack was big above her and she thought he was going to hit her.

All her reasonable feelings evaporated.

'It's not a baby, Jack. It's a fucking doll.'

He looked as if he was going to cry. Daisy saw him for what he was – a big, stupid man who didn't know what to do.

'I'm trying to hold her together.'

She watched him like a sly fighter guarding herself with big gloves, alert for the difference between trick and surrender. If trick, ready to hit hard.

'I have no idea. I have no mechanism for remotely trying to begin to think how she must feel. How you must feel.'

'I don't bother to think. Why couldn't our baby be like everyone else's baby?'

'A candle burning in heaven.'

'There's no heaven. How could there be a heaven and take away our child?'

There were tears in his eyes. Sentimentality wouldn't help, but in the short term it might pacify. She said, as gently as she could, 'Don't get her another doll.'

'Are you suddenly an expert on baby care?'

'Don't. I have taken insult after insult from Jill. Because she is a woman, and as a woman I will forgive her. But not from you, Jack. Much as I have loved you. Much as you are my friend. I need your help, I need your friendship. I will not take abuse from you.'

'She doesn't want to see you any more.'

'It'll pass.'

'I support her in that. You are bad for our family.'

Daisy smiled inside herself, thinking of one of Skunk Reilly's favourite expressions: get down to brass tacks. The air was becoming clear.

'Jack. I did not kill your baby. You did not kill your baby. Jill did not kill your baby. Magda did not kill your baby. When your baby was 15 days old she died in her sleep. It is not your fault. If you had been standing beside her, you could not have given back her life. Magda would say that God took her back because he was lonely. And perhaps Magda is right.'

For a while he stood looking at her. He spoke evenly.

'Thank you for your patronising lesson. We will grieve as a

family in our own way. If as part of that process, it helps my wife to pretend that our baby is still alive, she has my full encouragement. I would call that love. As for you. You killed our baby. Why you don't you kill yourself?'

Daisy went to the front door. On the point of opening it, she stopped and turned back, walked up to him.

'What a good idea.'

'I didn't mean it.'

Daisy pushed open the door to the library and put her briefcase on the desk. Opening the company cheque book she wrote a cheque. On a sheet of company letterhead, she wrote a long single paragraph. She called for Magda and asked her to witness her signature. Magda signed and dated her name and – sensing the mood – left.

Daisy handed the cheque and paper to Jack

She shook his hand and said goodbye.

Reilly was waiting outside to drive her to the office. On the way, she fell asleep.

○ ○ ○

A large glass ashtray sat on the desk in the library. Jill had won it for them at a fair in Hilly Fields Park, throwing rings over a hook with unexpected grace. Jack read the letter and cheque and burnt them in it, grinding the ashes with the stub end of a pencil. He found a fresh pack of Chesterfields in the drawer. The smoke in his lungs made him feel grand, and for a moment he soared, loving the height.

Taking a carrier bag, he went to Jill's bedroom and found her looking at the fragments of the doll. He kissed her, knelt on the floor and picked them up, putting each carefully into the bag until he had them all.

She watched him. Suddenly she burst into tears and let out a great wail. How ugly she looked, and how desperately he loved her. How right, he thought, the song is – all the rest is talk. I will never desert you, woman. He put his arm around her, and held her to him.

'Baby will be fine' he said. 'I'll put her back together.'

○ ○ ○

Daisy had an excellent view of the docks from the window.

Work didn't define life – not for most people, surely?

Since her father died, what she saw in front of her had been her single reality – home, school, university, family. Through it, she had learnt everything.

And now it had to go.

She picked up the phone and asked the company secretary to come to her office.

∘ ∘ ∘

Adam Brook opened the door as soon as Rachel Fonseca pressed the buzzer. Had he been waiting? It was the back way into the office – he'd drawn an elaborate map – because of a protest march at the front along Kingsway. As they went up in the lift, they could hear the shrieks and catcalls of the demonstrators.

He took her to a private office containing Sarah Carpenter, introduced them and left.

Rachel liked the look of Sarah Carpenter: her slight podginess and pleasant smile. Would her hair be better shorter? It rested on her shoulders, soft and blonde. Darker? Brown or even black? Rachel decided it was fine as it was – it framed her face and made the best of it.

She wore a black skirt suit with a white shirt and white necklace. The symmetry of this delighted Rachel, because she herself had chosen a black skirt and jacket with a white shirt (which she'd taken the unusual trouble to iron).

And a black patent handbag. Seeing this, Mrs Ballantyne had raised an eyebrow, asking if her third daughter had become a prostitute. Rachel replied that she might, to answer her question, be seeing Adam Brook.

There was milk, a bowl of chunky rough brown and white sugar lumps and a plate of white and milk chocolate biscuits. The march outside began to sound like a riot. Sarah Carpenter poured tea.

'Can I clarify? You're Adam's boss?'

'Adam would definitely prefer colleague.'

'Originally, I trained as a barrister in the office of the Judge Advocate General. That's the army, of course. Courts martial. I was a captain. I'm a civilian now, I hope you've noticed. It's quite

205

a transition. I'm a military type, born to it, army brat from age zero. Akrotiri, Hong Kong, Mönchengladbach.'

'You are a bit bossy. But you're probably nice.'

'I will accept that as a qualified approval. My job here is to keep all of us legal. So I read everyone's reports.'

'I'm going to make a bold guess, and I want you to tell me the truth.'

'I may be constrained by confidentiality. Otherwise I'll do my best.'

'It is easier to tell the truth. Why be caught out in a small lie? It ruins one's credibility for the big lie beneath the surface.'

'You want the truth?' Sarah Carpenter laughed. 'I'd like to run through rain like they do in films. But I'd be prettier. And careless.'

'Adam Brook wanted to tell me the truth. I stopped him.'

'We'd all love to be reckless. And that's what it is, the truth. Pontius Pilate: "What is truth?" I've never known what it is. You "tell the truth" and you ruin lives. Lives are important to us. Tell me about your son. I'm sure you didn't want him to burn to death.'

'I've met you before.'

Sarah went to a filing cabinet and pulled an A4 photograph out of a file. She handed it to Rachel.

'Taken at the inquest of your son at' – she looked at the back of the photograph – 'that's right, St Pancras Coroner's Court. Closed hearing, difficult to arrange, masses of forms. That's me, that's why you remember.'

'And me. You take photographs of people in court. How clever. How they react, I suppose. The way they look off-guard. And keep them. I imagine there are more of these?'

'Yes. We take photographs.'

'That's – Adam.'

'As a relevant officer, he would have been present.'

'What makes someone relevant?'

Sarah refilled Rachel's cup and sat back in her chair.

'Some connection to the case. Perhaps simply technical. It's not that this particular person would have any knowledge of those involved, not even their names. It could be a particular staff

206

member's specialism becoming involved.'

A gunshot exploded the window behind her. Rachel threw herself on the floor. Sarah continued to drink her tea.

'Are you all right?'

'I'm not absolutely certain.' Rachel sat in a heap on the floor. She felt dazed and afraid. Pull yourself together, girl. Fear was not one of Rachel's prime characteristics – at least, that was what she had always believed. No, she was sure of it. Sarah's voice was a soothing monotone.

'There's no need to be afraid. You are extremely safe here. The windows are anti-bandit glass. They can be shattered by gunfire or a high-velocity rifle shot. I think that is the type of weapon here. I'm not expert: Adam would know. But the glass breaks the velocity of the projectile – the bullet – and it becomes harmless even a millimetre after leaving the inner surface. The shattered glass has soft, blunt edges and a velocity of less than a centimetre a second.

'Civil disturbance can be disconcerting, and the sound of weapons discharging. May I examine your head?'

Sarah knelt. She drew Rachel up to a kneeling position, handling her gently and expertly. She parted Rachel's hair with her fingers and examined her scalp, looked carefully into her eyes, superficially over the rest of her, and lightly brushed her jacket. Finally, she helped her to her feet and sat her down in her chair.

'No scratches or bleeding, no bruising. I think you may have shock. Your pupils are slightly dilated. May I ask if you take drugs? We're not the police.'

Rachel shook her head. Sarah picked up the phone and ordered fresh tea and milk, and sandwiches.

'My invitation for you to come here was not entirely disingenuous. I wanted us to be able to speak because there are some serious and difficult matters we need to discuss. I think it is best if we leave that today and any questions you may have. It's been exceptionally stressful for you.'

'You didn't flinch.'

'If you hear the gunshot, you're not dead. But there's a much more direct explanation. I'm not afraid of dying. The process of death, yes. But each day, and night, I am perfectly happy to die.

Adam Brook is the same. Nobody isn't afraid of torture. But death, it's only a conclusion. A beginning too perhaps – but that is theology.'

'I don't know what I feel.'

'Somewhere in Walden, Thoreau says that he has never met anyone who was truly awake, and if he should ever do so, he wouldn't know what to say. Rachel, you are wide awake. We are here together.'

The refreshments arrived and Sarah served them both. Carefully cutting it, she put a sandwich on a plate and gave it to Rachel, with the gentle concern that an older sister might show if – playtime interrupted – her younger sister had suddenly been hurt. Rachel nibbled, realised she was very hungry, and ate it all. She knew that Sarah Carpenter was watching her, and liked it.

o o o

The company secretary, Nick Pershawe, senior partner in Pershawe Willmott, Solicitors and Commissioners for Oaths, sat at Daisy's desk taking notes on a yellow legal pad. She stayed by the window, looking out.

'Correct me Nick,' she said, 'but as Pöl Stuyvesant's executor, I'm allowed to vote for him?'

Pershawe was a precise man who felt that he had a reckless streak which must be kept under control. He was aware of how a solicitor was preferred to speak – soberly, the words measured as if carefully considered – and of how he longed to blurt that – yes! – he knew the answer. At school he had been intelligent and popular, a team player good at solo sports such as javelin and cross-country running, a gifted chess-player, an early smoker, a light though capable-of-being-heavy drinker, a competent and discreet kisser and fucker, successful at university and in the university of life. He said 'Yes.'

'In which case, make the valuations in preparation for selling the remaining ships, liquidating the assets and closing the company.'

Pershawe scribbled on his pad. He had no fantasies. Women? He had as many as he could be kind to – he was a considerate man. Drink? No further use for it. At school, it had been necessary to impress to obtain status and likeability. In life aged

40, he had nothing further to do: a slow coast to death. No point in a legacy of mastery in jurisprudence, cases triumphantly won. Who would care? Better to do what good could be done without show or boastfulness.

'Right.'

'I have severed the financial relationship with Jack Jouvry. I have given him a company cheque equal to his investment and interest to date. In anticipation of a negative verdict from the inquiry I have personally and corporately indemnified him for actions against me or the company as they might affect him, in writing, correctly signed and witnessed. Both of these dated this morning.'

Nick Pershawe wondered if female ejaculation was real or a fantasy. And the question of lying under glass tables while women – big women, possibly – shit on top: did it really happen? Where? In people's houses? Who cleared up afterwards? What about the carpet? Probably only over a stripped wood floor – but surely that would stain? Whipping had never appealed. All in all, Nick Pershawe was a straightforward man-on-top kind of a guy. They said it was equivalent to a five-mile run. Why run?

'OK.'

Daisy took the office keys off her keyring and left them, picked up her briefcase, shook hands, looked round for a last time.

○ ○ ○ ○ ○

6

Just before Tom and the crew died in the loss at sea of Daisy's merchant ship Turmoil, Daisy and Tom discovered that they were in love with each other. Daisy finds living without him very hard. Tom becomes acquainted with the afterlife. Mrs Ballantyne and Emilio Podro are old friends. Emilio is close to the official investigation of the subversive activities of Mrs Ballantyne's niece – brought up as her daughter – Rachel. Dianita (Diana) Lapraman, Helen Landesman's partner in an architectural practice, killed herself following mental illness.

EMILIO PODRO GLITTERED in the tart bright morning. Mrs Ballantyne opened her front door and appraised the excellence of his crisp soldier's uniform, shining leather boots, Sam Browne, pistol holster and peaked military cap.

There were two cars in the road: a well-used Volvo which she recognised as an embassy car, and a smarter one next to it. A lean and muscular woman, pretty and smartly-dressed, rested against the passenger door; a handsome, rugged man in a loosely-cut suit sat at the wheel.

'I see that today we are equipped as a toy soldier.'

'Mummy.'

'Not yet, thank God.'

Emilio sighed and stretched comfortably in his chair. He jumped up and made her a cup of tea, producing from his attaché case a package wrapped in hand-made paper, tied with a red bow.

'It isn't somebody's birthday but who cares?' He pirouetted on tiptoe and placed the package in her hand.

'Need we remember and it was a month ago?' But she opened the present and looked at the contents with satisfaction.

'Ah, now. This is something quite special.'

She cut the plastic film and extracted one of the bundle of twenty-five hand-made cigars. With a delicate flick of her tongue, she tasted the side of the wrapper at the lighting end, closed her eyes and whispered 'Maduro'.

∘ ∘ ∘

Helen Landesman sparkled in the tart bright morning. In sports kit, she set off for the office, fresh clothes in her bag, increasing her effort to the best she could manage. Disregarding the pain, and the furtive stares of passers-by at her ungainliness, she felt fully extended and alive. She showered, shook off the water, turned in front of the mirror and thought: I like the woman.

Casine sauntered into Landesman's office with a tray and laid the desk with coffees, boiled eggs, soldiers. 'Ta-da!'

She came round and cuddled Landesman. After a while, they sat and ate.

Casine burped, wiped her mouth. 'Congratulations.'

'Oh I mean to say for heaven's sake Francesca.'

'Off to the big house.'

'You won't even notice I'm gone.'

'The bunker.'

'I miss O'Brien though.'

'You'll probably be better.'

'Quite an endorsement.' She didn't laugh.

Casine leant forward. 'Helen. We need strong leadership. We need it now. From the word go, you must take command. You have to be robust.'

Landesman lit a cigarette, tossed the pack over to Casine.

'I'm ready.'

211

The kitchen floor had never been cleaned. It had been vacuumed. Sometimes it had been washed. The lino was rough to the touch and safe – no-one could slip on it, try as they might. No doubt it contained abrasive. As if anyone would try to slide on a kitchen floor!

But it had never been scrubbed, or if it had, it had never been scrubbed as Daisy scrubbed it now: dark grey to light grey, brightening the room. Rinsed and dried.

She had already cleaned the bathroom floor, bleached the scraps of mould from the edges of the bath. She wondered what the Romans had called hard water. She scoured the lavatory-bowl free of scale; beneath and around the taps; the lime-track down the porcelain of the wash basin.

Vacuuming the sitting room, she paused for a while and looked down into Hillfield Road. The police station was conveniently near, up at the corner of Fortune Green Road.

Walking through the past. The gentle curve past Aldred Road to Mill Lane and down to the Green. Three telephone boxes, different sizes. Frognal, and up to the Heath.

o o o

'Right, my boy. Enough shilly-shallying. As you're to join the family, you need hard facts.'

Podro sat upright.

'There's no need to stand to attention. And what's this damned military uniform? Are we going to war? I suppose these buffoons outside are meant to intimidate me?'

'No, no. Diplomatic Protection Service, nothing more. We have a tediously enhanced alert. It will pass.' He blew out smoke. 'Everything passes.

'And the droll uniform. Every now and again my employer likes to ring the changes, show the flag, whatever today's expression might be. I am, inter alia – many aliases – the military attaché. Occasionally, I am expected to dress accordingly. Ready for a part in Gilbert and Sullivan.'

'I don't think I believe any of that, but it will do.'

'Oh, but I assure you.'

'Emilio. We can switch to the intimate form. Tais toi, dear, and listen.'

'I shall be all ears, like a donkey. Oh, I'm sorry.'

'Gone to a better place. Though by now she has most probably made it worse. There will certainly be very little grass left.

'My parents were fornicators. My father was a philanderer and my mother was a philanderer, and their division was inevitable. My father remained, many years later to bear child – my dear sister – with another, and I was brought as an infant by my mother to this country, where by the grace of God I have remained ever since.

'By his further and continuing grace a good man came into my life and gave me the happiest years neither woman nor man could deserve nor merit by their own efforts, but only from the gift of the almighty.

'And I have sought to extend the love that I have been given to those placed into my care or made reasonably available: one natural daughter, one daughter by adoption, and one troubled and troublesome niece; each equally lovable and equally loved.

'Rachel did not have a difficult childhood, but she was a difficult child. Her mother – my sister, step if you prefer – was a good and decent mother but, and I will need to be honest on the understanding of complete confidentiality' – Mrs Ballantyne paused, and Podro nodded – 'not a gifted one.

'My father was a man with excellent political connections, as was his harlot. My sister inherited their ability to charm and exploit – I use the word in a benign sense – those connections and develop her own, so that her career in government – very properly – blossomed.

'There is only one thing that can most effectively damage a rising political career and it is neither sexual misconduct – generally welcomed as showing panache unless exceptionally perverted, and even that can mark one out as a card – nor corruption – which my sister is entirely free from. It is the misdemeanours of one's own family.

'Rachel was a troublesome and disobedient girl, who disliked her mother and delighted in embarrassing her. This is normal for girls, but her mother was not blessed with maternal understanding, and short of the love the child needed. Or perhaps

213

Rachel was born bloody-minded. I often debate this in my head but you see Emilio, I love the child and she, equally guilty m'Lud, has always given the appearance of loving me.

'The upshot was, Rachel was either achieved or thrust upon me, shipped like a monkey in a cage, howling and angry, and – I have no doubt – frightened and ashamed, and I have brought her up as one of my own. No. If I had, she might have been better or worse. As it was, I received a cross young woman, fully-grown and beyond alteration, whose first act of rebellion was to marry an unsuitable university lecturer, conceive and deliver a son whom she abandoned and later, if we are to believe speculation and the current attentions of an Adam Brook, destroyed.'

'Do you believe that?'

'Certainly not. If she had murdered her son there would have been uproar, or at the very least a demur. This is a country of high standards, even if the observance is low.

'I would ask, by the way, why you are marrying Rowena? Let us be frank. She is a plain girl. No, she is ugly. She is not a girl a man would rush to marry. Why are you marrying her? Is it for your own advancement?'

Emilio Podro looked contemplative. Mrs Ballantyne wondered if he would blub, and thought if so how embarrassing that would be. Foreigners! Stop. She had been foreign, though a long time past.

'Sometimes, I simply look at her face. I am amazed at how lovely she is, the sound of her voice is everything I want to hear. She smells of Rowena, which is the smell I want to smell, and she has Rowena's special laugh and smile. I think she likes to be with me.'

Mrs Ballantyne cleared her throat and prepared to say, yes, well, that sounds perfectly satisfactory, but the words remained in the dispatch room without being posted. She thought of the first time she had seen her husband, smart in his uniform, the overwhelming feeling of knowing, the golden moments and years.

○ ○ ○

If there were any prayers left, she had forgotten them. All she could find were pathetic words of her own. Do you remember me? I'm Daisy. I miss you Tom. Will you come for me? I'm lonely

214

Tom. Have you forgotten me already? I don't want to be here. Can you hear me Tom? Will you come for me? I love you Tom. Kiss me?

∘ ∘ ∘

Sugar Popsicle dug Tom in the ribs.

'Why the long face?'

Pleased to see him again, Tom wanted to be friendly, but couldn't think of the answer.

Sugar Popsicle waited patiently and finally gave up.

'That, by the way, is the punch-line of a joke.'

Sadly, he walked away.

∘ ∘ ∘

'You loved her?' repeated Magruder, incredulously.

'Utterly, completely, totally.

'I can imagine there was a miracle in her kiss.

'The thought of it transformed me from being an indifferent poet, a weak, masturbating, inverted, introverted bank-clerk of a nonentity – into a king.

'The idea of her kiss made me Omar Khayyam, Marco Polo, Attila the Hun – man, superman, super lover, super human.'

'And she's alive.'

Magruder said it neither with resignation nor finality. It was more an observation, as one might comment on the weather.

'Is that bad?'

'At the moment, I don't know. But I'm optimistic about this transformation in you, Tom. You appear to have been touched.'

Magruder nodded to himself. A critical point in their conference – interrogation? – had evidently been passed. Perhaps satisfactorily.

'You'll be given another chance, I'm sure.'

'I hid from love. Dodged the blast, crept out, caught its aroma – a wistful mixture of cunt and perfume which I could have licked, gargled with, if I'd had the guts to inhale.

'I should have stood up and said: I'm ready. Give it to me. Here's everything I am.'

'Who's to say she'd have taken you up, man? You, after all, are just a poet. Or a clerk, a cargo-meister. What are we today, Tom?'

215

Tom noticed that the ferry to Olkhon Island hadn't appeared. No sound of whistle or steam came from the circum-Baikal railway. No ripple of water from the five sisters of the Turka River.

Everything a mistake.

'I thought there'd be all the time in the world, and there was.
'It's just that all there was wasn't much.'

'I thought I could defer love, not realising that it had to be taken and risked the moment it was offered.

'If you find a woman, Mr Magruder, and she says she loves you, my advice is: give yourself immediately, readily accept her love, take her to you and give her your entire spirit, body, everything you own, forever, no profit-and-loss calculations.

'And when she is cruel to you, forgive her.

'When she fails to exceed your expectations, adjust them to what she – in good heart – can give.

'When she is unconfident, be her grace.

'When she offers you encouragement, be taken into her hands.

'When she says "I love you, love me, and by the way, am I fat?", say "thank you", "yes", and "no".

'And never look back.'

Magruder sighed.

'A shame you didn't take your own advice. It's too late for you now, Tom. It's too late for Daisy, for anyone you know or remember. There's no time. When there was time, there was time. It hasn't run out. It no longer exists.'

○ ○ ○ ○ ○

7

Father Julius Melendez is a priest at the Church of the Madonna of Sorrows in London where Captain Ballantyne's funeral service was held. Rachel Fonseca owns a radical bookshop in central London and is possibly unwell. She is being investigated for subversive activities. Her aunt and informally adoptive mother Mrs Ballantyne is able to receive some details of this from South American diplomat Emilio Podro. Dianita (Diana) Lapraman, business partner of Helen Landesman in their joint architectural firm, killed herself following mental illness: the theme of a little girl abandoned at Crewe station has been repeated in the story so far without explanation. Jill's baby died and her husband Jack is having an affair with their au pair Magda.

FATHER JULIUS MELENDEZ wondered why time passed so slowly. When he woke up and found there was half the night to go, time stretched, yawned, and refused to sleep. When he sat in the confessional and nobody came, time weighed out each of its seconds like a thrifty clock.

And today was motor-sport.

Even the most mild-mannered human being can be stirred to passion, and Fr Melendez had two, the other of which was making jams and preservatives. But if motor sport was ever pitched against marmalade – even Seville marmalade for the tiny envelope of time in which its oranges came to season – it would be game, set and match to motor sport.

Clearly no-one would come to confession in the last half-hour. If he were to leave now, he would catch the final ecstatic minutes of the world championship.

Fr Melendez had had worse temptations – better, really, because a beautiful woman could never be worse. To think so – Fr Melendez reasoned – would be to insult the God who made and loved her. But it was close. He was on the point of giving in, but didn't.

Fr Melendez stuck out the final endless minutes of duty in the confessional, and nobody came.

o o o

Doctor Lizzie Tillett wore white pumps. Her white lab coat hung open showing a white open-necked shirt beneath it. A grey pleated skirt came down to just below her knees. She stood on her desk – a fine wooden one with a roller top and compartments – tying a plastic shopping bag round a smoke-alarm on the ceiling.

Equipment filled the rest of the room, some esoteric, some basic: a stethoscope on the back of the door, scales, examination bed, wash basin.

Rachel sat in the visitor's chair.

Doctor Tillett jumped down, rocked back in her chair, put her feet up on her desk, lit a cigarette and exhaled.

'I've had my hands round two hundred testicles belonging to a hundred fairly pretty boys in their 20s.'

'Lucky you.'

'Hardly. Today is Men's Health Day, tomorrow is Women's Health Day. I will grasp two hundred breasts belonging to a hundred fairly pretty girls in their 20s. This is pointless. They will all die. They are all fit, thin, they exercise regularly. Their heartbeats are low, their blood pressure is exemplary. None of them has cholesterol, none of them will die of stroke, heart attack, emphysema. They will all die of cancer.'

'Really?'

'Nothing else left. And they queue up because with all this

218

vitality and perfect nutrition, they are neurotic. If I put them all together so that 100 women were holding the testicles of 100 men who were holding the breasts of 100 women, they'd have fun. And the last thing on their mind would be whether or not they have lumps.'

Rachel smiled non-committally. She was never quite sure with Dr Tillett. Trusted confidante? Yes. Friend? Certainly. But always the slight suspicion that her thoughts were separate from her words.

'Stick your head in this, chuck.'

Dr Tillett wheeled over a biomicroscope and propped Rachel's jaw on the chin-rest in front of the lens. She dimmed the room light and looked attentively first into one eye, then the other. She pushed the equipment away and switched up the lights.

'Am I dead?'

Dr Tillett looked grave. Rachel wondered if she felt it. Doctors had a vocabulary of relevant expressions: one for death, one for joy, one for extremely bad news. But what was extremely bad? We would all die. It was good to have certainties. The doctor was speaking.

'There is something. I can't say if it's a brain tumour. I think it probably is. What do you want me to do?'

'It's an X-Ray and then you see if you can cut it out?'

'Subject to size. Variants are: It's small, we shrink it. It's larger but not too large, we cut it out. It's too large, we can't. Or there's nothing there. I doubt the last. Results are: Shrink: slightly reduced lifespan, constant monitoring. Excise: death risk during operation, fairly normal lifespan. Too large and left in place: a few months. Nothing there: could get shot in the street.'

Rachel frowned.

'Random acts of violence have a lot to commend them.' With luck, the knowledge of impending death is short. And what is life but the risk of normality?

'What do you want to do?'

'Nothing?'

Dr Tillett looked calm.

'Headaches varying from zero to intense. Periods of irrationality. Periods of intense perception as the brain is squeezed. Likewise perception of pain or physical pleasure heightened. Non-existent or mild or severe hallucination.'

She got up, approximately tidied her desk, put on her coat, held Rachel's open.

'And the usual things we feel every day. Paranoia. Anguish. The knowledge of being forgotten.'

∘ ∘ ∘

'It's very. Isn't it?'

Francesca Casine ran her hand along the desk and sighed. 'I love luxury. It's a sin I suppose, but are there sins any more?'

'Have you finished?'

Helen Landesman laughed, put down the file she was reading and limped round to the front of the desk – an expedition, as it was long and deep.

'The workmanship. This must have cost. I am in awe.'

'It's an office, Casine.'

'It's a palace. The furniture. This is priceless. Curtains! In an office.'

'I imagine you'll have coffee.'

'I imagine you have staff to make it.'

'I have a pair of hands.'

Landesman poured coffee.

'Mugs? Keeping in touch with the common people?'

'O'Brien's office didn't work for me. I need space, and I need an office where I can have meetings. Apart from that, I am common, so I don't need to keep in touch.'

'You won't forget us, will you?'

'What do you think?'

'You won't forget Diana?'

'Probably. And O'Brien. It's time for a – realignment. And I have already put that in train.'

Gretl, unmentioned.

'It's a building, Helen. It's big, but that's all.'

'O'Brien was wrong. It's where Diana was wrong too, and me. And you. It's a society. It's a future. Look at everything that's gone wrong in the past. Can we make a perfect society? No we can't. But we can have a damned good try. We're going to get more things right, that's all. A better kind of imperfection. I'm not aiming for any kind of ideal because they don't work. But I want to give people chances.'

'Her mother killed herself.'

'I didn't know that, but it makes sense.'

'Makes sense?'

'Is that callous? Look Francesca. She was my best friend. We had good times, bad times, shared lots of secrets. She never told me that. If she had, I'd have thought of something to say. But she didn't and now she's dead. It's too late.'

'She was a little girl. Her mother left her on a railway station with a suitcase and stepped in front of a train.'

Casine wondered if Helen had heard. She said nothing and there was no reaction on her face, no reflection of tears, no stiffening of her body. Why had she told her? To bring her down to earth? Didn't she deserve her achievement? Hadn't she the right to enjoy it? Revel a little?

'I'm sorry.' It wasn't a whisper, and there was no choking of emotion. 'Where?'

'It was Crewe. Crewe railway station.'

'Very busy.'

'Very.'

'Clapham Junction in the south and Crewe in the north.' Landesman talked easily now. 'Two of the busiest in the world. I'm sure that's so. In the number of trains an hour rather than people going there. I suppose that not many people – relatively – live in Clapham Junction or Crewe. That's no shame on them as places.'

'No.'

'I'm revisiting the idea of a railway station in Square Mile.'

'I thought O'Brien had decided.'

Politely, Landesman cut her short.

'Thank you so much for coming in.'

As Casine left, Landesman called after her.

'And thank you for telling me.'

○ ○ ○

'My inclination, you see' said Mrs Ballantyne 'is to believe that now that my sister intends to honour us with her ambassadorial presence, her daughter has become an embarrassment.'

221

Emilio winked.

'You're a wily old bird, Mrs B.'

'I am that.'

'But I think your imagination is a step ahead of reality.'

'I am glad that reality is catching up.'

Emilio straightened the crease on his trousers, crossed his knees.

'We don't have the influence to initiate the arrest of a citizen of this country.'

'As I understood it, my niece is not under arrest.'

'Exactly.'

'But she is being detained for questioning.'

'Not detained, I think.'

Mrs Ballantyne went to the window and looked along the road. The woman leant against the car, regarding her casually. The man sat in the passenger seat, talking into a radio.

'And you know the detail of her interrogation?'

'That's a little strong. Chatting among friends. And there is the question of romance. I'm sure of it. It will all end happily.'

'You haven't answered the question, Emilio.'

He put on a boyish grin and gave her his most wheedling look. 'Strike a light, Mrs B, I'm just a poor boy from Sarf America by way of an English public school with beating and sodomy. I don't know nuffink.'

'And the answer?'

'Friendly countries keep each other posted. And to your unspoken question, I am not marrying your daughter to be a viper within the brood. I am marrying her because I love her. Some things are simple.'

o o o

The second meeting took place in Quiet Room 1.

Its door was faced and edged with felt, and opened off a quiet corridor in a secluded part of the building. The table was triangular – glass, and not large. Intimate. Knees could be seen almost to touch.

Sarah Carpenter explained that there was nothing electrical or electronic in the room apart from the lights and a whisper of electrically-propelled air. No cameras, microphones, computing equipment, no telephones. Paper and carbon duplicate sheets lay on a side-table beside a mechanical Remington typewriter.

QR1 – she called it that, and in her voice it sounded warm and homely – had no windows, and the floor and walls were carpeted. There was nothing that sound might bounce off – if that is what sound wished to do. Speech went only from face to face.

Rachel noticed that Sarah Carpenter was not perfectly dressed. The zip at the back of her skirt was held together at the top with a safety pin: neatly, but nevertheless. Her shirt had faint marks of sweat. Adam Brook looked dishevelled, but he often looked like that. She wondered if they had been fucking before she arrived.

To her surprise, Rachel didn't care. She was thinking of a different man, and the thought made her happy.

Sarah Carpenter and Adam Brook each had a spiral pad and pencil, and as soon as one of them spoke, the other took shorthand. Why not admit the room was bugged and get on with it? Rachel rested her elbows elegantly on the table.

○ ○ ○

Latchmere & Ferrandi Latchmere Solicitors' office was over the Golden Girls club in West End Lane, a comfortable place where married men from the suburbs met to smoke pipes – shishas were in fashion – and wear dresses. The pleasant aroma of charred molasses accompanied Daisy up the stairs.

'I would like you to look through this with care, and make sure it is exactly what you intend.'

The office was sunlit and peaceful and Daisy felt no sense of pressure nor time. There was, she thought, in its full meaning, all the time in the world, and only small tasks to accomplish.

'Thanks, Raffaello.' She looked up. 'That's it. Perfect.'

'It's not really my place to say it.'

'Say it.'

Tail-end Latchmere was the only one left. Ferrandi was dead; original Latchmere too. Both had handled her father's personal business.

'You won't, will you, need this to be executed for – a long time?'

Daisy hesitated. She was fond of Latchmere. Although she'd only met him from time to time over the years, in a way they had grown up together, and both were the end of the line.

'I won't lie to you, Raffaello.'

'Oh.'

'I want you to execute this.' She looked round the office. 'And I want you to be generous with yourself over your fees.'

He was taken aback, but she knew he was pleased; and less for the money than for the trust.

'This is an awfully big will. You know we're a very small firm now. It's only me. Don't you want your corporate lawyer to handle it?'

'How do we go about signing this?'

'I'll go downstairs and ask for a couple of witnesses. That is if you don't mind? They're really very nice.'

○ ○ ○

Emilio and Mrs Ballantyne kissed goodbye, and she stood at the door as he drove away. The woman police officer gave a last glance up and down the road, lingering for a moment on Mrs Ballantyne. The man briefly followed her look. Their car set off smoothly, catching up fast with Podro's. Mrs Ballantyne closed the door and remembered that the house was empty. The visit had ended pleasantly. But in small ways, everything had changed.

○ ○ ○

After a few minutes the police car turned back and parked further along the road, out of sight from the windows of the house.

○ ○ ○

Jack was thankful that the journey down to Bedlam had been peaceful. No screams or tears. It was difficult to interpret what Jill felt – certainly she couldn't express it in words. Perhaps inside, she accepted that this must be if not a final, then an extensively temporary solution.

Magda travelled with her in the ambulance: Jack drove behind. Jill had become comfortable with Magda. She treated her as a friend she didn't know quite well enough to confide in fully, but from whom she could accept affection and give some in return.

It was good that her condition had been given a provisional label, though Jack wasn't sure if anxiety fully covered the bewildered look in her eyes.

When they were alone together in the car coming back, Magda told Jack that she was leaving.

∘ ∘ ∘

'I won't lie to you, Rachel.'

Sarah Carpenter sounded sincere.

You do it all the time, Rachel thought, but didn't allow the smirk to show. Every word you say is a lie of some kind. But that's no bad thing. Don't we all lie, all of the time? And this is no time for profundity: I want a coffee.

'May I have a coffee?'

'Not just now.'

'Can I go?'

'If you want. I won't lie to you, Rachel. If your mother.'

'I don't have a mother.'

'If your country was not about to.'

'This is my country. I am a citizen and I have a passport.'

'And that is the point, Rachel. Under the Defence of the Realm Act 1914 (Re-enacted), as a citizen and with – as you say – a passport, we could refer everything to the police and you could be arrested and charged with – whatever they like.

'If your country – very well, the country of your birth – was not about to honour our country – yours and mine – with the appointment of a fine and senior civil servant as their new ambassador, and if that ambassador was anyone other than your mother, we would consider doing exactly that.'

'I'm glad to be significant.'

'Or a useful idiot. Lenin.'

'He never actually said that.'

'Alternatively we might have done nothing. Democracies need token revolutionaries to look like democracies.'

'How cynical.'

Sarah Carpenter sighed.

'Unfortunately, we don't have that option. Relationships with your – ex – country are deemed important to the national interest. Guns and bullets. You on the loose telling people how to make bombs out of starter-motors is an embarrassment to Mummy and therefore to them and therefore to us.

'And us, specifically – when the train hits the buffers – means

225

your two new friends, sitting here now.'

○ ○ ○

Emilio Podro would be a good addition to the family, Mrs Ballantyne reflected.

Rachel was a difficult girl, but loving, and able to find her way.

Daisy's beginning had not been ideal, but she had shown herself capable and – what would be, would be.

It was Rowena who had always worried Mrs Ballantyne. Often she woke and questioned whether she had been right to extend the family. No. Right it was, and – stemming from duty – it had become a deep and enduring love. But to the cost of the one person to whom surely she owed the most of her motherhood, her natural child?

Rowena was Rowena – stubborn, resistant, unbiddable, ugly. And capable of the simplest most pitiful love. She feared for Rowena because what she had needed most – her mother's undivided loyalty – had been taken away from her as soon as she began to think for herself and was able to appreciate the full extent of the treachery. And whereas the other two with their charm and mischievous grace were easy to favour, Rowena – clumsy Rowena – was left tagging along behind.

If it should transpire – Mrs Ballantyne suspected it to be true – that Emilio Podro loved the child – and Rowena gave every evidence of loving him – Mrs Ballantyne felt she could die in peace. But not just yet.

○ ○ ○ ○ ○

8

Daisy's lover Tom drowns when her merchant ship is wrecked. Rowena (the natural daughter of Mrs Ballantyne and the late Captain Ballantyne), Daisy (their adopted daughter), and Rachel Fonseca (their niece, daughter of Mrs Ballantyne's sister), have been brought up as sisters in the Ballantyne household. Fr Melendez is a priest in the Church of the Madonna of Sorrows in London, where Captain Ballantyne's funeral was held. After a reclusive life Rowena finds love with South American diplomat Emilio Podro who is kept informed of the official investigation into Rachel's radical activities.

'WHAT'S HER MOTHER like?'

It was evening and – her working day done – Rowena had come to Emilio's office looking forward to a weekend with the man she loved, to find him still at his.

'Identical to yours.'

'Big fat mamas are back in style.'

'Never would I be so offensive of your dear Mummy who is most certainly not fat, though of stature. Her sister is – how may I best put it? – the biggest ambassador you will ever have seen. A giant of the Corps Diplomatique.'

'Why are you wearing a uniform?'

227

'Appearances, appearances. They must be maintained.'

'Will you mind that I will only be able to give you ugly children?'

He laughed and kissed her on the nose.

'It isn't a snout.'

'Oink.'

He changed and she took him to a pub, bought them each crisps and a beer.

'Will she see Rachel?'

He hesitated.

'You know Rachel better than me. Isn't it more, will Rachel see her?'

'I don't really know Rachel. I put up with her. She tolerates me. No she won't.'

It was loud in the pub and welcoming: music, end-of-week voices, a degree of happiness, tobacco smoke, chicken-in-the-basket, cocaine, wedges of potato, fucks in the making, loneliness, gossip, some hysteria. The juke box played a slow waltz; they danced.

It was good to be in her arms. She smelt a bit, but not rank – when they married he would encourage her to wash more often – and she was beautiful.

She whispered in his ear. 'Your shoes are falling apart. First thing when we are married, we shall buy you a new pair.'

He stopped, held her away from him, laughing. 'Woman. You told me you loved me as I am. That you will never want to change a thing.'

'That isn't a change. It's an amelioration.'

He drove her home, and stopped some way short so that the car wasn't visible from the house.

'I'll see you tomorrow.' He kissed her.

'How's Daisy?' he added. He wasn't particularly interested – it was more of a politeness than a question – and he expected her to say she didn't care. He thought she hadn't heard. He was surprised to see her sad.

'We've got everything.' Rowena was wistful. 'She hasn't got each other. And every day she can't work out what's the point.'

'She's told you this?'

'I haven't seen her. Why should she? I've done nothing for her.

I have. I've shut her out.'

He put his arm round her, dried the tears with his sleeve and ignored the make-up that came off on it. It was getting chilly; he switched on the engine and ran the heater.

'Why don't you go and see her? I'm sure she'd like that.'

'Not at the weekend. It would be intrusive.'

'Next week? You could drop in one evening?'

'We're not on drop-in terms. I'd have to tell her beforehand.'

'Make an appointment?' He smiled, but didn't let her see it. 'I'm sure if you turned up unannounced with a bottle of wine and red, pink and white roses to cover all moods and occasions, she'd let you in for a couple of minutes while she read what you'd written on the card.'

Rowena sat up. She was becoming rock-steady Rowena, which he liked, but he liked tearful Rowena too, and the Rowenas in between. It was the whole package of Rowena that was good, in all her shades and vicissitudes. Virtues too. There was nothing complicated about love, he thought, overall. It was particularly like soil: thoroughly good despite outward appearances. And any dirt was easily washed away.

He said 'She might have a man with her.'

'She had an affair for years with a man called Jack. Jack Jouvry. She thought nobody knew and we all pretended we didn't, but she did. Not after Tom.

'Jack and his wife, their baby died.' She was crying again, softly. 'And the wife, she's gone crazy. They've put her in Bedlam. Where they queue up and pay money to see the lunatics, used to.'

'It's the Royal Bethlem now. It's a fine hospital. They'll make her better.'

'Mad as a badger.'

She leant over the seat to pick up her bag. He took her in his arms and kissed her. She was still crying a little and gently again he blotted the tears, this time on the other sleeve. He knew it wasn't about the baby or the woman or her husband, or about them: it was Daisy.

'Go and see her. You'll make her happy.'

'I will. First thing next week. She's my sister. And I love her.'

As he drove away, he passed the car he was looking for, and briefly flicked his lights.

○ ○ ○

Daisy surveyed the flat with a feeling of satisfaction. Now it was bright and clean and smelt faintly of bleach.

A stage perfectly set, its apparatus correctly disposed. She stroked the leather strop and admired its craftsmanship. Fruit of the earth – indirectly – and work of human hands.

One more appointment, and it wouldn't do to catch cold.

She wrapped herself up in her warmest coat and locked the front door behind her.

○ ○ ○

Jack walked upstairs, past the small bedroom. It hadn't been right to throw away her things – her cot, her toys, her baby clothes, her packages of clean nappies – and he wasn't upset to look at them. But he wouldn't dwell on them, and one day they could go. It would take time to adapt to the house being empty, but it must be. What had to be faced together had first to be faced alone, and there could be no life in the past. If the future was to contain love, it must be made in the present.

○ ○ ○

Saturday afternoon, the dog watch of the confessional. Fr Julius Melendez thought it was a good day to sin. The possibilities of greed in the weekly shop, the indulgence of extending Friday night's extempore fuck with a new and exciting lover into a weekend of languorous excess – perhaps with Stilton – and the lazy delight of a lunchtime drink blending into a welcoming oblivion. None of these did he begrudge his parishioners. As the poet had written – or was it St Paul? – human kind cannot bear very much reality.

The church was empty. Fr Melendez put aside his breviary and opened Forgotten Secrets of Professional Jam Makers by Evangeline Patropi at his bookmark, a title which sometimes puzzled him. Surely, Remembered?

A quarter of an hour later, enlightened as ever – this time on the setting point of apricot conserve – he closed the book, and switched off the light in the confessional.

There was a grand aisle along the centre of the church, from the main entrance doors – seldom used – to the principal altar, with seats on either side. In addition there were chapels with their altars along the side walls, with smaller aisles passing through them, giving three ways to pass from the back to the front of the church and the door which led to the priests' communal house.

Fr Melendez chose the one on the right, because it led through the chapel of St Mary Magdalene – the saint with whom he felt the greatest empathy – and he saw on reaching it that he had been wrong to assume that the church was empty.

∘ ∘ ∘

'If it's on the tip of your tongue.'

Rachel thought that Saturday was an unreasonable day to be questioned, however oddly. She had earlier replied '"The Beach Beneath The Street, The everyday life and glorious times of the Situationist International"', adding – to Sarah Carpenter's further question – author, publisher, date, and did she want the ISBN?

Rachel gave it without hesitation, because to a bookseller, the content of the title page verso is a small piece of heaven.

Sarah Carpenter wrote everything down.

∘ ∘ ∘

But she had only just arrived.

Fr Melendez wondered if she had come for confession and, finding it closed, knelt instead to pray.

He recognised her, the Ballantyne girl, from the funeral of her father, and more specifically because of the reception which followed it. Now as then he was struck by Daisy's beauty and a quality of – innocence?

No.

It was an older virtue, acquired only by its complement, experience. Resolution. And it chilled him because he had only before seen the look on her face on murderers, and suicides. He wondered whether to ask her if she had come for confession, but it seemed intrusive. Instead, he nodded politely and passed on his way.

There was a particular reason why he recognised her.

Fr Melendez was used to resisting the magnificence of

231

sexuality, perhaps even more so than Saint Anthony. Nightly he passed the winsome scullery maids of the Museum of Natural History at the corners of Exhibition Road, and heard their siren whisper: 'Forests of enchantment not on general display'. The scholars of the Organ College, too, with their brazen placards: 'Skin flute for raps and rhapsody'. But like everyone else, he was a fool for love.

He remembered the instant he had met Rachel Fonseca. Fr Julius was well-practised in the consoling small-talk relevant to a funeral reception, and when he turned to find her beside him, ready, he could see, to ask a question, the firing chamber of his unconscious was already primed with a useful platitude.

That was when he looked at her, and when she looked at him.

He blurted out: 'I can't hear your confession because I'm in love with you', and she 'I've never before met an honest man' / he: 'I've never met you before' / she: 'That's a fact' / he: 'I mean, what you are.'

She: 'Can I tell you that I love you?'

He had fallen in love? No, he had risen, and not in sexual innuendo. He had seemed to be looking up at her as if she was standing a little above him, inviting his ascension, and theirs together.

They giggled.

She hadn't spoken first, hadn't asked for confession. It was why she had so carefully approached him, and he had known. Known too that it was impossible to slink away from the reception to the church like two new lovers looking for a secret place of transaction. And they had never seen each other again, which was not the same as forgetting.

So it was dear Fr Leidenberg, honest and compassionate to his parishioners, a notorious fouler of his opponents in the annual charity football match against the priests and faithful of the London Oratory round the corner who, the next day, sat patiently in the confessional listening to her dreadful words.

○ ○ ○

Daisy knelt in the chapel of the Magdalene and wondered how many men she'd had. She grinned at Magda sharing her name. The painting over the altar showed St Mary looking up into sunlight, and she was glad that she'd found someone to love in the end. Not in the conventional sense, it was true, but someone who couldn't be lost.

Rachel was having a phase of Graham Greene with two copies of some. Daisy had borrowed one of The Heart of the Matter from which it was clear to her that confession was out of the question. But she wanted to be present to God, to ask if it was possible that by what she would do he would not turn his face from her. She walked to the back of the church – it would be vain to go to the front – and sat down, looking towards the altar. She apologised for returning herself, and that it wasn't his fault she'd fucked everything up.

○ ○ ○ ○ ○

9

Tom drowns when his lover Daisy's merchant ship is wrecked. He finds himself in an afterlife.

MR MAGRUDER ROWED nowhere in particular and Lake Baikal was gorgeously blue. There should have been waves, or at least a waver in their wake. But the surface remained placid, reflective as a mirror. Sugar Popsicle lay back in the prow gazing at the sun. Tom sat with the commissar under the canopy at the stern. All that was missing was a picnic. A wicker basket? Willow-pattern plates? Another story he could never remember, nor the significance of the bridge. Paté de foie gras? Jackson's tea – probably.

'I'm guessing this is a place of rectification?'

Magruder looked around, as if seeing it for the first time.

'A place of possibilities, Tom. I'll give you that. For doubtful cases.'

Tom felt a sudden elation, and with it the wariness that depression, the deflation of reality, might follow. 'Then I'm an optimist.' He laughed, and didn't care if he sounded like an idiot.

'Like Scrooge with the revelation of dreams?' enquired the commissar.

'Chance of a change.' He sang out the words, never minding

they were out of tune.

'There is scope for optimism.'

'I want to start living.'

Sugar Popsicle took a box of paints from the front locker, sticks of charcoal, and a wad of blank postcards. He began to sketch, rapid strokes, on card after card. He squeezed paint from tubes onto a white china palette – vivid colours, the brightest of blues, greens, pinks and magentas. Dipping a brush into the water, he laid down a wash on each of the cards. Once dry – a matter of seconds, Tom noticed – he blocked in colours, added highlights, finished each of them off with the finest of detailing and tossed them into the lake. As they floated away, Tom thrilled to their beauty.

Magruder pulled up the oars and for a while the boat continued with its momentum. Gently he said 'You can't love in the absence of the loved one.'

Tom knew it be true but it was Magruder's earlier caution that had stayed in his mind, shadowing it like a cloud. And clouds were only water. Time. I had no time, and now I have no time.

The commissar took his hand in hers.

I wasted or deferred time.

I reasoned there'd be time in the future, but now there is no time. Time could have been timed by useful notches – giving, good deeds, external actions. Instead I measured time in cups of coffee.

There was no doubt that they knew his thoughts as if he had spoken aloud. Even the fishes might. He looked at his new friends and spoke defiantly.

'Even worse – not milky Italian coffee from greasy-spoons in Museum Street, alleys off Tottenham Court Road, traditional expresso bars where Cliff Richard was discovered hard-by Tin Pan Alley, but American triple-shot extravaganzas in cardboard beakers. Un-recycled.'

He hoped that the commissar was familiar with the layout of streets around north-east Soho and wondered if it would be polite to provide a general description. To his relief, he saw Magruder discreetly pass her an A-Z, open at the page.

'I wasted the time allocated, the six-and-a-half-million seconds of a lifetime, three million pants, to introspection.'

The calculation could be wrong. Tom wished he had the reliable mechanical calculator from the bottom-right deep drawer of his office desk, with which he manually checked the distances of vessels across the curve of the ocean. These, he had found, differed entirely from those which might be supposed from Mercator's flat – though otherwise useful – projections.

I built a redoubt against ambuscade, perfectly sealed, and burrowed inside, no doorway, no entrance for the income of offered emotion.

Mr Magruder examined the rowlocks, finely-made and bronzed. He lifted each up in turn, and wiped them with a cloth dipped in linseed oil. Having replaced and checked them for balance, he inserted the oars and resumed rowing. He looked encouragingly at Tom, as did the commissar. Even Sugar Popsicle listened. Tom was surprised. Normally people didn't listen much to him, and often didn't bother to mask their lack of interest. He knew he was a bore, but at least he didn't have bad breath.

'I was solid. I didn't use my isolation to preach, hypocritise, pedestalise, pretend superiority. I looked down nor up, nor level. I neither ignored nor participated, I remained neutral, not married, single, never engaged. I voted the status quo, paid bills, tax, wrote "moderate" in satisfaction surveys, bought reasonable groceries: hand-thrown mascarpone, 8-percent wine from Eastern Europe. Never felled a tree, never owned a cat. I had the opportunity to stand and be loved. I sat. I had the chance to give my heart and penis – emotional offal tied in a pretty blue bow – to risk my love by creating it, allowing it to release to someone else ready to love me. I had no time, and now there is no time.'

∘ ∘ ∘

The lake began to freeze. Magruder tied the boat up at a jetty and led them ashore to find that Dr Friday had arrived. He had built a fire for them on the beach, and was roasting potatoes (lightly salted). They sat around it, warm in sable coats and hoods and sable boots; gloves and pink noses. An old enamelled kettle full of milk bubbled on a cooler part of the fire. Friday stirred in chocolate powder and poured a cup for each of them, together with a baked potato wrapped in a napkin.

Filled, they encouraged Tom to continue. Sugar Popsicle and the commissar gestured that he should stand. Tom rose to his feet and addressed them.

'If time existed, could be caught between my two hands, if I could swallow and exhale it, pummel it, I would throw away myself.

'I would offer her – my one beloved woman – Daisy – my – I would no longer exercise the petty restraint that could hold back the word – darling – the full love that my suddenly-opened heart releases.

'And – if she should judge my complete love worthy of and acceptable to herself – cherish her.

'I would be her love.

'She would be my love.

'And all would be complete.'

o o o

Magruder leapt to his feet and shook him vigorously by the hand.

'Good man' he said. 'Good man.'

There was a sniffle from Sugar Popsicle.

Doctor Friday embraced him. 'Jolly damn fine show.'

Magruder looked around the group, and then to Tom, with the formality – but the warmth – of an external examiner pronouncing on a thesis well done.

'I believe, Mr Devine. Yes. You may say goodbye.'

Doctor Friday disclosed a bottle of Veuve Clicquot and a handful of glasses. Quietly and without a toast, they drank to each other, with occasional tears.

'Dear Madame Commissar.' Tom slipped his arm round her.

He wiped her eyes with a clean handkerchief and kissed her.

Together, they looked at the lake – iced, inviting, and brilliant in the sun.

'There are no beaux now' she said. 'I wondered. Would you skate with me?'

10

Mrs Ballantyne and the late Captain Ballantyne bring up their natural daughter Rowena, their adopted daughter Daisy, and their niece Rachel Fonseca as sisters. Emilio Podro loves Rowena. He is an old acquaintance of Mrs Ballantyne. The bombed-out City of London is redesigned as an enclosed and segregated Square Mile City by the architectural practice of Dianita (Diana) Lapraman and Helen Landesman. Dianita commits suicide. Helen becomes disillusioned. Rachel is investigated about a plot against Square Mile City. Daisy's lover Tom drowns. Daisy is increasingly distressed because of his death.

EMILIO PODRO DROVE round the back of the Expatriate Trading Company in Knightsbridge to the section of the store known colloquially as the Foreigners' Supermarket. Exclusive to diplomats and tax-free, it sold them imported and scarce goods not available to the public.

What was on the shelves depended on what had arrived and from where. There was a glut of rum today – ten different colours and flavours in a shipment from Cuba – and, among other surprises, cases of canned sardines, pilchards, baby food, gin, corned beef, tins of chocolates from Shanghai, Spam.

Emilio strolled among the rows of goods. Catching sight of

something very special, he exclaimed with delight. How she would be thrilled! He bought two cartons, and chocolates for Rowena, and loaded them into the boot of the car.

∘ ∘ ∘

Helen Landesman looked at her new Rolex watch. She wouldn't dive to 200 metres and the calendar in her diary was enough. But the weight was comfortable, and she felt it said the right things. Shallow? It told the time. 14:00, Saturday. Helen was ready for bed. She'd worked through the night.

Her report had gone the day before. She'd spent the time since fine-tuning her answers to the storm that was bound to follow.

'A Separate Future Together' wouldn't make her friends – it was more like a rattlesnake among pigeons. But friends were something a strong leader must do without.

Helen hadn't used the sleeping tablets before, and wondered how many to take. She washed them down with water and fell asleep, clutching a photograph of Gretl.

∘ ∘ ∘

'It's an interesting analysis of Situationist theory.'

Sarah Carpenter looked meaningfully at Rachel. Rachel stared at her without interest.

'Am I expected to comment? Or are you an admirer of Guy Debord?'

'A lot of women were.'

'In which case may I recommend The Society of the Spectacle? He wasn't a great writer but there is some originality. Marx is there – and substantial borrowings from Hegel.' Rachel smiled slightly.

'"Never Work."'

'"Be at war with the world, but lightly." Platitudes by the dozen. Douzaine, being French.'

'Very good.' Sarah Carpenter took a document out of her bag. 'And the one we're interested in is his best-known quote, and indeed the central thesis of his work: "Divided We Stand". I believe you will know the corollary.'

She laid the document on the table facing Rachel so that she could read the title: "Square Mile City / Human Geography /

Summary Report / A Separate Future Together".

Rachel flicked through a couple of pages and handed it back.

'Helen Landesman is the human blotting paper of ideas she doesn't understand.'

'You of course do.'

Rachel wasn't paying attention. An odd feeling which she couldn't specify had crept into her. She knew it was important. It was stupidly elusive. Fear: and not for herself.

Their words passed over her. The usefulness of book codes, requiring only identical pairs. The limited and excellent vocabulary of a Graham Greene novel: 2,000 key words of common speech. The large and specialist vocabulary of The Beach Beneath The Street: 30,000 words including many of classical revolutionary theory.

If Rachel were herself, she knew that she would be bothered to point out that – if that were true – a book of 90,000 words would have one in three unique. Ridiculous.

Sarah Carpenter waved a hand in front of her face.

'Are you with us?'

'I have to go.'

'All right.'

Rachel stood, put on her coat, grabbed her bag.

'Can you drive me?'

'Within reason.'

'I have to go to my cousin.'

'Daisy Ballantyne?'

'I have to go now.'

'Is something wrong?'

'I have to go now.'

Rachel was shocked that she was screaming.

'Adam, will you drive Rachel? Or would you prefer me?'

'I don't fucking care which of you it is.' She felt sweat break out on the small of her back, forced herself to breath slowly. 'Excuse me, I don't mean to be rude. Adam. Please.'

After they had gone, Sarah Carpenter dropped her shorthand pad on the floor. She slid the bolt on the door and sat at the table. Out of habit she spoke to the ceiling, knowing that she could as easily speak to the floor.

'All clear?'

A voice replied 'Clear and complete. A useful idiot.'

∘ ∘ ∘

It was good to be home.

Not home. More like a bus stop, with a guess and a hope (but no definite idea) where the bus might go.

Daisy had decided not to leave a note: every life was only a different combination of the same clichés. All the gifts and experiences, the toys and half-successes, wrapped in a sheet of paper – explained, excused. Not worth reading.

Standing in the shower. Shampooing her hair, the soap not in her eyes, foam rinsing gracefully from her body. All the laundry into the rubbish chute. Nothing left that wasn't clean. She dressed carefully.

Brush your hair.

Of course.

∘ ∘ ∘

Two things occurred to Rowena.

There was no time like the present. Her mother would say that – was indeed saying it from the other room.

And the keys hanging up in the cupboard under the stairs were the spares to Daisy's flat.

With the excuse of returning them, Rowena set off at once.

If Daisy was out, she would let herself in. She would leave the keys on her kitchen table with flowers – and the tin of chocolates from Shanghai which Emilio had given her with promises of more to come. But I would give them to her if they were my last. Sisterhood may have arrived late, but now that it's here, I shall do it properly.

And there is no time like the present.

∘ ∘ ∘

Sarah Carpenter sat in the projection room listening to the playback. She doodled on her shorthand pad, making faces out of the limited opportunities offered by Teeline and wondering if there was time left in life to learn Pitman. She realised she liked Rachel, wasn't sure why.

Rachel was such a mixture of themes: often stylish, in a way

241

conventional, passionate. And with that little dash of feral which occasionally showed in her eyes, like a hare only mad in March. A nearly woman: nearly revolutionary.

And nearly mother – that was the difficult item.

Sarah Carpenter signalled to the projectionist. He switched off the lights and ran the film.

The camera pointed into the basement of Bound To Be Red from the staircase. It was above and behind Rachel, who stood a few steps up from her audience – standing – catching the 50 or so upturned faces clearly enough for identification. The back of Rachel's head was in the lower foreground so that the film showed them almost exactly as Rachel would see them: searching for their reaction, adjusting her delivery. An extra microphone delivered each nuance of her voice: natural, trustworthy, comradely, tutorly, mildly hectoring, theatrical whisper.

Flickering lighting, warm colour. Candle-light? Bodies and necks in darkness. Rembrandt – The Nightwatch, perhaps, or Belshazzar's Feast? Their faces focussed on her, valuing each word. Towards enraptured, short of fanatical.

Rachel began with Marx, great philosopher blah blah. Wat Tyler, Peasants' Revolt first English revolution, The Levellers, workshop manual of revolutionary tools, blah blah. And then:

'Do remember that to oppose capitalism and the ordered society implies that both are valid. They are not. Draw inspiration from the Situationist International of the 20th Century, Gary Debord in particular. May I commend The Society of the Spectacle, 1967, revolutionary politics.

'Marx is there – and substantial borrowings from Hegel.'

[Laughter]

'"Never Work" said Debord. "Divided We Stand". "Be at war with the world" he said, "but lightly." And every day, play Le Jeu de la Guerre.

'Let these words be our little red catechism.'

[Some cheers]

'Let us be the women and men Thoreau would have described as "truly awake". This is only possible by brushing against death.'

Carpenter wriggled in her seat. Playtime revolutionaries gathered round teacher for an afternoon story. She was tired and wanted to go home, lie in a bath for an hour, sleep.

On Monday she would ask for a complete staff list of Square Mile City Development Corporation and compare it with the list of Rachel Fonseca's associates, but only as routine.

'What is life? Periods of what others call irrationality. Periods of intense perception, heightened physical pleasure. The illusion of hallucination. The usual things we feel every day: paranoia, anguish, the knowledge of being forgotten. The absence of the fear of death.'

Fonseca's voice had become subdued, reflective, her speech rate slow, her head and – in tune – those of her audience slightly lowered. She looked up and spoke briskly.

'Smash. Burn. Delete. Ravage. It's a practical slogan.

'Here's another.' She took a stiletto knife from her bag, held up the blade. 'Kill one, frighten a thousand.

'Imagine the placid surface of a great untenanted lake. A single, unfamous, assassination is like a brick dropped casually into its centre. No man is an island. We are all part of the continent. The ripples reach as far as Surbiton, Tunbridge Wells, and all the way to Acacia Avenue.

'And to every home in which placid families live placid lives in the placid expectation of a placid future, a common purpose, a hopeful tomorrow.'

She replaced it, slipped her hands into her pockets.

'How much more lively to die pointlessly, unexpectedly. How much more glamorous to be a ripple, perhaps a wave. With your individual blade, create a small node of unbalance.

'And always remember: if you hear the bullet, you aren't dead.'

Sarah Carpenter yawned. Compared with what happened daily on the streets, this was trivia. The police? The file would come back with a polite note – we have no time.

She thanked the projectionist and went up to her office, intending to pick up her bag and go home. But once there, and surrounded by the things that she must do, should do, or push into the future, she slumped into her desk chair and put her head in her hands. Normally she didn't drink at the office, but there was an emergency bottle of cheap Scotch in the filing cabinet for communal use. Sarah filled a cleanish mug half full and swigged it down.

243

Sometimes – now – she felt overwhelmed. Logically, she knew that she was tired, and that after a day's rest she would see things in perspective. She thought of her parents, how they loved what she had achieved. And her? She wondered, knowing at the same time that she was being stupid. Of course they did. Didn't they?

Pride of place at their house was given to a table of photographs of her childhood. On the wall, there were framed certificates from her first swimming proficiency test – aged four – to her graduation, post-graduation, doctorate and every step of her professional career. Putting the shot had defeated her – not stocky enough – and the long jump – not long enough. No certificates for those. Neither for javelin, though her javelin had not been bad at all. The wall did however record excellence in skiing, gliding; long-distance running, high jump – and parachuting, something she hoped she would never have to do again.

She got on with people. Her colleagues liked her, and she liked them. She had enough money, believed what she did for a living was right and fair, remembered the quality of mercy when in doubt, had just enough savings for emergencies, her own flat, and an office car when she needed one. She should look at herself as others did, which seemed to be with approval, and often affection.

But for the moment, all Sarah Carpenter could feel was a lack of hope and – deep inside herself – despair.

∘ ∘ ∘

Rowena wondered how much longer the bus would stop for a change of driver. She'd bought a card: a smiling cat. Did cats really smile? She didn't know. Did Daisy like cats? She couldn't remember. The human menagerie plus dog and donkey had been enough. The choice in the shop had been a view of the Thames – Rowena thought water and ships weren't tactful. She wrote carefully and added a kiss. One didn't look right, and two was French and meaningless. She put three and sealed the envelope.

∘ ∘ ∘

Adam Brook looked quickly around as he drove out of the office basement into Portsmouth Street by the Old Curiosity Shop.

They'd run from the lift to find a flat tyre on the car, and he was sweating from the speed of changing the wheel, aware for every second of Rachel's extreme anxiety.

To his relief, the streets around Lincoln's Inn Fields were quiet and empty, and he negotiated them fast without incident. A mob rocked the car as they passed the fringes of a riot in Regent's Park, but it was a Saturday afternoon mob out for the fun of it, and all the damage amounted to a smashed headlight and a melon hurled against the windscreen, splattering it with red flesh.

∘ ∘ ∘

Daisy went into her bedroom and closed the door.

'Are you there Tom? Do you want to watch me undressing?'

She spoke softly, to wherever he might be.

Daisy began to take off her clothes, dropping them to the floor.

'I know you're watching. How close are you? If I reach out my hand, am I touching you?

'You can wank if you like. Actually I want you to wank. Is wanking allowed?'

There must be a protocol. Like Gormenghast.

'I'm a quick learner. I'll be Master of the Ritual. Did you know he was one of the first into Belsen? Yes. In 1945. With the army. A war artist. Yes, I didn't know.

'What he saw – he went mad. So Titus Groan, Gormenghast – and Titus Alone – but that wasn't very good, even his most die-hard fans admit that – with a grudge, but they admit it – are the kingdoms of a madman. They read like it, don't they?

'Is it like that?'

Shall the first thing we talk about be books?

I'm stripping for you.

'I can belly-dance.'

I trained. I'm not sure if an evening class at the City Literary Institute counts as trained, but I know you won't mind.

The open razor beside the bed, sharp. I'm disgusted by the process, but the destination is magnificent. Why be distracted from the beauty by the means?

Naked now, she looked for him encouragingly.

'Are you watching? Are you peeping through your fingers? Are you frightened? Don't be. It's only me.

'You can't wait to hold me, can you? You can't wait to sink yourself inside me.

'Do you like to watch me? Secretly? So you don't think I think you're watching me? Do you want to see me doing what you think I might be doing when I think I'm alone?'

Daisy cupped her hands under her breasts. She winked.

'Do you like these? You can weigh them in your hands. You can say "Weh-hey-hey". You can be vulgar about me – and I won't care. I know that you love me. You can flick these. I will prefer if you kiss them.

'Do you like this? Do you like inside here?

'It's all yours.'

The duvet had been washed, and its cover – all bright and white – and the pillows too. Daisy plumped them up and lay on top of the bed, stretched out her arms, marking the position of the radial and ulnar arteries with her fingers. She picked up the razor.

'Are you squeamish?'

Watch carefully.

'Do you like this? It goes here. And here.'

'You didn't like it? Come on – that wasn't real. These are the main lines.

'So don't look. I'll tell you when.'

Daisy checked the bedside clock to make sure the alarm was off. There was nothing more irritating than an absent neighbour's alarm.

The bright red second-hand swept round to the top.

'30 seconds. Counting?'

'Look away, Tommy. I'm coming home.'

○ ○ ○ ○ ○

11

Mrs Ballantyne and the late Captain Ballantyne bring up their natural daughter Rowena, their adopted daughter Daisy, and their niece Rachel Fonseca as sisters. Rachel is under investigation for radical activities by civil servants Adam Brook and Sarah Carpenter. Daisy's lover Tom drowns in the loss at sea of her merchant ship. In sudden concern for her, Rachel and Rowena hurry towards her flat, unaware that she has already killed herself.

THE PHONE CALL only lasted a couple of minutes and Adam Brook wasn't sure if he should be sombre or light and breezy. He took a look at Rachel's worried face staring ahead, and settled for breezy.

'Good news. No more me.'

She didn't reply; her hands were clenched.

'Sarah says bye bye. We don't have to see you again.'

'Can we just get there?'

'Sure.'

He didn't know if he should say, that means me personally too, means us, if there is an us. He took another sideways look, and decided to shut up and drive.

○ ○ ○

Rowena Ballantyne got off the bus at the corner of Fortune Green Road, walked the two minutes to Godolphin Gardens, and climbed the stairs to Daisy's front door. She rang the bell. There was no reply. She found the right key, and let herself in.

○ ○ ○

Not all the barristers, judges and solicitors whose offices and chambers surrounded Lincoln's Inn Fields were at home for the weekend. One particular judge sat at her desk in chambers catching up on her backlog of cases, starting with those which could be regarded as routine.

The verdict for The Department of Transport Marine Accident Investigation Branch Inquiry into the loss of Turmoil had seemed to the court to be straightforward at the time of the hearing. To refresh herself, she had the previous afternoon re-read her notes and summaries of the evidence. In some parts, she had gone to their detail.

Fully informed, she began the writing of her reasoned judgment, for issue to the parties in the coming week.

○ ○ ○

Adam Brook didn't ask Rachel if she wanted him to come up with her. He knew that he must. Pulling fast into the kerb, he raced after her as she got through the outside door by jamming her hand on all the buzzers and saying 'delivery'. He was right behind her as she ran up the stairs.

Rachel stopped as she saw Rowena.

○ ○ ○

Rowena was sitting on the landing – a marble floor, cold and uncomfortable. Never anything but graceless, she looked like a toy someone had thrown away.

The door to Daisy's flat was closed behind her, and she got up and backed against it. She put her hands on Rachel's shoulders to keep her away, but Rachel knew that it was without malice, rather for Rachel's protection.

She put her arms around Rowena and drew her to her; felt her arms come down and under her own, slip around her back. She held her cousin, patting her head, letting it rest on her shoulder.

'It's a bloody mess, Rachel.'

Rachel rocked her gently, waited until she became calm. After a while Rowena went to the car with Adam Brook.

∘ ∘ ∘

Seeing Daisy, Rachel surprised herself by kneeling down. She said a prayer, and smiled as she remembered.

'Your fucking catholicism.'

'You have it too, Daisy.'

'Not by birth. Only by infection.'

She comes into your life and fills it, and one day she's gone. There isn't much you can put your finger on. When she was here, days fizzed, days jumped. Daisy had – éclat de rire.

The bed and part of the wall were a mixture of blood colours. Rachel thought: a good part of 5 litres, neat work, gold star from a surgeon. There was blood over her face, in her hair, all over her body. No elegance. She looked like a dead cow before division into edible parts.

But she would have dignity. Rachel fetched a double sheet from the airing cupboard. She covered Daisy, leaned over and kissed her lovely face.

∘ ∘ ∘ ∘ ∘

12

Mrs Ballantyne and the late Captain Ballantyne bring up
their natural daughter Rowena, their adopted daughter
Daisy, and their niece Rachel Fonseca as sisters. Helen
Landesman, new director of Square Mile City – replacing
the City of London – has prepared a report for its design.
Father Julius Melendez, a priest at the Church of the
Madonna of Sorrows in London is in love with Rachel. Her
radical activities are investigated by the authorities and
dismissed as amateur. Daisy commits suicide after the
death of her lover Tom. Mrs Ballantyne had once
attempted to arrange a meeting between her and her
real mother, but this did not work out. Rowena blossoms
out of her reclusive life in the love of South American
diplomat Emilio Podro, a long-standing friend of her
mother. Daisy's natural father drowned in an accident
due to the negligence of naval submarine Instructor
Captain Verry, now an old woman. The late Captain
Ballantyne was responsible for her court-martial and
imprisonment, in revenge for which she has previously
tried to kill Mrs Ballantyne.

THE LANDESMAN REPORT was greeted with sniggers.
Everyone in the Development Corporation thought she had been
promoted above her ability. This, they agreed, confirmed it.

Dianita – there was a leader. Even crazy Jo-Jo O'Brien – with
his dipsy ideas and tropical rainforests every hundred floors – had
charisma. Helen Landesman was a nonentity, an amateur
fumbling with social engineering.

At best utopian, at worst segregationist, her report was an
embarrassment. The consensus was that she would have to go –
accompanied by a shrugged acceptance that nothing survived like
incompetence.

○ ○ ○

On the Tuesday, Fr Julius said early morning mass in the Saint
Mary Magdalene chapel. He had chosen the international form of

250

service for the benefit of visitors to the museums, careful to pronounce his Latin with a modern Italian inflection.

The delightful painting of the chapel's saint by Victoriano Codina y Langlin was the trophy of the annual football match between the Church of the Madonna of Sorrows and the London Oratory, won for the home team this year via a particularly vicious tackle by Fr Leidenberg.

Born in 1844 in Barcelona, dying in London in 1911 the artist had, Fr Julius reflected, straddled the century, straddled Europe, and probably many of the hundreds of bountiful and enthusiastically naked women featured in his works.

His rendering of St Mary Magdalene – kneeling quietly in prayer – was by contrast restrained, demure and fully clothed. Inspirational too, capturing her passion, a sense of her humility, and the warmth of her love.

It was when he turned to hold up the wafer of bread symbolising the body of Christ to the congregation that he saw Rachel. For a moment he stumbled to remember the words, before they came automatically out his mouth. Behold God, who takes away sin.

Fr Julius's classes for adults on sex in marriage and forays without were well-attended. Partly, he suspected, because – although bound not to express them in action – he shared the same desires. Partly too, because he came straight to the point in direct language.

His cock, therefore, rather than its medical term, stood on end to the extent that his trousers permitted, and he thanked God in person for the invention of vestments.

Rachel walked with the others to the communion rail. Her arms were crossed over her chest – the sign given by those not wishing to receive the communion wafer, or in serious sin, that they would like instead to be blessed.

A veil lay delicately over her hair; her jacket and skirt were black

Rachel looked straight into his eyes, and smiled.

They hadn't met since the first time, and every day in between she had been with him. He found himself smiling back, stunned for the moments before he recollected himself, placed his hands on her head and said the words of blessing.

He knew that she had come to say goodbye, and that he would never see her again.

○ ○ ○

The first bomb went off around midnight on the Wednesday, followed quickly by the second and third. Competently integrated with the structure, they destroyed the foundations of Square Mile City.

When they came to her house, they found it empty. Rachel had gone.

○ ○ ○

Rowena knew some of the people at Daisy's funeral, and others introduced themselves to her before the service. It was odd to be in charge, and it had worried her in the days of preparation.

Now it had arrived, she found herself competent.

Daisy's will – terse and even to a lay reader unambiguous – had shocked her. But that wasn't the reason she felt as she did today. It was a matter of duty – the duty to complete what her father had undertaken, and he had done it gracefully. She knew that grace didn't come naturally to her – to be frank, it didn't come at all – but she would give it her best shot.

Her mother was unusually well-behaved.

Rowena didn't know Jack Jouvry well, but liked him for turning up. He introduced a couple called Gretl and Jo-Jo who had married in the church – the woman sounded German and her face was slightly familiar.

Rowena had put on a black dress. Seeing it and her at the church, Emilio said she looked OK. She thought he looked OK, so that was two. He had chosen the uniform of naval attaché, which fitted in tactfully with the merchant and naval uniforms on some of the congregation.

Magda Baklanova explained who she was.

Colman didn't come, and in a way she wasn't surprised. Rowena had never called him Reilly, and certainly never Skunk. He'd been there since before she was born, and mainly she remembered being carried around on his shoulders. He was devoted to her, and later to Daisy, and to Rachel too – which for some reason had never made her jealous. It was perhaps that he was generous in his quiet affection: when giving it to one, there was no feeling of holding it back from another. Rowena knew that he felt deeply, and understood if he had thought it best to stay away.

Rowena missed Rachel. How funny. Days before, she'd have been thrilled never to see her again. Now, everything had changed. She must put out of her head that she was worried about her, until today was over.

The captain of Strident Bucephalus attended with his Third Officer, a pretty woman called Isabella Berthonella with gorgeous tousled black hair.

'I didn't know your sister well' she said, 'but I did love her.'

'Same here.'

They both laughed. Rowena wasn't used to being able to think of even half-clever things to say at the right time or ever; not things that made people laugh and perhaps opened the door. I am not familiar with being liked, but I could like to become accustomed to it.

It didn't matter that the wedding was delayed. It would find its time, and possibly bridesmaids. Two down, none to go.

∘ ∘ ∘

Fr Melendez had been spoken to – or rather, he thought with amusement, given orders – by Mrs Ballantyne. No woffle, sanctimony, no religious clichés. An adequate though sufficient amount of God. No rubbish about the celebration of a life. A proper funeral, with relevant music, and nothing from Saint Paul.

And accurate. She would be consigned – more in a moment – with her birth name of Tanechka Krestyanova and that for her new country, Daisy. Titania had been her parents' original idea, queen from a dream. As a baby, she was Tatti – little potato. Mrs Ballantyne had smiled. Dreamed, and lost.

Of course – Mrs Ballantyne had explained – as a suicide, burial was impossible. It would be correct, therefore, for her adopted daughter to be cremated and her ashes cast upon the ocean.

Fr Melendez replied that burial in consecrated ground was perfectly in order. Would it not also be kinder for Daisy to be buried in the name of the family in which she had – most

253

generously – been raised, and by which she was known?

Mrs Ballantyne gave way to the name, and remained adamant on cremation. Duly briefed, Fr Melendez prepared to address the congregation.

∘ ∘ ∘

The arrival of the telegram hadn't surprised Dr Jo-Jo O'Brien. There really wasn't anyone else, he supposed, they could call on at short notice – or call on, full stop. It could be the moment to return to the helm.

He'd asked for a copy of the Landesman report, and found in it volcanic possibilities – a nightmare mishmash of Noam Chomsky, Hans Eysenck, Karl Marx, Mein Kampf, Guy Debord, Michele Bernstein, Asger Jorn and More. Utopia, dystopia – neither could work here. But a meeting of the two – not a bad idea for a nation of compromise.

∘ ∘ ∘

'The old taboos of suicide are long obsolete.'

It was difficult to begin a sermon on death without the vapid and comforting words everyone expected so Fr Melendez had decided to plunge straight in.

∘ ∘ ∘

The German woman was there, a neat circuit of knotted hair on top of the rest like a children-kitchen-church hausfrau.

Fr Salman Jardine – never a patient man – had endured weeks of preparation for the ceremony of her marriage and finally got it over with, releasing his self-control only at her final confrontation with the organist to the Madonna of Sorrows, Dr Hayden Gombrich.

As bride-to-be and musician shouted at each other in German – Germans always seemed to shout, Fr Melendez thought, wondering if it was wrong to have presuppositions about God's creation, even in the case of the Germans – over the choice of music, Fr Jardine finally snapped.

'Stop fucking shouting.'

His tone silenced them.

'This is the house of God.'

Bride and groom walked down the aisle to Wagner's Ride of the

Valkyries, straining the Grand Organ – an early example of Reginald Goss-Custard's masterful engineering – and choir of the Madonna to their limits, and making Dr Hayden Gombrich a happy man.

○ ○ ○

Fr Melendez stared at his prompt card.

God's love.

What had he meant? That God loves us as we are, sees beyond the breaking of a rule, has mercy, aches to forgive?

'Yes. God loves every stupid, clumsy, burnt-cake mistake that we make.'

○ ○ ○

150 of the 750 seats in front of him were filled, concentrated at the front.

Towards the rear and left, a middle-aged woman sat alone, dour and skinny-faced, dressed for a funeral. At the back on the other side a dog lay on the floor by itself, apparently asleep, perhaps come from the street for the warmth. Or perhaps, Fr Julius thought – all creatures great and small – even the dumb animals are drawn to God. Two older men sat together in the middle of the empty seats – a couple maybe – paying attention to what he was saying. What am I saying?

'It's been on my conscience that perhaps I could have saved her life.'

It seemed natural to confess – how he'd wondered if she had wanted to and hadn't asked. Opportunity passed.

'God doesn't think there's anything wrong with being in love.'

And should death be the end of it?

The familiar glazed looks from the congregation, primed for a funeral, comprehension disengaged.

'I'm under orders from Daisy's mother not to give you the words of the apostle directly appointed by God.' Smiles. 'But it is impossible to talk about the love between a woman and man and its transcendence of death without him. Allow me therefore to quote to you from Paul.'

○ ○ ○

Fr Melendez noticed an old woman standing by the door peering

255

at the congregation, and recognised her from the photograph they'd shown him.

At the end of the sermon and as the altar girls – twin daughters of the organist, confirmed atheists at the age of nine and meticulous in their sacramental duties – prepared water and wine for the service, he left the altar and telephoned the number he had been given.

Reluctantly, he unlocked the drawer containing the Glock 17 service pistol kept for emergencies and loaded a magazine. When he returned the woman had gone, and the choir was singing Lacrimosa.

o o o

Dr Hayden Gombrich was unused to acting upon his dreams, but the suggestion of the opening chorus of Bach's Saint John Passion to accompany the final procession of the coffin to the waiting car met with the full approval of his conscious mind.

Daisy therefore departed to the choir's rousing delivery of 'Herr, unser Herrscher, dessen Ruhm in allen Landen herrlich ist!' – which he had hastily translated for their understanding as 'Lord, our master whose fame is wonderful throughout the world' – their voices joined by a member of the congregation.

o o o

Rowena had one of her mother's arms firmly in her own, with Emilio on the other side, but as they approached the rear of the church, Mrs Ballantyne released herself and spoke to the woman with the thin face standing alone.

'Come along Mrs Riskill' she said. 'We'll walk together.'

o o o

Rowena hadn't known what to think when tail-end Latchmere had handed her the will and explained that Daisy had left her everything. She liked him because he didn't rush her, understood, let her feel she could sit and consider as long as she wanted, made her a cup of tea and opened a tin of biscuits.

'And there is this.'

A crumpled old black and white photograph of Daisy that Rowena (during a truce) had said was her favourite, and a letter:

"Dear Pig-face. Sorry, generally. I'm leaving everything to you

256

because you'll know what to do. Mum and Rachel don't need anything except your love, and I'd like some of it too, you've got mine x"

She cried reading it. Latchmere handed her a box of tissues, a big full box as if expecting her to have a long heavy cry, but a short one was all she needed. It wasn't sadness: rather to be loved at last by the one she had longed to be loved by.

∘ ∘ ∘

The Electra's full service was due after its most recent flight. Under Reilly's supervision, the engines were dismantled, the circuits, rods, linkages, hydraulic pipework tested, the instruments re-calibrated, and the structure and surfaces of the fuselage checked and repaired.

The interior was intimately wiped and steam-cleaned, leaving not a trace of finger-prints nor DNA should these be of future interest.

The log book would require work. There were difficulties in concealing a round trip of that magnitude, but Reilly's experiences as a marine had taught him not to worry about trivia. On the flight, Rachel had passed the time sleeping and reading – unusually quiet for her. She had made a card for Rowena. On one side, a happy smiling pig's face. On the other 'And every day, play Le Jeu de la Guerre x'. In a week or two, he would think of a way for her to find it.

The next flight would be for the spreading of ashes. Reilly had given this considerable thought.

The third officer of Strident Bucephalus was training to pilot its helicopter. When it had landed with Daisy at Harbin Taiping, they'd met for the first time – eyed each other and approved. Now she had asked if she could sit in the co-pilot's seat, and Reilly had agreed.

Better, she'd worked out a way to stop the ashes whipping into a cloud from the engines and sticking to the airframe. Mix them with water. Pump them down a retractable tube. The apparatus looked promising.

∘ ∘ ∘

After the funeral, Mrs Ballantyne asked Emilio to take her home, and he understood. She had endured it: Rowena could handle the crematorium.

They drove where she wanted to go, with no particular pattern. A street to be revisited here, a view of a park with some memories, an incident recalled, a smile. Anything, he knew, to avoid arriving at the house, and remembering that she wasn't there. He kept an eye on the rear-view mirror.

'You see when she first arrived she was far older than later. She wouldn't cry at all. And finally, when she was seven I sometimes caught her smiling. She'd smiled before, but it was a polite grown-up kind of a smile. Always appreciative.

'I believe it was the competition of a sister. A resentful sister; but resentment is an acceptance, appraisal, love of a sort. Acknowledgement.

'I felt like one of those great sows, nosing her back into childhood. Then one night she cried.'

A quiet sob, nothing flashy. He said nothing to cover the silence.

'Then you see the memories could return. And when they return, they can fade.'

'Helped by a cup of warm milk?'

She patted his arm. 'Oh yes. That and a story.'

o o o

They'd reached the road, and he saw the police car, empty.

He parked, slipped out of his overcoat and came round to her door, helped her out, took her arm. They began to walk along the pavement to the house.

He saw the other car as it came towards them, driver's window open, saw the gun, Browning Hi-Power officer's side-arm, obsolete, effective.

Emilio turned in to Mrs Ballantyne, embraced her with his full body, pulled her to the ground on top of him, breaking her fall, and rolled onto her, protecting the back of her head with his hand, all with the continuous and elegant ease of a choreographer.

He counted the shots, heard the car smash into a wall, risked a look and saw the male officer standing back from the wreck. After a while the female officer joined him carrying a sniper's rifle.

Mrs Ballantyne rose unaided to her feet and brushed herself down. Emilio offered his arm, declined. They walked over to the car, looked at the old woman's blown-up head.

'Silly old fool' said Mrs Ballantyne. 'Instructor. Poor old thing. Silly, silly old fool.'

He took her arm successfully and they walked away.

'These – officers. Nothing to do with Rachel?'

He shook his head.

'I suppose they have been for me? How long has this poor woman been released?'

Emilio didn't answer, but squeezed her arm.

'The same time your friends have been here, I imagine. You can thank them politely, but it's a waste of time. You should have let the old bitch die.'

'Not till after the wedding.'

'I can't go on forever. I'm nearly out of steam. The race is almost run.'

'Another few furlongs. And besides, I have a surprise.'

Emilio hung up her coat and settled her comfortably into an armchair.

'I won't be long.'

Taking the front door key with him, he went to the boot of the car, took out the cardboard boxes, and returned to the house. Five minutes in all. He carried the boxes into the kitchen.

'Baked beans!' he called out. 'Lots of baked beans! All for dona Bettina!'

She didn't reply.

Thinking nothing of it, Emilio found a knife in a drawer and cut open one of the boxes. Removing a can, he checked the label to see it was genuine. She would be delighted.

Something was wrong.

Emilio ran into the sitting room. She was sitting exactly as he had left her, but with her eyes closed, apparently asleep.

'Dona Bettina!'

Her hands were folded in her lap, cool to his touch. He lifted her wrist and felt for a pulse.

○ ○ ○

It was a quarter of an hour before Rowena arrived. As she opened the front door she found him sitting on the stairs, smiled and came to him, kissed him.

'Have I kept you waiting? I've been as quick as I can.'

Emilio had words prepared, but at the right moment – nothing.

'It's the Mama. The Mama is dead.'

Rowena considered this.

'How do you know?'

He held her close.

'She is with the Lord.'

'I very much doubt it.'

Gently, Rowena removed Emilio and strode towards the sitting room. She threw open the door.

'Mother?'

'Yes dear?' Pianissimo.

'Are you dead?'

'I most certainly am not.' Robusto.

Mrs Ballantyne looked beyond her daughter to Emilio, her expression one of embarrassment, undershot with a modest gleam of triumph.

'It is a technique I learned from a guru in the Carpathian Mountains on a land-locked safari with the Captain.'

'Don't pay any attention to her. She has deep veins and appalling circulation. No pulse, cold hands. Rachel, Daisy, me – we've all fallen for it. Mother, you should be ashamed of yourself.'

'Oh very probably dear, all in good time. Did you say baked beans, Emilio? Or should I say, son?'

Emilio thought that he was easily pleased, and beamed nevertheless.

'Two boxfuls. All for the Mummy.'

'Heinz?'

'Would I pass off an imposter?'

'Do open a tin, be an angel, just as it is, and bring it to me. And a spoon. That will be splendid.'

∘ ∘ ∘

They took off from Lashenden Headcorn for the 50 km flight to Reculver.

'A tenner it doesn't work.'

260

Isabella grinned. 'Colman, you lose.'

It struck Reilly that he liked to be with her. Never had a daughter. Late in life to care about someone again.

In ten minutes they were over Reculver Bay, the twin towers of St Mary's Church sharply visible on its promontory. Isabella steered the Electra round in a circuit at 2,000 metres and handed over control. Reilly took them out to sea and headed south, steadily dropping down.

Isabella sat cross-legged on the cabin floor. There was a whip of air as she uncapped the tube they'd installed to the open air below. She pushed a thick flexible pipe through it, and watched through a camera on the underside as it payed out past the rear wheel, till its open end was clear in the slipstream.

A container beside her held the slurry of ashes. Another held the reservoir of clean water to flush away their residue. Between them was an electric pump. She opened the connecting valves, and lay on the floor with the pump-switch in her hand, the monitor beside her. They'd fitted an observation panel beside the tube, and she looked down to the water.

Reilly turned the aircraft back and headed up the coast, a few hundred metres out to sea, hugging the shoreline.

'Ready?'

As the church at Reculver came into view, he took them down low, almost touching the water. She started the pump, and watched as the ashes streamed into the ocean.

∘ ∘ ∘

Nick Pershawe never took for granted the senior partnership in Pershawe Willmott, Solicitors and Commissioners for Oaths, nor his role as company secretary for selected clients. Confidence must be won and renewed daily, achieved inch by inch.

He had prepared meticulously for the meeting with Rowena Ballantyne. He expected her to ask how much it was all worth. He had the answer. What the fall-out from the inquiry might be? None. In the clear? Yes. So, payment in full? Correct.

Rowena Ballantyne didn't say any of those things. When she did speak, what she said surprised him. Till then, maybe he had been assessing her and she him – but it seemed more a companionable

261

silence, with things being done beneath the surface. Supple thighs, Pershawe thought, firm hands. A different beauty, potent. Scandalous eyes.

○ ○ ○ ○ ○

Part Three

1

Within the afterlife, longstanding couples and friends John Lewis & Peter Jones and Fury One & Fury Two watch and try to help the stumbling relationship of Tom Devine and Daisy Ballantyne as first Tom and recently Daisy die. Daisy's once-estranged adoptive sister Rowena is surprised to be named the inheritor of her business. The death of Jill's baby daughter leaves Jill isolated and incurable in a psychiatric hospital, lost within her own world. Her husband Jack and their au pair Magda part as lovers. Architect Dianita Lapraman witnesses her mother's suicide at Crewe station as a child. As an adult, she kills herself. Mr Beldane and Mr Magruder pass between the present world and afterlife making running repairs.

THE VIEW FROM the top of the water tower was magnificent, a panorama of delight.

'You see' said John Lewis, briefly enveloping Fury Two in his free arm, 'if you stand exactly here you can see the lighthouse.'

'Oooh. It's pretty. How lucky you are to wake up here in the morning. Every day.'

'It was very kind of you to invite us' said Fury One.

'Thank you' added Fury Two.

'We are on our best behaviour.'

'Normally we're – furious. Slightly. We're not very good at it.'

'I know we've said it before. But it's true. Nobody's afraid of us. It's humiliating.'

'Even if they can see us.'

'It hurts the soul.'

'We do have souls.'

'Surely at the end, no-one will be forgotten?'

'Of course they won't' said Peter Jones.

'And we do have a little surprise for you.'

'I love surprises! Will it be later? All the best surprises are later.'

'Of course, dear Two. If you like.'

'It gives you time to prepare. To be surprised.'

'She's so primal' said Fury One. 'I apologise.'

'I am not so. I have complex emotions.'

'And this is the orchard' said John Lewis. 'Oh! Quickly everyone!'

o o o

Perhaps the meeting was accidental. They had taken separate routes around the garden, which now coincided.

'Hello' said Tom.

'Hi' said Daisy.

'Would you like an apple?'

'No. I hate apples.'

'Yes. Pointless.'

o o o

'Why doesn't she kiss him?' whispered Fury Two.

John Lewis sighed. 'It's not done. We have to be round-about; come to the point circuitously.'

'When I was on the stage' said Peter Jones. 'Oh yes. The West End has seen my Prince of Denmark. Morning noon and night we practised artifice. Indirectness. A certain dissembling. Mystique. Je ne sais quoi.'

'Supposing everyone spoke their minds?' added John Lewis. 'Catastrophe.'

'That's stupid.' Fury Two looked tearful. 'Kiss her! She loves you. Make her know how much you love her. She wants to kiss

266

you. You're terrified she'll reject you. She won't. You're afraid she'll laugh. She might. Kiss her! As if all your dreams will come true. As if there'll never be another kiss in the world.'

∘ ∘ ∘

Time meant nothing to Mr Beldane, and he wondered why he wore a watch.

He waved to the London Express as it growled and slid from Crewe station, and Casine blew a kiss to him, concealing it with her body from the sulky German woman beside her.

The watch had stopped at 5.15 – not a time of any significance, but somehow a sensible time – and he'd left the hands there on the basis of their being – from time to time – correct.

Mr Beldane paused to admire the magnificent Victorian station clock: an early John Brooke, if his memory served. If one were lost at sea – it occurred to him – here was the precise and correct chronometer for the calculation of longitude. And calibrated to railway time. Mr Beldane's knowledge of advanced mathematics was hazy, but he found himself questioning whether – without that first universal time – Albert Einstein's two-clock experiment would have been possible. And should it not have been, would this have denied the world his remarkable Theory of Relativity? Mr Beldane pondered this, unable to decide whether the hypothetical consequences were good or bad.

He crossed the bridge to the far platform, empty except for the small girl and her suitcase at the end.

'Hello Mr Beldane' she said. 'My, you've taken your time.'

'Have we met, Madame?' His eyes held a twinkle.

'My name is Diana. But if you like, you can call me Dianita.'

'You can't just go accusing anyone of being Mr Beldane. I could be a strange man.'

'You don't look strange.'

'How can you be certain?'

'I'm almost too tired of waiting, for riddles' she said. 'Would you like a sandwich?'

'Have you eaten?' he asked. 'There must be a buffet somewhere, or do they call it a canteen now, a café?' He looked around searchingly. 'There's never a porter when you have a reasonable question.'

267

'I have my sandwiches' she said. 'But I couldn't eat them right away. There'd have been nothing left for you.'

They sat together and she opened her suitcase. Inside there were clean clothes neatly folded – as an adult might pack them for a child to go on holiday – and a sandwich tin.

'It depends what they are. I really only like boiled egg ones, lightly peppered, in white bread, with butter and the crusts cut off.'

'Why' she said, 'that's exactly what I like.'

She unpacked the greaseproof paper and handed him a sandwich, adding 'My fingers are clean.'

Sometimes she kicked her legs under the bench.

After they had eaten, she looked for a bin. None.

'I'm sure no-one will know if I chuck them on the track' said Mr Beldane.

'God will know' she replied, a note of reproach in her voice.

'You're right, of course.' He blushed.

She stuffed the papers into her sandwich tin, closed the case and refastened its leather straps – not wanting to appear in a hurry, but sometimes looking at him expectantly.

'I'm ready' she said. 'I think you had better hold my hand. Shall we go home now? Shall we see mummy quite soon?'

They set off along the platform hand in hand – a man with a hat carrying a child's suitcase, the child skipping along beside him.

'Oh yes' he said. 'In really no time at all.'

○ ○ ○

Daisy looked quickly at Tom, looked away. 'I have one thing to say.'

'Ah.'

'You can't trust the weather this time of year. The weather is totally unreliable. Showers. Two hours later, piercing sunshine. Do you set out with an umbrella? Where do you put it? I hate having a bag. In your hand? Very irritating. Loop it through your belt. So, it rains. You have to undo your belt. That looks suggestive. It can appear improper. It depends who is watching – if anyone is watching. Suppose you aren't wearing a belt? Probably it won't rain today. It's hard to say.'

'I usually walk this way round the garden' said Tom. I proceed

268

in an anti-clockwise direction, because that is the way the water went down the plug-hole in either the northern or southern hemisphere. What happened at the equator? Who knows?'

'Who cares?'

'I have something for you.'

He gave her a plant in a bowl.

'It's gorgeous. What is it?'

'I don't know.'

'There's a label. Crocus. Do the buds open?'

'No idea. Never had one. I don't like plants.

'We could walk together' he added.

'We could.'

o o o

Lupins chatted to a sand-frog, who introduced them to the white heather and the purple.

Anabella Bee and Marika Bee held some of each other's hands while collecting pollen.

Everyone chatted that it was a sunny day among warm sunny days, and a charming morning. A snail who was French added 'Charmant'.

o o o

A rap of the door-knocker broke into Jack Jouvry's doze. It was ages since he'd slept well. He got up from the desk and opened the front door. She looked as beautiful as he dreamt her.

Magda.

'I have come to say goodbye.'

'I'm sorry.'

He took her coat.

'Most of my friends I have telephoned. Lovers I visit in person.'

It seemed crass to be mentally adding up hours against salary paid. Harshly practical, and surely something that could be done later, should have been done before. She must not be left in need.

'Do I owe you money?'

'You ridiculous man.' Final, affectionate. She patted his hand.

'I shall complete my doctoral thesis at the University of Uppsala.'

'Seven years?'

269

'Four.'

'I'm sorry that.' How to condense?

'I shall have time. I will travel. I have a ticket for Tanzania – I have never seen Africa. Next year, I shall visit Rawalpindi. Via Mumbai. I have never seen India. Apparently they have long wing-spanned birds. Quite like vultures, I've heard.' She said it wultures. 'I believe it is pleasant. The climate near or on the equator has a low diurnal range. The temperature is almost unchanging, between 28 and 32 degrees Celsius. Humidity is frequently 100%. A few degrees of latitude further north it becomes, of course, cooler.'

'She won't get better. They've said that.'

Magda held his hand.

'Then you will be resolute. Courage. Endurance. Fortitude.'

'I must give you money.'

Concern, or continuing to possess her?

'No.'

'How do I start? I'm sorry. Thank you. Without you.'

'Jack.'

A tone of conclusion. He changed the subject.

'And. What will it be called, your thesis? The full title?'

'"Only Disconnect: The 30 Years War and the Epistemological" – sorry I can never pronounce this word – "the Epistemological Consequences of Internecine Strife: 1500 to the Present Day."'

'I'll look forward to reading it.'

'I have a present. It is a recording I have made for you in which I read aloud the 18,000 word summary of my preliminary dissertation.'

'Oh.'

She glanced sideways at him, her mischievous look.

'At the beginning, I read slowly. Towards the end, I quicken the pace.'

∘ ∘ ∘

Very discreetly, John Lewis had been watching Fury One, hoping that she might begin to feel at ease. He'd come to recognise the ways she held herself as she listened, the stiffening of her body as she prepared to speak. Happiness washed upon John Lewis with the abundance of sea upon shore, and he longed for her to share in it.

'Fury Two wants to make an announcement. Look at her. Whenever she knows she's being clever, she swells.'

'I do not, One. All I want to say is, I know why Tom is difficult about love. He was a sensitive boy. He grew up in a lighthouse. We've seen it.'

'Sadly that was a metaphor. He was raised in Tiptree.'

John Lewis wished that Peter Jones wasn't sometimes so literal. At those moments, all one could do was to follow in his wake. 'Famous for its jam. And little gangsters. The ones that can't afford Dagenham. His parents still live there. Charming people. Chintz and anaglypta.

'So he's a fake' said Fury One. 'Like Noël Coward. Noël Coward grew up in a house like that. His parents were boring. He invented himself. If it's alright for Noël Coward, it should be alright for Tom.'

'I wasn't belittling. Simply alluding. There's nothing wrong with his parents. They are merely – sub-standard.'

'Are you a snob, John Lewis?'

'Yes.'

Up till now, Fury Two had controlled herself. No longer.

'Ooh. Ooh. Ooh. I don't want to know about Tom's childhood. I don't care. I only want to know. Him and Daisy. Will they find true love?'

John Lewis pondered this.

'Is Tom capable of love? He's emotionally shrivelled. So's Daisy.'

'His heart is clamped shut' said Peter Jones. 'Tight as a crocus bud.'

∘ ∘ ∘

'If I water it' said Daisy, 'I think the buds might open.'

'That's certainly a possibility.'

∘ ∘ ∘

From where they stood it was impossible to overhear the conversation: no cliffs to transport an echo; no breeze to carry a whisper. John Lewis, philosopher, feared the worst.

'Days passing more quickly. In the least painful way. That's how

271

life is for some, and we shouldn't despise it. Love isn't always an explosion. And if it is, it soon accommodates.'

'That's awfully depressing' said Fury Two. 'I thought – if she loves him, everything will be all right. I want to cry.'

'Don't.' Fury One rolled her eyes. 'When she starts, she never stops.'

'I do.'

'She's such an exhibitionist.'

'I am not. Dear Peter Jones. I have feelings. They're not very well-trained yet. But one day they will blossom.'

'They will, they will! Like pretty private flowers on parade. In any case, you're right. They're being absolutely stupid and self-indulgent. They should simply go up to each other and tackle it head-on. John Lewis doesn't believe us. Look at his dear face.'

Fury Two stared at the ground, uncertain, made up her mind. 'Can I kiss you, John Lewis?'

'I'm shocked.' He blushed unconvincingly.

'This is an experiment.' She put her lips carefully on his and kissed him for a long time. The others watched, counting the seconds. She drew back. 'Is it working for you?

'It's working very much for me. Heavens.'

'Oh Lor' said Peter Jones. 'It's not just the barometer that's rising.'

Fury Two kissed him again. 'You see! You see!'

o o o

Nick Pershawe took a document from his briefcase, handed it to Rowena.

'These are the valuations of our vessels from Clarksons at close of business last night. As you can see, most of them will sell at reasonable prices. We'll take a loss on Soubricant, easily outweighed by the cash gain on Turmoil.

'On liabilities, early surrender of the lease here' – he gestured round the office – 'possibility of an assignment, I can enquire. An indemnity to Mr Jouvry is no longer needed, so no loss there. Repayment of Mr Jouvry's loan on a cheque issued by Ms D Ballantyne. I simply await your instructions to sell our ships, pay what we owe and wind up the company.'

272

'How much will it cost to buy Strident Bucephalus?'

○ ○ ○

It was no effort to be quiet together, and there was no need for words.

But as Tom looked at Daisy, he knew how much he longed to hear her voice.

'Your feet are dainty.'

'When I was a little girl, I did ballet.'

'Perhaps you could be a ballet-dancer now.'

'Perhaps you could.'

'I've never danced. I liked to swim, but the changing-rooms of public baths – sordid. I often didn't like to undress in front of other men.'

'Is your penis extra small?'

'Not really. I'm not sure what is large or small. About 25 centimetres when erect. Sometimes 20, sometimes 30.'

'Thirty? That's a very large penis for a man.'

'Small for a porpoise.'

A familiar head popped up from a stream.

'I'll say.'

And discreetly withdrew.

'Incredibly small for an elephant', Daisy added.

Tom could never tell when she was serious. Was that bad, or an inevitability to get used to?

'I've never had sex with an elephant. It's not going to arise.'

'Joke?'

'No. "Why the long face?" is the punch-line of a joke. Unfortunately, I don't know what the joke is. I never mastered jokes. "40, and still believe in leprechauns?" is another. And "What? Eric?" If I could remember jokes, I suppose I'd have been popular. Another is – "Tell me, are you still dancing with Ginger Rogers?"'

'I had hundreds of friends. Once I'd left school. I hated school. All those fucking sports.'

'It's very rude to say fuck.'

'I don't care.'

'Do you smoke marijuana as well?'

'Sometimes. If I want to. I love smoking. My favourite

273

cigarettes are Sobranie Cocktails. They have gold tips, and come in lots of different colours. Do you smoke cigarettes? I hope you do.'

Tom felt like the left-out boy at school, not brazen enough to pretend. He grunted, hoped it sounded like agreement, loved the music of her talk.

'If my father was painting the house, I'd light cigarettes and pass them up to him. I am sitting in a chair, reading a book. I am watching him in the side of my eye. He can paint elegantly. He picks out the detail of cornices. He paints the edge of window frames without putting a spot of paint on the glass. All without masking-tape.'

'I can't do that.'

'I can taste the smell of emulsion, oil paint, thinners, stripper, paraffin, meths – Virginia tobacco. He smokes Senior Service. They have a ship on the packet. And Players. There's a sailor on the front. On his cap, it says Hero. My father is a hero. A modest man. You don't have to live up to anyone.'

'Daisy, I'm not good at anything. I can read. Of course I can read. A lot of people can read. I can write poems. But I lived most of my life out of books. I have never smoked a cigarette. I would very much like a cigarette now. I want to inhale smoke and feel lighter than air.'

'Colour?'

'Red.'

'Me too.'

She giggled, put a cigarette into his lips, lit it and stroked his cheek as he inhaled.

'This feels fabulous. I wish I'd smoked all my life.'

She took the cigarette, put her finger into his lips. 'Open your mouth.'

'I've always wanted to do this.'

'You have to seal your lips exactly where mine are, and breathe in.'

The kiss.

Is heaven.

∘ ∘ ∘

Nick Pershawe put his hands together in front of his mouth, and

274

rested his chin on his thumbs – a gesture he'd learned from other solicitors and found useful when pausing to re-group.

'Interesting.'

'How much?'

'Madame, you are full of surprises.'

'Only one so far – hopefully a lot more to come. Are you in for the ride?'

'Oh yes, I feel so, Ms Ballantyne.'

'Rowena. I will feel a lot easier to call you Nick.'

She held out her hand, they shook.

'Out of the question at the moment, not saying for ever. What do you have in mind?

'A big ship. We'll work the assets for a year, not sweat them, but a ten-per-cent rise in productivity makes sense. I've read what you sent, thank you, well-prepared, cogent. When the figures look healthy, talk to China Lines, let them in on the secret. I want that ship. Next year, ten years, junior partnership in a joint venture heading north to an outright sale. I don't care how, we'll get it.'

'So we're not selling out?'

'Nick. My sister, Pöl Stuyvesant, her dad. Thirty years in the business. I'm the fourth pair of hands. Am I going to let them down? We're going all the way till we have that ship. And that'll just be the start.'

'Right.'

'And we'll give her a new name. The Daisy. The Daisy Ballantyne.'

∘ ∘ ∘

Peter Jones and John Lewis gave the Furies a complete tour – with commentary and historical anecdotes – of the water tower – down to the last nook, staircase and hiding place. Finally they sat together in comfort in the sunlit room at the top.

'Now' said Peter Jones. 'Our little surprise. We've decided. John Lewis dear?'

John Lewis smiled anxiously at the Furies, and looked self-deprecatingly at the floor.

'Peter. Peter Jones. Peter Jones and I have decided. That does sound pompous, I do apologise. We want. I'm quite overcome by emotion. We would like. You really must come and live with us.'

275

Peter Jones put an arm round his shoulder. 'We can't bear to think of you out in the cold when we have a house. Sortie-ing with the Wild West Wynde.'

'So unkind.'

'Anyhow. There's a roof terrace. Perfect for take-offs and landings.'

'Oh we couldn't possibly', Fury One blurted out.

'Yes we could.' Fury Two bounced on the sofa. 'Thank you. Oooh. Thank you.'

'But we are – others. We were made different.'

'We were too, dear' said Peter Jones.

John Lewis looked eagerly around them.

'We shall be different together.'

'I always wanted to be unconventional' Fury Two said, wistfully. 'Live in a house. Get dressed. Sleep in a bed.'

'I've never lived in a house', murmured Fury One. 'I've peeped through windows. Warm fires. Armchairs. Comfortable beds. Soft eiderdown pillows to hide your face in when you are afraid. When you are alone. When nothing can ever be right.'

'But we'd take up space' said Two. 'We'd get in your way. We'd be a terrible imposition. Then you'd tire of us and want us to leave. And we would be sad.'

John Lewis hugged her. 'As you have seen. In this house, there are many rooms. If there were not, we would never have suggested it.'

Fury Two ran round the room, looking first from one window, before darting to another.

Realising that everyone else was sitting thinking, she suddenly felt shy. She sat down quickly next to One, and tried to look demure.

Peter Jones cleared his throat.

'We did think of one thing.'

'But only for your consideration' said John Lewis. 'There are no conditions. And you won't be guests. This will be your home.'

Fury Two tried it to herself.

'Home.'

'Home' said One. 'Home.'

John Lewis knelt in front of them.

276

'One and Two. Say if you are offended. We suggest – no more, no less. You might like to have names.'

'Oh.' Fury One looked shocked. 'We've never thought.'

'It's quite a nice idea' said Two.

'It's never come up. I'm One, she's Two.'

'I'm Two, she's One.'

'Couldn't you be Queer One and Queer Two?'

Peter Jones sighed.

'It would never work. I'd always want to be first, and so would John Lewis. Anyway, it's de-humanising.'

'We aren't' snapped Fury Two. 'Human.'

'Oh dear. My mouth.'

Fury One stood.

'We're not ruling out names. But they can't be imposed.'

Fury Two stood beside her.

'We don't want to be imperialised.'

John Lewis rose awkwardly to his feet.

'No no no. You won't be. Dear One and Two, Two and One. If you don't want names, there will be no names.'

'We thought it would help you feel welcome' added Peter Jones.

'Included' said Fury One.

'Yes.'

'What names?' said Two, diffidently.

'It's not up to us. It'll be your name.'

Fury One sat down, put her hands together. 'I like Beatrice.' Fury Two joined her, patted the space between them for John Lewis.

Peter Jones smiled.

'Welcome, Beatrice. Here you belong. And you, dear Two?'

'I like Grace.'

'Oh?'

'It's sweet and girly. I'm a girl. It's old-fashioned. Grace. I want to have a ribbon tied in my hair and wear pink shoes. Now that we have a home.'

∘ ∘ ∘

It was night-time at the Royal Bethlem Hospital.

In a private room, windows curtained for sleep, Jill Jouvry woke to a visitor.

'I don't understand who you are.'

She peered at the name on his badge.

'Magruder? Are you a doctor?'

'How are your dreams?'

His voice was gentle, barely above a whisper.

'Why doesn't it say doctor? I can't recognise your voice.'

'I'm a Scottish man.'

What did he take her for?

'It's not Scottish.'

'I'm a wee bit Scottish.'

She turned away from him, eyes open.

'My baby is dead.'

'And you, Jill. Are you alive?'

'I killed my baby.'

'What is her name?'

'How do you know she is "she"? Was "she"? How do you know me?'

'Every body has a name.'

'Do you know Jack? Do you know my friend?'

Daisy. Why can't I say her name?

'Would you like to see your baby?'

Won't cry.

'My baby is dead. Why do you torment me? I killed my friend. I can't see my baby.'

'Look.'

Beyond him, there was a garden.

'Daisy. Tom and Daisy. Happy.'

Jill realised she was laughing. She remembered that she hadn't laughed, must let it subside – keep up appearances.

The garden faded.

Magruder was still there, quietly regarding her.

'Are you alive?'

'Am I asleep? I don't believe I am asleep.'

'Then you must be alive?'

'Can I see my baby?'

He stood back, and again she looked beyond him.

'My baby. Baby! Ah. She's waving to me. She's waving goodbye.'

278

She realised she was waving too, blowing a kiss. No need to cry.

'Goodbye?' murmured Magruder. 'Do we have a name?'

Jill sat up.

'Dawn. My baby is Dawn.'

Magruder smiled.

'Then let us begin.'

o o o o o o o

WILD ELUSIVE BUTTERFLY

LIST OF CHARACTERS

THE MAIN CHARACTERS IN WILD ELUSIVE BUTTERFLY INCLUDE: Daisy Ballantyne (born Tanechka Krestyanova), Rachel Fonseca, Rowena Ballantyne, Mrs Bettina Ballantyne, Tom Devine, Emilio Podro, Jill Jouvry, Jack Jouvry, Pöl Stuyvesant, Isabella Berthonella, Adam Brook, Magda Baklanova, Sarah Carpenter, Gretl Lorelei, Helen Landesman, Diana (Dianita) Lapraman, John Lewis, Peter Jones, Fury One, Fury Two, Dr Friday, Madame La Commissar, Mr Magruder, Fr Julius Melendez, Dianita Lapraman (as a child), Turmoil (trawler), Turmoil (tramp ship).

And: Aloyshaha Krestyanov, Captain Verry, Captain Ballantyne, Paul, Colman Reilly, Strident Bucephalus (ship), Andrew Beacruft, Dulcie, Electra (aeroplane), Dr Lizzie Tillett, Dr Jo-Jo O'Brien, Francesca Casine, First Officer Renn, Sugar Popsicle, Porpoise, Mrs Riskill, Lake Baikal (lake), Fasil Iskander, Mr Beldane, Nick Pershawe, Police Officer Female, Police Officer Male, Raffaello Latchmere, Dr Hayden Gombrich, Dawn.

Also (alphabetical order): Abena, Admiral Susanna, Admiral Susanna's Husband, Anabella, Audience of Rachel Fonseca, Beatrice, Bosun, Captain of Briardeus, Captain of Defender, Captain of Ramona II, Captain of Strident Bucephalus, Chemist, Counsel for the Government, Crew Member, Daisies, Daisy's mother, Dandelions, Defender (submarine), Diana Lapraman's Mother, Dock Leaves, Dog-roses, Doll, First Engineer, First Mate, Fr Leidenberg, Fr Salman Jardine, French Snail, Gary

Malanuik, Girl standing on Crewe Station, Grace, Guest, Ingo, Judge, King Neptune, Lagonda (car), Lupins, Magda Baklanova, Man who burnt to death in a car, Marcus D, Marika, Mary P, Member of Deck Crew, Merry Kimber, Miss Jouvry, Mob, Mrs Ballantyne's Father, Mrs Ballantyne's Father's Harlot, Mrs Ballantyne's Mother, Mrs Ballantyne's Step-Sister, Mrs Evangeline Patropi, Navigation Officer, Nettles, Officers and Crew, Pan, Pilot at London dock, Pink-purple Lupin, Pöl Stuyvesant's father, Pöl Stuyvesant's Grandfather, Pöl Stuyvesant's Great Grandfather, Priest at the Church of the Madonna of Sorrows, Primroses, Projectionist, Purple Heather, Queen Amphitrite, Rebuke (ship), Sand-Frog, Sarah Carpenter's colleagues, Sarah Carpenter's parents, Second Officer, Soubricant, Staff at Imperial Institute Laboratory, Staff at Square Mile City Development Corporation, Steward, The Countess Constanza (ship), The Expatriate Trading Company, The Foreigners' Supermarket, The Furies, The Golden Girls Club, The Queen, The Scholars of the Organ College, The Scullery Maids of the Natural History Museum, Tom's Father, Trees in Hyde Park, Vicar of Holy Trinity Headington Quarry, Victoriano Codina y Langlin, Voice, Waitress, Weapons officer, Wheel Crew, White Heather, Young Man.

○ ○ ○ ○ ○

THANK YOU

THE FIRST THANK YOU IS TO YOU for reading the book, I've included a separate page to you.

Wild Elusive Butterfly started ten years before this novel as a theatre play script, then became a radio play en route to sitting here in your hand. On the way it's involved a lot of people and I'd like to thank as many of them as I know here – the book wouldn't exist without them. Any omissions are my fault. And muses? Of course. They're at the end, because muses like to have the last word.

Thank you to all including (in alphabetical order and any omissions will be rectified): Rohan Acharya, Fabian Acker, Lesley Ackland, Christopher Ager, Elina Akhmetova, Anthony Alderson, Josephine Arden, Ken Armstrong, Lucy Ash, Brian Attwood, Paul Aves, Catherine Balavage, Rose Theatre Bankside, Edith Barnard, James Barrett, Zena Barrie, Joe Bateman, Lucy Beale, Peter Benedict, Eleanor Bennet, Steven Bernstein, Caterina Bertone, Alan Birkinshaw, Robert Black, Marc Blake-Will, John Blandy, Angela Bleasdale, Gary Blissett, Susanna Bologna, Rachael Booth De Perea, Jack Bowman, Andrew Boxer, Josh Boyd-Rochford, John Bradford, John Bradley, Debbie Bright, Rae Brogan, Adrian Brown, Franz Budny, Peter Bulloch, Craig Bulpitt, Eleanor Burke, Gillian Caffrey, Paulette Caletti, Graham Cantwell, Sarah Carpenter, Chandrika Chevli, Barbara Chomicka, Steve Cleary, David Collins-Rivera, The Wireless Theatre Company, Jason Cook, Richard Costello, Andrew Cox, Spotted Cow Creations, Professor Tim Crook, Simon Dale, Samantha Darling, Sue Scott Davison, Eva del Rey, Nolia Devlin, Petar

Dimitrov, Alex Dower, Andrew Down, Aurore Down, Richard Dragun, Jeremy Drakes, William Dubes, Dhiraj Dudhia, Barry Eccles, Richard Fitzmaurice, John Fleming, Michelle Flower, Diana Franco, Flavia Fraser-Cannon, Wendy French, Gilda Frost, Ray Gardner, Isabelle Georges, Marja JA Giejgo, Nadia Gilani, Roger Gilles, Michael Gluckman, Nik Górecki, Penelope Granycome, Sara Griffiths, Elliot Grove, Victoria Grove, Christopher Gutteridge, Susanne Guyler, U-Wei bin Haji Saari, Jean Graham Hall, Bill Halson, Penrose Halson, David Hardcastle, Bruce Harris, James Harris, Malcolm Harrison, Rosemary Harrison, Will Harrison-Wallace, Elaine Hartley, Amy-Joyce Hastings, Lina Hayek, Dalh Haynes, Colman Higgins, Peregrine Hodson, Cecilia Holmes, Tracy Howl, Sheridan Humphreys, Mike Iles, Bill Jacklin, Bernadette Jansen op de Haar, Frank Johnson, Jill Jordan, Richard Jordan, Gareth Kane, Irina Karatcheva, Tracy Keeling, Rupert Keenlyside, Damian Kell, Dylan Kennedy, Jennifer Kidd, Dee King, Tshari King, Simon Kitts, Charles Knowles, Regina Kohl, Isabel Lagos, Keith Larkin, Philip Lawrence, Phil Lawson, Pam Lee; All the staff at Leicester Square Theatre, Museum of Comedy, Players Theatre, Raindance Film; Lucy Llewellyn, Stefan Lubomirski De Vaux, Nick Lucas, Henry Luxemburg, George Maddocks, Chris Manning-Perry, Marcus Markou, Mike Maurice, Bill McLean, Gill McMullan, Andy McQuade, Lynn Ruth Miller, Mike Miller, Rachel Miner, Steve Newton, Timothy Nicholls, Audrey Nicholson, Johnnie Oddball, Dominic O'Flynn, The Apollo Symphony Orchestra, David Palmer, Julia Papp, Serene Park, Holly Penfield, Sarah Pickering, Chantal Pierre-Packer, Sarita Plowman, Fleur Poad, Chris Polick, Gareth Potts, Gillian Best Powell, Pepe Pryke,

Daniel Pursey, Jack Rebaldi, Sonja Rein, Christopher Richardson, Eric Rickett, Victor Ridley, Jude Rigby, Johanna Rigg, Suzy Robinson, Adam Robinson-Witts, Luca Romani, Guy Rose, Jessica Ruano, John Rubinstein, Jenny Runacre, Mariele Runacre Temple, Morgann Runacre Temple, Professor Alyson Ruskin, Kevin Sampson, Samantha Sanns, Kate Saunders, Alexander Scherbak, Aki Schilz, Russian International Theatre School, Joe Sedgwick, Fr Michael JSW Seed, Richard Shannon, Adeela Sharif, David Shepherd, Paul Sherreard, Jennifer Skapeti, Tom Slatter, John Sleep, Sally Sleep, Sarah Smit, Pete Smith, Matthew Smith, Victor Sobchak, Maureen Spurgeon, Bloomsbury Studios, Borough Studios, Becky Talbot, Greg Tallent, Philippa Tatham, Emma Taylor, Brian Temple, Canal Café Theatre, Tabernacle Theatre, Diana Thomas, Fumiko Thomas, Wendy Thomson, Malcolm Thorp, Turkan Tijen, Chris Timms, Jason Tribe, Alison Trower, Sandra Turnbull, David Vickerstaff, Olivia Vinall, Brett Vincent, Marion Vivien, Alex Walker, Jonathan Walpole, Peggy Walpole, Michelene Wandor, Becky Webster, Sarah Whitehouse, Kevin Wilson, Martin Witts, Karl Woods, Eliza Wyatt, Pete Wyer, Sarah Louise Young, Andrei Zayats, Carlos Ziccarelli.

And finally, the muses. Writers always have muses, whether they tell you or not. They usually come in threes, and no-one who has read the terrible consequences of the Judgment of Paris would dream of listing them in any kind of order. Timidly, I'll go for alphabetical and you'll know if I survive. Thank you to my three wonderful friends and constant inspirations: Josephine Arden, Isabel Lagos, Sarita Plowman.

○ ○ ○ ○ ○

DEAR READER

THANK YOU for being there.

I write for readers and if you like Wild Elusive Butterfly it's worked. If you've hated it, burnt it or used it as a weapon I've failed completely and will re-read Pilgrims Progress for directions to the Slough of Despond.

Do you occasionally react violently to books? Would burning them be too drawn out? Excellent. I tore up a massive one by Don DeLillo at page 30 (starts with a baseball game). Another by someone else (Don and I have never met but have a tacit agreement that I don't read any more of his) I destroyed and threw in a bin on Charing Cross Road just after buying it.

If I've accidentally triggered a 'DeLillo' in you, please do write a review saying what you've done with the book or your ebook reader. Writers often ask for great reviews but what fun is that? I'd much rather you say what you think. If of course you adore it, I'll be thrilled. You're the important person here, so do write a review if you'd like to, and say what you think.

I wrote Wild Elusive Butterfly first as a play for the theatre. With a cast of 20, a full orchestra and a full choir it won't surprise you that 10 years later it still awaits its West End debut (but you and I know it will come).

It's since had a very successful and continuing life as a radio play by Wireless Theatre Company thanks to the brilliant work by the cast, director George Maddocks and producer Mariele Runacre Temple. If you like audio, you can download it from their website.

The play tells the central story of this book, in 3 acts roughly corresponding to the book's 3 parts. The book is much wider in scope and with more background to the characters. I wrote the book as a new work rather than a novelisation: I don't think they usually work.

A later novel, Rachel Is Bookish, will tell more of the story of the characters in this book from a slightly different angle. In all I'm planning 3 or 4 books, together forming a whole, and each complete in itself, readable in any order.

Contact details: Please get in touch if you'd like to - my email is contactjohnpark@gmail.com. Twitter is @wildelusivebfly. The website is contactjohnpark.wordpress.com.

Thank you very much for reading Wild Elusive Butterfly and I'll look forward to hearing from you,

Best wishes

John Park

∘ ∘ ∘ ∘ ∘